BEYOND THE SHROUD OF THE UNIVERSE

BOOK TWO OF THE CODEX REGIUS

Chris Kennedy

Chris Kennedy Publishing
Virginia Beach, VA

Chris Kennedy/Chris Kennedy Publishing
2052 Bierce Dr.
Virginia Beach, VA 23454
http://chriskennedypublishing.com/

Publisher's Note: This is a work of fiction. Names, characters, places, and incidents are a product of the author's imagination. Locales and public names are sometimes used for atmospheric purposes. Any resemblance to actual people, living or dead, or to businesses, companies, events, institutions, or locales is completely coincidental.

Ordering Information:
Quantity sales. Special discounts are available on quantity purchases by corporations, associations, and others. For details, contact the "Special Sales Department" at the address above.

Beyond the Shroud of the Universe/ Chris Kennedy. -- 1st ed.
ISBN 978-1942936428

Praise for "The Search for Gram" by Chris Kennedy:

"Chris Kennedy's Search for Gram takes humanity, the most recent newcomers to interstellar space -- and the reader -- on a roller coaster exploration of alien cultures with ancient animosities and startling technologies. There's action and skullduggery in plenty, and along the way Kennedy gives the reader a look inside questions of morality, ethics, and the true meaning of personal responsibility, not simply to others, but to one's self."

- David Weber
Author of the Honorverse
and Safehold Series

As always, this book is for my wife and children. I would like to thank Linda, Beth and Dan, who took the time to critically read the work and make it better. Any mistakes that remain are my own. I would like to thank my mother, without whose steadfast belief in me, I would not be where I am today. Thank you.

I would also like to thank Jim Beall for his assistance with several aspects of the physics in "Beyond the Shroud of the Universe." Any remaining errors are mine, in spite of his expert aid.

Author's Note

When more than one race refers to a planet or star, the same name is used by both races in order to prevent confusion. Also on the topic of planet naming, the normal convention for planets is to add a lower case letter to the name of the parent star (i.e., Tau Ceti 'b'). The first planet discovered in a system is usually given the designation 'b,' and later planets are given subsequent letters as they are found. In order to prevent confusion in this book, the closest planet to the star in a star system is given the letter 'a,' with the rest of the planets given subsequent letters in order of their proximity to the star.

"For fools rush in where angels fear to tread."

— *Alexander Pope,* "An Essay on Criticism"

Chapter One

Throne Room, Planet Utopia, MOA-2007-BLG-192L System, September 27, 2021

You told me our ships would not have to worry about the Aesir," High Lord Sarpedon said, "and yet, the *Agnostos* has been destroyed *with its entire crew*." All four eyes turned to glare at the emissary. "What do you have to say for yourself?"

The emissary of the Jotunn Empire, Skrogg Ottarson, knew he was on dangerous ground. Sarpedon was not known for his patience with people who failed him, regardless of their status in court. He usually didn't just shoot the messenger who brought him bad news, he usually ate the messenger, as well. "The ship that destroyed your vessel wasn't an Aesir vessel," he said; "it was a Terran ship."

"Terran?" High Lord Sarpedon asked. "I am unfamiliar with this word. What is a 'Terran' ship?"

Ambassador Ottarson breathed an inaudible sigh of relief; he would get to keep his head a little longer. "We don't know," he admitted. "We haven't seen this race before, so they are either new to our area of space, or they recently achieved space flight. Their ship looked like it was from a class that existed 3,000 years ago. We believe the Terrans must be a client race the Aesir hired to find out why their ships were disappearing; they are probably nothing more than expendable underlings." He paused and then added, "We are still trying to determine exactly who and what they are."

High Lord Sarpedon's eyes narrowed. "So, an Aesir client race with a 3,000 year-old ship annihilated one of my new, front-line destroyers? How exactly did you let this happen?"

Perspiration began flowing again; he wasn't out of the woods yet. "We did nothing to allow it to happen, my lord," Ambassador Ottarson said. "The reports I received indicate the Terrans were barely able to scratch your ship; however, when the *Agnostos* transferred into our universe, it did so on top of one of the Terran's fighters. The fighter happened to hit the *Agnostos'* armory, which blew up, and both the fighter and your ship were destroyed in the blast. The loss of the *Agnostos* is nothing more than bad luck."

"There is no such thing as luck." The high lord sat back on his throne. "I read the same reports. My crew was sloppy. After easily defeating three Aesir vessels, they took the Terran ship too lightly." He leapt to his feet and turned on his military advisor. "*That will not happen again!*" he roared, pointing both of his right arms at the military advisor. Sarpedon's anger was a palpable force in the room, and Ambassador Ottarson was overjoyed it was no longer directed at him.

"Yes, my lord," Admiral Rhadamanthus replied, showing no outward sign of fear. "Since he is not here to account for himself, the family of the *Agnostos'* captain has been put to death as an example of what happens for such incompetence; in fact, I believe we will be having his wife for lunch today. It will not happen again."

The high lord glared at the admiral for another few seconds, looking for weakness, but Admiral Rhadamanthus met his unblinking tetrahedral gaze without flinching. Mollified, the high lord took a slow breath and returned to his throne.

"Ultimately, I care little for how it happened, Admiral Rhadamanthus," High Lord Sarpedon said; "I only care that it *did*. The Terrans destroyed one of my ships. They must be destroyed."

"It shall be done," the admiral replied. "We will find and destroy the Terrans. They will be annihilated."

"Good." The high lord's eyes returned to the ambassador, and the high lord nodded once.

"Ugh—"the ambassador said as the breath was driven from his body. He looked down to see a spear point and two feet of shaft emerging from his stomach. The guard behind him was far shorter, and the tip of the spear pointed up at him as if in accusation. He dropped to his knees, his life fading quickly. The wound might have been survivable on its own; however, he knew the guards' spears were poisoned. His life was over. "Not…my…fault…" he said as he fell forward onto his face.

"Of course it's your fault," the high lord said as four of the guards dragged the ambassador's body toward the door to the kitchen, leaving a green smear behind. "Your people should have advised my ship's captain better. And besides, we needed dessert."

Chapter Two

President's Conference Room, Terran Government Headquarters, Lake Pedam, Nigeria, September 27, 2021

"That concludes my report," Lieutenant Commander Shawn 'Calvin' Hobbs said from the podium. "Are there any questions?" He looked around the room and involuntarily cringed. While he had known there would be *some* questions; he hadn't expected that *everyone's* hand would go up.

The president's conference room was unlike any other Calvin had ever been in. At its center was a table which could easily seat 20 people to a side. The floor of the room sloped upward on all sides, with 10 rows of stadium seating.

The leaders of the Terran Government sat at one end of the table, with the president seated at the head of the table in her customary chair. The vice president, the secretary of state and the speakers from both houses of parliament filled the chairs closest to her. The rest of the seats at the table held members of the Terran Republic's Security Council; their staffs and other interested representatives filled the audience seats, as well as most of the aisles. The place was packed.

The people at the table had brain implants which translated any Terran language; every seat in the room also had jacks that allowed users to plug in and get a running translation of the conversation provided by a small artificial intelligence (AI) which had been replicated for that purpose. The AI also kept notes and logs of all the conversations within the room, unless specifically told not to.

Seeing the forest of hands, Calvin sighed. This was going to take forever. With a mental shrug, he pointed to the closest representative.

"We have only just finished the war with the Drakuls," the senator from Japan said, throwing her hands up in the air, "and now this…this…soldier has gone and involved us in another one. Who is he to think he has ambassadorial powers or the right to speak for us?" She looked around the enormous room for support and smiled when she saw most of the heads in the audience nodding.

"I certainly didn't intend to get us into a war, ma'am," Calvin said. "We were helping the Aesir, as we were ordered, when the Efreeti vessel appeared and fired on us unprovoked. We didn't even know it was *there* before then, much less do anything to cause them to attack us. And actually, ma'am, I'm a naval aviator, not a soldier." Although Calvin currently led a space fighter squadron and a platoon of Terran Space Marines, he still considered himself a naval aviator at heart. It had only been a couple of years since the aliens had shown up on Earth and drafted him to be a janissary in their wars; until recently, a Navy F/A-18 pilot was all he ever wanted to be.

"Not only has he involved us in a war with the Efreet, but also a war with these Jotunn frost giants?" the senator from Romania asked. "Both of these are creatures out of myth and legend. And new universes? What's next, vampires? How are we supposed to fight things that don't exist in places our best scientists say are impossible?"

"The Jinn Universe does exist, sir," Calvin replied. "My men and I have been there several times, and in a number of different systems. Their universe is just as real as ours. I lost a lot of good people there."

One of the senators from Domus raised her hand, and he pointed to her. The planet had been discovered on one of Calvin's first missions to space, and their society had joined the Terran Republic the year before. The world was home to two races; one of these was humanoid in appearance, while the other, the Kuji, looked like 6-foot-tall Tyrannosaurus Rexes. Having been recognized, the Kuji princess stood.

"Unlike the rest of this august body, we are less focused on what is already done and can't be undone," said the princess, nodding to the other Domus senator, the humanoid princess. "We are more worried about what will happen next. Lieutenant Commander Hobbs has already shown these races inhabit a number of stars and planets in their universe, most of which are also inhabited in *our* universe. How do we know they won't all of a sudden pop up on our planet or jump into our system and start dropping bombs on our cities?"

"I'm sorry," Calvin said, "but the bottom line is that we *can't* know whether they are there until we go into their universe and see. Even then, there is no way to protect against them; we can't stop them from jumping into our universe. The only thing we have going for us, we think, is that there aren't any stargates in the other universe. The Jinn have to transfer into our universe to use our stargates if they want to move around quickly. They don't have faster-than-light space travel in their universe, so it would take many years to go from one system to another."

"So the only ones we really have to worry about would be the ones already there, or those that come through the stargate into our system?"

"Yes, ma'am," Calvin said. "At least, that's the way we understand it now. There may very well be creatures that inhabit your planet in the other universe; in fact, I would bet there are. It seems like most of the planets that support life in our universe are also inhabited in the Jinn Universe."

"A follow-up, if I may?" the princess asked. Gaining permission, she continued, "It is necessary for our continued security to determine if they exist on our planet. How do we find out if they are there?"

"There are a couple of ways to find out, ma'am. If we want to do it stealthily, we can use one of the transportation rods we brought back to send a few people to their universe and look around. Unfortunately, we only have a few of them, so it will probably be a little while before we can do so. We are working on making more rods, but there is a substance we need that is only found in the other universe. In order to make all the rods we need, we are going to have to find a supplier in the other universe."

"What about the friendly race you met? The Sila?" Terran President Katrina Nehru asked, happy to be headed back in a positive direction.

"Yes, ma'am," Calvin replied. "We have had contact with the Sila on a couple of occasions. They all left a common planet when its star went nova, and they now inhabit several planets we know of, but they don't have contact with each other. Most of their planets have been conquered by the Efreet and ruled by them ever since. We helped one planet throw off the Efreeti yoke; I'm sure they would help us against the Efreet."

"How big is the Sila Navy, exactly?" the Russian representative asked.

"Almost nonexistent," Calvin admitted. "The Sila only have a single destroyer; however, they have been artificially held back in their technological development by the Efreet. If we give them a boost, I think they'd make great allies."

"Oh, so now you are qualified to give us treaty advice?" the French representative asked. "After involving us in a war with two previously unknown star nations, you are going to tell us who we should have as our allies too?" He spread his arms as he looked across the entire auditorium. "Honestly, I don't see the need for this body to exist since we already have you to determine who our allies and enemies should be."

With that, many of the representatives began shouting their own comments and criticisms. As the moderator struggled to regain control of the meeting, Calvin opened up his in-head calendar display and began cancelling his other appointments for the day. This wasn't going to end any time soon.

The Situation Room, Fleet Command HQ, Lake Pedam, Nigeria, September 29, 2021

"That concludes my report," Calvin said for the second time in three days. "Are there any questions?"

Unlike the chaos that followed this question in the governmental headquarters building, the mood in Fleet Command was somber. Everyone in the room could see the magnitude of what the fleet had been tasked with. How could you defend an entire planet, much less its individual cities, when aliens could emerge anywhere, at any time, and attack? What did they have that could stop an Efreeti ship from appearing and conducting an orbital bombardment of Earth before any of the Terran forces could stop it?

Nothing.

It could happen in the next five minutes, and the military would be completely unable to prevent it. Everyone knew it, and no one had a solution. All the eyes in the room turned to Fleet Admiral James Wright, the head of the Terran Navy, who sat at the head of the table.

For his part, the admiral looked out the window at the Terran Governmental Headquarters, visible across the lake, deep in thought. Finally, nodding to himself, he returned his gaze to the podium. "So Calvin," he said, "you've had the longest to think about it, what are your recommendations?"

Although the question might have seemed out of place to some of the non-American members of the staff, Admiral Wright had a long, personal relationship with Calvin, going back to the Sino-American War of 2018. Although their working relationship had been strained at first, the admiral had come to count on Calvin's decision making. That trust was rewarded with a string of Terran victories across a number of systems in two universes. And, more to the point, Calvin had more off-world fighting experience than any other Terran officer.

"I don't think we have a lot of choices," Calvin said. "We have to take care of Terra first. Don't get me wrong; I'd love to help the Aesir, and they need all the help they can get. Even with the information we gave them, they are going to be overwhelmed by the combined forces of the Efreet and Jotunn if they don't get any help. Still, we have to take care of Earth first."

"I'm sorry," Admiral Ackermann said. "Who were the Jotunn again?"

"The Jotunn are frost giants allied with the Efreet," Calvin said. "They stand about 16 feet high and weigh over a ton. Not only does their size make them difficult to stop on an individual basis, their ships are similarly oversized. For example, their battle cruisers are about the size of a Mrowry dreadnought."

"That is about 1.5 of your miles in length," Captain Andowwn, the Mrowry attache to the Terran military, replied. A felinoid race, the Mrowry were the Terrans' closest allies on the galactic stage, with the elven Aesir close behind.

"That is…quite large," the German admiral said. "We will need more ships if we are to meet them in combat."

"That's the problem," Calvin said. "Well half of it, anyway. As much as I'd like to help the Aesir, I don't think we can. Unless something changed while we were gone, we barely have enough ships to defend our own planets in the face of this new threat; if we send some to aid the Aesir, we are leaving ourselves perilously open to attack."

Admiral Wright's eyes found the only civilian in the room. Not surprisingly, he was tapping on a data pad. "Mr. Brown, could we get a status on ship production?"

Andrew Brown jumped as his name was called. Brown ran the Fleet Material Management Network, or 'Replicator Command,' whose sole purpose was to ensure the Republic of Terra's replicators ran as efficiently as possible. Products of advanced alien technology, the replicators could take raw materials and turn them into any finished product for which they had a blueprint. The biggest replicators could even produce super dreadnoughts, the largest class of ships.

Calvin had first met Andrew Brown when he was the plant manager for Boeing's Airplane Programs Manufacturing Site in Renton, Washington, during the war with China. Brown's experience managing aircraft production facilities had been instrumental in his success with Replicator Command...although it looked to Calvin like Brown's hairline was rapidly receding, probably due to the stress involved.

"Ah, yes," Mr. Brown replied. He tapped the pad two more times. "Our fleet remains at three ships, the cruiser *Vella Gulf* and the battleships *Terra* and *Domus*. We also have the former Efreeti cargo ship *Spark* that Lieutenant Commander Hobbs brought back, if you count it. Although we do not have many active ships, our ship building facilities are just beginning to hit their stride."

He looked at his pad. "The republic is up to five replicators—"

"Excuse me," Calvin interrupted. "Did you say *five?* You've been busy."

"Yes, we have," Brown replied with a smile. He looked around the room and saw questions on several of the faces. "For those of you outside of Replicator Command, replicators range in size from Class 1, which can only make minor items, up to Class 8, which is capable of producing a super dreadnought. Class 1 replicators are found on some of the medium-size and larger ship classes where they are used to replace equipment that breaks. Class 8s are enormous in size, and are relatively static."

Brown's focus returned to Calvin. "In addition to the Class 2 replicator on the moon and the Class 6 we got from the Mrowry, we also towed the Class 8 you captured back to our asteroid belt. I knew that wouldn't be enough, so we made a Class 5 replicator with the Class 6, and another Class 6 with the Class 8. We sent the Class 5 to

Domus so they could begin shipbuilding, and we stationed the new Class 6 in the asteroid belt with the Class 8. It took some time to do all of this, as well as to create the infrastructure required to operate them effectively."

He smiled. "I'll tell you what, though," Brown said, pausing for effect; "once you get a Class 8 set up, it can generate infrastructure *fast*. The amount of material it consumes in a day is nothing short of staggering…but you wanted to know about our ship status. All five replicators are now in operation making ships, and you will see a number of new ships very soon."

He motioned, and the lights dimmed. "If you look at the screen, I can show you what I mean." He tapped on his pad, and a picture of a tube in space appeared on the screen. "This is the Class 8 replicator four months ago. For scale, do you see these little points of light?" He indicated a group of about 50 small dots. "Those are *Reliable*-class shuttles, and each is over 200 feet long. The replicator is over two *miles* long."

There was a collective intake of breath. Even though the officers knew the replicator was big, few realized just *how* enormous it really was.

"For the record," Brown continued, "the dots represent one *day's* worth of production." The crowd gasped again. "Of course, that was one day's worth before we had all of them to help tow asteroids to the replicator. We actually ran out of raw materials at 8:00 in the morning. If we hadn't, we could have built several hundred more that day." Another gasp.

"Here's the Class 8 today." The picture changed, and the crowd had its biggest gasp yet. Emerging from the replicator was a ship that dwarfed it. "The super dreadnought *Thermopylae* should be ready next week. It is fully three miles long and masses over 10 million tons."

"Oh, man," Calvin said. "I am soooo ready to have that on my side."

"In addition to the *Thermopylae*," Brown continued, bringing up the next picture, "we also have the battleship *Hood* within a week of completion at one of the Class 6s and the battleship *Yamato* finished at the other." The picture changed to a battleship alongside one of the replicators. "Now that we have everything in place for mass production, we will have the makings of a fleet soon, but even with a Class 8 replicator and two Class 6s, it still takes time."

"Time we don't have," Calvin said. "And, even when we get them, they won't be able to make the jump to the Jinn Universe until we get the metal required to make their jump modules…and the time required to refit the modules into the ships. Also, we're still working on developing effective weapons and tactics for fighting the Efreet, but we haven't figured *them* out yet, either. And even with implants, training the crew isn't going to happen overnight. The bottom line is we simply aren't ready for a fight with the Efreet."

"Speaking of which," Admiral Wright said, looking at Brown, "Do we have a source for getting the unobtanium, or whatever the hell you need to make the jump modules?"

"The caliph in the anti-Keppler-22 system has said he would be happy to let us mine it there."

"Anti-Keppler-22?" one of the wet navy admirals asked.

"Anti-Keppler-22 is the system in the Jinn Universe that corresponds to Keppler-22 in our universe," Brown explained. "The problem with getting the needed material from there is the system isn't close to here, and the material decays in this universe if it's untreated. Somewhat explosively. If a ship left anti-Kepler-22 with 100 pounds, there would only be 10 pounds remaining by the time the ship arrived here, if the ship wasn't destroyed in the attempt. It has to be kept very closely confined and processed immediately, or it is quite dangerous."

"How much do we need for a jump module?" Admiral Wright asked.

"We need a little more than a pound of the metal for each module," Brown replied, "and the larger a ship is, the more modules it needs to be able to jump; for example, battleships need eight." He sighed. "I hate to suggest it, but I think the best thing we could do would be to send the Class 2 replicator from the moon to Keppler-22 'b,' or, even better, to jump it into the Jinn Universe and have it make the jump modules there. It could also fashion more of the transportation rods needed to jump people between the universes while it's there."

"What about the indigenous people on Keppler-22 'b'?" Admiral Babineaux asked from down the table. "Will they mind if we set up on their planet?"

"I doubt it," Calvin said. "The people there are the equivalent of the Mayan Indians of a millennia ago. They still think of us as gods or demi-gods when we go there. They shouldn't be an issue. I don't think there'd be a problem with running the replicator in the Jinn Universe, either. I'm sure the caliph would love to have us there to help defend the system while his nation learns to defend itself."

"As I understand it, we can't stay in the other universe long-term, though, can we?" Admiral Wright asked. "Isn't there some sort of disease or something you get?"

"Yes sir," Calvin replied. "The two universes aren't completely compatible. Just like some of the metal we need from their universe breaks down here, silver and gold from here break down in their universe. Something also happens to people who stay too long in the opposite universe. Eventually, they sicken and die. We can operate the replicator in the other universe, but any Terrans manning it will have to come back to our universe periodically, or they will die. One of our pilots, Lieutenant Dan Knaus, was trapped in the other universe for a couple of months, but he crossed back and forth several times and doesn't appear to have any long-term health issues."

"Got it," Admiral Wright said. "Although the situation won't be remedied within the next couple of months, we're making progress on our lack of ships and jump modules. But I think you said that was only half the problem?"

"Yes sir," Calvin replied. "In addition to not having enough ships capable of taking the fight to the enemy, the other part of the problem is that we don't know the nature of our enemy; we don't know what we're trying to defend *against*. We don't know for sure what's on anti-Earth and anti-Domus although we have anecdotal evidence that the Efreet are across the shroud of the universe from Earth."

Admiral Wright raised an eyebrow. "Shroud of the universe?" he asked.

"Yes sir," Calvin said. "That's what the Sila call the boundary between our two universes. They think of it as a veil that can be pierced, and, to answer your earlier question on what we ought to do, I think we need to pierce it here on Earth and find out what the hell's on the other side."

"Wouldn't it be better not to antagonize them?" Admiral Babineaux asked. "Perhaps they don't know we exist. Shouldn't we build up our strength first and then cross over in force?"

"No sir, I don't think so," Calvin replied. "Captain Nightsong, one of the Aesir, was here several hundred years ago, and he said there unequivocally *are* Efreet on anti-Earth. Even worse, they already know we exist too, because some of them have crossed over in the past. If anti-Earth is really the Efreeti capital, as we've been told, then it's better if we find out first, before they find out about us. I'd rather negotiate with our ships holding their orbitals than vice versa."

"They may know we exist," Admiral Babineaux said, "but it is unlikely they know we are the same people who destroyed their ship. They probably don't even know about the attack. How could they? Wouldn't the Efreet have to use our stargate to get to their capital to tell them?"

"We have been *told* the Efreet don't have faster-than-light drives, but we don't *know* that for sure," Calvin replied. "Are you willing to bet the future of the Earth on that, sir? I'm not." He turned to Admiral Wright. "Honestly sir, I think we need to mount a small operation across the boundary to find out what we're dealing with, not only here, but on Domus, too. That is the *only* way we're going to be able to prepare for them."

"I take it you are volunteering to lead this mission?" Admiral Wright asked.

"Yes sir," Calvin said. "My platoon has the most experience with cross-boundary operations. The first few times you go beyond the shroud, you are violently sick when you get there. I wouldn't want to take a bunch of people who had never been to the Jinn Universe before and have them throwing up while we're taking enemy fire. My troops have been there, and we are acclimated to the jump. We can do this, sir. And then, once we determine the nature of the threat, we need to do the same on Domus." He paused, then added, "It's the only way to be sure."

Bachelor Officers Quarters, NAS Oceana, Virginia Beach, VA, September 30, 2021

"**D**id you get authorization for us to go?" Captain Paul 'Night' Train asked. The executive officer (XO) for the special forces platoon Calvin commanded, he had arrived at Calvin's room with a six-pack of beer shortly after Calvin returned from Nigeria. He twisted the top off one and toasted, "Cheers!"

"Cheers," Calvin returned. "Yeah, the admirals had to discuss it for about three hours to come to an agreement, but they finally bought off on it." The XO frowned, and Calvin grinned. "Hey, the Terran Security Council discussed it for two whole days, and they never actually came to a conclusion. Only having to discuss it for three hours was a *huge* win!"

"Still, it was obviously the right thing to do," Night said. Due to a combat wound sustained earlier in his career, his voice was gruff at the best of times; it got worse when he had to deal with stupidity. Or politicians, who were usually the ones committing the stupidity. "How could they not see that?"

"I don't know," Calvin replied. "Some of them were more worried about letting the Efreet know we exist."

Night snorted, spraying some of his beer. "Really?" he asked. "According to Captain Nightsong, they've known about us for hundreds of years. They know we're here. It's time for *us* to find out more about *them*."

"No kidding," Calvin said. "Still, they came to the right conclusion in the end and authorized us to go."

"So what's the plan?"

"Well, I'd like to go as soon as possible, before they change their minds," Calvin said. "We will go across with Captain Nightsong. Apparently, he knows an out-of-the-way place we can cross over and not be detected. The only holdup is manning and arming the troops."

"The manning is all set," Night replied. "The platoon is over at Dam Neck where they have been training with the SEALs. I spent most of the day with them and can tell you even the newbies are working out pretty well."

"Good," Calvin said. "The only problem we're going to have is that some of the new folks haven't made a cross-universe transit before. We'll have to send over our experienced people first to cover them while they…adjust."

"Yeah, I remember how I felt on my first jump," Night said.

"Since it sounds like the platoon is ready," Calvin said, "we'll use tomorrow to make final preparations, and we'll go the day after that."

"Sounds good, sir," Night said. He stood up and walked to the door. "In that case, I'm going to turn in."

"G'night," Calvin said. He started to shut the door, but then he remembered something. "Hey, Night…um…when we came down, do you remember me bringing down my Progenitor's Rod?" The rod had been given to him by an ancient civilization, along with a quest.

"I swear I had it in my hand when I walked off the shuttle, but now I can't find it in my quarters."

"I think so, sir," Night said. He thought for a second. "Yeah. You definitely had something golden when you walked across the tarmac. I was walking behind you, and the sunlight kept flashing off it into my eyes."

"Damn," Calvin said. "For the life of me, I have no idea where it went. I thought I put it in the closet here, but now I can't find it."

"Maybe I was wrong, and it's still on the ship," Night said. "I'll help you look when we get back. Sure would suck to lose it. It's not like you can go pick one up at the corner market."

Chapter Three

Cockpit, *Shuttle 02*, Enroute to Fredensborg, Denmark, October 2, 2021

"Hey, sir," *Shuttle 02's* pilot, Lieutenant Kenyon 'Bucket' Salo, said, "Wouldn't it be easier to just replicate a bunch of jump modules, equip all of our ships with them and then jump in there and kick the ever-lovin' shit out of the damn salamanders?"

"Perhaps," Calvin said.

"Then why the hell aren't we doing that?" Bucket asked.

"Because we don't have any idea what's there," Calvin replied. "We don't know what types of ships or what ground forces they have, and Fleet Command wants us to jump across and find out…as quietly as possible. If we jump a ship over, they're definitely going to see us coming."

"So?" the Weapon Systems Officer (WSO), Lieutenant Neil 'Trouble' Watson, asked. "If we jump in there and hold the orbitals, what are they going to do to us? I'm sure they'll get the message when we drop a few rocks on their heads."

"What if their reply to our message is to jump into our universe with a few nukes and set them off in our cities?" Calvin asked.

"Can they do that?" Bucket asked.

"We don't know," Calvin replied, "and that's why we're going. We don't know anything about the forces there, either on the ground or in space. Wouldn't it be better to know we can win *before* we jump in there with all of our forces, rather than jumping in blind and find-ing ourselves vastly outnumbered?"

"Yeah, I guess it would," Bucket said.

"That's our mission today," Calvin said. "We're going to jump over and get the lay of the land. Once we've done that, and once we've determined the Efreet don't have the capability to nuke the Earth, *then* we'll replicate a bunch of jump modules, equip all of our ships with them and jump in there and kick the ever-lovin' shit out of the salamanders."

Entrance to Grendel's Cave, Fredensborg, Denmark, October 2, 2021

"That is the entrance to Grendel's cave," Captain Nightsong said. "The passage leads to a large cave below sea level."

"I still think this is a mistake," Master Chief said, looking at the fissure in the side of the cliff. The shuttle had landed on the plateau above, and the soldiers had climbed down the cliff to a narrow beach on the Oresund Bay. "I think we should transfer both groups in at once," he added.

"Each of the control rods only lets us take three people in at a time," Captain Nightsong said. "Since we can't go in with enough people to make a difference at the start, we should go in small so there is less of a chance the Efreet will see us. They may have some kind of monitor or sensor that lets them know how many people are around, and three people are a lot less suspicious than six. While three people could be friends on a walk, six people are likely to be conspirators up to no good. It's just the way the Efreet think."

"Okay," Calvin said, coming to a decision. "Here's the plan. I'm going to jump in first with Captain Nightsong and Lieutenant Knaus. We're going to make sure everything is still the way Captain Nightsong remembers it, and then we'll come back and get the rest of the platoon."

"Do you really think that's wise, sir?" Master Chief asked. "Captain Nightsong and two aviators?"

"What do you mean?"

"I mean that every time you go somewhere without me, you always seem to get into some kind of trouble I have to come rescue you from. Wouldn't it be smarter and save us all a lot of time and trouble if we sent in some combat troops first? If nothing else, wouldn't it be better if I went with you now, instead of the lieutenant?"

"I'll be fine, Master Chief," Calvin said. "Captain Nightsong has been here before and knows the way. K-Mart has more experience with the Sila race than anyone else we have. If there are Sila there, he's the best person we have to interact with them. We'll just take a quick look and then send Captain Nightsong back to get everyone else. It makes sense to find out what's going on over there before we bring in so many people that we can't get back out again quickly. It also lets us find out from the start whether we can wear our combat suits or not."

"You know sir, I've been thinking," Master Chief said after a pause.

"Damn," Calvin said. "Master Chief's been thinking? Now I really *am* scared."

"That's funny, sir," Master Chief replied; "it's just fucking hilarious. Seriously, what if the damn Psiclopes got it all wrong? What if

I'm actually the hero, and you're just one of my sidekicks? Have you ever thought of that? I seem to have to save the day all the time; wouldn't that make me the hero? Perhaps you should let the hero lead on this one for a change. Besides, I've got a bad feeling about this jump."

"Now Master Chief, if you were the hero, you'd be the one to have to go to all of the press conferences and do all of the media interviews. Is that what you want? To be in front of the press all the time?"

"Screw that," Master Chief said. "Okay, you got me there. You can go, but please be careful for once, won't you?"

"I will," Calvin said with a smile.

"Don't worry about it," said Captain Nightsong. "He'll be with me. What could go wrong?"

Captain Nightsong led them into the tunnel opening, turning on an Aesir lantern as he entered the narrow passageway. The troops followed him into the shaft, turning on their flashlights as they reached the darkness inside. The passageway sloped steeply, forcing the soldiers to carefully pick their steps, and after a few minutes Calvin knew they were well below sea level. The passageway eventually leveled out, snaked back and forth several times and then opened into a large chamber.

Captain Nightsong walked to the center of the cavern and turned around to face the group.

"Ready?" Captain Nightsong asked. He held out a hand, and Calvin and K-Mart made skin-to-skin contact with him. Seeing two nods, the Aesir pressed a button on the transportation rod he was holding in his other hand. With a flash, the three vanished.

Chapter Four

Anti-Denmark, Anti-Earth, Unknown Date

The trio reappeared in a cave complex similar to the one they left on Earth, but one that was substantially larger and showed signs of habitation: a sword was mounted on one wall and a table sat in the far corner, with a small golden rod on top. The biggest differences Calvin could see were the addition of a second room, visible through an open archway, and that the chambers were lit with some sort of light emitting strips stuck to the walls.

From what Calvin could see through the archway, the new compartment looked like a workshop, although one that didn't appear to be in use. A bellows sat next to a cold fireplace, and empty tables and barrels were scattered throughout the room. An enormous anvil bolted to a massive wooden block stood as a lonely sentinel by the fireplace.

"Wow, it's so clean," Calvin said. "It doesn't smell musty at all, and there's no dust or dirt anywhere. It's almost like someone was living here and just moved out yesterday."

"Three days ago, actually," Captain Nightsong said.

"What do you mean?" Calvin asked.

Both aviators turned to look at the Aesir, and they saw he had drawn his laser pistol. Without a word, Nightsong shot K-Mart in the center of his forehead. The aviator fell backward, dead before he hit the floor.

Calvin paused in shock, then started to draw his pistol in reflex. Before he could get it clear of its holster, Captain Nightsong picked up K-Mart's pistol, turned and leveled both weapons at Calvin. "Don't do that," he warned. "I'd hate to have to kill you, too. This soon, anyway."

"What the…?" Calvin asked, looking down at K-Mart's body. "Why the hell did you kill him?"

A wicked grin crossed the Aesir's face. "Why?" he asked. "Because he was unnecessary to my plans. You are the only one who matters." He crossed the room and removed Calvin's laser pistol from its holster. "I've been looking forward to having a real hero soul to experiment on for centuries. To finally have one given to me so freely is simply divine providence."

Captain Nightsong pulled the battery pack out of Calvin's pistol, inserted something into the battery well and reinserted the battery. A high-pitched whine filled the close confines of the cave. He made the same alteration to K-Mart's pistol, and the whine doubled in volume.

"I moved out three days ago," Captain Nightsong said. "I had to remove the rest of the equipment I left here; I didn't want it destroyed in the explosion."

"What explosion?" Calvin asked.

"The one that's going to destroy this workshop, of course," Nightsong said, looking up. "We certainly wouldn't want your people to follow us. I'm overloading the batteries so they will detonate. When they do, I expect this cave will collapse. Anyone who follows us will find themselves under 50 feet of water…assuming they don't materialize within the rubble. If they can't breathe water, I expect they will die." He chuckled.

"Let's go," Nightsong added, motioning Calvin through the doorway into the new chamber. As he entered the room, Calvin saw a familiar figure off to the side.

"Father Zuhlsdorf!" he cried, running to where the priest was zip-tied to a chair. The priest had seen better days and, judging by the wounds and bandages, had been subjected to an enormous amount of torture. Father Zuhlsdorf's head was on his chest, but when he heard his name, he lifted it and tried to focus bleary eyes on Calvin.

"But…you're dead," Calvin said.

"Nothing so exciting…as a return from…the Existential Peripheries," the priest replied. "The truth is…much more mundane." His gaze turned to Nightsong and turned into a glare. "He kidnapped me."

"What the hell did you do that for?" Calvin asked. "What the hell is going on?"

Captain Nightsong laughed. "Did you really think I could stay undetected by the Psiclopes for as long as I did? You obviously have no idea how good they are at spying. Those busy-bodies have reconnaissance devices that can go anywhere and remain undetected. I'm good, but they're better. Arges caught me a long time ago and offered me a deal. This is all just part of the plan."

"Arges caught you? Caught you doing what?"

"Rather than tell you, why don't I show you?" the Aesir asked. He put his hands over his face. When he removed them, he looked completely different. "My real name is Wayland, or "Wayland the Smith" as I was often called on this planet. For a time, I was also known as Beowulf. What you choose to call me matters not. You can continue to call me Nightsong if it simplifies things for you. I have lived long enough with that name I am used to answering to it."

"So if Arges caught you, he obviously didn't turn you in," Calvin said. "What did he get out of it? Nothing is free with him."

Nightsong barked a short laugh. "No, nothing is free with him." He shrugged. "I did some odd jobs for him. Does it really matter? They were things I was good at. An arch-duke here, a president there…"

"You…you killed people…for Arges?"

"Indeed. Arges and I had similar plans although our ultimate goals diverged in the end. He was looking for hero souls to study; I was looking for them to continue my experiments."

"How many people did you kill?"

"For Arges? Many. He was always trying to foment some kind of revolution or civil war, something that would cause heroes to come to the forefront of society."

"I don't believe you," Calvin said. "Next you're going to tell me you're the one who killed President Kennedy."

"Was he the one with the top hat or the one that kept the United States on the gold standard?" Nightsong asked. "They all kind of run together after a while." He smiled. "Oh, wait, I've got it. Kennedy was the one in the convertible, right? You've *got* to give me that one. It was a great shot, even with heat-seeking bullets."

"You really killed Kennedy?"

"No, the man in the car wasn't Kennedy; it was just a doppelganger…someone I had modified to look like him. *I'd* actually been posing as Kennedy for a while."

"If Kennedy didn't die, where is he?"

"Thanks for reminding me," Nightsong said; "I almost forgot." He crossed the room and took the sword off the wall. He turned and held it up. "Here's your president. Arges was watching him because the Psiclopes thought he was a hero spirit. When the Psiclopes decided he wasn't a full hero spirit, I got to have him." He smiled. "You may find it interesting to know Marilyn Monroe said I was the best she ever had."

"Didn't she die before Kennedy was assassinated?"

"Yes she did. The Psiclopes were watching him for quite a while." Captain Nightsong looked down at the sword, lost in thought.

While he was distracted, Calvin looked at his watch. Seeing the movement, Nightsong looked up. "Yes, it is time we left. It wouldn't do to be here much longer." He crossed to where Father Zuhlsdorf was sitting, motioning Calvin to step away from him.

"Testing a hero spirit's helpers is always so much fun," he said as he cut loose the zip ties. "It does, however, take something out of them. You may have to carry him if you want him to come along with us." Nightsong motioned for the Terrans to precede him up the passageway. "Let's go."

Calvin reached down to help the priest to his feet and found him greatly reduced; the cleric was nothing more than skin and bones. He pulled the priest's arm over his shoulder and lifted him easily from the chair.

"Let's go," Nightsong repeated. "We don't want to be here when the pistols explode."

Grendel's Cave, Fredensborg, Denmark, October 2, 2021

"Damn it," Master Chief swore. "I told him not to run off without me. Now look!"

"What?" Night asked.

"They've been gone too damn long, sir," Master Chief said, pointing at the watch on his wrist. "They should have reported back by now."

"Yes, they should have."

"Well? Aren't we going to jump in and find out what went wrong?"

Night looked at his watch. "Yes, we are," he said. He turned and started back toward the tunnel leading out of the cave.

"I thought we were going in after them," Master Chief said.

"We are," Night said, "but I'm a naturally suspicious kind of guy. I don't think I want to jump into the same place where they went in. Whoever got the CO may still be sitting at the jump point waiting for us to show up so they can bag us too. I know it's dangerous to jump in somewhere that hasn't been surveyed, but it's less dangerous to do that than to jump in where we already suspect there's a problem."

A smile crossed Master Chief's face. "I like your thinking, sir," he said, nodding. "Let's go kill some damn lizards."

Chapter Five

Anti-Denmark, Anti-Earth, Unknown Date

"I don't get it," Calvin said. "I thought you said you killed Wayland."

"You're really not very smart, are you? I *am* Wayland. Nightsong came to kill me, but the sentimental fool just couldn't do it when it came time to pull the trigger. I killed him, instead."

"What? He let you go?" Calvin asked.

"Oh, no, he shot me," Nightsong said, lifting up his tunic so Calvin could see the scar in the center of his chest. "His mistake was in caring too much for me. He flinched as he pulled the trigger and hit me too high." He pointed to a spot about three inches below the scar. "If he'd shot me here, he would have hit my heart, and I might not have been able to save myself, nanobots or not."

"Obviously you had the nanobots, or we wouldn't be having this conversation."

"Indeed. As awful as you are at your own history, even *you* have to realize how horrifically primitive medicine was on your planet at that time. I mean, really. Leeches? How is a leech supposed to cure anything? Praying to your peoples' miserable gods wouldn't have helped either. I had to come up with a better medicinal plan, or I would have died from their treatments if I had ever been wounded in battle." Nightsong's eyes lost focus as he went back in his memories.

"So, what did you do?" Calvin asked when the silence had gone on for several seconds.

"I made a deal with Arges to supply me with medicinal nanobots and taught myself how to be a life-based Eco Warrior. I became so good at healing the locals believed I could speak to the gods. I refused to worship their pathetic gods, though, so one day I made up my own pantheon on a whim. Odin, Thor, Freyr..." he stopped to laugh and then continued, "I gave them a better religion, even though it was completely made up."

"Wait; you said Arges helped you?"

"Of course he did. He was always there to provide me with whatever I needed, as long as I did what he wanted." Nightsong picked up the rod from the table and again motioned for the Terrans to precede him through the fissure. "When I first met you, I told you I knew two others who had been given progenitor's rods, and that both died before accomplishing their task," he added. "That much was true. What I didn't tell you was how they died. I killed them." He held out the rod so Calvin could see it. "You only had two of the symbols, but I need one of them. I imagine it was the one for the Psiclopes' home world."

"You didn't have Olympos?" Calvin asked. "I would have thought getting the Olympos symbol would have been easy. They were your allies, after all."

"Yes, I could have gone there on several occasions, but I could never stand the little twerps. They're always spying and trying to find out your secrets so they can use them against you. Go to their planet and let them inspect all my belongings? No thanks. I nearly left your planet when I found out there was a Psiclopes outpost on it; however, by then I had the Efreeti control rod. Since it let me turn invisible and change my appearance, I decided to see how long I could outwit them. That was my mistake, as Arges eventually caught me."

"What did he want for not turning you in?" Calvin asked.

Nightsong shuddered. "Victims, usually."

"What do you mean, 'victims?'"

"Arges is, and always has been, a sick and twisted creature. The reason he was always trying to cause international conflicts was he loved finding hero spirits' helpers. He would happily follow a hero spirit around for days…but what he enjoyed even more was seeing how long the hero spirit's helpers would last while he tortured them to death."

"You mean, like what you were doing to me?" Father Zuhlsdorf asked. "Coming from you, that's really saying something."

"Sticks and stones," Nightsong said with a smile. "Unlike his experiments, mine have a purpose. I am trying to advance the science of sword-making; Arges just does it because he likes it."

The group paused as Calvin switched Father Zuhlsdorf from his left side to his right. "I digress," Nightsong said as the group started forward again. "You asked about Nightsong. He didn't know I was a functional Eco Warrior, and took me for granted. Nightsong was already an Eco Warrior and should have killed me with his fire. He could easily have done it; however, it wouldn't have been a good way for me to go. Instead, he decided to go for the clean kill of a laser. When Nightsong flipped me over to see if I was dead, I shot him through the head." He sighed. "Salvan Nightsong and I really *were* best friends when we were young. Still, when Arges told me Nightsong was coming to kill me, I knew I only had one choice. Believe it or not, killing him really *was* the hardest thing I've ever had to do…but then again, it was either him or me."

"So you killed your best friend."

"I did," Nightsong agreed. "The irony of it all was the real Nightsong was a hero spirit himself, and I was one of his helpers. Nightsong never realized it, and I didn't figure it out until it was too late. I spent all that time trying to find a hero spirit and then killed the first one I met without being ready to catch his soul. The gods must have been laughing at me that day."

"And you've been impersonating him ever since?"

"Indeed." He chuckled. "People were amazed at how quickly I advanced as an Eco Warrior. With several hundred years' of nanobot experience at that point, advancement was trivial; I had to intentionally make mistakes so I wouldn't be found out."

As they topped a hill, Calvin looked down to see a ship sitting in the valley. Although the ship was bigger than the space fighter Calvin flew, it was much smaller than a combatant. The ship's silver skin was shapely, and it was obviously intended for atmospheric flight. "What is that?" Calvin asked.

"It's my ship," Nightsong replied. "We're going to go for a ride."

As they started moving toward the ship, Father Zuhlsdorf spasmed out of Calvin's grasp, then collapsed and lay groaning on the ground. Before Calvin could do anything, there was a flash as Nightsong shot the priest with his laser pistol. Father Zuhlsdorf stilled, his last breath escaping as a sigh.

"What the hell did you do that for?"

"He was extraneous to my plans now that I finally have you," Nightsong said. He motioned toward the ship with his pistol. "Now shut up and get going."

Fredensborg, Denmark, October 2, 2021

Night held up one finger to Master Chief as he passed along a status report to their superiors. It was a report Master Chief was happy he didn't have to make.

"Okay," Master Chief said, his eyes sweeping across the platoon. "We jump in one minute." "Is everyone suited up and ready to go kill some liz—" Master Chief interrupted himself as his eyes stopped on Bob and Doug, two of the reptilian Kuji from Domus. Thinking back, he remembered an earlier "let's go kill some lizards" comment, too.

"Umm…," Master Chief said. "When I was talking about killing lizards, you know I didn't mean you two, right?"

"Why would we think that?" Bob asked. "We're people, not lizards. How would your comment apply to us?"

"Uh, right," stammered Master Chief, at a loss for words for one of the few times in his life, "that's what I meant." His gaze moved back to the rest of the platoon. "All right; gear up! We leave in one minute."

Bob looked at Doug and twitched an ear, the equivalent of a shrug for a race that didn't have shoulders.

"Humans," Doug said in his native tongue, as if that explained everything. Bob nodded. In this case, it did.

Anti-Denmark, Anti-Earth, Unknown Date

"What are we waiting for?" Calvin asked.

"Are you in a hurry?" Nightsong asked. He nodded to the handcuffs chaining the Terran to the co-pilot's seat. "Relax. It doesn't look like you're going anywhere." He chuckled, then added, "Don't worry; you won't have to wait long."

Calvin looked back out at the landscape, hoping to see one of his friends. He tried calling the platoon on his comm, but there was no reply. While he was distracted, Nightsong reached over and touched him on the cheek. Calvin's face burned with the contact. "What was that?" he asked.

"Those were some nanobots of mine. If you get more than 25 feet from me, they will stop your heart. Also, if I should happen to die, you will die too. Just a little precaution in case you decide to try something foolish." He smiled. "Oh, yeah, I also turned off your implant's ability to transmit and receive, so you needn't bother trying to contact your friends."

Calvin glared at the Aesir, too frustrated to come up with a response.

Nightsong looked at his watch. "Five seconds," he said. He looked out the canopy as a rumble was felt throughout the ship, and a large section of land lifted a mile away, turning into a massive fireball.

"That's what I was waiting for," Nightsong said. "I just wanted to make sure your friends have an interesting welcome when they come looking for us."

"Bastard," Calvin spat.

"No, just cautious," Nightsong replied, unperturbed. "Speaking of which…" He turned a dial on the instrument panel and pulled the boom microphone down from his headset. "*Base, this is Faery,*" he transmitted. Although Nightsong spoke in Farsi, Calvin's implant was able to translate, as he had received a download of all the common Terran languages. *"I've delayed them all I can. You need to execute Plan Tempest."*

"But we are not ready," a voice replied from a speaker, also in Farsi.

"If you do not do it now," Nightsong said, *"the Americans and their allies will be here to talk with the Efreet soon, and you do* not *want that."* After a moment, he added, *"Do what you do best. Bluff."*

"You leave us no choice," the voice said. *"We will move forward with the plan. Make no mistake, though; we are not bluffing."*

Nightsong looked over to Calvin. "The scary thing is, he really isn't bluffing." Nightsong shrugged. "And they call *me* crazy."

"You're never going to get away with this…," Calvin said. "…no matter what *this* is. Night will come for you. He will never give up."

Nightsong smiled at Calvin, then looked back out of the cockpit. "I rather doubt he will come after us," the Aesir said as he pulled back on the control stick. The ship leapt from the ground and soared skyward. "Even if he somehow survives his entry into this universe, I think he is going to be rather busy with other things very soon."

Chapter Six

"Ready," Master Chief said, reaching over to make skin-to-skin contact with Staff Sergeant Alka Zoromski.

"Me too," Night said, putting his free hand on the staff sergeant's.

"Here goes nothing," Zoromski said. He pushed the 'transfer' button on the control rod, and the three men jumped into the Jinn Universe. They immediately dropped into ready positions, each facing outward, scanning their surroundings. Like all the other planets they'd been to in the Jinn Universe, the sky was a light green. The sun shone down on barren hills…and not much else.

"Hey, sir," Zoromski said after a few seconds, "isn't there supposed to be some sort of civilization here?"

"Yeah," Night said, surveying the empty horizon, "Nightsong said the Efreet were supposed to be nearby. Apparently, we've been lied to. Go back and get the next group." He gestured toward a small hill that stood between them and the cliff housing the mouth of the cave. "C'mon, Master Chief, let's go take a peek and see what there is to see."

As they reached the top of the small rise, Night and Master Chief were thrown to the ground as something below them detonated, the blast throwing huge pieces of dirt and rock in all directions. A massive fireball rolled past them.

"Ugh…" Master Chief said, rolling to his stomach and pushing himself up. "It appears someone didn't want us in the cave."

"I guess not," Night said. "I think that pretty much confirms we've been had."

"By who, though?" Master Chief asked. "Not by Nightsong. The Efreet must have found out somehow we were coming."

"If it wasn't that bastard Nightsong," Night said, "then I don't know who else it could have been. How else would they have known exactly where and when we were coming?"

The two began walking back to where platoon was assembling. As they neared the unit, Zoromski returned with the last group, who promptly threw up.

"What's up, Captain Train?" Master Gunnery Sergeant Bill Hendrick, the leader of the Ground Force, asked. "Any sign of them?"

"No—" Night said.

"Hey, sir," Sergeant Pierce 'Big Sky' Tomas interrupted, "what the hell's that?"

The platoon's leadership turned in time to see a silver ship rising in the sky a mile away.

"Beats the hell out of me," Night replied, capturing several images of the ship for future analysis. "It looks like it's about twice the size of one of the shuttles, but I've never seen anything like it before."

"That bastard can move," Master Chief said as the silver ship rocketed into the sky. It vanished from sight faster than any ship he had ever seen.

"Whoever was in that ship, we missed them," Night said. He looked around to see all of the troops staring up at the sky. "I don't imagine they're coming back, either," he added to the group. "If everyone would like to *get back to doing their fucking jobs*, we'll do a quick survey of this planet and then get back to our world to figure out what we're going to do next."

Master Chief closed his own mouth, and his gaze dropped to the men and women under his command. "What the hell is everyone doing staring up at the fucking sky?" he yelled. "The enemy is probably near here somewhere. Get your heads out of your asses and start acting like a military organization. Let's go! Scouts out! Everyone else, set up a defensible perimeter. Let's *move*, people!"

Anti-Denmark, Anti-Earth, Unknown Date

"**D**ude, what's that up there?" Sergeant Jamal 'Bad Twin' Gordon asked, motioning toward a lump 80 feet in front of them.

"Don't know," Sergeant Marcus 'Spud' Murphy replied. "Looks like a body. S'pose we ought to check it out?"

"Beats me, dude. Maybe they leave bodies on the ground here. Looks human, though." Bad Twin switched to his comm system. *"Hey, Master Chief, it looks like there's a human body up here. Want us to go check it out?"*

"No, I'd like you to wait for the second coming and see if it gets up on its own and starts walking," Master Chief replied. *"Of course I want you to check it out, you moron! Just be careful in case it's booby-trapped."*

"Roger that," Bad Twin replied. He looked at Spud. "You heard the man. Let's go check it out."

The soldiers advanced on the body, rifles at the ready, watching for enemy activity.

Bad Twin reached it first. "Holy shit!" he cried. "It's Father Z!"

"Oh, man, someone fucked him up *bad*," Spud said. "Who'd do that to a priest? *Medic!*"

The squad's medic, Corporal Shaun 'Lucky' Evertson, ran up and knelt down next to the body. "Careful," Spud said; "Master Chief said he might be booby-trapped."

"Well, then move back, because I can't check him out without touching him."

Seeing the troopers were more interested in finding out if Father Zuhlsdorf was alive than they were worried about possible booby-traps, the medic shrugged and felt for a pulse in Father Zuhlsdorf's neck. "I'll be fu…guys, he's got a pulse. It's weak, but it's there." He started stripping out of his combat suit. "Quick! Help me get him in the suit. I can stabilize him better that way."

The three soldiers raced to get the inert priest into the combat suit. As they connected the last seal, the suit came to life, analyzed Father Zuhlsdorf and began injecting him with a variety of analgesics, fluids and life-saving medications.

"*Can anyone see Lucky?*" Master Chief asked. "*What the fuck just happened to him? His suit is showing him as almost dead.*"

"*I'm good,*" Corporal Evertson said. "*We just found a human who was near death, so I gave him my suit. It will be close, but it looks like he may make it.*"

"*It's Father Z,*" Bad Twin added. "*Looks like someone beat the crap out of him and then shot him with a laser. Of course, that's after they brought him back from the grave since he was dead and all.*"

"I'll need one of your suits, too," Lucky said, who was monitoring his suit. "My suit isn't going to have enough meds in its pharmacopeia."

Anti-Iran, Anti-Earth, Unknown Date

"That's it?" Calvin asked, looking down on the Efreeti capital of Belshazzar. "It doesn't look like much, considering this is the capital of their home world." Judging by the geography, Calvin guessed he was somewhere over what would be Iran on Earth. Nightsong had overflown the Black Sea, then Calvin had seen the Caspian Sea go past on the left. The city they were overflying had tall buildings made of adobe and brick, arranged in narrow winding streets. Even though the city spread out to cover a fairly large area, each of the houses had its own enclosed courtyard, so there weren't as many residences as there would have been in a modern city on Terra. Altogether, the city couldn't have housed more than 10,000 individuals.

"Home world?" Nightsong asked as he guided the ship past the city toward an enclosure that housed a number of buildings and looked far more modern. A tall, Efreet-manned wall surrounded the buildings, including what looked like an enormous warehouse. "This isn't their home world," Nightsong continued. "The real Efreet home world is a long way from here. Whatever gave you the stupid idea this was their home world?"

"You did," Calvin said as the shuttle swooped in to land between two large adobe buildings in the enclosure's central courtyard. "You told us this was their home world."

"Did I?" Nightsong asked. The ship touched down without even a tremor, and Nightsong looked across the cockpit at Calvin. "Oops. I lied."

"It looks like you lied about a lot of things," Calvin said.

"Yeah, well I needed to make getting here important enough that you would come running back to Earth and cross over with me, without thinking about it much first. Sue me."

Nightsong smiled. "When I first met you," he added, "I told you that Aesir are less worried about short-term gains than we are long-term successes. This success has been a *long* time coming…and it's even sweeter for all the planning and work that has gone into it."

Chapter Seven

General Assembly, Terran Government HQ, Lake Pedam, Nigeria, October 4, 2021

"We searched a mile in every direction," Night said, "but there was no sign of civilization. The only sign of life on the other side was the silver ship we saw leaving, but we don't know whether our forces were onboard it or not." The general assembly meeting room spread up from him in a 90 degree cone, 45 degrees on either side of the center aisle. The room was packed, with every seat taken; all the representatives' aides had to watch from their offices.

"Why can't you tell if they were aboard?" President Nehru asked. "Wouldn't you have been able to contact them over your implants?"

"Yes, ma'am," Night replied. "If they were on the ship, we should have been able to contact them. Either they weren't onboard, they were incapacitated or there was some sort of interference that kept us from reaching them. We are unable to determine which of these happened. I think our personnel were captured by a third party, who then blew up the initial landing zone, but that is just a guess; we don't have any hard evidence to confirm it."

"What are your recommendations?" the president asked.

Before Night could respond, he saw motion out of the corner of his left eye and dove to the right away from it. He rolled and came up on one knee, reaching for the laser pistol in his holster…except he hadn't been allowed to bring it into the session. It was outside the conference chamber in the weapons storage facility.

Just to the left of where he had been standing now stood a man and a creature that looked like a seven-foot-tall salamander. An Efreeti! He had to protect the president!

Night's senses went into overdrive, and he looked around for something he could use as a weapon. Seeing nothing, he gathered himself to charge the alien as several of the representatives screamed. He could see movement as doors opened throughout the auditorium; he knew it was the security force personnel responding to the threat.

Night turned back to the man. Swarthy in complexion, the man was dressed in the long robe worn by Muslim men, along with a ghu-tra headdress. The man had dark hair and eyes, and badly needed a shave. Night could also see the man held a package wrapped in chains.

"Nobody move," the man said in Farsi, holding up his bundle. "This is a bomb!" He brought his left hand out from under the par-cel and held up a joystick. His thumb held down the button on top of the controller. "And this is a dead-man's switch," he added. "If I release this button, or if you kill me, the bomb *will* blow up. I suggest no one does anything that might make me nervous." He turned to Night.

"Captain Train," the man said, "I would appreciate it if you would come out to where I can see you. You can stand over by the president if it makes you feel better."

Night slowly got to his feet and moved to the president, his eyes on the intruders the entire time, looking for an opportunity he could exploit. It did make him feel better to be near the person he most needed to protect, even if he didn't have a plan for how he was going to do so. Yet.

President Nehru waved the security forces back. "What is it you want?" she asked.

"I am not here to hurt anyone today, and I do not intend to take up much of your time," the man said. "I just have a few announcements I need to make. You may call them demands, but they are not demands, so much as statements about how your lives have changed, and what you must do to adapt to the new reality you find yourselves in. If you want to live, that is."

"Yes?" President Nehru asked. Night had never heard so much sarcasm loaded into a single syllable.

The man smiled. "The Supreme Leader wishes you to know the so-called "Republic of Terra" is no more. All ties with off-planet civilizations are dissolved as of today. Any aliens currently polluting our soil are to leave or be exterminated immediately. All the nations on Earth have now been absorbed into the Fourth Persian Empire, and Sharia law is now in effect across the entire planet. Any infractions will be dealt with accordingly. The Supreme Leader will have more information on what this means to you, and how the new laws are to be enforced, soon."

The Efreeti next to him grunted something, its tongue flicking in and out of its mouth. "Additionally," the man added, "all technology research is forbidden from this day forward. Anyone found conducting research into any area of technology will be summarily executed. As of this moment, all replicators are to cease functioning and be turned over to us. The penalty for disobedience is simple. Your nation's capital will burn in a nuclear fire for the first infraction. After that, your entire country will feel the wrath of Allah, and all will die in the fires of his anger."

"How do we know what you say is true?" President Nehru asked.

The man smiled again, but there was no warmth; it was the most evil expression Night had ever seen.

"I hoped someone would ask that," the man said. He nodded to the Efreeti, who vanished. He looked at his watch as if counting time. "If you would all monitor your news feeds, I believe something bad is about to happen to Tashkent."

"Who's Tashkent?" a voice called.

Within moments, Night's newsfeed was swamped with pictures of a mushroom cloud rising over a city. The text beneath it read "Nuclear Bomb Destroys Tashkent." Gasps could be heard throughout the room.

"Tashkent *used* to be the capital of Uzbekistan," the man said. "Pity. It was quite a nice town before the Soviet invasion. Don't worry, though. Our people recovered the Samarkand Kufic Quran before the…demonstration." He surveyed the audience and saw several hands shoot up.

"There will not be any questions taken today," he continued, "but you may be sure more information will be forthcoming. For now, return to your countries and await further instructions. This meeting, just like this government, is at an end. Go!" He pointed to the exit.

When no one moved, he set down the package and pulled a pistol from a holster at his side. "Perhaps I didn't make myself clear. It is time for you to leave. If you don't leave immediately, I will begin shooting people until you do. You have five seconds." He began counting backward from five.

At "three," several people sprinted for the exits; at "two" the stampede was on. Night headed for the exit at "one," but only after memorizing the man's face. Someone who could so casually destroy a city of two million people needed to die. They would meet again; Night was sure.

As he passed through the door, he felt a nudge at his side and looked down to find a short, nondescript man walking alongside him. Night hadn't noticed the man before, nor had he seen him approach.

"Can we talk somewhere privately?" the man asked without looking up.

Night ran an online facial recognition scan on what he could see of the man's face, but it came back with no matches. That hadn't happened since he got his implant. Some of his confusion must have shown on his face, for the man added, "An online search won't find me. I don't exist."

"Yeah," Night said. "Come with me. My shuttle is parked on the landing pad. We can talk there."

Chapter Eight

**Cargo Bay, *Shuttle 02*, Terran Government HQ, Lake
Pedam, Nigeria, October 4, 2021**

"So," Night said. "We're here. What is it you wanted to talk about?"

"When the Psiclopes made their presence known, the world became focused on the stars," the man said, "with very few people looking after things on this planet. While this was sufficient for most nations, my country has many enemies, including those who didn't join the Republic of Terra. Everyone thought North Korea and Iran had been marginalized enough that they couldn't make trouble." He shook his head. "Those people were wrong."

After a sigh, he continued, "My organization, however, has con-tinued to monitor them. And it is a good thing we never lost our focus. Our world…no, our very race, has traitors, as you just saw."

"It might help me trust you," Night said, "if perhaps I knew who you were."

"You can call me Moshe Arens," the man said. "That is not my name, of course, but it will do well enough for now."

"If that's how you inspire trust, you're not very good at it. You'll have to try a little harder."

The man shrugged, waving off Night's concern with a flip of his hand. "My real name is unimportant; it was erased many years ago to protect the remaining members of my family. I exist for one purpose and one purpose only, to ensure the safety of my country."

"I guess you didn't get the memo," Night said. "We don't have countries anymore; we're all part of the Fourth Persian Empire now."

"I do not consider myself part of the Persian Empire any more than you do, Captain Train. If it will help you move on, I am authorized to tell you I am part of the Mossad, although my organization is not one you would ever have heard of. You may be familiar with my organization's motto. If not, it is very relevant now. 'Where there is no guidance, a nation falls, but in an abundance of counselors, there is safety.'"

Night recognized the biblical quote, and he knew it to be the Mossad's motto. "So you are an Israeli?" It was more of a statement than a question.

"I am," the man said with a nod. "Despite the world's recent focus on the stars, we still have many enemies here; it is only prudent we keep our eyes on them. I have been watching Iran nearly all my adult life."

"With a secret organization?"

The man shrugged. "We all have our secrets. By the way, how is Father Z doing?"

Night raised an eyebrow. The priest's reappearance was a closely-guarded secret; only a *very* select few were aware of it. Whoever the man was, his sources were good. Very good. "Touché," Night said. "If you really care, he is expected to recover."

"I do care," the man replied; "he may be able to provide additional information about what the traitors are doing." He paused, seemingly lost in thought.

"So," Night said, growing impatient after a few seconds, "this would be a good time to tell me what you know. That *is* the reason you made yourself known to me, correct? So I could do something about it?"

"Partially," the man said. "While we do want your involvement, we also want you to take *all* the credit for it; we would prefer our involvement…even our very existence…never comes to light. We are ghosts, and we would like to stay that way."

"If you can help us stop these assholes, I'll be happy to forget I ever saw you," Night replied. "My focus is on killing bad guys, not revealing the identities of quasi-allies."

The man smiled. "We *are* allies," he said. "We want what you want, a peaceful Earth where everyone can prosper. We just have different methods of achieving it."

"I understand," Night said. "The Kidon has been responsible for a number of successful assassinations; however, that's something we Americans generally don't go for."

"There are two things wrong with that statement. First, Americans *do* go for assassinations; they just aren't honest enough to admit it when they're caught. Assassinations can be very effective in stunting an organization's growth. The other thing wrong is that, while the Kidon *is* the department responsible for executing our nation's enemies, I am not part of it as you are suggesting. Now, can we dispense with the verbal sparring? We do not have much time before irreversible changes will be made."

Night stared at the man, trying to take his measure; the man endured it without shrinking until Night made up his mind.

With a small nod, Night indicated his approval. "Okay," he growled. "What do you know that can help us kill these bastards?"

Cargo Bay, *Shuttle 02*, Lake Pedam, Nigeria, October 5, 2021

"I don't have a lot of time," Admiral Wright said, walking into the cargo bay with Night to find Lieutenant Bradford waiting for them. "As you can imagine, the world leadership wants to know what the hell I'm doing about the terrorists. What is so damn important you dragged me out here to see?"

"There isn't anything to see, sir," Night said, "but I think I have a line on your terrorists."

"Well that would be the first good news I've had today," the admiral said. "What have you got?"

"After the General Assembly meeting yesterday, I was approached by a man with some information. I think he's from the Mossad, but can't prove it. He claims to know where the terrorists are hiding and how to get them."

"And you believe him?"

"I think so. He certainly is well-connected, if nothing else. He knew we had found Father Z and brought him back."

"Why did he contact you and not someone in the government, then?"

"He said our communications are compromised, and all our phones are monitored. He's also pretty sure our satellite and network communications are being monitored. I can't tell if he's just paranoid, but he's worried about our implant comms too. I don't know how the terrorists could breach the implant network, but he swears they have. If you're transmitting anything, he says the Persians can probably pick it up. The bottom line is if your conversation isn't face-to-face and in a secure location, you're being monitored."

"That's scary," the admiral said. "Total comms breakdown."

"Yes sir. The Israelis also believe we only have global communications so the terrorists *can* monitor them for intel. If the Iranians thought we were onto them, the man said the Iranians could take down *all* our comms nets."

"But how? Who do they have positioned to do this?"

"I don't know, sir. He did tell me where to find their headquarters, and he let me know that we've only got a small window of opportunity to stop them."

"Based on the fact we're now part of the 'Fourth Persian Empire,'" the admiral said, "I'm guessing the headquarters is in Iran."

"That's a good guess," Night said. "What do you know about the Iranian nuclear program?"

"Umm…they lie until they're caught, they confess and we forgive them? Then they go back to doing it again? Something like that? Honestly, my focus has been on aliens, not what the Iranians have been doing."

"Unfortunately, almost everyone's focus has been on the stars," Night replied, "and that's what's biting us in the ass right now." He paused to pull out a map and spread it across the central web seating.

Night pointed to a spot in southwest Iran. "This is Lashkar Abad. In 1998, the Iranians built a plant here for the laser isotope separation of uranium in support of their nuclear program. The site was exposed in 2003, leading to an inspection of the site. Soon after that, the Iranians said they were shutting the plant down because they no longer had any intention of enriching uranium using that method. The plant stayed vacant until 2006, when claims were made that the site had been revived by Iran for laser enrichment."

Night met Admiral Wright's eye. "But that isn't what happened. It was revived, all right, but it was revived to serve as a portal between our world and anti-Earth. Ever since, there has been trade and communications between the two worlds."

Admiral Wright's eyes widened in shock. "You mean they've been in contact with the Efreet *for 15 years?*"

"Yes sir. That's what our new friend told me, anyway. It even escaped *their* attention for a while. At first, they thought the site had been restarted to conduct laser separation again, and they really didn't think much about it. Sure, they cared, but it was lower priority than a lot of other things they were following, and they didn't have enough assets to follow up. They noticed security had been beefed up and a number of scientists and workers were coming and going from the plant, and they just put it down to the plant's original purpose."

"What changed?"

"Nothing changed for a while, which is something our contact felt very ashamed of."

"Still," the admiral said, "at least they were watching it, if only a little. That's more than we were doing."

"Yes sir, but it was only an accident the site truly came to their attention. During a routine analysis of some photoreconnaissance, their intelligence officer recognized the face of a scientist going into the plant. He had just seen that face on TV and knew who it was, a Dr. Dalir Shir-Del, a very prominent biologist. He was part of a group of 12 men who were going into the plant."

"What's a biologist doing in a nuclear plant?"

"That's what their intel guy wondered, so he tried to figure out who was with him. As it turned out, they were *all* biologists. One biologist might have had a scientific reason to be there, but 12 of them? At once? He knew something else was going on and alerted his superiors."

"When did that happen?"

"August 20, 2018. You may remember that date."

"Yeah, the start of the Sino-American War."

"Yes sir, you and I were a little distracted at the time. Then, as soon as it ended, the Psiclopes showed up and 'boom;' off we went to the stars. We missed it."

"But the Israelis didn't?" Night could hear the hope in the admiral's voice.

"They didn't miss it," Night replied; "unfortunately, by then the Iranian's security was *tight*. The people involved in the program all knew each other, and weren't letting anyone else in. It was difficult for the Israelis to get an operative close to the site."

"What did they do, kill someone to take their place?"

"He wouldn't say, but I imagine they took out more than one. However they did it, the Israelis finally got someone into the plant and found out what was going on."

"When did that happen?"

"Two weeks ago."

"Shit; *just two weeks?*"

"Yes sir, they *just* found out. That's why we haven't heard anything about this; they haven't had time to tell anyone. They haven't even finished briefing their *own* chain of command. Then, before they really even had a handle on everything going on, their inside guy said something changed a few days ago and the Iranians accelerated their plans. Tashkent wasn't supposed to be the target; Chicago was. They just didn't have time to get someone to our side of the planet in their universe. Tashkent was close…and the fallout wouldn't affect them. Picking Tashkent also let them steal the Samarkand Quran, the oldest Quran in the world, because the Iranians thought having it would give them more legitimacy."

"What changed?"

"We went into their world."

"So we spooked them into kicking off their plans before they were ready?"

"No sir, I don't think so. Well, at least not on our part."

"What do you mean?

"I mean the plan changed when, quote, 'an elf and his prisoner,' unquote, landed in the main city of the Efreet on anti-Earth."

"You think that's Captain Nightsong and one of our men?"

"I would bet money it's Nightsong and one of our men. Sir, I think he's been playing us all along. The only reason we went to anti-Earth was because he told us to. He's the one who said anti-Earth was their capital, and then he scared us into taking a look. He even talked us into letting him take Calvin across with him."

"Why did he do that?"

"I don't know," Night said. "But I do know when I see that bastard again, I *will* kill him."

"Well, I don't know if there's anything else we can do about it right now, but I agree with your sentiments. Did your new friend have any ideas on what we can do to stop the Persian Empire from taking control of our infrastructure, aside from trading nuclear bombs with them?"

"Yes sir, he had an idea. We talked about it a bit, and then I brought Lieutenant Bill Bradford, our representative from Department X, into the discussion. You're familiar with Department X, right, sir?"

"Familiar with it?" Admiral Wright asked. "Of course I am; it was my idea. I knew we needed an organization to exploit the alien technology we've been acquiring, so I set it up."

"Okay, so when I tell you about some of these things, I just wanted you to know the equipment exists, and I'm not making this shi—I'm not making this equipment up…even if we haven't used it yet."

"What equipment?" the admiral asked.

Night turned to Lieutenant Bradford. "It's your plan, hot shot," he said. "Why don't *you* tell the admiral?"

Lieutenant Bradford took a breath and let it out, looking at the floor. Night could tell the lieutenant was building up his courage; he suspected the lieutenant had never briefed an admiral before. With a nod to himself, he looked up and met the admiral's eyes.

"Here's what we know, sir," he said. "First, almost all the cross-universe operations occur at the plant. The Israelis said this is because the Iranians have built an operational portal that will let people cross over—"

"Wait," the admiral said. "The Iranians *built* a portal? Have we ever seen one of these before?"

"No sir," Night replied. "The portal is a new capability, and the fact that the Iranians have it makes our position extremely precarious. They could transport people into the other universe and have them show up *anywhere* on this planet. We might wake up one morning to find Washington has been destroyed…or the world headquarters…or anything. We need to destroy the portal, along with any other facilities they have that could be used to make more."

"Complicating this," Lieutenant Bradford added, "is the fact there's a portal on anti-Earth like the one in our universe. Both of these will need to be destroyed."

"Got it," the admiral said. "What else?"

"Second," Lieutenant Bradford replied, "the Efreet also have two transportation rods to go back and forth between universes; we saw one at the General Assembly building." He handed the admiral a digital photograph of the Efreeti. "These rods will have to be either captured or destroyed. The good news is both of them are usually kept at the plant in the other universe; they don't trust the Iranians with them."

"Good thinking on their part," noted the admiral.

Lieutenant Bradford nodded. "Finally," he said, "we think Captain Nightsong is holding Lieutenant Commander Hobbs at the facility in the other universe. It could be Lieutenant Knaus, but the description in the reports more closely resembles Calvin. Lieutenant Commander Hobbs would also be more valuable as a hostage. Nightsong has a ship, which is probably the silver ship Captain Train saw leaving when they went across to anti-Earth. Nightsong might leave or move the hostage at any time."

He took another breath and continued, "All these missions will require lightning raids in order to be successful. The Israelis are prepared to destroy the facility in Iran, but they have no way of reaching the facility on anti-Earth."

"But we do," the admiral said.

"Yes sir, we do," Lieutenant Bradford said.

"It will have to be my unit," Night said. "We're the only ones with the training and equipment."

"If, and I do mean *if,* I authorize this, it is going to have to be a perfect, foolproof plan," the admiral said. "If we try and fail, there *will* be repercussions. There's no telling how many of our cities they will nuke in retaliation."

"There's no such thing as a foolproof plan," Night said; "you know that as well as I." The admiral nodded. "With that being said, I believe we have come up with a workable plan that gets us there and allows us to accomplish the missions."

"What about getting back?" the admiral asked.

"That's going to be more difficult," Night acknowledged. "The problem is we don't know if there are any Efreeti ships in anti-Earth orbit. We have a couple of plans, but we won't know which one we're using until we get there."

"I don't like that," the admiral said.

"Honestly, sir, I don't like it much either," Night said; "however, it's got to be done. The longer we wait, the more control the Iranians will have, and the more chance they'll have to proliferate nuclear warheads around anti-Earth. We need to go now, before they take control of all our facilities."

"What do you need from me?" the admiral asked.

"We just need authorization to make a box with the Class 2 replicator on the moon."

"Didn't the Iranians say we weren't allowed to use the replicators anymore? Won't they be watching?"

"They might," Night said, "but they are probably watching the big ones to make sure we don't build more ships. As the replicator I want to use is on the far side of the moon, they won't be able to see it. If we black out comms, we can be done and out of there before anyone notices."

"One other question," the admiral said. "How are you going to keep them from noticing the *Terra* is gone? Won't they be expecting an attack when the *Terra* jumps to the other universe?"

"*Terra?*" Night asked. "Who said anything about the *Terra* taking us over?"

Chapter Nine

Starboard Cargo Bay One, *TSS Spark*, Dark Side of the Moon, October 6, 2021

Master Chief watched the ungainly craft as it floated into the box. Nearly 100 feet long and 50 feet wide, it barely fit. Despite the driver's best effort, the starboard side made contact with the box, smearing the paint on the number '85' and eliciting a squeal that could be heard over the screaming of the vessel's four gas turbine engines.

"With all the advanced alien technology at our disposal, *that's* the best we could do?" Master Chief shouted. "I've ridden on those pieces of shit. Really? That's the best we could do?"

"What *is* that thing?" Sergeant Anne 'Fox' Stasik asked.

"It's an LCAC," her brother, Gunnery Sergeant Jerry 'Wolf' Stasik said, pronouncing it 'el-cack.' "That's short for Landing Craft, Air Cushioned. Basically, it's a big hovercraft the wet navy uses for transporting people and gear from amphibious assault ships to the beach."

"The navy folks also used to take us SEALs out with them sometimes," Master Chief added. "They break down a lot." He looked back to Night. "Really? We couldn't do any better than that?"

"No, we couldn't, so stop your bitching," Night said. The flying boat made it into the box, landed on four giant blocks inside it and shut down its engines. "All right," he continued as silence returned to the cargo bay; "gather round. Here's what we're going to do."

Cockpit, *Shuttle 02*, Dark Side of the Moon, October 6, 2021

"Is this the dumbest thing you've ever done?" Lieutenant James Alfred 'Jamming' Miles, the Weapon Systems Officer (WSO) of *Shuttle 02,* asked.

"While flying anyway," his pilot, Lieutenant Jeff 'Canuck' Canada, said. He watched as the *Spark* vanished from sight. "Huh," he said, "maybe this will work after all." He clicked the radio's transmit switch twice to let the crew of the *Spark* know they were invisible. The system of microphone clicks had been arranged to keep any voice transmissions from being intercepted. The cargo ship reappeared.

"Here goes nothing," Jamming said. He flipped the switch on the shuttle's stealth system. After a couple of seconds, two microphone clicks were heard, indicating it was working as well.

"Well, I'll be damned," Canuck said. "It worked."

Jamming turned the stealth system back off, and Canuck flew the shuttle into Starboard Cargo Bay One.

"How long do we have to wait?" Canuck asked.

Jamming looked at his notes. "About five minutes," he said. "It took a lot longer to get the stealth module attached to the shuttle than they thought. We almost didn't make the timeline."

The five minutes flew by as they went over the mission profile in their minds. Finally, right on schedule, there was a flash as they made the jump to the Jinn Universe…followed by waves of nausea.

"Is it always this bad?" Jamming asked when he finished puking.

"It gets easier," Canuck said.

"I hope so," Jamming said. He tied off the airsickness bag. "All right, I'm ready to go."

Canuck lifted the shuttle off the deck. "Are we cloaked?"

"Coming on now," Jamming said. He flipped the switch. "Should be good."

Canuck could tell from the look on the lineman's face that it worked. "Okay," he said, "here goes nothing." He guided the shuttle out of the cargo bay and began flying to the drop point.

As they crested over the anti-moon, they got their first look at anti-Earth. "Looks about the same," Canuck observed. "Aside from the atmosphere being kind of green."

They flew the rest of the way in silence, each hoping there wouldn't be a system that could see them.

"Oh, crap," Jamming said as they neared the drop point. "I'm picking up something. Looks like there's a ship in orbit." He did some calculations. "It won't affect us now, but the pickup could be...interesting."

"I hate interesting," Canuck said. "Are we ready?"

"Yeah," Jamming agreed. He reached up to flip a switch. "Cargo bay doors coming open." When the green light illuminated, he pushed a red button next to the switch. "Cargo deploying."

"Good luck, boys," Canuck said as the box rolled out the back of the shuttle. "And now, we wait..."

Port Cabin, *LCAC 85*, Anti-Earth, Unknown Date

"I've done an awful lot of crazy shit in my time," Master Chief said as they felt the giant box roll out of the shuttle's cargo bay with jolt. The officers and senior enlisted were watching the evolution from the port cabin of the LCAC, while the rest of the troops waited in the 'Personnel Transfer Module,' a big box strapped to the center of the LCAC's cargo bay. "I've even done some really stupid shit too," he continued, "but this has to be the stupidest and craziest thing I've *ever* done. Have I mentioned that?"

"Repeatedly," Night said.

"Actually, I reviewed the records, and the assault drop box is one of the safest means of assaulting a planet," Lieutenant Bradford noted. "Not only does it get us down quickly, but with the various coatings the box has, we appear to an unsuspecting nation like a meteor falling from the skies." His eyes widened a little as a thought came to him, and he turned to Night. "They aren't expecting us, are they?"

"Not that we know of."

"Good," Lieutenant Bradford replied, although his eyes darted back and forth as if he was still unsure. "I didn't realize we would be weightless this long."

"This is the easy part," the LCAC's Loadmaster, Petty Officer Steve Johnson, said. "The fun part is going to be when we try to fire up the engines. Hopefully we will get them all running before we hit."

"What are the odds of that happening?" Lieutenant Bradford asked.

"Pretty poor," Petty Officer Johnson replied.

"Shitty," Master Chief said.

"What happens if the motors don't all run?" Lieutenant Bradford asked.

Petty Officer Johnson shrugged. "We make a big splash when we hit."

"We're not going to sink, though, are we?"

"Nah, we'll hit pretty hard, but assuming nothing breaks too badly, we'll still float like a normal boat…we just won't be able to do any of the flying stuff."

"Which means we'll be a lot slower on the water, and the Efreet will have a lot more warning we're coming," Night added. "And we'll have to hump all our gear about 18 miles, too, which will suck."

"And we won't make our mission timeline," Master Chief concluded. "We'll be pretty screwed."

The men were quiet as they contemplated all the ways the mission could go wrong…until they reached atmosphere, and the shaking began.

"Is it supposed to vibrate this much?" Lieutenant Bradford asked. "I mean, this is normal, right?"

"No idea sir," Master Chief said. "You're the expert on these things. I've never used a box before."

BANG! BANG! BANG! It felt like somebody was outside the assault box hitting it with a massive sledgehammer.

"Sounds like someone's outside," Night said. "Hey, Lieutenant, why don't you go answer the door?"

"Not…funny," Lieutenant Bradford replied, his eyes tightly shut.

The hammering continued for several more minutes, then the shaking became more violent.

Master Chief winked at Night. "Hey, Lieutenant, is the side of the box supposed to get so red? It almost looks like it's glowing…"

"What? Where?" Lieutenant Bradford asked. "The manual didn't say anything about that! I hope it's normal; I mean, it's got to be normal, right?"

"Actually, the sides of the box *are* turning kinda red," said Petty Officer Johnson. Seated up on a platform, he was the only person able to look out the port observer dome window.

All the color drained from Lieutenant Bradford's face.

"Guide parachutes deploying," Petty Officer Johnson noted. The sounds of wind noise could be heard from outside.

"Wee!" Master Chief yelled as the capsule began to yo-yo back and forth. "This is fun, isn't it, Lieutenant?"

"This is worse than a roller coaster," Lieutenant Bradford said. "How can it feel like we're being pulled in every direction at once?"

"Main chute deployment," Petty Officer Johnson said. The ride smoothed and everyone, including Lieutenant Bradford, began breathing again. "Time for the fun to begin." The passengers were thrown from side to side as the LCAC rocked. "There go the sides of the box. Time to pray that the engines will start…"

"There's one…" Over the wind noise, the troops could hear a jet engine spin up to full power.

"Two…" The jet noise doubled in volume as the second engine came online.

"Three…" The craft started shaking as the roar intensified.

"And four…fuck!"

"Unless that's a technical term in the navy," Night said, "I can't imagine 'fuck' is good."

"Nope," Petty Officer Johnson replied. "The fourth motor won't come online. There's a stuck valve."

Reacting to something he heard over his headset, the other member of the port cabin, the LCAC's deck mechanic, pulled a wrench out of the tool box next to him. He released his seat belt and jumped out of his seat.

"Sit down, Jones!" the loadmaster yelled, but the other man ran to the cabin door, catching himself on a bulkhead as the craft rolled in a wind gust. "The craftmaster said we'd get it once we're down!" the loadmaster added.

The deck mechanic opened the door, and a blast of wind swept through the cabin. The temperature was below freezing at their altitude, and all the troops shivered in the icy gale. Jones turned around, gave the loadmaster a thumbs-up and went out the door, closing and dogging it shut as he left.

The ship rolled again, even further than before, as another gust hit the craft. Master Chief saw the loadmaster's eyes grow large in shock. "Man overboard!" he screamed into his microphone. He threw off his headset, released his harness and jumped down from his platform.

He crossed the cabin to the door, before turning back to Night. "I just hope this is worth it, sir," he said. Another icy blast lashed the cabin, chilling the troops, as he went out. The door slammed shut with a note of finality.

Chapter Ten

Transfer Facility, Lashkar Abad, Anti-Earth, Unknown Date

"I don't get it," Calvin said as they walked into the warehouse. Unlike the rest of the buildings and houses in the area, the warehouse looked modern and very Earth-like from the outside, almost as if it had been lifted from a Terran facility and brought to the Jinn Universe intact. "Why are you doing this? You're helping your civilization's enemies. Your entire *race* could be destroyed because of you."

"True," Nightsong replied; "the civilization *could* be destroyed. I don't think it will be, at least not before we get back, but that was a risk I had to take. If they can't hold out until we get there to save the day, then it wasn't much of a civilization anyway, was it?"

"That still doesn't tell me why you're doing it," Calvin replied.

Nightsong stopped walking and leveled a piercing glare at Calvin. "You really want to know? Well let me tell you a story. A long time ago, especially as your race reckons time, there was a set of twins, a boy and a girl, who were born to the rulers of our race. This was during one of our wars with the Jotunn. As was often the case, the giants struck without warning, hoping to surprise us and take back their planet. As part of their plan, they sent a number of assassins along with a diplomatic party to our capital. While there, the assassins struck, killing our king and queen. The Jotunn also captured the twins, who they hoped to take back to their world as hostages to ensure our obedience to their wishes."

"Unfortunately, the girl was tremendously headstrong. Once she got something in her head, you could never talk her out of it. She decided she would escape and, if that failed, she would kill herself rather than become a hostage. Unable to escape, she killed herself before I could stop her. Minalwen died in my arms, and I watched her spirit leave her body. I swore then I would find a hero and return to destroy the entire Jotunn race. All of them, no matter how far they ran or how well they hid."

Calvin's brows knitted. "So…you want to take me back to fight the Jotunn for you?"

"Indeed. I intend to fight and destroy the Odin in single combat, and you will help me."

"How can I help you in single combat?"

Nightsong smiled. "You will be in my sword; together, we will destroy the Odin and his entire line. Then we will destroy the entire Jotunn race. And finally, I will kill my uncle and take my place as Thor of the Aesir."

Port Cabin, *LCAC 85*, Parishan Lake, Anti-Earth, Unknown Date

The cabin door opened, but this time the blast of air was much warmer. The loadmaster struggled to enter the cabin, his right hand tucked into his left armpit. Blood was splattered across his entire front.

He dogged the door shut and sagged against it, his face pale. Master Chief released his seat belt and sprang to the man's aid, helping him to a seat on one of the web benches. "Let me see it," Master Chief demanded.

Petty Officer Johnson removed his hand from the protection of his armpit and Master Chief could see he was missing most of the little finger. Blood continued to well up from the stump. "What happened?" Master Chief asked, pulling gauze out of his pack.

"You know how they say, 'beware of rotating machinery?'" Johnson asked in a weak voice. "They really mean it." He coughed and winced. "Hurts like a son of a bitch too. The good news is the fourth motor is running." He nodded toward his seat. "Give me the headset please."

The headset's cord was long enough to reach where he was sitting, and Master Chief put it on the loadmaster's head, adjusting the microphone so he could speak into it.

"*Duke, Smoke, we're all set back here,*" Petty Officer Johnson said. "*No, there's no chance. He went overboard at about 30,000 feet. I saw him go.*" He paused, listening, and then moved the microphone to talk to the soldiers.

"Stand by; they're about to blow the box!" The LCAC's engines screamed as the ship's craftmaster brought the engines and lift fans to full power. *Bang! Bang! Bang! Bang!* The explosive bolts holding the LCAC to the bottom of the box were fired and the LCAC's fans blew the rest of the box down and away from them. The boat lurched, and Master Chief could feel the craft drop as the parachute was jettisoned immediately afterward.

"Hang on!" Johnson called.

Master Chief didn't think the engines could get any louder. He found he was wrong, as the engines were brought to full power. The ship shook like a wet dog, seemingly trying to tear itself apart, and then slammed into the water of Parishan Lake. Miraculously, nothing further broke and the craft lifted back off the water to its operating altitude of six feet. The craftmaster spun the craft around to the southeast and began accelerating.

"The navigator sends her compliments and says we're 40 miles away from the target. We will be there in 39 minutes."

Master Chief looked at his watch and nodded to Night. "Right on time."

Chapter Eleven

Lashkar Abad, Iran, October 6, 2021

The nondescript man looked over the crest of the hill at the warehouse three miles away. It was well lit, and he could see activity throughout the compound. Trucks continued to come and go, all day and night, as they had for the last week. Everything was normal.

He looked up and saw a flashing light high above as an aircraft flew over. Pushing himself back from the crest, he stood up and struggled into his suit. He hated wearing it, but it was necessary. He only had 43 seconds to get it on and sealed, but he had grown up on the Lebanese border. He could suit up twice in that time. He smiled to himself as he closed the last seal.

Aircab 207, **Enroute from Baku to Abu Dhabi, October 6, 2021**

"Coming left five degrees," the pilot of the Gulfstream G550 aircraft said.

"Think they will notice?" the copilot asked.

"Unlikely," the pilot replied. "They are lazy bastards."

"Aircab 207, *this is Shiraz Approach Control*," a voice crackled over the radio, "*We show you deviating left of course. Come back right 10 degrees to resume track and avoid restricted airspace.*"

"Aircab 207, *roger, coming right 10 degrees,*" the pilot replied without touching the controls.

"This place must be important to them," the copilot noted.

"It must be," the pilot agreed. "Too bad they won't have it much longer." He switched to the plane's intercom. "*We are within range. Deploy the weapon.*"

"*Roger, deploying the weapon.*"

The pilot felt the plane shudder slightly as a door opened in the back of the aircraft. After 30 seconds, the shuddering ceased.

"*The weapon is deployed.*"

"*Understood.*" The pilot brought the plane back to the right. He looked back to the area of Lashkar Abad. "Leh lehizdayen," he said in Hebrew. "*Fuck you.*"

The copilot nodded. "I think they'll get the message."

Starboard Cabin, LCAC 85, Approaching Lashkar Abad, Anti-Earth, Unknown Date

"Oh fuck," the craftmaster said, a note of awe in his voice. "Hey, Klemarczyk, what's our target again?"

The navigator didn't look up from her chart. "It's a warehouse. Just follow the wadi to the southeast, and we'll run right into it. It sits just past a small village."

"We'll run right into it?" the craftmaster asked.

"Yeah," the navigator said without looking up. "It should be right in front of us. You can't miss it."

"You mean *that?*"

"Holy shit…"

Port Cabin, *LCAC 85*, Approaching Lashkar Abad, Anti-Earth, Unknown Date

Master Chief heard the engines come back up to full power and felt the craft jump forward as the craftmaster accelerated to attack speed.

"Five minutes," Petty Officer Johnson said from his normal position up in the observation bubble. The platoon's medic, Corporal Shaun 'Lucky' Evertson, had patched him up and given him some drugs, and the loadmaster had resumed his duties.

"Five minutes, everyone, stay sharp!" Master Chief commed. *"Gunners ready?"* With the loadmaster injured and the deck mechanic lost overboard, the platoon was manning the LCAC's two M60 machine guns.

"Mount One is ready," Sergeant Milan 'Gunner' Vranjesevic said.

"Two is manned and ready," Sergeant Dan 'Giseman' Geisenhof added. *"I can see the facility. It's lit up like a Christmas tree. At a guess, I'm probably going to need a bigger gun…I may need more ammo, too, but definitely a bigger gun."*

Master Chief looked up to the loadmaster. "Can you see the target?" he asked. "What's it look like?"

"It's big," Petty Officer Johnson said. He slid out of the seat so Master Chief could climb up to look out the bubble. "Here, take a look."

Master Chief looked at Night. "Want to go first?" he asked.

"Go ahead," Night said as he went to the door. "I'm going outside."

Master Chief climbed into the loadmaster's seat and his eyes widened in surprise. "Fuck…" he said involuntarily under his breath. He had been told the facility was about the same size as the one on Earth, but it wasn't. It was much, *much* bigger.

Where the warehouse building on Earth was only two stories, this one was at least three stories high, and probably closer to four. It was hard to tell, though, because part of it was obscured by an enormous wall. It wasn't a chain link fence like on Earth, but a no-kidding *wall* that any medieval castle would have been proud to call its own. The wall was at least 15 feet high and looked thick…far too thick for the LCAC to knock down. The only opportunity would be the gate, but the gate doors were closed and looked like they were made of metal and at least as solid as the rest of the walls.

Fuck.

"Grenadiers and cyborgs to the bow, now!" he commed. He looked down at the loadmaster. "Tell your craftmaster to aim for the gate. We're going to take it down." He switched back to the comm system. *"Aim for the gate and try to take out the hinges. 25 nanogram setting!"*

"Hey, Master Chief," the loadmaster said, "he wants to know what you think you can do against that wall."

"Tell him—" Master Chief started and then reached for the headset. "Give me the damn headset, and I'll tell him myself."

He took the headset and put it on. *"Craftmaster, this is the platoon's master chief. I have my grenadiers and cyborgs going to the bow. They are going to blow down the gates. Don't stop; they'll get them down."*

"Grenadiers? Are those the guys with the trident things?"

"Yeah, those aren't tridents, they are antimatter projectors. They are going to be firing rounds with about five times as much explosive power as a hand grenade. If that doesn't work, we'll up the ante."

"Unless they have a pretty good range, they're only going to get a couple of shots."

"You just drive the damn bus and leave the gate to us. We'll take care of it."

Master Chief handed the headset back. "I'm going outside," he said. He switched to his comm. *"The craftmaster is worried you won't get the doors down. Use the 50 nanogram setting."*

Chapter Twelve

Bow, *LCAC 85*, Approaching Lashkar Abad, Anti-Earth, Unknown Date

The wall approached with alarming rapidity. *"Fire!"* Master Chief commed over the noise of the engines and the rush of the wind.

There were six fire teams in the platoon, and each team leader was equipped with an alien trident that launched a round of antimatter within a magnetic containment field. The magnetic field dissipated upon impact, and the antimatter reacted explosively with whatever it hit. The six rounds impacted the gate's doors and the ground in front of it, and the blasts threw several of the Efreet from the walls. Three of the four cyborgs had rocket launchers, and they added to the maelstrom.

As the smoke cleared, Master Chief could see the right gate was only hanging by one hinge, although the left gate was still in one piece. *"Fire!"* he ordered again, and another round of projectiles raced in front of the speeding LCAC to collide with the gates. The right door was blown completely off its hinges, and the left one sagged, two of its three hinges destroyed.

Both machine guns opened fire as the defenders began firing at the craft. Unsure what the craft was, the defenders had held their fire while they waited for orders; as the Terrans made their intentions known, the defenders returned fire. They had never trained to hit something moving as quickly as the speeding LCAC, though, and their first volley went high and long. They didn't get a second volley as the LCAC crashed through the remains of the gate, yawing slightly as its left front impacted the left door, still hanging from the wall.

Transfer Facility, Lashkar Abad, Anti-Earth, Unknown Date

"Let's go," Nightsong said, bursting through the door. The ground shook and multiple explosions could be heard from outside.

"What's going on?" Calvin asked.

"I imagine your friends are here to try to recover you, despite the warning they were given." He motioned toward the door with his laser pistol.

"And what if I'd rather stay here and wait for them to rescue me?"

"Then I would have to shoot you," Nightsong said, as the sound of jet engines and tearing metal could be heard. "That's not what I want to do, especially now that my plans are starting to come together, but shoot you I shall. Then I'll use my nanobots to sew your hands behind your back to make you easier to transport. It won't be fun." He smiled. "Well, it won't be fun for you, anyway." Nightsong motioned toward the door again. "We don't have any time to waste. Move!"

LCAC 85, Transfer Facility, Lashkar Abad, Anti-Earth, Unknown Date

Master Chief surveyed the buildings while his troops did everything possible to knock them down and kill everyone in the compound. The troops had formed a perimeter around the LCAC and were firing at everything that moved. Some of the buildings were already a *lot* worse for wear.

"*Hey, Gurn,*" Master Chief commed. "*I think that's enough for that building. Dial your trident back a little. We don't need to level* everything *out here, especially since the skipper may be in one of them.*"

"*You got it, Master Chief,*" Staff Sergeant Ryan 'The Big Gurn' Gurney replied. "*Is this all they've got? Flechette guns and flamethrowers?*"

"*No, we know they also have big combat robots that are armed with powerful lasers, so be on the lookout for them.*"

Master Chief surveyed the compound. Unless some of the robots showed up, the battle was in hand. All the Efreeti flechette guns were the little handheld ones; they had a few of the big crew-served guns on the wall, but the Efreet couldn't swivel the mounts to point into the interior of the compound. Even if they could, the Terrans' weapons would still have completely outclassed them. The flamethrowers the Efreet had were extremely nasty, but only from a fairly close range. As long as the Terrans kept the Efreet back, they weren't going to be much of a danger…unless they brought up some of the bigger stuff.

He went back to identifying the buildings. The giant warehouse housed the transport device, or so they'd been told; anything else that might reside in its cavernous depths would remain unknown until they went into it. There were several buildings that looked like they could be barracks, several that looked like administration of some sort, maybe, and at least another six or seven that could have been anything.

Searching all the buildings for the transportation rods would take forever…especially if the troops continued to destroy them.

"So, sir," Master Chief said, "how are we going to do this?"

"I'm still working on that," Night said. He frowned. "It's going to take a long damn time to search all the buildings, even if we're able to narrow it down some. There's no telling how much backup they have available, but I'm sure they've called it in. We're going to need to evac pretty quickly."

He thought for a few seconds, then came to a decision. "Have First Squad take the devices into the warehouse and let's get that party started. Send a fire team from Second Squad through the facility and see if we can find any indication of where the transport rods or the skipper might be. The rest of Second Squad can guard the LCAC."

Transfer Facility, Lashkar Abad, Anti-Earth, Unknown Date

Calvin tried to cover a smile as he looked over the tops of the nearby buildings. Smoke rose from several places, and the only sounds of combat he could hear were his soldiers' weapons.

Nightsong saw the smile. "Taking this facility is not a great accomplishment," he noted with a shrug. "The troops here are poorly armed and armored compared with your forces. The Efreet might have been ready if they had another year to prepare." He pulled back on the stick, and the silver ship rose quickly from the courtyard.

"Still…" he added after a couple of seconds, "there are probably a few surprises they haven't found yet."

Chapter Thirteen

Transfer Facility, Lashkar Abad, Anti-Earth, Unknown Date

Master Chief watched as the silver ship climbed rapidly into the sky and disappeared. "I'm getting really fucking tired of watching that ship fly away," he said. "I can't wait to find out who's inside it…and then kick the living shit out of him or her."

He turned back to the LCAC. "All right, let's get a move on. They ain't paying us by the hour." He stepped back to allow the two cyborgs to sidestep down the front ramp of the craft holding a large box between them. "That goes to the big warehouse."

"You got it, Master Chief," the cyborg on the right, Sergeant Jacob 'Chaos' Braig, said.

"What *is* this thing, anyway?" the cyborg on the left, Sergeant Pierce 'Big Sky' Tomas, asked.

"There are two silver thermite bombs inside," Lieutenant Bradford said. He walked behind the cyborgs, staring at the box like it was a long-lost love.

"Sounds nasty," Big Sky said. "I've always been a fan of thermite, white phosphorous…things like that. 'Cept if the enemy's shooting them at you, in which case it ain't quite so cool."

"Oh, these bombs are cool, all right, although the thermite really isn't anything more than a dispersal mechanism for the silver," Lieutenant Bradford replied. He smiled. "It's way cooler than any of those other things."

"Why's that?" Chaos asked.

"Silver isn't stable in this universe, so when the bomb goes off, the silver will start energetically decaying, making it *much* worse than burning magnesium or Willie Pete. Think about how hard it is to put out those two substances once they are burning. Carbon dioxide extinguishers don't faze them because they make their own oxygen. Water doesn't do anything, either, except maybe remove a little of the heat and spread them around some. Meanwhile, this is a *nuclear* reaction, and the hose teams will be dying from the radiation it's putting off."

"That's coooooool," the two cyborgs chorused.

"Even better, the thermite/silver mixture is going to spread and burn through anything it touches. Then it's going to spread and burn through the next level. If we can get it to the top of the building, nothing is going to stop it from burning all the way down to the lowest basement. There's enough mass here to take care of this building several times over."

"These little bombs are going to destroy the whole building?" Chaos asked.

Lieutenant Bradford nodded. "These bombs are going to create a substance that's unlike anything this universe has ever seen before. It's like…I don't know, it's like perpetual lava. It will burn through anything it touches. It's kind of like the corium you would get if a nuclear reactor melted down, but that reaction only uses the heat from nuclear decay; this will have its own source of new thermal energy."

"What's corium?" Big Sky asked.

"Liquefied nuclear fuel. Nasty stuff."

"All you knuckleheads need to know," Master Chief said, stepping in between the troopers and the lieutenant, "is that it's a big box of shut the hell up and focus on what you're supposed to be doing. Like the lieutenant said, the stuff inside that box reacts badly with this universe, so don't drop it and *definitely* don't open it before it's time. It's amazing the damn thing didn't go off when we parachuted in here."

As the cyborgs continued their march toward the plant, Master Chief realized with a start the Efreet had stopped attacking, and it made him decidedly uncomfortable. An enemy that stopped attacking blindly was an enemy who was planning something…and he really wasn't in a mood to find out what.

He advanced with First Squad to the warehouse, with the cyborgs bringing up the rear. The building was immense, and he wondered how the Efreet had built it. They must have had help, he decided, probably from the Iranians. Bastards.

The building was almost 200 feet wide on the end he approached and over 500 feet in length. The side of the building had a large, central door that would have accommodated a dump truck, as well as people-sized doors on either side. *"Fire Teams One and Two on the left door and Fire Team Three on the right,"* he ordered. *"Cyborgs in front. Take no chances, but be careful with your explosives. I don't want anyone fragging us because they forgot to dial their tridents back from the initial assault. Everyone got that?"* He looked around and could see heads nodding through the visors of the troopers facing him.

"All right, we go on three. One… Two…"

Cockpit, *Shuttle 02*, TSS *Spark*, Unknown Date

"Here's where it gets fun," Jamming said as he watched the tractor holding the shuttle's broken stealth module drive away. "Don't know why the damn thing picked *now* to die."

"Nah," Canuck said. "This run shouldn't be a problem, even without the stealth. We race down, pick up the troops and get back up here before the destroyer can attack us. Nothing could be easier."

"Unless the destroyer's moved."

"Yeah, unless it's moved." The lineman signaled the tractor and all personnel were clear, "Here we go." He lifted the shuttle from the *Spark's* deck and flew into space. As he cleared the stealth field of the *Spark*, he turned toward the planet and accelerated to full power.

"Shit," Jamming said. "It's moved."

Fleet Command Headquarters, Lake Pedam, Nigeria, October 6, 2021

"Excuse me, sir," Admiral Wright's aide said, after a quick knock on the door. Admiral Wright could see the aide was out of breath.

"Yes?" Admiral Wright asked.

"You asked to be made aware of…immediately…any geopolitical events…that were out of the ordinary," the lieutenant replied, gasping for air; "we just got word that a…nuclear bomb exploded…about 15 miles southwest of Shiraz, Iran. The information…still pretty sketchy, but it looks like…it looks like it was a big one, sir…Somewhere on the order of 400 kilotons."

"Thank you, lieutenant, that will be all," Admiral Wright said with a smile. His smile faded into the grin of a predator as he switched to his comm system. *"Captain Griffin, you're up."*

LCAC 85, Transfer Facility, Lashkar Abad, Anti-Earth, Unknown Date

"Look who we found," Staff Sergeant Park 'Wraith' Ji-woo said as she prodded her captive forward with the muzzle of her weapon.

"Yeah, I found him hiding like a sissy under a desk in the admin building," Corporal Calvin 'Bossman' Davis said.

"Nice," Night replied, looking into the eyes of the Iranian who had threatened the General Assembly, and who had been responsible for the bombing of Tashkent. He was still wearing the traditional robe and headdress, but now had on a ceremonial orange cloak over the robe, which probably meant he was a politician of some sort. Night hated politicians, maybe even more than terrorists. "I knew we'd meet again."

"I am not afraid of you," the man said.

"Even though you were hiding under a desk?" asked Bossman. "Yeah, you're pretty brave, all right."

"All of you infidels will die!" the man yelled. He pulled a ceremonial dagger out of his robe and charged Night, but only made it two steps before the lasers of Night, Wraith and Bossman dropped his smoking corpse to the ground.

"I'm sure I'll die someday," Night said, flipping the man over with the toe of his boot. "However, it won't be today."

"Captain Train!" a voice called from the LCAC.

"Here," he said. He looked up to find a woman in a flight suit coming down the ramp. The woman carried an M-16, scanning the compound for threats as she crossed the ground between them. Night approved. Not bad for a swabbie.

"I'm Petty Officer Klemarczyk," she said as she reached Night. "The craftmaster asked me to come out and tell you we've got a problem with the boat."

Transfer Facility, Lashkar Abad, Anti-Earth, Unknown Date

"*Three!*"

Shoulders down, Corporal Robert 'Fury' Scott and Big Sky crashed through the two doors, tearing them off their hinges and sending them spinning to the side. As they brought their weapons up, the combat robots waiting for them began firing.

"Ziiiiiip-PEW!" "Ziiiiiip-PEW!" "Ziiiiiip-PEW!"

Five robots waited in a firing line, along with a large number of Efreet on both sides armed with crew-served flechette throwers.

The second person through the left door, Master Chief was familiar with the robots. Although he hadn't fought them personally, the platoon had, and he knew their capabilities. He dove to the side, narrowly avoiding the three centimeter laser bolt that passed through where he had been. "*Keep moving!*" he ordered. "*They don't anticipate movement. We've got to get behind them!*"

All the Terrans could see of the Efreeti combat robots were the thick, rounded shields that protected the seven-foot-tall machines behind them. The robots fired through small slits in their shields, while the shields shed the return fire from the Terrans like rain.

The troopers pouring into the building ran into a firestorm as the robots fired bolt after bolt, and Corporals Donald Drake and Brenton Davis were felled on entry, three-centimeter holes burned through their suits and chests. There was about a two-second lag between shots as the robots' lasers charged, and the Terrans used it to disperse.

They looked for cover, but there wasn't any to be had; the interior of the building was almost entirely open. A large metallic device sat on a six-inch high concrete platform in the center of the building, with nothing between the device and the troops except the robots and Efreet. Overhead, several levels of metal grid work extended throughout the building. The overhead levels appeared to be for storage, but there was very little actually being stored inside the building, and nothing at their end; there was no cover.

The cyborgs, Fury, Chaos and Big Sky, marched straight ahead at the robots, firing their heaviest weapons. Although able to withstand the majority of the fire with nothing more than melted proto-flesh, the cyborgs were also unable to break through the shields of the robots in return.

The Efreeti flechette throwers focused on the cyborgs, and all three were hit by numerous slivers of metal. One jammed in Fury's knee joint, locking it up. The offending flechette crew received a return volley from Fury's Mrowry autocannon, spreading most of their remains 50 feet behind their weapon.

As the Terrans continued to pour into the room, the balance of fire changed, especially as the tridents came into play. The Efreet were quickly eliminated, and two of the robots were put out of action by rounds that exploded immediately behind them.

Seeing the rest of the soldiers sprinting around behind the robots, the cyborgs continued a slow, straight-ahead advance, happy to receive the brunt of their fire while their teammates got into position to take the robots from behind. One of the robots tried to turn to follow the suited figures, but that exposed it to Big Sky's chain gun, and it was wrecked.

Within 15 seconds, the Terrans were behind the robots, and the last two were destroyed, although not before one caught Corporal Rus 'Overkill' Rogers with a bolt through the head.

Master Chief surveyed the interior of the building, shaking his head at how quickly the Terrans had lost three men. He promised the dead that the Efreet and the Iranians would pay for this…starting with whoever was on the damn silver spaceship. With a sigh, he shrugged it off; there was nothing he could do about it now.

"Fire Team Three," Master Chief commed, *"help Lieutenant Bradford position the bombs. The rest of you, get the dead and wounded out of here and back to the boat. Our evac should already be on its way, and you do* not *want to get left behind!"*

Chapter Fourteen

"**M**other—" Canuck swore as he pulled the shuttle back into a tight corkscrew turn. The ship shuddered as it flew through the ionized air. "That was close. Can you do something over there about that?"

"Uh, no," Jamming replied; "I can decoy a missile, but I can't trick a laser beam. Just a little further, and they won't be able to shoot at us without risking hitting their guys on the ground." He paused. "And...we're in the clear. If they miss us, they'll hit their base, so I doubt they'll shoot anymore."

"That's great and all," Canuck said, "but how are we going to get back to the *Spark* again?"

"I asked that after the brief and was told, 'don't worry about it.' They've got something planned, but they didn't want to say what it was for operational security purposes."

"Opsec, huh?" He snorted. "Sure would be nice for the operators to know, now that there's an enemy destroyer breathing down our necks," Canuck said as he touched down in front of the gates of the enemy complex. "Hey, weren't they supposed to destroy that building?"

"Ramp's coming down for recovery," Jamming said as he pushed a button on the console. He looked up and out the window. "Yeah, they must have some other plan for it. They sure did a number on the gates, though."

Bridge, TSS *Terra*, Earth Orbit, October 6, 2021

"Our mission is to go to the anti-Earth system, take out any enemy ships there and bring our people home," Captain Lorena Griffin, commanding officer of the *Terra*, said. "We know the Efreeti ships have been difficult to hit with missiles, so we're going to have to get in close and take them out with energy weapons. We also know they can fire a torpedo that we *do not* want to hit us. If they launch one at us, we jump back to our universe pronto, and hope it doesn't jump with us. Any questions?"

Heads shook across the bridge. Although there was a significant feeling of trepidation among the crew, based on the capabilities the Efreeti ships had shown in the past, every member of the crew knew his or her job, and they were much better prepared to meet them in battle…this time. The last time, a single Efreeti destroyer had almost destroyed the much-bigger *Vella Gulf*, and it was only through blind luck the *Gulf* had escaped.

"Terra," Captain Griffin said to the ship's artificial intelligence, "if it looks like one of their torpedoes is going to hit us, I want you to jump us back to this universe three seconds prior to impact, and then return us three seconds after the weapon would be clear of us. Can I count on you to do that?"

"Yes, Captain Griffin," Terra replied, "I can easily do that."

"Thanks," Captain Griffin said. "We don't know the turning radius of one of their torpedoes; I'd like to jump back in time to find out its capabilities. If you are in doubt, keep us in our own universe. I don't want to take even a single hit from one of those torpedoes."

"Understood, Captain Griffin," Terra said; "my priority will be to keep us from being hit."

"Outstanding," Captain Griffin agreed. "Standby to jump. On my mark…*Now!*"

With a flash, the *Terra* disappeared from the Solar System.

Transfer Facility, Lashkar Abad, Anti-Earth, Unknown Date

"*T*he bombs are set and we're on our way back to the boat," Master Chief commed.

"*Negative, the boat just had an engine failure,*" Night replied. "*It's down hard. Meet us at the shuttle. It just landed in front of the gate.*"

Master Chief arrived at the shuttle with First Squad to find Night waiting for them.

"Everyone else is onboard," Night said. He turned to Lieutenant Bradford. "Blow the building."

Bradford pulled a small transmitter out of a cargo pocket, removed a wire cage and pressed the button underneath. Two small 'thumps' were heard, but the building seemed unaffected by the bombs.

"That's it?" Master Chief asked. "I thought you had some new super-special bomb."

"Wait for it," Lieutenant Bradford said, his eyes never leaving the building. After a couple of seconds, he pointed to the right side of the building. "There! See that bright spot? That's it. Just watch."

Bright spots appeared all over the building's roof and walls as the silver thermite ate though the metal. Once the silver reached the exterior of the building, gravity pulled it toward the planet's surface, and the silver cut through the sides of the building like hundreds of welders' torches.

"That's burning at about 5,000 degrees Fahrenheit," Lieutenant Bradford said. "About three times as hot as lava."

Within 15 seconds the silver had cut the building from top to bottom in hundreds of places. The warehouse shuddered in the light breeze, and then collapsed like a house of cards. As the metal of the building came in contact with the silver thermite on the ground, it liquefied, and the wreckage continued to crumple in upon itself.

The larger mass of silver, where the second bomb had gone off next to the transport machine, ate through the transporter in seconds, and continued to dissolve the walls and roof as they collapsed down into the silver puddle.

Within a minute, all that was left of the massive building was a few metal plates that had fallen outside the thermite's area of destruction.

"There's no 'bang,'" Lieutenant Bradford said, "but it still took care of the facility pretty well."

"No shit," Master Chief said. "I think it's safe to say they won't be using that building again." He nodded with his head at the LCAC sitting in the compound's courtyard. "Got another one of those things for that piece of shit?"

"Here's where we stand," Night said. "I suspect Lieutenant Commander Hobbs was taken away on the silver ship, again. It doesn't appear we are going to get him back today. I would say the transporter is pretty much wrecked, so we at least accomplished that. The other mission was to find the transport rods, which we haven't done. As much as I would like to have them, I'll be just as happy if they are destroyed, and we don't have to fight whatever reinforcements I'm sure are on their way here. Master Chief, set one of the tridents to overload, and let's get the hell out of this universe."

"Overload one of the tridents?" Lieutenant Bradford asked.

"Yeah," Master Chief replied. "They've each got a gram of antimatter inside, or they did when we started. One gram of antimatter contacting one gram of matter has the same explosive power as twice that of the nuke we dropped on Nagasaki, Japan. That bomb had the equivalent of about 20 kilotons of TNT; a trident will detonate with the equivalent of 42 kilotons. Even though we used a little in our attack, there's still going to be way more than enough to wipe out this facility."

"What about the town nearby? Will that be affected?"

Night turned to look at Lieutenant Bradford, and his gaze narrowed. "I can sum up my feelings for the town in one word." He turned and began walking toward the shuttle. "*Let's go, people!*" he commed. "*The shuttle leaves in one minute. Be on it or get left behind.*"

Lieutenant Bradford ran up behind Night. "Wait, what was the word?" he asked.

Night looked back over his shoulder. "Tashkent."

Chapter Fifteen

Bridge, TSS *Terra*, Anti-Earth Orbit, Unknown Date

"System entry into the anti-Earth system," the ensign at the science station said. "Launching probes; looking for any Efreeti ships."

"Got one," the defensive systems officer (DSO) called. "Just coming over the crest of the planet. It looks like a single ship, destroyer-sized."

"I've got him," the offensive systems officer (OSO) replied.

"Missiles free; kill the bastard," Captain Griffin ordered.

The OSO looked up from her station.

"I know the *Vella Gulf* couldn't hit the Efreet with its missiles," Captain Griffin said, "but maybe we'll get lucky."

"Anti-ship missiles launching," the OSO said. "32 missiles launched; hang fire on tubes three and 18."

"Ma'am, the Efreeti ship is turning toward us," the DSO advised. "It's accelerating toward us to engage."

"Let him," Captain Griffin said. "We've got him outgunned, unless he has a bunch of those torpedoes. The closer he gets, the better it is…for us."

"Ma'am, he doesn't have any shields," the OSO said. "Missile impact in three…two…one…*holy shit!* Ma'am, we got at least 30 hits on the destroyer, almost all of them on the forward half of the ship. Those missiles were meant for taking out battleships and dreadnoughts…there isn't much left."

Cargo Bay, *Shuttle 02*, Anti-Earth Orbit, Unknown Date

"Sir, I don't get it," Master Chief said. "This just doesn't add up."

"What doesn't add up?" Night asked.

"All of this. On one hand, you have an Efreeti ship that is nearly untouchable. If we hadn't gotten lucky, we would all have died aboard the *Vella Gulf* the first time we fought them."

"That's true," Night agreed.

"And yet, we have the base we just hit. It was barely defended, almost as if they expected the walls alone to hold out whoever they thought was going to attack. I don't know who they were defending against, but it sure as shit wasn't us."

"Yeah. Keep going," Night urged.

"Okay, so the Efreet are the most uncoordinated race we've ever seen. They have a couple of great weapons, but generally, most of their stuff is crap. Flechette guns and flamethrowers are cool and all, but our weapons can kill them well before they ever get in range of us."

"Unless we're on a ship or in a tunnel."

"Okay, granted, their weapons are great for enclosed spaces, but certainly not for defending a fort against modern forces."

"True."

"And then you have Captain Nightsong, who appears to be a respected member of Aesir society, but I'll bet my next three paychecks he's the one who has the CO. What the hell is up with that?"

"Are you saying the Aesir can't be trusted, or just Nightsong?"

"I don't know. I mean, we really don't know the Aesir. Maybe their whole race is a bunch of liars. Steropes vouched for them, though, so I'm guessing it's just Nightsong. Besides, it's easier to believe there's one bad apple than an entire race of liars."

"I'd agree with that. The Mrowry seem to trust the Aesir, too, and the Mrowry have been nothing but honorable since we met them."

"So what does Nightsong get out of taking the CO?"

"I don't know, but I agree with you…it doesn't make sense." Night thought for a minute. "Here's something else that's odd. When we came down from the *Terra,* the CO brought his Progenitor's Rod down with him. I'm sure of that; I remember seeing it. But then, a couple of days later, it was gone, and he had no idea where it went. Before this mission, I went and looked at the Bachelor Officers' Quarters' security tapes, and you know what I found?"

"It walked off on its own?"

"Close," Night replied. "Shortly after we arrived, Calvin went into his room, took the rod and left with it. Why would he have done that? Even better, why wouldn't he remember doing it?"

"He did get hit on the head a month or two ago, so it's possible there's some brain damage. But to not remember taking it out of his room? I doubt it. You're sure it was him?"

"Positive."

"Okay, so how is it possible for him to do something, and yet not have done it? The only answer is that he didn't. But if *he* didn't, *who did?*"

"I don't know," Night replied. "My mind keeps returning to the Aesir Eco Warrior teams. It's almost like we had a Life Warrior here…you know, someone who could change their shape to match the CO's."

"But the only Aesir here is Nightsong, and he is fire-based."

"Is there any reason he couldn't be both?"

"I don't have any fucking idea how that works, sir. I guess it's possible…but if he *is* life-based, then he could be anyone he wanted to. He could appear like anyone or anything he wanted to, and we would never know it."

"No, we wouldn't."

"Sir…work with me on this. What if…what if Nightsong really wasn't Captain Nightsong? Remember all those times he talked about Wayland? I mean, he knew *everything* about the man. It was almost like he *was* Wayland. What if Nightsong didn't kill Wayland…what if Wayland killed Nightsong and took his place? Instant credibility. No longer is he a man on the run; he is now a senior member of their space navy, and he's in charge of a ship that can take him anywhere he wants. Once there, he can change his shape and become anyone he needs to be."

"Like Calvin, when he walked into his room and removed the Progenitor's Rod."

"Exactly. The other thing he always talked about, besides the things Wayland did, was the fact that Wayland was able to outsmart the Psiclopes. What if that isn't true, either? What if the Psiclopes caught him and turned him to their own purposes?"

"What could that be? Steropes was with us the whole last mission to help the Aesir. What was he getting out of it?"

"Nothing. But what if it wasn't him, sir? What if the one who caught him was Arges, and he never said anything to anyone else? Or at least not to Steropes? He could run Nightsong however he wanted. He could probably get him to do almost anything in order to avoid being exposed."

"Son of a bitch," Night said. "It would explain a lot if they were working together. Arges runs all the news and information services…what if he used them as information collecting devices?"

"That might go a long way to explaining our information leak. He would have access to all our ships' movements, too, and would know where they were at all times."

"But why? Why would he work with the Iranians and the Efreet? What could he hope to gain from that?"

"I don't know," Master Chief replied, "but I do know how to find out."

"Call him up?"

"No sir, I don't want to risk alerting him to the fact that we know about him. I think we ought to go to his house and surprise him. Besides, that way, I can be the one to wring his scrawny neck."

"I think that's a damn good idea, Master Chief," Night replied. He switched to his comm and called the pilot. "*Hey, Canuck, once we get back to our universe, we're going to need to make a little stopover on our way back home…*"

Chapter Sixteen

"**Y**ou know, sir, I'm starting to think this was a bad idea," Master Chief said as the platoon marched up the hill. "Really. Who needs to build themselves a castle at the top of a mountain?"

"Two types of people," Night replied. "Those who like the view, and those who want a defensible position. The fact there isn't enough room for a shuttle landing zone anywhere close by gives me an idea on which one Arges is."

"And that confirms it," Master Chief agreed as they came around the final bend in the road. A large number of men could be seen patrolling the castle's walls and the grounds around it.

"Yeah," Night said. "It's got a great view of Lake Lucerne, but it looks like we've found the source of at least some of our problems. Not even the president has that much security."

Master Chief spat as they approached the gated entrance into the castle. "Those are mercenaries on the walls," he said under his breath. "I recognize a couple of them. They tried to get into the SEALs but weren't disciplined enough. They just like killing. Sir, we might want to rethink this…"

"Platoon, halt," Night said. "Master Chief and Master Gunnery Sergeant Hendrick, you're with me."

The three Terran Space Marines advanced toward the gate, and three heavily-armed men came out to meet them. "That'll be close enough," the one in the lead said, "especially if you're coming armed. Is this an official visit?"

"Yeah, we'd like to talk to your boss," Night replied. "We've got a few questions we'd like to ask him."

"Well, I'm sorry," the leader said, not sounding sorry at all, "but you aren't on the list of visitors for the day, so I'll have to ask you to come back another time when you have an appointment."

Master Chief noticed all the security forces in view had stopped patrolling and were following the ongoing confrontation. Although their fingers weren't on their triggers, yet, their rifles were now pointing in the general direction of the platoon.

"Hey, Scabby," Master Chief said to the leader, "we don't have to make this into a big deal. I know it would certainly make me feel a lot better if your men kept their fingers well clear of their triggers."

"My men are doing their jobs," the leader gruffly said, "and you know I don't like that name."

"Sorry," replied Master Chief in the same not-sorry tone; "must have slipped my mind." He took a step closer to the leader and lowered his voice. "Now, rather than continuing to posture in front of your men, why don't you just call up to the house and see if a few of us can come in and talk with your boss? As much as I'd like to kill you, I hate doing paperwork, and I really don't want to start anything here that is going to end with me having to justify why I killed all of you."

The leader looked over Master Chief's shoulder at the members of the platoon. Their rifles were pointing in the general direction of his troops, with fingers close to *their* triggers, including the six tridents pointed at the wall. Master Chief watched his eyes as he did the math and came to the correct conclusion.

The leader backed down, taking a step back from Master Chief. "Stand by." His eyes glazed over, like someone who had recently received an implant and hadn't figured out how to hold two conversations at once.

Master Chief took the time to survey the other members of the security force and didn't like what he saw. Both the lieutenants' faces came up in internet searches as persons of interest in a number of killings; he recognized both by reputation. Several of the men on the wall were also wanted by the police, including one listed as a deserter from the U.K.'s special forces.

"*Stay frosty boys and girls,*" Master Chief commed. "*These are bad men, and this could go south without warning. They have implants, so an attack could come without any notice.*" He stretched, using the motion to gain a little space from the closest lieutenant, who was going to be the first to die if they attacked. While the leader was a braggart and a bully, the two lieutenants were stone-cold killers who would have to be taken out first.

While he waited, he started assigning targets to the platoon to kill the time, all the while smiling at the closest lieutenant. The lieutenant, a man he knew only as 'Jackson,' smiled back, well aware of what Master Chief's gaze meant and obviously relishing the opportunity to go toe-to-toe with Master Chief if given the opportunity.

I'm getting too old for this shit, Master Chief thought.

"Okay," the leader said finally. "Mr. Arges will see Captain Train, and only Captain Train, but he is to go in unarmed. Mr. Arges is well aware of Captain Train's particular…skills."

"*Mr.* Arges now, is it?" Night growled as he began setting down his weapons.

"Yes," the leader said, "that's *Mr.* Arges to you."

"I'm ready," Night said, stepping back from an impressive pile of weaponry. Figuring he would have to go through a metal detector, he left it all behind.

"Come with me, then," the leader said.

As Night passed between the two lieutenants, they stepped together, blocking anyone else from following. "Just 'im," the lieutenant that had been eyeing Master Chief said.

"So that's how it's going to be, huh Jackson?" Master Chief asked.

"Oh, you know who I am, do you?"

"Yeah, I can recognize shit like you when I step on it."

"I'm going to enjoy killing you," Jackson said.

Master Chief nodded, biding his time.

Arges' Office, Chateau de Arges, Beckenried, Switzerland, October 7, 2021

"You don't seem surprised to see us," Night noted as he was ushered into Arges' office. As could be expected of a media mogul, the large office was tastefully outfitted with a mix of bookcases and a number of screens that gave up-to-date information on a variety of topics at a glance. Arges' desk would have dwarfed a human; the shorter Psiclops looked like a child sitting behind it.

"I try not to be surprised by anything," Arges replied. "Now, what is it I can do for you today?"

"Well, you could die," Night suggested. "That would be helpful."

"Helpful to you, perhaps, but not helpful at all to the accomplishment of my plans."

"Let's talk about those plans," Night said. "What are you hoping to get by helping the Iranians and the Efreet?"

"Who says I'm helping them? Are you accusing me of treason?"

"Yes, I am, you bastard. I know you've been helping them and passing on information to them. You're going to pay for it."

"I am?" Arges asked. "How? Are you going to kill me?"

"If that's what it takes," Night replied, "I'd be happy to kill you myself."

"You accuse me of passing information to your enemies," Arges said. "Whatever could I hope to gain from doing something like that?"

"I don't know," Night admitted, "but I notice you said 'my' enemies and not 'our' enemies."

"*You don't know,*" repeated Arges, ignoring the last part of Night's statement. "That's a problem for you, isn't it? When it comes right down to it, success in life and politics is all about information and knowing where the bodies are buried. If you have the information, you can act from a position of strength. If not, well, look where it's got you."

Sensing a trap, Night dove to the side, but he was too late. Four glass walls erupted from the floor, and slammed into the ceiling. Night was trapped in the resulting glass box.

Arges came around his desk to stand in front of Night. "You don't look quite so dangerous now," he said. "Would you like to threaten me some more?"

"No need. Just let me out and I'll kill you. No threats are required."

"I don't think letting you out would be a good idea," Arges replied. "Killing you would be much better for my own long-term health." He turned to the security force leader. "Go to the armory and begin passing out the special weapons and equipment." His gaze returned to Night. "And now it's time for you to die." He walked back to his desk and pushed a red button.

Gas began billowing into the glass box.

"I've been waiting a long time for this."

Gates, Chateau de Arges, Beckenried, Switzerland, October 7, 2021

The leader of the security force returned, carrying a portable television. "Mr. Arges wanted you to see this."

"What is it?" Master Chief asked. The screen came alive with a picture of Night in a glass box. A visible gas filtered into the box, and Night fell over after a few seconds.

"It's a video of your captain dying," the security force leader said. "He threatened my boss."

"Just putting him into the box wasn't enough? Arges had to kill Captain Train?"

"This is a live feed to show you how much Mr. Arges believes in permanent solutions."

"And why are you showing me this? Both you and your piece of shit boss have to know seeing this is going to make me have to kill you."

Arges stepped in front of the camera. "I just wanted you to have one last view of your Captain Train before he dies. He attacked me, and I was forced to defend myself."

"If you have him trapped, why do you need to kill him?"

"I have ruled this planet since before you first ventured forth from your caves, and I have done so because I do not tolerate threats, either to me or to my rule. I have killed off far bigger threats than you, and I thought it appropriate to make an example of your captain so you know what will happen to you if you decide to strike at me again."

"I can't wait," Master Chief said.

"You can't wait for what?" Arges asked.

"I can't wait to get my hands around your throat so I can choke the living shit out of you."

"You are going to kill me?"

"Damn right I'm going to kill you, you worthless bastard, in the most painful way I can imagine! Just let me get ahold of you; your ass is mine!"

Arges looked to the side. "Did you get that?" he asked. He turned back to face Master Chief. "I'm sorry you feel that way. I'm afraid you leave me with no choice but to defend myself until the authorities get here."

As one, all of the security force pointed their weapons at the platoon.

"What's it going to be?" the leader asked. "Are you going to leave quietly, or do you want to throw down?"

Master Chief looked around the area of the gate. In addition to the men he could see, there were several other thermal blooms that were probably people hiding in the woods to either side of the path.

Even with their combat suits on, half of the platoon would be dead before they could return fire. Not good odds.

"We'll leave," Master Chief said, "but we'll be back. Count on it."

"I'll look forward to it," the leader said.

"Me too," Jackson added, winking at Master Chief.

Master Chief turned and began walking away from the gates. "Let's go," he said.

"*We're not leaving, are we?*" Sergeant Hattori 'Yokaze' Hanzo commed. "*We can't let him keep the captain's body. It would not be honorable.*"

"*We don't even know if he's dead,*" Master Chief replied. "*We just know they* said *he was dead. They might be keeping him alive for some purpose. Either way, we're not leaving him here.*"

"Damn right," several voices said.

"*So what's our play?*" Master Gunnery Sergeant Hendrick asked.

"*When I give the word, we are going to throw ourselves off the road and into cover, and then we are going to assault back up through his piece of shit castle. The overuse of explosives near the gates is authorized, as there were people hiding in the woods on both sides. We'll smoke them out with superior firepower.*" He paused. "*Anyone* not *ready to do this?*"

Dark Side of the Anti-Moon, Jinn Universe, Unknown Date

Calvin stopped and set his third load onto the pile. Although bulky, it wasn't as heavy as it would have been on the planet. "What *is* all of this stuff?" he asked.

"Currency of various types," Nightsong said. "It turns out the moon is just as good as a bank. Aside from…uh… not getting any interest on your money, that is. Arges would never think to look here." He saw Calvin had stopped. "Keep moving! We don't have all day."

Calvin knew his chances for rescue were fading fast. After fleeing the planet, Nightsong had brought them to the far side of the moon where he had made Calvin help load boxes and bags onto the courier ship. They were headed somewhere, but Calvin doubted it was going to be home.

Gates, Chateau de Arges, Beckenried, Switzerland, October 7, 2021

"*Now!*" Master Chief ordered, and the platoon dove off the road and engaged the invisibility on their suits. The security guards had obviously been expecting it; machine gun fire sprayed both sides of the road and grenades began bursting. The soldiers continued to disperse, but Master Chief saw the status bars of Corporal Anderson and Sergeant Al-Sabani rapidly heading toward zero. Damn. Al-Sabani had been with the platoon a long time.

Master Chief went further off the road into the forest and began advancing on the castle. He could tell from the sounds of the battle that the platoon's heavier weapons were having an effect; most of the largest explosions were coming from the area of the castle gates. The automatic weapons on the four cyborgs were also firing near continuously.

"*Holy shit! I'm visible!*" Sergeant Geisenhof commed.

"*Me too!*" several others added. The life signs for Second Squad's medic, Sergeant John Russert, went to zero.

"*All right, don't get jumpy,*" Master Chief ordered. "*Stay in cover and advance by fire teams. Arges has more money than God; it's not surprising he has a disrupter field. He's bound to have some other tricks lined up too. Go slowly and kill everyone that isn't part of the platoon.*" He paused and then asked, "*Can anyone see Sergeant Russert?*"

"*Yeah, he was working on Staff Sergeant Hirt when the invisibility went out and took several laser bolts to the head.*"

"*Lasers? They've got lasers?*" Master Chief asked.

"*Yeah, we're taking laser fire now and…holy shit! They've got tridents! Down!*"

An enormous explosion came from Master Chief's right.

"*Fuck, they got Fury!*" The life signs for the cyborg and Master Gunnery Sergeant Hendrick zeroed.

"*Screw this!*" Master Chief commed. "*Hit them with everything you've got. 100 nanograms on the tridents! Level the fucking walls!*"

The ground shook as the platoon complied with his orders and began lobbing the explosive equivalent of bombs at the castle.

Master Chief advanced at a jog, hoping to outflank the castle defenders and hit them from where they weren't expecting it. "*Hold fire!*" he commed as he reached the tree line. Looking across the open killing zone, he could see that the platoon had taken him at his word; the castle wall was down across the majority of its front. The right gate post still stood, with a section of the gate hanging limply from it, but there was only rubble for 50 feet on either side.

There were no live defenders to be seen although a number of bodies were strewn across the courtyard. Master Chief hoped one of them would be the smart-ass lieutenant, but doubted he would die that easily.

"Move up!" Master Chief commed as he picked his way through the rubble. The castle would need repairs too; pockmarks from shrapnel covered its façade, and almost all of the forward-facing windows had been shattered.

Master Chief waited for the rest of the platoon and then crossed the courtyard with them. As they approached the front door, they could feel the grinding of machinery in motion, and a familiar silver shape rose from the side of the hill below them, although this one had Arges' logo on the side. It raced upward in a full power climb and was out of weapons range before anyone could think to shoot at it. Master Chief raised his laser rifle and fired several shots, anyway.

"Fuck!" he said in frustration as the ship disappeared into the sky.

"Hey Master Chief, this is Lieutenant Canada at the shuttle. I just tried to get Captain Train but couldn't reach him. It looks like the entire Swiss police force is headed up the hill to you. Well, except for the group stopping here to arrest us, anyway."

Chapter Seventeen

The Situation Room, Fleet Command HQ, Lake Pedam, Nigeria, October 7, 2021

A lieutenant poked his head into the meeting. "I'm sorry to interrupt, sir, but there is an incoming transmission for Admiral Wright from Terran President Nehru," he said.

"Thank you," Admiral Wright replied. "I've got it." He pushed two buttons on the panel in front of him and his monitor came to life with an image of the Terran president already on it. *This can't be good,* he thought. *She never waits around for anyone.*

"Yes, ma'am," Admiral Wright said. "What can I do for you?"

"Did you authorize an assault on Arges' home?" President Katrina Nehru asked.

"An assault on Arges home?" Admiral Wright asked. "No, I didn't. Why? What happened?"

"He just complained to me that members of the Terran Space Navy attacked his house, killed his guards and threatened his very life. He has video documentation of all of this! Aren't the Efreet big enough problems for you? Why do you feel the need to attack law-abiding Terran citizens too?"

"Uh, yes ma'am. The Efreet are enough trouble on their own," the admiral replied. "I don't know what was going on or who was doing it, but I will look into it immediately."

"You don't know who was involved?" President Nehru asked. "Your people assault one of the leading citizens of the Terran Republic and threaten the local police force, and you don't know anything about it? Perhaps you have lost control of your forces and need to step down. You know what? That is a good idea. You are to arrest the perpetrators of this crime, then you are to tender your resignation to my office, immediately. It is obvious you are no longer in control of the people under your command."

"Yes, ma'am," he replied automatically, but the monitor had already gone dead as she terminated the connection. He looked up to see the concerned faces of his senior admirals and ship captains. "Does anyone know anything about the attack the president referenced?"

Heads shook all around the table.

"There's only one unit I know of that would, or even could, try to take on the security at Arges' mansion," Admiral Wright said. "You are all dismissed. Captain Sheppard, please stay a moment."

The meeting room emptied, somber looks on the faces of the men and women as they shuffled, heads down, out of the conference room.

"Yes sir?" Captain Sheppard asked after everyone had left. "You think it was Lieutenant Commander Hobbs' platoon?"

"I know it was Lieutenant Commander Hobbs' platoon," Admiral Wright replied. "What I don't know is *why* they did it. Sure, they sometimes do things that might be a little unorthodox, but there has always been a good reason for what they did in the past. You have been around them more than anyone else…have you ever known them to do something that completely defied reason or the rule of law?"

"Sir, I have known that group for as long as anyone, and I have worked closely with them on a number of occasions. They are courageous, aggressive and not afraid to do whatever they think needs to be done to save the human race. But to just attack someone's house with no reason? No sir, that doesn't make any sense to me. They must have had a reason, and a damn good one at that. I don't have any idea what it might have been…but I *know* they didn't just do that on a whim."

"My thoughts, exactly," Admiral Wright replied. "Unfortunately, my orders on this are quite clear. I am going to have to arrest them, and then I am going to have to tender my resignation."

Admiral Wright paused for a moment, deep in thought, before looking up. "It would, however, be improper of me to arrest them without first confirming they were actually the ones responsible for the attack, so I suppose I need to call Arges to confirm the identities of the attackers. That might take…a while, as he is a busy man and might have fled. In the meantime, I would like you to find Lieutenant Commander Hobbs, if he was rescued from the Efreet, or Captain Train if he wasn't, and use your best judgment on what needs to be done."

"I understand, sir," Captain Sheppard said.

"Do you?" Admiral Wright asked. His eyes narrowed. "Do you really? Because I can't offer you any protection if this goes badly. I am probably done here, so it's your own career that is on the line."

"Yes sir, I know. I also know I wouldn't be alive today if it weren't for Lieutenant Commander Hobbs and his troops. I'll do what needs to be done."

"Thanks," Admiral Wright replied. "Now, get the hell out of here. I've got some calls to make."

Bachelor Enlisted Quarters, NAS Oceana, Virginia Beach, VA, October 7, 2021

Master Chief slammed his suit down on the couch in his room and tossed the rest of his gear onto it. The day couldn't get any worse. Half of the platoon wiped out, the CO abducted by an overgrown fairy and the XO dead. And now he had to go file all of the paperwork because he was the senior person remaining in the unit. He kicked the couch in his frustration and broke the bottom board with his augmented strength.

Great, now he'd have to pay for that too. What else could go wrong?

A smear from floor to ceiling appeared on the other side of the room, and it coalesced into a uniformed black man wearing the insignia of a captain in the Terran Space Navy. As the transporter beam cleared, Master Chief recognized Captain James Sheppard, the commanding officer of the *Vella Gulf.*

"Uh, hi sir," Master Chief said, recovering from the shock of seeing someone beam in. No one was supposed to use the transporter system, as none of the Terrans had been scanned. Without a molecular scan, the person being transported ran a much higher chance of being incorrectly combined on the opposite end, or ending up off target. Both outcomes were usually fatal. "Can I help you?"

"I hope so. Where is Lieutenant Commander Hobbs?"

"I don't know, sir. He was taken away by that bastard Nightsong."

"Where?"

"I don't know, sir. He left the planet in a spaceship, but that was in the other universe, so I have no idea. He could be anywhere."

"Well, what about Captain Train? Where's he?"

"Dead, sir. Arges killed him. We just delivered his body to the morgue."

Captain Sheppard's gaze narrowed. "Just tell me one thing, Master Chief. Was there a reason for attacking Arges' mansion?"

Master Chief met his eyes. "Yes sir," he said without a trace of doubt. "Arges is the person behind all of this. He has been helping the Iranians and the Efreet."

Captain Sheppard looked into Master Chief's eyes, searching for deception, but didn't find any. He nodded. "Okay, Master Chief," he said. "I believe you. Grab your gear. We're beaming out of here."

"Beaming out, sir?" Master Chief asked. "I didn't think we were supposed to use the transporter."

"We're not," Captain Sheppard said, "but Fleet Command is looking for you, and they are going to arrest you. We've got to get you out of here."

"*Arrest me?*" Master Chief exploded. "Arrest me for *what?*" Even as he asked the question, he began picking up his gear.

"Arges has filed charges against you and the rest of the platoon for attacking his home," Captain Sheppard replied. "They specifically name you as the leader of the invasion force that killed most of his security detail and destroyed millions of dollars of his property. He also said you attacked him because he found out your platoon was helping the Iranians."

Master Chief dropped his gear. "*What?* That little rat bastard accused *us* of attacking him? *He's the one who has been helping Nightsong and the Iranians!*"

"Apparently, he also has a video of you saying that you hate him and want to kill him."

"Well, of course I want to kill the little son of a bitch; *he's been helping the enemy!*"

"Do you have any evidence of that?"

"Well no, not really."

"That's the problem. He has video of your attack on his castle and a recording of you threatening to kill him.

"*He killed Captain Train!*"

"He says it was in self-defense." Captain Sheppard sent Master Chief an audio file. "Is this your voice?"

"*Go slowly and kill everyone that isn't part of the platoon.*"

"Well yeah, I said that, but it was on a secure comm set and it's taken out of context. We were taking heavy fire, and they had just canceled out our suits' invisibility."

"He says you threatened to kill everyone there."

"But, but…he's lying!"

"Yeah, well you've been had by a master manipulator," Captain Sheppard said. He nodded to Master Chief's gear, still sitting on the floor. "Grab your gear; we've really got to get out of here. I hear the Swiss are standing in line to get their hands on you. Did you really threaten to tear off the police chief's arms and beat him to death with them?"

Before Master Chief could answer, a window opened up in his mind, and Admiral Wright appeared in it.

"*Master Chief Ryan O'Leary,*" Admiral Wright said, "*you are under military arrest for a variety of crimes stemming from the assault on Arges' mansion. You are to proceed immediately to the brig and turn yourself in.*"

"*Sir, you have to know all of that is bullshit,*" Master Chief replied. "*Captain Sheppard just told me about the charges, and you have to know they're all bogus.*"

"Captain Sheppard is with you?"

"Yes sir, he's standing right here."

There was a pause, and then Captain Sheppard was brought into the conversation.

"Captain Sheppard, you are to take Master Chief O'Leary and the other members of his platoon into custody."

"Yes sir, I am rounding them up," Captain Sheppard replied.

"Good; see that you do," Admiral Wright said. *"Wright, out."* The windows all closed.

"Oh, shit," Master Chief said.

"See," Captain Sheppard said. "I told you it was serious."

"It's worse than you said. Did you see the flags behind Admiral Wright?"

"Yeah, there was the Terran flag and a U.S. flag, why?"

"The U.S. flag was upside down," Master Chief said. "That's what you do when you're under duress. There must be more going on than we know."

"Well, he told me to take you into custody, so you are now my prisoner," Captain Sheppard said. He cocked his head and looked at the enlisted trooper. "So, prisoner, what do you intend to do next?"

Master Chief shook his head. "Sir, I don't have any idea beyond the fact we can't stay here." He paused, then added, "This is where Lieutenant Commander Hobbs usually comes up with a great idea for what we're supposed to do."

"Unfortunately, Lieutenant Commander Hobbs isn't here."

"No sir, he isn't," Master Chief said. He met Captain Sheppard's gaze. "I guess we ought to go find him then, don't you think?"

Transporter Room, TSS *Vella Gulf*, Earth Orbit, October 7, 2021

Two smears appeared on the transport pads, turning into Captain Sheppard and Master Chief. Both of the men arrived six inches above the platform and fell to the deck.

"Sorry about the landing," Captain Sheppard said. "I told Solomon to aim six inches high so we didn't end up fused into the deck or something else catastrophic."

"Works for me, sir."

"Solomon, are you available?" Captain Sheppard asked.

"Of course, sir; I am always available for you," the ship's artificial intelligence responded.

"Good," the CO replied. "Please beam aboard the rest of Master Chief's platoon, using the same guidelines. Six inches high. If there are any complaints, tell them to come see me."

"Yes sir; I will start transporting them now."

"I need to get to the bridge," the CO said, "and we need to talk. Walk with me."

"Yes sir," Master Chief said, following him out the door. "What do we need to talk about?"

"Several things, like how we're going to find Lieutenant Commander Hobbs. First, though, there's the matter of your platoon's leadership. With Lieutenant Commander Hobbs gone, there is a vacancy in the leadership of both the space fighter squadron and your platoon. While his executive officer, Lieutenant Commander Brighton, can take over the squadron, the platoon doesn't have that luxury."

"Are you going to ask Fleet Command for a replacement?" Master Chief asked.

"No, I'm not. I want to minimize my face time with them. Out of sight; out of mind. If I check in with them, someone might very well remember I'm supposed to be transporting you to jail and start asking questions I don't want to answer."

"So what is the plan? Send over one of the ship's officers or one of the squadron's officers? I never would have thought an aviator would fit in with my troops, but Lieutenant Commander Hobbs has been doing pretty well. That would be my choice, anyway."

"No, there is a third choice you haven't considered. Battlefield commissioning."

"Battlefield commissioning? You mean, like turning an enlisted person into an officer? I don't know if I can really recommend any of the folks in the platoon for that, sir. We have a lot of good folks, but none of them are really experienced enough for that. Not yet, anyway."

Captain Sheppard stopped and turned to look at Master Chief. "No one?" he asked. "No one, *at all?*"

Master Chief's eyes widened in surprise as it finally sank in. "Oh! No sir. No way, sir. I'm not officer material. That is the one thing that is *not* in my contract."

"You wouldn't happen to have a copy of this contract you're referring to, would you?"

"Well, no sir, I don't," Master Chief replied. "But that doesn't mean you can do it. In fact, I don't think anyone's gotten a battlefield commission in at least 20 years, even with all the wars we've had. It just isn't done."

"Longer than that," Captain Sheppard said. He began walking again. "It hasn't been done since Vietnam. It is, however, still on the books."

"Well, that's a good place for it to stay. Right in those books. Besides, sir, why do we need an officer? Why can't I just lead it as a master chief until we catch up with Lieutenant Commander Hobbs?"

"Two reasons. First, The Book says a platoon is commanded by an officer. And it really does say that; I looked. Second, we don't know where Lieutenant Commander Hobbs is right now, and the odds of us recovering him are getting smaller and smaller. The platoon needs an officer, and you're it. Congratulations, First Lieutenant O'Leary."

Captain Sheppard stopped as he reached the door to the bridge and turned to add, "It's already done, so stop bitching about it and get to work. Your men and women need you."

"Yes sir," First Lieutenant O'Leary said with a sigh. Then he straightened and saluted. "Lieutenant O'Leary reporting for duty, sir!"

"That's more like it," the CO said with a nod as he walked onto the bridge. "So, Lieutenant O'Leary, you mentioned finding our wayward lieutenant commander. How do you suggest we do that?"

"Well sir, the only thing we really have to go on is the silver ship. We need to find out where that ship went. Do we know if it ever came into this universe? If it didn't, then it has to still be in the anti-Earth system."

"You're looking for a silver ship?" Steropes asked from the science station. "What kind? Did it look like this?" He pressed a couple of buttons on his display and the fuzzy outline of a ship appeared on the front screen.

Even though the image was blurry, Lieutenant O'Leary recognized its shape. "That's it!" he cried. "That's the ship we're looking for."

"Oh," Steropes said, sounding disappointed.

"What's wrong?" Captain Sheppard asked.

"That ship is a courier ship that jumped into our universe. It's headed toward the stargate that leads to Domus. Fleet Command hailed it several times, but it isn't responding. They sent the *Spark* to intercept it, but the *Spark's* too far away; she won't catch it before it reaches the stargate."

"Is a courier ship capable of making the jump?"

"Unfortunately, it is. The courier ship is the smallest class of ships able to use the stargate. The only thing that could stop it is the minefield at the gate. Fleet Command is still trying to decide whether they want to use them or not."

"What happens if they use the mines?" Lieutenant O'Leary asked.

"Hard to tell," Steropes said. "If they wanted to stop it, they could, but they would probably have to destroy the ship to stop it."

"So, if Lieutenant Commander Hobbs were onboard the ship, we wouldn't want them to use the mines."

"No sir, not if we want to recover him alive."

"Solomon," the CO said, "have you transported up all the platoon and aviators?"

"Yes sir," replied Solomon, "although I couldn't find a few of them. Also, I was unsure whether or not your directive applied to Father Zuhlsdorf, as he isn't officially a member of the platoon. As he has fought with the platoon in the past, and their numbers were depleted, I anticipated his presence would be welcome. He is not yet operational, but is expected to recover."

"You anticipated?"

"I found it 74% likely either you or Lieutenant O'Leary would want him onboard. When I added in the possibility he might know something about Captain Nightsong's plans, having been his hostage for so long, the likelihood increased to 87%. It was a logical deduction, put into what I determined to be the correct phrase. Is 'anticipated' not the correct word?"

"It *is* the correct word," the CO said. "I've just never heard you say it that way. Nicely done." He turned to the front of the bridge. "Helmsman, all ahead flank; make for the stargate. Comms, call Fleet Command and let them know we are in pursuit of the courier ship and to deactivate the mine field. Don't answer any further communications from Fleet Command without my permission."

"Heading to the stargate," said the helmsman. "Coming up to flank."

"I told them, sir," replied the communications officer. "They ordered us to maintain our position until told otherwise."

"Noted," Captain Sheppard said. "Continue the pursuit."

Bridge, TSS *Vella Gulf*, Solar System, October 7, 2021

"Sir, Fleet Command is calling," said the communications officer. "They're ordering us to break off the pursuit and remain in the Solar System."

"Did you answer them?" the CO asked.

"No sir, I did not."

"Good; continue radio silence. There is a problem at Fleet Command. I don't know what it is, but Admiral Wright personally ordered me to recover Lieutenant Commander Hobbs, and that is what we are going to do."

"Sir, we're not going to catch the courier ship before it reaches the stargate," Steropes said.

"Then we're going to follow it into the next system," the CO replied, "and the next one, and the one after that, too, if that's what it takes. We *are* going to run it down, recover Lieutenant Commander Hobbs and find out what the heck is going on. Any questions?"

The bridge was silent.

"Steropes, how long until the courier ship reaches the stargate?" the CO asked.

"Two hours."

"And how long until we hit the gate?"

"Five hours."

"Good. In that case, I want a staff meeting in my conference room right now so we can figure out what we're going to do after that."

Chapter Eighteen

CO's Conference Room, TSS *Vella Gulf*, Approaching Stargate #1, October 7, 2021

"So that's what we know," Lieutenant O'Leary said. "Arges has been helping the Iranians and the Efreet. Based on his troops' weapons and technology, Arges either has a replicator of his own or access to one. It appears Captain Nightsong has also been helping the Efreet although I have no idea why or how. We believe the courier ship we're following is his ship, and that he has Lieutenant Commander Hobbs onboard as a captive."

"We really don't know if that's true, though, do we?" the *Vella Gulf's* executive officer, Commander Russ Clayton, asked. "We may very well be chasing a ship that has neither Lieutenant Commander Hobbs nor Captain Nightsong aboard. We don't have any hard evidence that confirms Lieutenant Commander Hobbs is even alive, much less onboard that ship."

"That's correct," Lieutenant O'Leary replied, "but it's the only lead we have. He could have been killed when the cave blew up, and he might have been killed when we destroyed the Efreeti facility in the other universe. Both times, though, a ship just like the one we're following lifted off. Whoever is in it has been a couple of steps ahead of us ever since we went to the other universe, which shows they have a foreknowledge of our plans. They may have received that information from Arges, but they may also have gotten it from Nightsong. We just don't know."

"And, as the lieutenant said," Captain Sheppard added, "that ship remains our best lead in figuring out what is going on. Its pilot was almost certainly involved in the cave explosion, and it was also at the Efreeti transport facility. Whoever is onboard has to know *something* about what's going on."

"I have a question," Lieutenant O'Leary said, looking at Steropes. "What did Arges mean when he said he had ruled the planet since before we ventured forth from our caves?"

Steropes eyes twitched from side to side. "He said that? Um…I was afraid of that…"

"You were afraid of *what?*" the CO barked, knowing that none of the Psiclopes liked to reveal more than they had to. "Out with it! All of it!"

"Uh, yes," Steropes stalled. "You see, this is a problem with people who live as long as we do; it is not uncommon for us to develop a degree of megalomania. In its most basic sense, a little bit is helpful in defending against loss, and trust me, loss is something we Psiclopes already knew a great deal about, even before we lost our home world. When one of us has been in a position of power for an especially long period of time, like Arges has, it can also lead to feelings of personal omnipotence and grandeur. As the leader for our mission to your planet, Arges *was* theoretically in charge of all the activities on it for many millennia."

"And you think this has happened to him?" the CO asked.

"I believe it has," Steropes replied. "I realized some time ago he was overly fascinated with information, and this has grown worse as time has gone on."

"What type of information?" Commander Clayton asked.

"All types," Steropes replied. "He wants to know it all. Not just important things, but *everything* there is to know. Knowledge is power, and if he knows everything, then he will also be all-powerful. He sees the human race's ascendance as a blow to his power base, and I do not believe he wants to share. He probably started the global news network so he could keep track of everything going on, system-wide, and use it to stir things up. He started the Sino-American War; this could be his latest effort to take your society back a few steps."

"I thought he started the war to help find your hero souls," Lieutenant O'Leary said.

"That is what he told me, but it is also possible he had plans within plans. Wars serve all of his vices well. As he has often said, 'where there is chaos, there also is profit.'"

"Okay, so Arges likes wars," Captain Sheppard said. "That much I can get. There's profit and megalomania for him. Why did he start a war between the Efreet and the Aesir? Why not just start the war here if this is the planet he wants to control? Does he have bigger goals? The takeover of the entire galaxy?"

"One reason to start somewhere else may be the state of the Efreet on anti-Earth," Lieutenant O'Leary said. "Their technology level was pretty low; maybe the plan was to build them up until they were ready to take us on. He probably knew they wouldn't be much of a fight for us right now." He thought about it a moment, then added, "Well, aside from being able to jump in and nuke us at will, anyway."

"Yeah, that makes sense," Lieutenant Commander Sarah Brighton, the acting CO of *Vella Gulf's* squadron of space fighters, said. "If we were focused somewhere else, that might give him a chance to build up the Efreet on anti-Earth to the point where they were a credible threat."

"There is something we are still missing," Steropes replied. "If Arges was trying to build up the Efreet, why did Nightsong lead us to anti-Earth before they were ready? It seems like all the reasons we went to anti-Earth were based on things Captain Nightsong said. If they were working together, why would he have led us there before both were ready? If he wasn't working with them, why was his ship at the Efreeti transportation facility? We are missing a piece of the puzzle."

"Okay, we could go around chasing our tails on this all day," the CO said; "let's focus. What do we know for sure?"

"The Aesir are at war with the Jotunn and the Efreet," Lieutenant Commander Brighton said.

"We are at war with the Jotunn, the Efreet and the Iranians," Lieutenant O'Leary added.

"I'm not sure we're officially at war with the Jotunn," Captain Sheppard said, "but I'm pretty sure we've blown up enough of their stuff that war with both the Iranians and the Efreet is a given."

"We also know Arges is helping the Efreeti/Iranian alliance," Lieutenant O'Leary noted.

There was a long pause. "That isn't very much," the CO commented. "So, what do we *think* we know?"

"We think that Arges and Nightsong are working together, and that Nightsong has captured Lieutenant Commander Hobbs and is taking him somewhere," Lieutenant O'Leary said.

Silence again filled the conference room. "It seems to me," Captain Sheppard said, "that we don't know enough about what's going on to make good choices, and there are only two people who do know. The first is Arges, who is virtually unapproachable right now due to the attack on his castle, and who wouldn't have told us anything in the first place. The second is Captain Nightsong, who we *think* is still alive, and who we *think* is in the space ship we're chasing. He also won't want to tell us anything, but at least he isn't being protected by the Terran government."

"We don't have very many choices," Captain Sheppard concluded. "We can either continue to chase the courier ship in front of us, or we can go back and live under Arges' rule like good little girls and boys." He shook his head. "When you look at it that way, there really isn't much of a choice. I have no desire to live under the rule of a megalomaniac. We will continue to follow the courier ship and see if we can get our hands on Nightsong. Meeting adjourned."

Bridge, TSS *Vella Gulf*, Approaching Stargate #1, October 7, 2021

"Sir, Fleet Command is calling us again. They are ordering us to break off pursuit and return to Earth."

"Understood," Captain Sheppard replied. "Solomon, I would like you to transmit the following via standard radio. 'Fleet Command, this is Captain Sheppard onboard the *Vella Gulf*. We are experiencing a communications failure and only have our standard radio operational. We are chasing down an intruder, but the ship has too big of a head start for us to catch it prior to the stargate. We intend to continue pursuit and capture the interloper. We will return once we have apprehended the fugitive."

"If I send that via standard radio, rather than the faster-than-light communications set, it will be several hours before Fleet Command receives the message," the ship's AI said. "We will not receive an answer prior to making the jump into the Vulpecula 452 system."

"Understood," Captain Sheppard said. "Please transmit as requested."

"Done," Solomon replied.

"Well, we're committed now," Lieutenant O'Leary said.

"Yes we are," the CO replied. "Now we just have to catch him."

Chapter Nineteen

"The last thing I remember is visiting a friend of mine who was in the hospital," Father Zuhlsdorf said. "I got into the elevator with a man I had never seen before, and I don't remember getting back off. When I came to, I was in the cave where I have been ever since. During my time there, I only saw two creatures: the man who looked like an elf, and a creature that looked like a large walking salamander. My time there does not bear repeating as it was a mix of starvation and torture. I'm afraid I must confess to having had some very non-Christian thoughts about the elf from time to time."

"The elf is a person who goes by a number of names," Captain Sheppard said. "We know him most recently as Captain Nightsong; however, he has also been known as Wayland and Beowulf, among many other aliases."

"I believe he called himself 'Wayland' while I was in captivity, but most of it is kind of a blur now."

"Do you remember how you came to be outside where we found you?" Lieutenant O'Leary asked. "You had been shot with a laser."

"Yes! It is all coming back," the priest replied. "Calvin came in with Wayland...no, wait, Calvin was his prisoner too. Wayland said we had to leave and cut me loose from where I was tied, and Calvin helped carry me outside. I walked as far as I could, carrying my own cross, as it were, but when I stumbled, Wayland shot me and left me to die."

"Did you see where they went after that?" Lieutenant O'Leary asked.

"No, I didn't. I'm afraid I may have passed out for a while."

"That's okay," Captain Sheppard said. "Go ahead and rest." He looked up to Lieutenant O'Leary. "Well, if nothing else, I think that confirms Nightsong is our bad guy."

"Yeah, now I have an even bigger score to settle with the bastard," Lieutenant O'Leary said. "Not only did he abduct my CO and torture a priest, but he also blew up the cave, knowing I'd be the first person to jump into it. He obviously intended to kill me and Captain Train. Just let me get my hands on that murderous bastard. All I want is five minutes alone with him…"

"You do remember he is one of those Aesir Eco Warrior people, right? And he can manipulate fire and life-based nanobots?"

"You're right," O'Leary said, "better make it 10."

Bridge, TSS *Vella Gulf*, 61 Cygni System, October 17, 2021

"Sir, it looks like he's heading for the Epsilon Eridani system," Steropes said.

"Any change in his speed?" the CO asked. They had chased the unknown ship through four systems but had been unable to make up any ground. Strangely, they hadn't lost any ground, either.

"No sir. He continues to maintain a two-hour lead on us. Whenever we speed up, he speeds up. Whenever we slow down, he slows down."

"So he's just toying with us?" the CO asked.

"Unknown," Steropes replied. "He may be trying to lead us somewhere; it may also be he is slowing to maintain a more efficient speed to conserve fuel. There are a couple of things we could attempt to determine which is correct, like slowing down further to see if he does the same or running our engines at full thrust to see whose motors blow first."

"No, I don't think we're quite ready for that yet," Captain Sheppard said. "Maybe some time, but not now. We'll continue to follow the ship to Epsilon Eridani, if that's where it goes. Maybe the Domans will have a ship in position to capture him."

Bridge, TSS *Vella Gulf*, Epsilon Eridani System, October 20, 2021

"*D*omus Control, Vella Gulf, *checking in entering through Stargate One.*"

"*Good to see you,* Vella Gulf. *Did you bounce in and out? We thought another ship came in before you, but it disappeared immediately upon system entry.*"

"*That wasn't us, Domus Control; that was the ship we are chasing. Interrogative, do you have any ships available you can send to block the stargates?*"

"*We have one cruiser available.*"

"*We'll stay here and guard this one; please send your cruiser to the other. We don't know if the ship we were chasing jumped to the other universe or cloaked, but if we can trap them here, we can figure it out.*"

"*What do you mean, 'jumped to the other universe?'*"

"*We will send a shuttle to the planet to meet with your leaders. We'll explain everything.*"

"Got it, Vella Gulf. *Domus Control, out."*

Chadnezzar, Anti-Domus, Unknown Date

"Well, we're here," Nightsong said as he brought the courier ship in for a landing on the airfield in the center of the city. Chadnezzar covered the area within a ring of seven hills, with the outlying urban areas climbing well up onto the hills. A modern city would have housed several hundred thousand; however, as the tallest building was only three stories, Calvin doubted the city had even 100,000 inhabitants.

"You're going to hide in the middle of the city?" Calvin asked. "Our forces will find you anyway and come for you."

"You forget the ship following us is the *Vella Gulf.* It doesn't have the ability to make the jump. They can stay in your universe while we stay here. When I'm ready to leave, I have the stargates plotted very accurately; I will stay in this universe and only jump back to yours at the last minute."

"What if Fleet Command sends the *Terra* or the *Spark?*"

"They won't. They are more worried about the Iranians and the Efreet. You heard them trying to call the *Vella Gulf* back. I don't believe the *Gulf's* CO will still have a job when he returns to Terra."

Calvin felt a surge of pride as he realized the CO of the *Gulf* was more worried about trying to rescue Calvin than his career. "So what do you intend to do here?" he asked.

"I don't plan to be here long," Nightsong replied. "I have some things to pick up, I need to refuel my ship and you have a date with a sword. After that, it is off to kill some Aesir and some Jotunn…but not necessarily in that order."

Palace, Remurn, Domus, October 21, 2021

"So we chased the ship to this system," Lieutenant O'Leary said. "We have discussed it and we do not believe the courier ship had stealth modules on it, nor would it have had the capability to stealth without them. The ship isn't anything more than an engine and a minimal shell around it. It is meant to get diplomatic messages and an ambassador or two from point to point as quickly as possible. If the ship didn't have stealth, it must have jumped to the Jinn Universe."

"Which would mean there is an Efreeti presence on this planet in the Jinn Universe," the Kuji queen, Queen Risst, said. She turned to the humanoid queen. "I like this not."

"Nor do I," the humanoid queen, Queen Glina, replied. She turned to Captain Sheppard. "We know so little about the Efreeti society, and now you tell us they could jump to our planet at any moment and destroy our cities and everything we've worked so hard to achieve in the last few years. This is unacceptable."

"I agree," Queen Risst said. "You must jump through to the other universe and destroy their planet before they do the same to ours."

"Just like that?" Captain Sheppard asked. "Destroy their planet without any warning? That would make us no better than they are."

"It would also ensure that we are the ones who continue living," Queen Glina replied. "My responsibility is to my people first, and then to the Republic of Terra, a republic which seems to have some problems lately recognizing who its friends and enemies are."

"We have no such issues here," Queen Risst added. "Everyone on the planet in *this* universe, I deem 'friend.' The creatures on the planet in the other universe? 'Enemy.' What do you do with implacable enemies who won't talk or negotiate with you? You exterminate them like a nest of vigrebs." Captain Sheppard's implant brought up an image of a vigreb, a creature which lived in the swamps of Domus. The creature was five feet long and looked generally snakelike, but had four sets of small, razor-sharp claws to hold onto prey while delivering its poisonous bite. The vigreb was nearly impossible to detach without killing it.

"I understand that, ma'am, and can sympathize with you," Lieutenant O'Leary said. "I've fought them on several planets and have yet to find any of them willing to negotiate. The problem I have with nuking their planet, or whatever it is you wish us to do, is that Lieutenant Commander Hobbs is probably on it, along with Nightsong. Unless the need is great, I'm generally not a fan of nuking my friends and, at the moment, that stupid elf is the only person we know of who might be able to tell us what is going on."

"I want to be perfectly clear," Queen Glina said. "If it is a choice between them and us, I choose us."

"We have read the reports of the last war," Queen Risst added. "We saw there was a device called a black hole generator. We would like you to go to the other universe and set one of those off on their planet. Then, we will not have to worry about them crossing over, ever again."

Captain Sheppard rubbed his chin. "Umm…according to what the Mrowry told us," he said, "using that bomb goes against the rules of war. Our society is already going to be looked down on for using one of them; I can't imagine detonating a second one will win us any points on the international stage."

Queen Risst smiled, showing a great number of very sharp teeth. "There are only seven of us here. Queen Glina and I aren't going to say anything. Ambassador Flowers is a career politician; he knows how to keep his mouth closed when necessary. The rest of you are military. You can always say that we ordered you to do it, as the legitimate political rulers of this system."

"That excuse hasn't always worked well in our past," Captain Sheppard said. "We also have another problem beyond my reluctance to kill an unknown number of unarmed civilians. We don't have the ability to jump the *Vella Gulf* into the other universe. We don't have jump modules for our engines."

"They can't be that big," Queen Glina said. "We have a Class 5 replicator. We will make some for you."

"It's a slightly bigger problem than that," Captain Sheppard said. "One of the components is a metal that only exists in the other universe; it is unstable here. We don't have any of it with us, nor do I expect you have any, either. In order to replicate the jump modules needed to go to the other universe, a few people are going to have to go over first and bring back some of the metal."

"How much do you need?" Queen Risst asked.

"Not much; we only need about a pound per module, and we only need four modules, so we only need about four pounds total. We can bring that back using a transportation rod. Going over ahead of time will also give us the ability to get the lay of the land there. We can find out what the planet's like and what forces they have. Hopefully, we can even find out about their navy, so we don't jump the *Vella Gulf* into a battle bigger than we can win."

"What do you need from us to make this happen?" Queen Glina asked. "We would like this to be done quickly, before they can do something to one of our cities."

"We would like to do it quickly too," Captain Sheppard replied. "The longer we wait, the longer Nightsong has to plan. I would rather keep him reacting to what we do, rather than giving him time to act on his own accord."

"My platoon is down quite a few men," Lieutenant O'Leary said. "Would it be possible to borrow a squad from your armed forces? Perhaps one from the platoon Second Lieutenant Cristobal Contreras is in charge of?"

"The 'Princess' Own' platoon?" Queen Risst asked. "I will see what can be done."

Chapter Twenty

Captain's Office, Army Training Facility, Remurn, Domus, October 21, 2021

"Why did you ask for me, Master Chi—I mean, Lieutenant O'Leary?" Second Lieutenant Cristobal Contreras asked. "I never thought you liked me when I was in your platoon."

"Whatever gave you that idea?"

"All the times you called me a fuck-up, perhaps?"

"Contreras, you've got me all wrong. I use that as a term of endearment."

"Really, Master Chi—I mean, really, Lieutenant O'Leary?"

"Of course not, you fuck-up. That term means you're an idiot, not that I love you. I spent a lot of time training you, though, so hopefully you still remember the difference between your ass and a hole in the ground. And anyone you've trained ought to be better than some run-of-the-mill jarhead, so that's why I asked for you. The fact you're a second lieutenant and I'm a first lieutenant, so I can boss you around again? That just makes it more fun for me."

"Really, Lieutenant O'Leary? You just asked for me so you can boss me around?"

"No, you fuck-up, I asked for you because I thought you knew what the hell you were doing, but maybe I was wrong. *Now go and get the platoon formed up for inspection!*" Contreras left at a jog.

Lieutenant O'Leary turned to his old friend, Captain Aaron Smith, who had been in charge of creating the Doman Army from scratch. "I'd almost forgotten how much fun new officers are."

"The same could be said about you," Captain Smith said. "Whatever happened to, 'no matter what they do, they'll never make ME an officer?'"

"Too many good men and women died."

"Oh." With that one word, he conveyed the shared sorrow of a lifetime of friends lost in the military service.

They shared a moment of silence for fallen comrades, then Lieutenant O'Leary nodded once. The lost would understand his need to move on so he could try to save the living. "Well, let's go see what our combined militaries have done to me now."

The Terrans walked outside to where the new, integrated platoon was drawn up by squads. The sun was high overhead, and the smell of Remurn reminded Lieutenant O'Leary of Lancaster, Pennsylvania…right after the Amish fertilized their fields 'the natural way.'

"Atten-hut!" Lieutenant Contreras shouted, from where he was waiting in front of the platoon. He saluted as the two officers approached. "The platoon is formed and ready for inspection, *sir!*"

"Very well," Captain Smith said. "Precede me in inspection."

The three officers walked through First Squad, which had only lost three people in the Jinn Universe mission and assault on Arges' house. Two of them had been replaced with members of the Kuji race and one with a member of the Doman humanoid race.

"This is Bill," Lieutenant Contreras said as the officers came to the first Kuji.

"Corporal Obillossilllolis, *sir!*" Bill said.

Lieutenant O'Leary nodded. "Got it; Bill."

"And the other new Kuji member of First Squad is 'Skank,'" Lieutenant Contreras said.

"Corporal Misssollossissos, *sir!*" Skank said.

Lieutenant O'Leary looked at Lieutenant Contreras and raised an eyebrow. "Okay, I'll bite. How did you get 'Skank' out of that?"

"We didn't," Lieutenant Contreras replied. "The corporal emits an odor when he gets excited that is…unpleasant to be around. We are looking forward to having him in a suit as often as possible. That way, we don't have to smell him."

"I see."

The officers reached the end of the squad and returned to the beginning of Second Squad. There were more new faces in Second, as it had borne the brunt of the platoon's combat losses. In addition to two more Kuji and three members of the Doman humanoid race was a new recruit who stood out from the others.

"That has got to be the biggest gun I have ever seen," Lieutenant O'Leary said as he inspected the unit's newest cyborg.

"Sergeant Declan Jones, Princess' Own, *sir!*" the cyborg shouted. "My main weapon is a modified 81mm mortar. My other weapon is a Barrett M82 .50-caliber rifle. Peace through superior firepower, *sir!*"

Lieutenant O'Leary turned to Captain Smith. "An 81mm mortar?"

Captain Smith shrugged. "What can I say? He likes big guns. On the good side, he provides his own fire support, and he is the one individual capable of carrying a good number of reloads for that beast. After my time in the infantry, I'm really happy to have someone *else* carry the heavy ordnance."

"Makes sense," Lieutenant O'Leary replied with a nod. At almost 10 pounds each, the rounds got heavy *fast*.

The officers finished the inspection and returned to stand in front of the platoon. "At ease!" Lieutenant O'Leary ordered. "Okay, here's what's going on. After we're finished with this brief, we're going to get our shit together, and then we'll be jumping into the other universe. For those of you that haven't done it before, the feeling sucks, and you'll probably spend the first five minutes puking your guts out. It gets easier, which is why the veterans will jump first."

"I'm sure you're wondering what it's like there. If the planet is like most of the others we've been to, the sky will be somewhat greenish, but you'll get used to it. Your vision won't be quite as good there, so make sure you use your other sensors. We will be wearing our suits. We have been told the Efreet can track them, but I think it's better to have their capabilities. Just remember, if this is your first jump, you might want to jump with your helmet off, unless you want to smell puke for the next several hours."

"Our mission on this jump is to secure 10 pounds of a metal that doesn't exist in this universe. When we get it, the *Vella Gulf* will be able to replicate the jump modules needed to jump in with all our gear. Right now, we only have one transport rod, so we will jump in three at a time. Also, we won't be able to bring the cyborgs because they tend to break the rods, and no one wants to get stuck in the other universe. Not only is the sky green, but it smells and you will eventually sicken and die."

"I'm sorry we weren't able to do any exercises to help integrate the new folks into the platoon, but we are under a big time crunch. Our country is at war with several nations, and we don't know why. The only person who can tell us, an Aesir named Nightsong, is in the other universe. We also believe he has the platoon's real commanding officer with him as a hostage; our ultimate goal is to recover Lieutenant Commander Hobbs and take Nightsong prisoner. If we can do that on this jump, so much the better."

Lieutenant O'Leary's eyes roamed across the men in ranks. "Any questions?"

One of the Doman humanoids raised his hand. "Yes?"

"Sir, Corporal King," the soldier said. "What are the chances we will find them there?"

"Tremendously small," Lieutenant O'Leary said. "We don't know anything about what exists on the planet in the other universe. The odds we will jump close to their position are minimal. If we can get the material we need, we can search for them with the *Gulf* and find out where they are hiding."

"What can we expect in the way of resistance?" Sergeant Jones asked.

"We won't know until we get there, but most of the planets we've found have had two races, the Sila and the Efreet. The Sila are generally humanoid, although their arms and legs are thinner and their knees are jointed the opposite of ours. They are generally peaceful and have not been unfriendly to us. The other race, the Efreet, looks like walking salamanders and are both warlike and aggressive. On every planet where we've found both races, the Efreet have ruled the Sila. The Efreet have also attacked Terra and set off a nuclear bomb in one of our cities. They are our enemy, and they will probably attack on sight."

"I hope they wait until I get there to do it," the cyborg replied, waving his three-inch mortar. "I've got a present for them." When the laughing stopped, he asked, "What type of weapons do they have?"

"They tend to use flamethrowers and a flechette gun. Some versions can be large, but generally our weapons are much better than theirs. We have also seen them deploy a robot that is very tough to kill from the front. If you face one of them, try to get behind it where its armor is weaker."

"Anything else?" Seeing no other questions, Lieutenant O'Leary ordered, "Atten-hut. At the command of 'fall out,' fall out and grab your gear. We'll start transporting in 10 minutes. Fall out!"

Nightsong's Abode, Anti-Domus, Unknown Date

"Welcome to your new home," Nightsong said, motioning Calvin into the room. "For what's left of your mortal time, anyway."

Calvin inspected his quarters, which took all of three seconds. The 10-foot square room had a hospital bed with shackles, a table and two chairs. And a door with three locks on the outside. Nightsong motioned to the bed, and Calvin sat down on it.

"So when are you going to tell me your plan?" Calvin asked.

"My plan?" Nightsong asked, pushing Calvin back onto the bed. "Why would I want to tell you my plan?"

"I thought that's what all psychopaths did, right before they killed the good guy."

"Oh, so you're the good guy now? Since when did you start seeing yourself that way?"

"Well, it's obvious you're the psychopath, so I figured that made me the good guy."

"And why would I want to tell you my plans?"

"So I can thwart them once I break out of here."

"Break out of here?" Nightsong laughed, locking the cuff on Calvin's right wrist. "You can't break out of here. Even if you could, where would you go? You'd still die soon anyway, as you aren't native to this universe. No one here has a transportation rod except me, so you couldn't make it back to your universe even if you escaped and made it out of the city. The point is moot, in any event; even if you escaped, my nanobots would kill you as soon as you got out of range." He snapped shut the cuff on Calvin's left wrist, pinning him to the bed.

"Then what do you have to lose by telling me your plans?"

"Nothing." Nightsong smiled. "Goodbye." He walked out of the room and shut the door; the sound of locks being thrown adding a note of finality to his words.

Anti-Domus, Unknown Date

The female Sila screamed as Lieutenant O'Leary, Gunnery Sergeant Jerry 'Wolf' Stasik and Staff Sergeant Alka 'Z-Man' Zoromski appeared next to her child. After a quick scan for danger, Lieutenant O'Leary commed, "*Z-Man, go back for the next group. Wolf, clear the landing zone.*" Bending down, he picked up the small child and carried him to the woman.

"We come in peace," Lieutenant O'Leary said, handing over the child. After several encounters with the Sila, the Terrans' suits were able to translate his words into her language. "It would help us a lot," he added, stepping back to give her some space, "if you would stop screaming."

She stopped screaming momentarily, but then yelled "Ah!" and ran away as Staff Sergeant Zoromski reappeared with two more soldiers. The woman ran into a small adobe house and slammed the door. Lieutenant O'Leary took a moment to assess his surroundings. The terrain features were similar to what they had left on Domus, with rolling hills surrounding them. Some forest still remained to the west of their position in the Sila Universe; it had been clear-cut on Domus.

A field of something that looked like grain extended to the south, with a male Sila answering the call of the scream at a run. "*Keep 'em coming, Z-Man,*" Lieutenant O'Leary commed. "*Wolf, set up a perimeter with the troops as they come in. Keep the LZ clear.*"

Holding his hands well away from his weapons, O'Leary went to meet the man, who was carrying what looked like an old-time sickle. The man's run was interesting to watch with his backward-jointed knees…or would have been if he weren't holding the large, very sharp blade. "We aren't here to hurt you," he said as the man stopped in front of him, sickle at the ready.

"Whatcha here fer, den?" the man asked with a back-country accent the suit struggled to translate.

"I am Lieutenant Ryan O'Leary," he said. "I am the acting commander of these people. We have come from a different universe, hoping to find one of our people who is being held by the Efreet. If we can't find him, we need to obtain 10 pounds of a metal you use to make jewelry so we can transport our ship here to look for him."

"Efreet," the man said. He spat onto the ground. "Hate 'dem bastards. Don't mind if you kill every last one of 'em. Of course, if'n you don't kill 'em all, you'll just piss 'em off and make life a lot harder fer us. It's probably better if'n you all left real soon. Like now."

"We'll be happy to go," O'Leary said, "if you could point us in the direction of where we might find the metal."

"What kinda metal you be looking fer?" the man asked, grounding the end of the sickle now that the apparent danger was past.

"It is a black metal often used to make necklaces and bracelets," O'Leary said.

"You'll need to go into town fer dat." He pointed to the north. "It's about three miles in dat direction."

"*Lieutenant O'Leary, we've got what looks like a shuttle coming in,*" Gunnery Sergeant Stasik commed. "*Definitely not a fighter…it isn't much more than a box with wings.*"

"*Okay everyone, go invisible,*" O'Leary replied. "*We don't want to start anything if we don't have to.*" He spoke to the Sila. "My men tell me there is a shuttle coming this way. We are going to hide from them." With that, he turned on his suit's invisibility and watched as the man jumped back in surprise.

The man had just enough time to walk to the house and shout something inside before the shuttle landed in front. The boarding ramp came down and nine Efreet marched out. The first four were dressed in solid black suits of combat armor and boots with gold trim, and they carried flamecasters. The next two Efreet wore the same combat armor, but carried flechette guns.

The last two troopers wore golden greaves, with brown robes covering their torsos. Each carried a double-tube apparatus under their robes that O'Leary knew from personal experience was similar to a Terran taser.

The last Efreeti wore a black leather, form-fitting suit, with an abundance of blue and silver piping and braid. A band of blue and a band of purple encircled his left arm. He stepped off the ramp, and the two taser-carrying Efreet walked next to him as he marched over to the Sila.

"We have received electronic emissions from this area," said the Efreeti. "If you hand over the equipment now, we will only take you away. If you do not turn it over to us, all your family will be slain. Choose."

"Skipper, we're not going to let them kill that family are we?" Wolf asked. *"They've got to be looking for us."*

One of the taser-bearing Efreet spun around. "Sir, I'm picking it up again," he said, looking at a device on the back of his wrist. "It's close." He started walking toward Wolf.

"Lead him away if you can," O'Leary said.

As he transmitted, the Efreeti with the tracking equipment spun around. "I'm getting something from this direction too. There are at least two sources."

"Lead them away from the family and over the hills to the east," O'Leary commed, already moving in that direction. *"We'll deal with them there."*

"Sir, the source is moving."

"Are you sure you're reading it correctly?" the Efreeti leader asked.

"Yes sir," the trooper said. "There are at least two sources, and they are moving."

One of the troopers in armor fired a blast with his flamecaster, narrowly missing O'Leary. "Sir, I saw a footprint appear. I think they must be invisible."

"Everyone hold where you are," the leader said. "Watch for any other signs of movement. If you see something, shoot it. Until then, flechette casters, search the house and take anyone you find to the shuttle."

"Wait!" the Sila said. "We ain't done nothin. You can't take us!"

The leader waved a claw at the Sila in an offhand manner. "Fine. We won't take you," he said. He turned to his men. "Kill them all!" he ordered.

"*Kill the Efreet!*" O'Leary commed.

Everyone fired at once, and almost all the Efreet troopers fell. One of the flamecasters was left standing, and fired his weapon in a semicircle around him, until he was killed by a second round of shots.

O'Leary turned to see a full pattern of flechettes hanging in mid-air, two feet in front of the Sila. Sergeant Dan Geisenhof appeared, the flechettes stuck into his chest like a backwards porcupine. He fell forward onto his knees, blood spreading from at least five of the metal slivers.

"Tried to…save him…" he said before falling over onto his side.

Becoming visible, the squad's medic, Corporal Shaun Evertson, ran over. He looked up after a couple of seconds, shaking his head. "Sorry sir, one of them went through his heart. He's dead."

"Don' get me wrong," the Sila man said, "I'm grateful fer his sacrifice and all; however, he might as well not have done it. By killing dat patrol, you've killed us, too. By the way, the name's Umar, in case you want to put it on my burial marker."

Second Lieutenant Contreras became visible. "We will take care of your family," he said. "We brought this upon you; it is our duty to take care of you, right Lieutenant O'Leary?"

When the CO didn't respond, he asked again. "We will take care of the family, right Lieutenant O'Leary?"

With a start, O'Leary realized he was staring at Sergeant Geisenhof's body. Coming to his senses, O'Leary became visible and turned to the Sila. "Yes, we will take care of them," he said. "We will get you out of here, and we need to do it quickly before their response force comes. Before we go, do you have any of the metal we're looking for?"

Nightsong's Abode, Anti-Domus, Unknown Date

"Ah, you're awake," Nightsong said. "Just in time, too."

"Just in time for what?" Calvin asked. He turned his head to see Nightsong sitting at the table, with two Progenitor's Rods in front of him. Being pinned to the bed cut down his ability to see anything further.

"You are just in time to see me take credit for the lousy job you did collecting symbols on your rod," Nightsong replied.

"What do you mean, 'lousy job?'"

"You only have two symbols, and I already had one of them. If you had the right two, I would be finished."

"I'd like to say I'm sorry for not helping you more, but it wouldn't be true."

Nightsong shrugged. "Indeed. Well, no bother. At least I am able to get the symbol for Olympos without having to go to that godsforsaken planet. Of course, it is going to be difficult for *anyone* to get Olympos since you idiots put it into a black hole." He paused and cocked his head, considering. "On second thought," he added, "I guess I really should commend you Terrans for doing that. Now, I won't have to worry about those meddling little pains in the ass."

"What about your boss, Arges?"

"*He is not my boss!*" yelled Nightsong. "I am the rightful Thor of the Aesir," he said in a more controlled tone. "I work for no one besides myself. Ours was nothing more than a business arrangement."

"A business arrangement? I thought he caught you and forced you to work for him."

"He did *not* force me to do anything! I *chose* to work *with* him, so he could supply me with the things I needed for my plans."

"Okay, if that's how you want to remember it," Calvin replied with a shrug, although being bound to the bed lessened the motion somewhat.

One side of Nightsong's lips quirked upward in a half-smile. "I see what you're doing," he said, nodding. "You're trying to make me angry. Perhaps you hope I will accidentally kill you quickly. Maybe you hope I will make a mistake of some other kind, allowing you to escape. Maybe I'll even tell you my plan." The half-smile grew into a full smile. "It won't happen. I have waited far too long for this. And trust me, your death will be a long time coming. You won't die until I am completely ready for it; my nanobots will simply not allow it to be otherwise." He chuckled. "No, you aren't going to die quickly or easily. Prepare yourself for pain…a *lot* of pain."

He turned back to the table and picked up one of the Progenitor's Rods and inspected it closely. "Yes, you did a lousy job, but at least you have one of the symbols I need. That's better than being completely worthless, I guess. Only one more, and I will get the prize."

"What is the prize?"

"No one knows," Nightsong admitted, "but I am going to be the first to complete the task and find out. I suspect it is access to the Progenitors' technology…which I will use to completely wipe out the Jotunn. Whatever the prize is, it will be interesting. Too bad you won't be around to see it."

Nightsong picked up the other rod and brought the two of them together. Both glowed red, and Calvin could feel a hum that increased in intensity until Nightsong pushed a button on one of the rods. He set both onto the table and stepped back. One lost its glow; the other lost its form, disintegrating into a pile of ash.

"You have done that before," Calvin noted.

"Indeed."

"Why did you set it down? Would it disintegrate your hand as well?"

"I do not know," Nightsong conceded, "nor do I intend to find out."

Nightsong picked up the remaining rod and examined it. "One more to go," he said to himself. He set the rod down gently on the table after brushing the ash off with a sweep of his hand. Nightsong watched the dust fall to the floor, then turned with a smile. "Now, about you…"

Anti-Domus, Unknown Date

"It's just over dis hill," Umar said. After sending his wife and two small children to the Terran Universe with some of their valuables where they would be safer, if not exactly "safe," Umar had agreed to help the platoon collect the metal they were looking for. Although relatively poor, his family had almost a pound of the metal, mainly in his wife's necklaces. After the Terrans secured the metal in a vacuum box, he agreed to lead them to the neighboring farms.

"Incoming from the east!" Gunnery Sergeant Stasik yelled.

Lieutenant O'Leary turned to see a fireball streaking across the sky in their direction. "Down!" he ordered, and the platoon threw themselves off the path. Moving over 10 times the speed of sound, the round struck several miles behind the platoon with the kinetic energy equivalent of over 120 tons of TNT, tossing the soldiers around as the ground shook.

"Dude," Sergeant Austin 'Good Twin' Gordon said, watching the mushroom cloud rise over the farm they had just left "these guys are *seriously* against technology."

Nightsong's Abode, Anti-Domus, Unknown Date

Bright, flashing lights pulled Calvin from his dream of roaring down a valley in his F-18 fighter. Reality was considerably less enjoyable, and he wondered if he could fall back asleep. He decided additional rest was unlikely; his whole body ached from being strapped to the bed.

"Ah, good to see you're awake," Nightsong said from Calvin's right; "it's almost time to start."

"Start what?" Calvin asked, rolling as far as he could in that direction. Nightsong had been busy while Calvin was unconscious; a new workbench filled most of the space between the bed and the wall, with a number of unfamiliar devices resting upon it. The flashing lights were from the machines as they fulfilled some aspect of their programming.

"The capture of your soul, of course," Nightsong said. "Why else would I have brought you here?"

"To play a really bad practical joke on me before letting me go?" Calvin asked.

"I see you haven't lost your sense of humor yet," Nightsong replied. "We'll see how long that takes. Usually, it occurs somewhere during either the third or fourth day. I'll bet you make it to the fourth. No one lasts throughout the fifth."

"What happens on the fifth day?"

"That's when I cut you open to see what makes you tick. That process usually leaves the prospect somewhat worse for wear...and far less jovial."

Chapter Twenty-One

Anti-Domus, Unknown Date

Umar looked at the two small bracelets and shrugged. "We're poor farmers," he said. "Most of us ain't got but just a little. If'n you really want to get a whole bunch of it, you should go into town and rob the bank. Our money is based on this metal, and every bank has gotta keep some in their vaults in case someone wants it."

"Why are you only telling us about this now?" Lieutenant O'Leary asked.

"Well, shit," Umar replied. "If'n you go an' steal all of it from the bank, what's our money going to be worth? If'n the bank ain't got the metal, our money ain't got the value either, you know?"

"Won't the Efreet or someone from your government bring in more to replace it?"

"'Dem bastards? They'd as soon as let us rot as help us out. If'n we want our money to have value again, all of us have got to contribute some of what we got. In my case, I ain't got none of it no more; I've done given it all to you."

"What do your taxes go for, if not to provide services when needed?" Lieutenant Contreras asked.

"Our taxes?" Umar spat. "Our taxes go toward not waking up with one of 'dem 'mushroom cloud' things rising from the remains of your farm," Umar replied. "Ya' know? Like the one 'dat destroyed my farm after you bastards came?"

"We are sorry about your farm," Lieutenant Contreras replied, "and about any inconvenience we have caused you. We will make it up to you as soon as we are able. It is the only honorable thing to do."

"In the meantime," Lieutenant O'Leary interjected, "this bank of yours seems like the fastest way for us to accomplish our task and get you reunited with your family. If you lead us to the bank, I will do everything in my power to restore whatever we take from the bank, once we have the ability to do so."

"Ya' give me your word on 'dat?"

"My word as an officer of the Terran Space Marines," Lieutenant O'Leary replied.

The man spat on the ground again. "Ain't got no reason to trust no damn soldiers," he said, shaking his head. "I'd take your word as a man, though."

O'Leary looked him in the eyes. "I will do everything I am able to bring back your money."

"Fair 'nuff," Umar replied. "Least ways, it's as good as I'm likely to get."

Nightsong's Abode, Anti-Domus, Unknown Date

Nightsong attached the wire lead to Calvin. It joined nine others leading back to the machinery on the table.

"What are the wires for?" Calvin asked.

"Monitoring."

"Monitoring what?"

"Most are for monitoring your vital signs," Nightsong replied. "Can't have you dying too soon." He looked up. "You know, you ask a lot of questions."

"Well, I'd kind of like to know what you plan to do to me."

Nightsong smiled, but there was no humor in the expression. "Are you *really* sure you want to know what I'm going to do to you?" he asked. "I would bet money you do not. Still…if you want to know, I will tell you."

"Yeah, I want to know," Calvin replied.

"Well, it's your funeral," Nightsong said with a shrug. "Literally. Just remember, I warned you." He pointed to one of the wire leads. "Most of the wires are for monitoring your vital signs. This one is different." He pointed to a second wire. "So is this one."

Nightsong turned back to the equipment on the workbench, humming to himself.

After a long pause, Calvin couldn't take it any longer. "So what do those two wires do?"

"I thought you'd never ask," Nightsong replied. "They complete the electrical circuit to this machine right here." He patted one of the boxes, then looked at his watch. "Well look at that," he said; "it's time to begin." He threw a switch and electricity coursed through Calvin's body.

Calvin screamed until he passed out.

Anti-Domus, Unknown Date

Lieutenant O'Leary eased over the crest of the hill so he could see into the small town on the plain below. Calling it a town was an overstatement; it was no more than four blocks in any direction. Despite its size, the town was busy, with foot traffic and animal-drawn carts crowding its narrow passages. All the traffic was going to complicate things. "Which one is it?"

"Ya' see the second street from the left?" Umar asked.

"Yeah."

"Follow it up past two roads. It's the blue building on the right."

"Oh, fuck."

"Good, you see it, 'den. 'Dat is the other reason I didn't suggest it before. It is somewhat heavily guarded."

"Somewhat?" Lieutenant O'Leary asked. "Security looks to be as tight as my first girlfriend's...never mind."

"See the cluster of buildings north of town?" Umar asked.

"Yeah," O'Leary said. "They important?"

"Only if'n you are worried about more Efreet showin' up. 'Dat's where 'dey live."

"That compound is almost half the size of the town," Lieutenant Contreras said from the other side of Umar; "there's got to be a bunch of the Efreet there."

"Still think you want to try going 'dere?" Umar asked.

"Not anymore," O'Leary said. He could see guards at the door as well as roving patrols. "But we need the metal so we're still going to have to try."

"What do you think?" Lieutenant Contreras asked. "Overwhelming force or stealth?"

Lieutenant O'Leary paused, considering, while he looked at the vista below. Finally, he turned to Umar and asked, "Do you think the Efreet would blow up an entire town, including their own people, to stop us?"

Umar made a face. It didn't take a Sila expert to guess that he considered O'Leary's question the height of stupidity. "Would da' lizards blow up a town to stop technology? Yeah. Faster than a hinn can run."

"What's a hinn?" Lieutenant Contreras asked.

"See 'dose things 'dat some of the patrolling lizards have on leashes?" asked Umar. "'Dose are hinn."

"They look like dogs," Lieutenant Contreras said.

"Well, I don't know what a 'dog' is," said Umar, "but I know a hinn when I see it. 'Dey ain't very smart, but 'dey are *fast* and can smell you a long way off."

"We need to get in there without the alarm being raised," Lieutenant O'Leary said, "and then get back out again. We can all jump back to our universe, but I'd rather not have the Efreet destroy the town."

"'Dere's gonna be punishment for anything you do to the lizards," Umar warned.

"But what will they do if their soldiers just vanish?"

Nightsong's Abode, Anti-Domus, Unknown Date

Bright lights shining in Calvin's eyes dragged him back from the depths of unconsciousness.

"Why, why, why—" Calvin stuttered.

Nightsong looked down on Calvin. "Why am I doing this?" Nightsong asked.

"Yeah," Calvin said, breathing heavily. Every muscle in his body ached, including some he wasn't aware existed.

"It's all part of the process," Nightsong replied. "I want to focus your spirit, so I get all of it, not just part. Electro-stimulation works wonders on focusing your attention." He smiled. "Or, was this the part I do just because I like it? I can never remember which parts are meant to focus you and which parts are meant to focus me." He shrugged. "Either way, I know it's important."

He threw the switch, and Calvin screamed again as the electricity flowed through his body.

Anti-Domus, Unknown Date

One of the things Lieutenant O'Leary liked about leading an elite unit was he could count on everyone to be professional and get the job done on time. But sometimes accidents happened, so he stood in an alcove worrying about everything that could go wrong. He couldn't transmit to see if everyone was ready; transmitting anything might give them away. Similarly, he couldn't comm to see where everyone was or if they were ready, so he kept coming up with ways the plan might fall apart.

He checked the time on his in-head display; 30 seconds to go. He hoped everyone was ready. He hoped no accidents happened. He continued watching the countdown.

If nothing else, the Efreet at least seemed unaware of their impending doom. Invisible, the Terrans had encircled the town and were creeping ever closer toward the bank. Five of his troopers also waited outside the Efreeti compound north of town. Should the alarm be raised, he was confident no support would be coming from that direction.

Unfortunately, he couldn't stop an orbital bombardment round.

15 seconds to go.

Everyone should have been in position for five minutes by now. Of course, his troopers had to dodge all the foot and vehicular traffic on the roads and what passed for sidewalks in the town. Invisible wasn't immaterial, and any Sila inhabitants who bumped into them would know something was there. Happily, the walls of the adobe houses had enough imperfections in them that you could lean into them and almost be out of the way.

5 seconds. He aimed his rifle at the hinn across the street. Reptilian and hairless, the creature was dog-shaped and about the size of a medium Labrador retriever. Lieutenant O'Leary had decided to take it first and then its holder.

A woman screamed from around the corner, and the hinn jumped. O'Leary's shot went wide, striking the side of the bank.

The Efreeti handler dropped the hinn's leash and started to raise his weapon, a flechette thrower. Although O'Leary wasn't worried about the weapon, much, he was worried about the Efreeti's ability to call for help, so he switched targets and shot the Efreeti in the face.

The creature fell backward.

O'Leary looked for the hinn, but it had disappeared. He scanned back and forth with his rifle, looking for the animal, but it was nowhere to be seen. As O'Leary started to lower the rifle, the hinn appeared in full stride, five feet in front of him. Without breaking stride, it launched itself at O'Leary as if it could see him.

Instinctively, O'Leary brought his rifle up sideways in both hands to defend himself, and jammed the upper receiver assembly into the creature's mouth as he fell backward. The hinn bit down on the metal, and O'Leary flung the rifle up, throwing the hinn over his head as he hit the ground.

The creature twisted in the air, and landed on its feet, facing Lieutenant O'Leary. The hinn's momentum carried it a little further, its feet scrabbling for purchase on the slick surface of the sidewalk. As it started to gain momentum, Lieutenant O'Leary rolled to his stomach, brought up his rifle, and shot it through its left eye.

The hinn screamed, sending shivers down O'Leary's spine, and kept coming.

O'Leary shot it in the head again, but the creature didn't slow down. O'Leary fired a third time, but the creature jumped and the shot went below it.

The hinn's jaws opened wide as it dove onto Lieutenant O'Leary, and he saw a mouthful of sharp teeth. O'Leary knew he didn't have time to get his rifle back up to defend himself; the creature was *fast*.

He pushed off with his left hand, trying to avoid the hinn's leap, and rolled to the side. He heard the creature's claws scraping on the sidewalk again, and he spun around, raising the rifle.

The creature was already in the air, descending toward him, and O'Leary realized he was too late. As the hinn descended, there was a silver flash, and the beast's head spun off to the side, separated from its body. A spray of yellow blood filled the air, most of which landed on O'Leary, as the creature's leash flew free.

The rest of the animal landed next to O'Leary, and he watched in horror as it got back to its feet. The weapon struck again, this time severing the body into two pieces, with the noise of a machete going through a watermelon. The hinn fell to the ground, and Lieutenant O'Leary looked up to find a male Sila standing over the corpse with a small axe.

"Hate those damn things," the Sila said, spitting on the hinn.

He turned to where Lieutenant O'Leary lay and said, "If you're still there, its brain is in the main part of its body, making it hard to kill. Ya' gotta hit it in the chest."

O'Leary turned off his invisibility and got to his feet. He didn't hear anything from the bank, so he figured he had a minute. "Thanks," he said. "It was going to get me that time."

"My pleasure," the man said, pulling out a rag and wiping off the blade. He threw the rag into the street and strapped the axe to his back. "They're nasty critters," he added. "Don't let 'em bite you. It ain't a matter of *if* you'll get infected, but *how many* things you'll get infected with."

"Thanks again," Lieutenant O'Leary replied. "You might not want to stay here in case the Efreet come back."

"Oh, they'll come back," the man said. "They always do; however, it was right fun to see some of 'em gettin' what was coming to 'em. But you got the right of it; it's time to be gettin' back to my farm a'fore they do. Good day." He nodded, turned and left, humming a happy tune to himself.

Lieutenant O'Leary ran over to the building, just as Lieutenant Contreras came around the corner. "There you are, sir," he said. "I wondered if something had happened to you."

"One of the damned hinn almost got me," he said. He turned and indicated the pieces of its body. "It's over there. Let the clean-up crew know if you would, please."

"Aye aye, sir," replied Lieutenant Contreras. "By the way, the bank is secure. We didn't take any serious casualties, but Spud Murphy's suit is messed up. There was a woman about to get run over by a cart. He dove in front of it to save her. Turns out, the carts have spikes in their wheels…for traction, I guess. He took one through the leg but will be okay."

"Are we in?"

"Yeah, no problem. All the Efreet were out here except for one. I shot him, and the bank manager was more than happy to let me into the vault." He smiled. "We did pretty good; there has to be over 100 pounds of unobtanium in the vault."

Nightsong's Abode, Anti-Domus, Unknown Date

Nightsong held the vial up to the light and smiled; Calvin's blood sparkled. "I'll just run a few tests on this, and then I will be back for some more." He walked over to a work bench where the testing instruments waited with flashing lights and began analyzing his latest sample.

Calvin hoped the platoon would show up soon; this was getting scarier by the hour. Chained to an alien hospital bed, he had more wires and tubes attached to him then he wanted to count. Ever. Nightsong had already run a series of tests on his blood and DNA. The only good thing about being the captive of an Eco Warrior was he could draw blood without it hurting. And the Aesir had stopped electrocuting him for the moment, which was nice.

"So, you're not going to tell me your plan?" Calvin asked, trying desperately to take his mind off his current situation.

"Nope," Nightsong replied without turning his head or looking up.

"Well, can you at least tell me one thing?" Calvin asked.

"Maybe."

"How is it an anti-technology race like the Efreet is able to develop an advanced technology like the time bomb they hit the *Vella Gulf* with?

"Easy. They can't."

"What do you mean?" Calvin asked.

"You assumed we were fighting the Efreet in the 14 Herculis system. We weren't. I just never corrected you."

"Who was it, then?"

"Someone else."

"You're not going to tell me?"

"Nope."

"You told us a lot of things about the Efreet," Calvin said, trying a new tack; "was any of it true?"

"I'm sure there were random bits of truth in there, in order to make it believable," Nightsong replied; "however, most was made up in order to get you to do the things I needed you to do."

"And we fell right into your trap."

Nightsong turned and smiled. "You're here, aren't you?"

Chapter Twenty-Two

Army Training Facility, Remurn, Domus, October 21, 2021

Lieutenant O'Leary, Gunnery Sergeant Stasik and Staff Sergeant Zoromski returned to their universe several hundred yards in front of the Doman Army's training facility.

"The platoon is coming back!" the sentry yelled from the wall.

Lieutenant O'Leary and Gunny Stasik cleared the jump zone as Zoromski went back for the next group, and O'Leary saw Captain Smith hurrying toward him.

"We were starting to worry about you," Captain Smith said as he approached.

"Yeah, I was starting to get worried about us, too," O'Leary replied. He turned to Gunnery Sergeant Stasik. "Get the unobtanium to Lieutenant Bradford ASAP, and then get everyone ready for pickup."

"Yes sir!" the gunny replied. He turned and began issuing orders to the next group that had just arrived.

"Can I talk with you a minute?" O'Leary asked.

"Yeah, let's walk back to my office. I know the queens are going to want to talk with you when they hear you're back. What's up?"

"This whole officer thing," O'Leary said.

"What about it?"

"It's different."

"Well, yeah, it is. Is there something specific you wanted to discuss?"

"Yeah," O'Leary replied quietly. "We lost Sergeant Geisenhof."

"Okay," Smith said. "It's not the first time you've lost someone. What was different with him?"

They walked for a few seconds, not saying anything. Captain Smith waited patiently for his friend to come to grips with what was obviously troubling him.

"It's different because he was my responsibility," O'Leary finally said. "Not only was I the person in charge, I got him killed. We'd been told that the Efreeti monitor electronics, yet I had everyone wear their suits. I should have done it differently."

"How did your suits get him killed?"

"The Efreeti must have tracked our suits because they showed up where we were. There was a firefight, and Geisenhof was killed trying to defend some of the local civilians."

"So they homed in on the suits? I don't see how that's your fault. The suits are part of your battle gear. They give you an edge the Efreet don't have. I would have told you to wear them if you had asked me."

O'Leary thought back. "You know what? I don't think they intercepted our suits. They followed us when we commed. They must be able to pick up our transmissions."

"See? It's nothing to worry about," Captain Smith said. "It's not your fault."

"No; it *is* my fault," O'Leary said. "We knew they had some sort of intercept capability, and I was the one using the comm system. It's my fault the Efreet picked us up, and it's my fault Geisenhof died. I knew it immediately, and I froze when I saw him go down."

"Froze? What do you mean?"

"I couldn't stop looking at him as he lay there on the ground. I should have been giving orders to get the platoon moving, but all I could do was stare at his body."

"Ryan, when you were in the SEALs, did you ever lead a mission when you lost someone?"

"Yeah," O'Leary replied. "A couple of times we lost folks in the Sandbox. But that was different. I wasn't the one in charge; I was just following our mission tasking."

"No, it's no different at all. You were in charge of those operations, the same as you were in charge today. It doesn't matter if you're an officer or an enlisted; if you are the leader, you are responsible for the outcome. The mission is more important than all of us; we're talking about the future of our race here. If all of us have to die to accomplish it, then that's what we'll do. Geisenhof knew that, and you used to know it too. It doesn't matter what rank you have. People under you have died in the past, and it's an unfortunate truth people under you are going to die in the future. You accomplished the mission and brought back what we need to make the jump modules, so now we can go and kick their asses. While I am sorry for Geisenhof's loss, you need to look at the bigger picture. We won today, and we need to keep winning, regardless of who we lose along the way. Anything else is less than irrelevant."

Captain Smith watched as Lieutenant O'Leary processed his comments. With a sigh, O'Leary nodded as he accepted the truth in them. He stood a little straighter as he met Captain Smith's eyes. "So, how long until we can go back?"

Palace, Remurn, Domus, October 22, 2021

"The modules have been installed and are being tested," Lieutenant Bradford said in summation. "Solomon, the ship's artificial intelligence, will control the jump. We learned the hard way with the *Terra* that everything has to be done perfectly, or the ship won't make the jump."

"When will you be ready to go?" Queen Glina asked.

"Within the hour," Captain Sheppard replied.

"When the platoon was in the other universe, were they able to get an idea of the forces you will have to fight?" Queen Risst asked.

"No," Captain Sheppard said, shaking his head. "Based on historical patterns, we expect there will be an Efreeti destroyer in orbit, although we don't know if it will have the time-based weapons we've seen from some of their ships. My cruiser is more than a match for their less-capable destroyer class. Now that we can make the jump between universes like they can, the fight will be a lot more even if we have to fight one of their better destroyers too."

"We don't know if their torpedoes will be able to track us when we jump back and forth between universes," Lieutenant Bradford added, "but it's one of the things we want to try to defeat that technology."

"One of the things?" Queen Glina asked. "There are more?"

"Yes, we have several options we're working on," Lieutenant Bradford said as he looked at his shoes. "Unfortunately, it is taking a lot longer than expected to convert our existing technology to do what we want it to."

He looked up as a thought occurred to him. "Although, with all the unobtanium the platoon brought back, I'll be able to conduct some experiments I had to put off. They will give us some new capabilities…if they work.”

“Whether they work or not, our positions haven’t changed,” Queen Glina said, with a nod to indicate Queen Risst’s agreement. “If you get the chance to destroy their world while you are there, take it.”

Bridge, TSS *Vella Gulf*, Domus Orbit, October 22, 2021

Captain Sheppard looked around the bridge. The air was electric with sweat and adrenaline, but no one seemed scared. Just professionals going into combat with the unknown. Again.

Captain Sheppard had decided to make the jump from orbit, rather than pulling away from the planet. It was a gamble that the Efreet wouldn’t have anything the *Gulf* couldn’t handle waiting on the other side, but it was a gamble he was willing to take. They would have to fight the Efreet in the system at some point; better it was on his schedule than the Efreet’s. Besides, fighting them in the anti-world ensured that if anything fell from orbit, it would land on the Efreet and the Sila, not on the Domans. The queens had been very clear on that.

One thing made Captain Sheppard uncomfortable; this would be the first time he went into battle without Calvin. The aviator had been the ship’s good luck charm; everyone knew Calvin would pull something out of his hat to save the ship when things looked worst. Not having that little corner of security blanket made him…not frightened, exactly…just a little bit apprehensive. He shrugged it off. They’d get through the fight; they had to. And if they had to throw the planet into a black hole to carry the day…it wouldn't be the first time the Terrans had destroyed a world on his watch.

Not that he was proud of that fact.

"All right," Captain Sheppard said. "Around the bridge, is everyone ready?"

"Helm's ready and standing by," the helmsman reported from the front console. "Solomon is standing by to make the jump at your command."

"Engineering reports ready," the duty engineer said from his seat next to the helmsman. "General Quarters is set, and all repair lockers report manned and ready. Shields are at full strength."

"Sensor operator ready," Steropes replied. "All equipment operational, with a full spread of sensors ready to launch after we make the jump."

"Anti-ship missiles (ASMs) ready in all tubes," the offensive systems officer (OSO) said. "All gamma ray laser (graser) mounts extended and ready, except for mount 15 which is being worked on."

"Anti-missile missiles (AMMs) ready in all tubes," the defensive systems officer (DSO) said. "All defensive laser mounts extended and ready."

"All fighters manned and ready," Lieutenant Carl 'Guns' Simpson said. The squadron's acting executive officer, he had drawn the short straw of having duty on the day they went into combat. Captain Sheppard knew Guns had been in the majority of the squadron's combat missions and could tell he didn't want to sit this one out. If there was anyone who looked more intense on the bridge, Captain Sheppard couldn't see him. "The platoon is onboard *Shuttle 01*, which is waiting for your command to launch. *Shuttle 02* is also ready for launch."

"Very well," Captain Sheppard said. "Comms officer, please let Domus Control know we will make the jump in one minute." He switched to the ship-wide comms network. "*All hands, this is the Captain. In 30 seconds, we will jump into the Jinn Universe. We do not know what is waiting for us there, but we know Lieutenant Commander Hobbs and his abductor are in the system. It is our mission to track them down, rescue Lieutenant Commander Hobbs and apprehend Captain Nightsong.*"

"*It is likely there will be enemy ships in the system,*" he continued. "*We will deal with them first, and then land on the planet if necessary. Captain Nightsong is an Aesir Eco Warrior, so we know he is armed and dangerous, even when he doesn't have any weapons. No one is to communicate with him until we are ready to apprehend him. Once we get him onboard, take no chances with him.*"

"*We've been in combat many times together, and I am confident in your abilities. The Efreet nuked our planet; it's time to get some back. For Terra!*"

"Helmsman, make the jump!"

Chapter Twenty-Three

Bridge, TSS *Vella Gulf*, Anti-Domus Orbit, Unknown Date

"System entry," Steropes said. "Launching probes."

"Fighters launching," Guns said.

"Contact!" Steropes said. "Starboard bow, 300,000 miles! Designate contact as 'Sierra One.' Contact is destroyer-sized."

"Fire starboard missiles and grasers at Sierra One!" Captain Sheppard ordered. "Have the fighters stay clear. We'll take this one ourselves."

"Taking Sierra One with starboard batteries," the OSO said.

Captain Sheppard could feel the ship shudder as the ASMs began launching.

"Second contact!" the DSO called. "Port beam. Just coming over the curvature of the planet. Also destroyer-sized. Designate contact 'Sierra Two.'"

"Port batteries fire on Sierra Two," Captain Sheppard ordered.

"Aye, sir," the OSO replied. "Taking Sierra Two with port batteries."

Captain Sheppard looked at his tactical display. "Is that it? Just the two destroyers?"

"Holy shit!" the DSO exclaimed. "I've got activity on the moon, sir, and there's *lots* of it!"

"Coming on screen," Steropes said. He put the image on the front view screen.

"Oh, shit," Captain Sheppard said under his breath. Louder, he added, "Better get the fighters on that."

Cockpit, *Asp 07*, Anti-Domus Orbit, Unknown Date

"We were just ordered to strike the moon," Lieutenant Commander Sarah 'Lights' Brighton said.

"Just 'the moon?'" her pilot, Lieutenant Denise 'Frenchie' Michel, asked as she yanked the fighter around toward the moon 'above' and 'behind' them. "Not, 'Strike the missile facility on the moon?'"

"They said the Sea of Serenity but didn't specify after that," Lights replied. "Just a second; I'm looking." She peered into her weapon system's monitor. "Oh, bloody hell…that's no moon. That's a fucking military base!" She frantically searched for the best target among the forest of antennae, buildings, weapons and craft. The center of the crater held the largest base she had ever seen. As she scanned, a missile lifted off from an underground silo. An anti-ship missile from the size of it. "*Vampires inbound from the moon!*" she commed back to the *Vella Gulf*.

She was at a loss. Too many targets; not enough missiles. Think, Sarah, think…They can't shoot us if they can't see us… "*All Asps, synch up with my targeting. Asps 01-06, target your missiles on any radars you see, especially if they look like tracking radars. Asps 07-12, shoot the fighters on the ramp. We need to thin them out before they come up to play. After that, strafing runs by section; we need to hit them hard before they can respond! Fire when ready!*"

She peered back into her monitor. The fighters sitting on the ramp next to the runway looked like bugs, squat and ugly. If it weren't for the missiles hanging on some of them and sitting next to others, she might not have recognized them as such. She picked five of the armed fighters in a group of 16. Figuring they were the alert squadron, they needed to be the first to go. She designated them to her individual missiles, then transmitted the targeting to the other fighters so no one else would target them.

"Master armament panel is 'on,'" she said to Frenchie. "Targets designated. *Fire!*"

Frenchie squeezed her trigger and their missiles began launching, leaping out to begin the assault. Lights wished she had more…but that's what the laser was for.

Bridge, TSS *Vella Gulf,* Anti-Domus Orbit, Unknown Date

"Both targets destroyed," the OSO said. "Looks like we surprised them, sir; they never even got their shields up."

"Understood," Captain Sheppard replied. "Comm, any luck reaching the government or the military?"

"No sir," the communications officer replied. "No replies so far. I think I found the frequency they are using, but my system is unable to break into their comms."

"Solomon, can you break in?" the CO asked.

"Without a complete database of their language or communications systems, it is difficult. I believe they are also using some level of encryption. I will attempt to decipher their communications, but it will take some time."

"Sir, the facilities on the moon are responding," the DSO replied. "I've got a mass launch inbound. Still trying to get an accurate count, but there are almost 100 missiles inbound. I've also got fighters launching from there, as well."

"Didn't the fighters hit their base?"

"Yes sir, they did," Guns said, "and they are continuing to do so, but from what I'm hearing, the base is immense. There were *hundreds* of fighters on the base and more targets than we had missiles. Most of our fighters are now engaged in dog fights, rather than attacking the base. I ought to be out there."

"Launching AMMs," the DSO announced. "There are going to be leakers."

"More missiles launching from the moon," Steropes said.

"Thanks," the DSO muttered; "I *so* needed to know that."

Cockpit, *Asp 12*, Anti-Domus Orbit, Unknown Date

"Two more behind us," Lieutenant Tobias 'Toby' Eppler warned.

"Damn," his pilot, Lieutenant Phil 'Oscar' Meyer, swore. "Where the hell did *they* come from?" He pulled hard on the stick to get the enemy fighters out of his blind spot as Toby destroyed one with the fighter's laser.

"No idea," replied Toby, "but they're everywhere. At least 300 must have made it off the moon."

"Individually, they suck as fighters," Oscar noted. "I can run rings around them. Literally, rings. Their technology sucks. They must not have any of the thrust vectoring and inertial dampeners we do. I mean, they can't turn at *all*; they have to stop and then accelerate in the opposite direction."

"Yeah, but there's just *so* freakin' many of them," Toby said. "I can't keep up with them all, even with assistance from the targeting computer."

"No shit!" Oscar exclaimed, swerving to the left to avoid two more Efreeti ships. "Their missiles are crap too," he added as he continued the turn, "but there is a metric ass-ton of them out here." He didn't see the two missiles coming from the left.

Cockpit, *Asp 10*, Anti-Domus Orbit, Unknown Date

"Gotcha, you little bastard," Lieutenant Jim 'Sweets' Sweeny said as he destroyed the fighter he was chasing. The Efreeti had made the mistake of missing his fighter with a two-missile salvo, and Sweets had spun it in a tight 360-degree turn, looping in behind the Efreeti fighter and his wingman as they flew past. While they frantically tried to slow their fighters, Sweets had rolled in for the shot.

"And now for your little brother too," Sweets added, switching to the wingman.

"Hurry up!" his WSO, Lieutenant Poon 'Harpoon' Yee, urged. "There are three coming from the right!"

"No problem," Sweets replied. "This won't take but a second."

"Two coming from the left, too!"

"Got this…"

"They're launching!"

"I know, just a second, almost done…"

"We need to turn *now!*"

"Got him!" Sweets exclaimed as his laser speared through the cockpit of the Efreeti fighter. "One dead salamander! Pulling out!"

Three missiles impacted the starboard side of *Asp 10*, a second before two more from the left detonated in the debris.

Bridge, TSS *Vella Gulf*, Anti-Domus Orbit, Unknown Date

"Lasers and AMMs firing!" the DSO cried. His voice had risen an octave as the horde of missiles got closer. "We're killing them fast; they're just shooting them faster." He switched to the ship-wide communications network. "*Missiles inbound; all hands brace for shock!*"

The ship was buffeted, but didn't rock like when missiles had hit it previously.

"Sir, the shields stopped most of the missiles," the duty engineer reported. "We have some minor damage in the galley and officer's showers. Damage control parties are responding."

"More missiles launching from the moon," Steropes said.

"Sir, we just lost *Asp 10* and *Asp 12*," Guns reported. "It's getting pretty bad out there. Their fighters are crap and their anti-fighter missiles are just as lame as their anti-ship missiles, but they've got several hundred fighters compared to our 12. Well, 10, now."

"Are we in range of the moon?" Captain Sheppard asked.

"Yes sir," the OSO replied.

"Pull the fighters back," the CO ordered, "and blast the moon with everything we've got."

Cockpit, *Asp 07*, Anti-Domus Orbit, Unknown Date

"*Break right,* Asp 06!" Frenchie commed. She fired, and her laser lanced out, destroying the Efreeti following *06.*

"We need to pull back," Frenchie said. "There are too damn many of them. Individually, they aren't a match, but they out-number us about 20-to-1 now, and I can't see everywhere at once. If they keep launching more fighters, we're going to be overwhelmed."

"You just got your wish," Lights said as Frenchie destroyed another Efreeti ship, then maneuvered wildly to avoid a pair of missiles. "*All Asps, clear out of the space between the* Vella Gulf *and the moon. I think Mom's had enough of this bullshit, too. Rendezvous at the coordinates I'm sending you, and we'll delouse ourselves.*"

She watched as the remaining fighters gyrated wildly to get clear of the fur ball they had allowed themselves to become embroiled in. *Asp 02,* with its crew of Lieutenants Brian Bouchez and Jerry Johnson, didn't make it, succumbing to a barrage of missiles from at least three sides. Lieutenant Bouchez almost got them clear, but they took a missile he hadn't seen coming from 'below' the fighter.

Once the fighters were clear, it didn't take the *Vella Gulf* long to sanitize the moon. ASMs and grasers were retargeted onto the lunar surface, flattening buildings and turning the lunar soil to fused glass. The space in between was swept clear with a barrage of the ship's AMMs and anti-missile lasers.

"*Holy shit,*" Lieutenant Erika Smith commed as she watched the ship fire broadside after broadside. The ship rolled after each launch to bring the other set of launchers to bear, doubling the effective rate of fire. The fighter's view screen allowed her to see the laser strikes raining down like a fierce lightning storm on the lunar landscape. *"They're getting pasted down there."*

"And good riddance to them bastards, too," her pilot, Lieutenant Samuel Jakande, added.

After four broadsides, no more missiles or fighters rose from the surface. Four more broadsides followed…just to make sure.

"Guns is going to be pissed," Frenchie said.

"Why's that?" Lights asked.

"He thought he was going to be the first space ace," Frenchie replied, "but he's not."

"Did we get five kills today?"

"No," replied Frenchie, sounding embarrassed. "We got 12."

Chapter Twenty-Four

"I think that will be sufficient," Captain Sheppard said. "Hold fire; let's see if there's anything still alive down there."

"I see a couple of hostile fighters still operational," the DSO reported. "Want me to take care of them?"

"Are they headed toward us or our fighters?" the CO asked.

"No sir," the DSO replied. "They appear to be going back to the moon."

"I think we made our point. Keep an eye on them. If they stay on the moon, let them be. If they come back up, you are cleared to fire without further direction."

"Aye aye, sir."

"Captain Sheppard," Solomon interrupted, "I believe I have broken into their communications net. Would you like to hear what they are saying?"

"Yes, I would."

"The queen is still at risk from the intruders. Gather all your remaining fighters and send them in a coordinated attack with your remaining missiles. The intruders must be destroyed!"

"General Skeeeeezzis, that is impossible. I value the queen's safety as much as you, but sending out what remains of the fighter wing is nothing short of ludicrous. How are seven fighters going to do what 347 couldn't?"

"Perhaps if you were to pilot one of them, Colonel, the men would fight better."

"And perhaps if you hadn't siphoned off all the money for improved equipment, the men might actually have had a chance."

"Solomon, can I transmit to them?"

"Yes sir, just speak and I will overpower their transmitters."

"Efreeti officers, this is Captain Sheppard of the Terran Spaceship Vella Gulf," the CO said.

"Wait; who is this?" General Skeeeeezzis asked. *"What are you doing on our network? This is a secure transmission!"*

"I am the commanding officer of the Terran ship in orbit," Captain Sheppard said. *"I am interrupting your conversation to give you my terms. They are simple. There are two foreigners on your planet. One of them is an Aesir by the name of Nightsong; the other is one of our countrymen whose name is Lieutenant Commander Shawn Hobbs. We will send a shuttle down to the surface of the planet. If you return the two foreigners to us, we will then negotiate your surrender. If you don't return the foreigners, we will destroy your towns until you do; I will instruct my forces to look for likely places your queen might be and will have them destroy those places first. It's up to you; give us the foreigners, or you* will *lose your cities and your queen."*

"You're bluffing," the general replied. *"You wouldn't lay waste to our cities, as you might inadvertently kill the people you are looking for. If they are so important, you wouldn't dare!"*

"Perhaps not," Captain Sheppard replied. *"However, is that really a risk you are willing to take? Even if we don't destroy your cities, we will certainly slag your facilities on the moon."* Captain Sheppard motioned to the OSO. "Resume graser fire on the moon."

"Continue kicking the shit out of the moon, aye, sir!" the OSO replied in a happy tone.

"*You have got to make them stop!*" the colonel exclaimed. "*The base cannot take much more. We have already lost atmospheric integrity in several places. We will be completely open to space before much longer, and with most of our shuttle craft destroyed, we will be unable to return our survivors to the planet.*"

"*You have failed the queen,*" the general replied. "*What value are your lives?*"

"*What is the value of your life, general?*" Captain Sheppard asked.

"*What do you mean?*"

"Solomon, can you determine where the general's transmission is originating from?"

"Yes sir, the signal is coming from a military facility on the largest continent. I do not know whether that is where he actually is, though. He may be somewhere else and just using that transmission facility. Standby."

There was a pause as Solomon traced the signal through their network, then the AI added "The general is at the facility, as well. I found a map of the base in their computer network; I am displaying it on the front view screen."

"Good," Captain Sheppard said. "OSO, slag one of the buildings on that base. Pick one with maximum psychological value."

"Graser firing," the OSO noted.

"Sir, it is done," Solomon said. "The general's house has been destroyed."

"*You asked what I meant by the value of your life, general,*" Captain Sheppard said. "*Your house has been destroyed. We can kill you at our discre-*

tion just as easily. Perhaps we should do that right now; your replacement may be easier to reason with."

"No…um…I don't think that will be necessary," the general replied. "*I will, however, need to talk to our officials as I do not know who or where the individuals you are looking for are residing.*"

"*That is not factual,*" Solomon transmitted. "*The communications logs indicate Captain Nightsong checked in with their space command establishment upon his arrival. At a minimum, they are aware of where he landed.*"

"*Well, it may be true someone from this organization talked with him,*" the general replied, "*but I couldn't tell you how long ago that was or who it was that spoke with him. I will need some time to research those details. I'm sure I can have an answer for you by mid-day, our time, tomorrow.*"

"*I do not believe that is necessary,*" Solomon said, "*as you were one of the people who spoke to him. The records indicate you asked if he would be landing at the 'normal place,' and he replied in the affirmative.*"

"*You have two hours to have the people we're looking for ready to travel. If they aren't, I will find out if your successor is better able to get things done. Captain Sheppard, out.*"

"Do you think the Efreet will have them ready in two hours?" the OSO asked.

"It will depend on their relationship with Nightsong," Captain Sheppard replied, "but I would expect the answer is, 'probably not.' I doubt Nightsong is going to give himself up to us willingly, and he is a pretty capable individual. Work with Solomon and develop a list of targets for us to strike in case they don't. I would like a number of options."

Nightsong's Abode, Anti-Domus, Unknown Date

Nightsong smiled down at Calvin, strapped to the bed. Additional restraints had been added to keep him from moving. "This is where the fun begins," he said. He tested the point of a scalpel with a finger. Green blood welled up from the cut momentarily, but then the cut closed on its own and the blood disappeared. "Well, I guess I should say that this is where the fun begins *for me*," he said with a giggle; "your experience, of course, may differ slightly."

"Why are you *doing* this?" Calvin asked.

"I already told you why," Nightsong replied. "I need your spirit to help me with my quests." He saw Calvin staring at the scalpel. "If you mean, 'why am I going to remove most of your organs first, before finally killing you?' it is because I have found pain focuses a soul wonderfully prior to death. I don't want any soul energy to escape when you die; I want to get every last bit." He smiled again. "As your culture says, it's good to the last drop."

He ran the scalpel down the right side of Calvin's abdomen, and Calvin screamed in pain and terror. "Did that hurt?" Nightsong asked.

"Yes, you bastard, you know it did," Calvin moaned in pain.

"Good. I told you pain was part of the process. I could make this not hurt if I wanted to, but that would be defeating the purpose. By the way, I would try not to struggle so much if I were you. This has to be done in a certain order, and if you cause me to make an incorrect incision, I will have to put you back together again and start all over. While it might be fun for me, I doubt you would like it as much, and I *am* on somewhat of a schedule. You know, giants to kill and regicide to commit…things like that."

Nightsong drew the scalpel across the bottom of Calvin's stomach, eliciting another scream. Nightsong shuddered in delight. "I had almost forgotten how much fun this was."

The Aesir drew the scalpel across the top of Calvin's abdomen and lifted up the flap of skin he had cut. "This is so much nicer as an Eco Warrior," he noted absently. "As you can guess, this process used to be *so* bloody before I became one. Clean up was always *such* a chore."

The sound of pounding on the door interrupted his reverie.

"Go away!" he shouted.

The pounding continued.

"*Go away!*" he shouted even louder.

The pounding also grew louder.

Nightsong gave a theatrical sigh. "Good help is *so* hard to find." He turned and walked to the door. "Don't go anywhere," he said with a giggle; "I'll be right back."

Calvin could hear voices. Their tone sounded urgent, but the voices were too low for him to understand through the searing pain. After a few moments, Nightsong returned to the doorway.

"I'm sorry, my presence has been requested by the queen, and she is the one person that cannot be ignored. If I do not go see what she wants, her troops will continue to interrupt us, regardless of how many I kill. They really *are* quite persistent in following her orders."

He crossed to Calvin. "Unfortunately, going to the palace means I will have to go outside the control range of the nanobots in your system; I am going to have to turn them off so they don't kill you."

Despite Calvin's intentions, Nightsong saw the smile that flickered across Calvin's face.

"I'm sure you believe this is a reprieve, but let me assure you, it is *not*. First of all, your implant's transmitter and receiver are turned off, so even when I disable my nanobots, you still won't have the ability to communicate. Not that there's anyone to talk with here. Second, no matter how much pain you think you are in now, it is about to become much, *much* worse. The nanobots have been blocking some of the pain to keep you from passing out; you are about to feel it all now. Enjoy."

He smiled and leaned forward to touch Calvin's cheek, and pain blossomed across Calvin's body. He screamed until he passed out.

Chapter Twenty-Five

Palace, Anti-Domus, Unknown Date

"What is this all about?" Nightsong asked as he was greeted outside the palace by the captain in charge of the palace guard.

"I don't know," the captain replied. "You know the rules," he added, all business, "I must search you."

"I don't have any weapons," Nightsong said, "but you are welcome to look." *For all the good it will do you,* he added silently.

Confident the Aesir was unarmed, the captain led him into the palace. Nightsong hated the palace, and he avoided it whenever possible. Partly because it smelled. Badly. On a good day, the Efreet smelled like Terrans after they worked out. When their pheromones were running high, like today, it was worse. Much worse.

The stench was suffocating as he walked into the waiting room, accompanied by four Efreeti troopers with flamecasters. They looked like they expected him to be trouble, he thought; they had their armor secured and looked ready for combat operations. He expected a large number of troops armed with tasers would accompany him into the queen's presence.

On any other day, he would have welcomed the opportunity to display his superiority by killing them all...*but today he was busy*. He focused on that truth as the desire to kill started to get the better of him.

Another reason for hating the palace was this room. They always made him wait, as if their time was more important than his. He knew this was part of the queen's protocol, but it only served to infuriate him further. Focus, he thought to himself. He drew several deep breaths to let some of the anger go. It didn't help much.

The captain came into the room. "The queen is ready to see you now," he advised.

Nightsong walked past the troopers, ignoring them, and into the queen's audience chamber. It was unlike any other audience chamber he had ever been in, and he had been in more palaces over his lifetime than he could count. Every other audience hall was designed to impress its visitors, with huge, vaulted ceilings, ornate stonework and tapestries, and other grandiose displays of wealth.

The Efreeti version was much different.

While the Efreeti audience hall still had the displays of opulence any palace-goer would expect, it was overdone, with ornamentation and felt-like material covering all the walls, the ceiling and the floor in garish patterns of blue and orange. Nightsong had decided long ago the Efreet must have a different visual acuity to appreciate it; the display just made his head hurt. Worse, the audience hall was a miniscule 10-foot square, which focused all the smells and the riot of color into an inescapable putrid collection of nauseating sensory overload.

The Efreeti race had developed in flooded subterranean chambers and passageways, and they were more comfortable in smaller areas. This queen felt the agoraphobia more strongly than any of the previous queens, and had shrunk the size of the audience hall to the minimum required; it was not much larger than herself.

More than anything else, she was the reason Nightsong hated coming to the palace.

Larger than the male Efreet, the queen looked like an overweight eight-foot long sausage with the ends of her arms and legs sticking out from the central mass of flesh. While the males had some vestigial webbing between their claws, the queen's hands and feet were fully webbed, and she still had a fin on the top and bottom of her over-sized tail. From the additional odor, she had also laid eggs recently; that stench, when added to the stink of the taser troops in the room, made him want to vomit, and it took all his self-control not to.

The bowl of Efreeti flesh the queen kept nearby to snack on didn't help.

All-in-all, every visit to the palace was an event to forget, and he couldn't wait to begin forgetting this one as soon as possible.

"How may I be of service to you?" he asked in Efreeti. Meetings with the queen were things to get through; being polite accelerated the process, so it was something that had to be done, despite his real feelings for the queen and her underlings.

"You may serve me by taking your prisoner and going to the starport, where you will meet a group of people called Terrans. You will turn yourself over to them, so they will leave our system. That is how you may serve me best."

"*The Terrans are here?*" Nightsong asked. "How did they get here? They shouldn't be able to make the jump to this universe with the equipment they have available."

"I don't know," the queen replied, "but here they are, and their one ship destroyed my entire space force and all the facilities on the moon. You will go meet them at the starport, and you will do so now."

"I see," Nightsong said. "So this is how you repay me for all my help through the years. Despite everything I have done for you, you are willing to turn me over like a common criminal."

"While we appreciate your prior service, there is nothing else we can do. The Terrans will bomb our towns until they get you and your friend."

"I know the Terrans well. I seriously doubt they will indiscriminately bomb your cities. They don't have it in them to kill to get what they want."

"In this case, you would be wrong," the queen replied. "They obliterated our base on the moon…the one you said was 'impregnable.'"

"Nothing is impregnable. If I used that word, it was only in relation to the Sila's capabilities, which are laughable. I never expected it would withstand a concerted Mrowry or Archon assault. If you had listened to me and built what I said, though, it would have at least held off the Terrans."

"What's past is past," the queen replied, "and it cannot be changed. I am not interested in speaking of past events, only in moving forward. And for that, you must leave, and you must leave *now*. No further delays will be tolerated."

"Indeed," Nightsong said with a sniff. "So be it. I will go to the starport and meet with the Terrans, although I must go back to my house first. There are things there I will need for my journey, and I will also need to get my companion, who is, I'm afraid, not in very good traveling condition."

"That is acceptable," the queen replied.

"Then I will be on my way," Nightsong said, as he turned and walked out of the audience chamber. As he passed through the door, he saw a flash of movement to the right and dove away from it. The taser leads went over him, missing by several inches; however, his dive took him into the path of a second taser attack, and both leads penetrated his skin. He fell to the floor, twitching, as the electricity coursed through him.

While he writhed on the floor in agony, two of the queen's 'shock troops' grabbed his arms with thick rubber gloves and placed metal cuffs on his wrists and irons on his ankles. Once secured, the Efreeti trooper turned off the taser, allowing Nightsong to lay on the floor and catch his breath.

"I will…kill you…for that," Nightsong said when he had control of his muscles again.

"Queen's orders," the captain said. "She knows you are smart and tricky, and she wanted to make sure you followed through with your promise."

"I promise if you take these cuffs off, I will go with you and turn myself in," Nightsong said. "I just need to go by my house first."

"I don't think so," the captain said. "I'm sure you have any number of weapons in your house, and I don't want them used on me. We will all just walk nicely to the starport, where you will be turned over to the Terrans. And then *they* can then go get the other person they're looking for."

The Aesir's comm went active. "*Nightsong, this is Lieutenant O'Leary,*" the voice said. "*I'm coming for you…We have some things I want to discuss before I send you back to Santa like the naughty little elf you are. By the way, once I get there, please feel free to resist…I'd like it a lot if you did.*"

Nightsong didn't reply as he took stock of his situation, although he did turn off his implant so he couldn't be tracked by it. Getting tased was the worst possible thing for him. He would have done or said anything to avoid it; the electrical current fried his nanobots. The life 'bots were low power because they had to be sensitive to the electrical current in living organisms; he had lost well over half of them. His combat 'bots were hardened against attack so he had considerably more of them left; unfortunately, without the life 'bots, he lost the element of surprise. He could do a few things with what remained, but didn't have anywhere near enough to disguise himself as an Efreeti. Growing a tail, in particular, was right out.

And he hated having a tail, in any event. They were just gross.

The Efreet were right to tase him, but were wrong in thinking the cuffs could hold him. And only five troops to guard him? Laughable. The two flamecasters were next to useless against a fire-based Eco Warrior, and the captain's over-confidence would be easy to use against him. The two shock troopers were the only ones who concerned him; both were alert and had the ability to damage him. They would be the first to go.

The walk to the starport was only about half a mile, and he used most of that looking for an opportunity. The problem was all in the timing. He needed to break free before they came in range of the Terrans, but not so early the Efreet could put out an alert on him. His ship was at the starport, so he was at least headed in the right direction for an escape. Losing Calvin would be an annoyance, but he knew there would be opportunities to reacquire the Terran. More annoying would be the loss of his Progenitor's Rod; that was something he was seriously considering going back to the house to get, especially since he only needed one more system to find out what it did. He had a pretty good idea where the last system was and had been practicing the skills he'd need to blend in there. He *would* be the first to figure out the riddle of the Progenitors; he was sure of that.

As they neared the starport, he saw the Terran shuttle coming in to land, and knew his time was growing short. He wouldn't have time to go back and get the Rod, after all. He didn't know why the gods had chosen today to laugh at him, but he would laugh at them on the day he took the Rod back. There was no doubt in his mind he would recover it eventually; the Terrans were simply too gullible to prevent it.

Adrenaline and other natural stimulants flooded his body, speeding his reactions. With a thought, he grew a lump on his leg and used it to push the only thing in his pocket, a coin, up to the lip of the pocket, where he palmed it with his walking motion. As they passed an alleyway, he stumbled, and the coin flew from his hand into the alley.

"My lucky coin!" he shrieked, stumbling ahead of the Efreet into the alley. He lurched as his feet withdrew into his legs, allowing him to step out of the leg irons, while his arms elongated and slimmed. The hand cuffs fell off. Spinning, he found the two shock troopers close by, as expected. One was already aiming his weapon, and Nightsong had to dive past him to avoid the leads fired from it.

Nightsong touched each of the shock troopers on the neck as he passed, turning the dive into a forward somersault that brought him up and running on his stumps between the two flamecaster troops. He mentally thanked his former team leader, Landslide, as he ran a hand under the tanks on the flamecasters' backs.

With a small 'bang,' the nanobots in the shock troopers' necks exploded, blowing out their main arteries. The detonation wasn't strong enough to completely decapitate them, but was more than sufficient to kill them.

Nightsong swung his hand in a chopping motion as reached the captain, and the knife-edged bone Nightsong extruded slashed through the captain's throat in an explosion of blood and gore.

Spinning, the Aesir found both flamecasters being slammed into the wall by the propellant spraying from one of the tanks on their backs; fuel puddled on the street as it poured from holes in the other. He sent a command to the earth nanobots that had eaten the holes to shut down, while triggering the fire 'bots. Both troopers ignited in a 'whoosh' of flames. He could hear their screams through their helmets and shivered in delight.

He looked up to see the black, oily smoke rising above the alley. That would serve as a nice distraction, he decided. His legs grew feet again, and he loped out the other end of the alley. He had wanted to use one of the flamecaster's armor as a disguise, but didn't have enough time to put it on. He also found that he couldn't stand the smell of roasted Efreeti.

It was even worse than how they normally smelled.

Cargo Bay, *Shuttle 01*, Anti-Domus, Unknown Date

Lieutenant O'Leary led the platoon down the ramp at a jog. As befit a hostile landing, all the troops were in their suits and armed to the teeth; their weapons were out and ready. With a truce 'sort of' in place, they didn't aim their weapons directly at the three Efreet who met them; however, it wouldn't have taken more than a split second to do so.

The 'welcoming party' was led by an officer in black leather, with two flamecasters in sealed black combat armor accompanying him. Apparently, they weren't ready to let the hostilities go, either, as their weapons were carried in a similar manner to the Terrans. Ready, but not quite aimed at their foes.

"I am Lieutenant Sllleeekss," the Efreeti in leather spat. "I would welcome you; however, the manner in which you come is hardly a welcome one."

"I'm Lieutenant O'Leary. For my part, I'd say I was sorry for how we arrived, but having already fought you guys on two other planets, I'm really not in much of a sorry mood."

"I do not know what you are talking about," the Efreeti said. "We are at the end of our communications chain; we are unaware of any conflict prior to you appearing and attacking us."

"Well, that's something for the higher-ups to discuss later, I guess," O'Leary said. "As of right now, I just want to get the two foreigners you have."

"I would love to give them to you," the Efreeti replied; "however, there has been a problem."

"A problem, eh?" Lieutenant O'Leary asked. "Why does that not surprise me?"

The Efreeti hissed. "This is not a problem of our making, but of yours. The person you asked for killed five of our soldiers, including my captain, and escaped. Had you not come here, my captain would still be alive."

"Oh yeah? Well the little cookie maker took my commanding officer hostage. I've got my own score to settle with him." O'Leary paused. "Where would he run to on this planet? Where could he get aid?" A thought struck him. "*Where is his damn ship?*"

"I will ask," the Efreeti said. He spoke into a circular box on his uniform. "He maintains a house in town, but his ship is at the far end of the starport. Let's go; we can be there in five minutes."

The Efreet and the Terrans set off toward the end of the landing area, but had only gone halfway when a familiar silver shape rose from a building in front of them. It rose several hundred feet into the air and disappeared.

"Mother *fucker…*" Lieutenant O'Leary muttered. "I am *so* going to kill that little tree hugger when I get my hands on him." He switched to his comm. "Vella Gulf, *Nightsong just lifted off and jumped back into our universe.*"

"*We saw him go. The CO says to get back here ASAP so we can go after him.*"

"*Don't wait for us; go get him! You can come back and get us afterward.*" O'Leary looked at the Efreeti lieutenant and decided he would probably be okay until the *Gulf* got back. They now shared a hatred of a common enemy as a bond. And the Terrans had better weaponry, if it came to that.

"*You don't have the ability to get back to our universe on your own. Shag ass to the shuttle and get back here ASAP.*"

"*On our way!*" O'Leary turned to the Efreeti. "We've just been called back to our ship, but I'm sure we'll be back."

"I'm sure of it too. You said you wanted the other person with the Aesir. I understand he is still back at the Aesir's house although he is not in very good shape."

"*What?*"

"It appears the Aesir was operating on him; he has been cut open."

"Take us there. Right *now!*" O'Leary switched back to his comm. "*Vella Gulf, disregard our previous intentions. Lieutenant Commander Hobbs is still here on-planet. We are going to try to rescue him. The Efreeti here says*

Nightsong was experimenting on him, and he is in bad shape. If he's bad enough the Efreet can recognize he's messed up, we've got to get him now!"

"Roger, the CO says to get Lieutenant Commander Hobbs. We'll wait."

The Terrans followed the Efreeti lieutenant at a jogging pace out of the starport and into the city. The Efreeti "run" involved a lot of side-to-side swaying that would have been humorous under other circumstances. As it was, O'Leary just wished they could run *faster*.

After about half a mile, O'Leary could see what had to be the Aesir's house; it was surrounded by Efreet in combat gear who were obviously guarding it. As the Efreeti lieutenant leading them slowed to a pace not much more than a walk, O'Leary sprinted past him.

He immediately slowed as all the Efreet in sight leveled their weapons at him. "Seemed like a good idea at the time," he muttered.

After a couple of seconds, they lowered their weapons, and O'Leary sprinted the rest of the way to the house. Not knowing what he'd find inside, he kept his weapon ready as he entered.

The first room was some sort of sitting room. He gave it a quick scan and continued on as the rest of the platoon followed him through the door. The second room was equally unimpressive, a bedroom, and he continued into what had once been the kitchen. Now, however, it was some sort of weird lab, with a number of apparatuses and monitors along the walls. The object of his search was strapped down on the room's sole piece of furniture, a bed in the center of the room.

The Efreeti had been right; Lieutenant Commander Hobbs was a mess. His stomach was cut open, and all his organs were exposed. At least he was unconscious as the pain would have been excruciating.

"Medic!" he commed as he started taking off his suit.

"Holy shit!" Corporal Shaun 'Lucky' Evertson exclaimed as he arrived in the kitchen. He switched to his comm. "*Everyone stay the fuck out! I don't know if the germs here will infect him, but I know ours will, and he is extremely susceptible right now!*"

"Stay with us, skipper," he said as he gently closed the flap and sprayed some liquid skin over it to hold it in place. Without looking up he said, "We need to get him into your suit ASAP, sir, and back to the *Gulf* even faster. Is there any way we can get the shuttle closer?"

"I don't know," Lieutenant O'Leary replied, "but they're damn well gonna try."

Cockpit, *Shuttle 01*, Anti-Domus, Unknown Date

"Roger that," the shuttle's WSO, Lieutenant Neil 'Trouble' Watson, replied. "They found Lieutenant Commander Hobbs, but he is pretty screwed up. Lieutenant O'Leary wants us to move closer so we can get him back to the *Gulf* ASAP."

"I don't know how well that's going to work," replied Lieutenant Jeff 'Canuck' Canada. "I didn't see a lot of open space in the city when we came in." His suit twitched as he shrugged. "Bring the ramp up and we'll go take a look."

Nightsong's Abode, Anti-Domus, Unknown Date

"*There's no place to set down,*" Trouble commed. "*There are houses for a good quarter mile in all directions.*"

"We don't have much time, sir," Lucky said. "The suit just went into stasis mode to try to keep the Skipper alive as long as possible, but even the suit has limits. We've got to get him back *now*."

"Let me see what can be done," Lieutenant Contreras said. "I used to be a forward air controller, and making landing zones was part of the job." He ran out and surveyed the houses around them.

No matter what he did, he wasn't going to make any friends with the Efreet. The houses were all built with something that looked like adobe; when he dropped one of the houses, the others around it were probably going to sustain severe damage as well.

If it were a choice between the Efreeti houses and the life of the Skipper, though, it wasn't a choice at all.

He waved over the Efreeti lieutenant. "See that house over there?" He pointed to one a couple doors down and across the street. "I need to level it so we can get our shuttle in here. The ones on both sides will probably be destroyed too. You have two minutes to clear the occupants."

"Over my dead body," the Efreeti said, seething. "I forbid it."

"Your death can easily be arranged," Lieutenant O'Leary said, coming out to supervise the process. His weapon was once again almost-aimed at the Efreeti. As O'Leary glanced around, he saw the Efreet who had been guarding the house were now also holding their weapons in the same position. The platoon outnumbered the Efreet and had better weapons and armor; it would be a slaughter.

"We are wasting time," Lieutenant Contreras said. "I am sure our government will reimburse the occupants for what they lose, but let me make one thing clear. We *are* going to blow up that building. If you want to add your death and the deaths of all your men to the list of people who got killed today, then so be it. I have done my part to warn you; I don't care. Are you going to go evacuate those buildings, or should we kill you first?"

Contreras watched as the Efreeti looked at the forces arrayed against him. Not only did the Terrans outnumber his forces, but Contreras also guessed the Efreeti had no idea how capable the Terrans' weapons were. The Terrans also held the planet's orbitals so Contreras was pretty sure the Efreeti would come to the correct conclusion.

"We will evacuate them," the Efreeti said in capitulation.

"Thank you," said Contreras with a sweeping bow. It never hurt to be gracious in victory.

Chapter Twenty-Six

Medical, TSS *Vella Gulf*, Anti-Domus Orbit, Unknown Date

Calvin opened his eyes a crack and tried to focus. Bright lights. White walls. Everything else stainless steel. He had seen this vista too many times. He was in medical, *again*. Then everything flooded back, and his eyes sprang wide open. Being in Medical was *good!*

"How'd I get here?" he asked, hoping the computer would answer since he didn't see anyone in the area.

Master Chief leaned into his vision. "Welcome back, sir," he said. "It was touch and go with you for a while. That bastard Nightsong really did a number on you."

"Yeah, I remember him turning off his nanobots and then the pain hit. I've never hurt that much in my life; I must have passed out. How did I get here?"

"Well, that's kind of a long story, but the bottom line is we figured out you had been taken by Nightsong, and we followed you to anti-Domus from Earth. We even got a little help along the way from some old friends."

"Hi, sir," Second Lieutenant Contreras said, leaning forward into Calvin's line of sight.

"Wait a minute," Calvin said, finally recognizing the silver bars on O'Leary's uniform; "you're a first lieutenant now?"

"Yes sir, I…uh…sort of got promoted."

"What, I'm out of it for a little while, and everyone starts getting delusions of grandeur? What's Contreras now, a lieutenant colonel?"

"No sir," Contreras said, "I'm still a second lieutenant."

"And it's a damn good thing we had him, too," O'Leary said. "He leveled an entire block in the Efreeti city so we could get a shuttle in to rescue you."

"Si," Contreras said, lapsing into Spanish. "I hadn't blown up anything in a while so I was sort of out of practice and, you have to admit, those houses really weren't built that well."

"No, they weren't," O'Leary agreed; "however, you still used too much antimatter."

Contreras shrugged. "We were in a hurry. Better too much than not enough."

"So," Calvin said, "back to the point. Please tell me you guys caught Nightsong."

"No," Lieutenant O'Leary replied; "however, I did recover this for you." He held up the Progenitor's Rod he had found at Nightsong's house.

"That one's Nightsong's, but since he destroyed mine, I'll be happy to claim it. Seriously, you didn't catch him?"

"I wish," O'Leary said. "When I get my hands on him, he's going to tell us everything. And then I'm going to kill him."

"Hey," Calvin said, looking around. "Where's Night?"

"I'm sorry to have to be the one to tell you this," O'Leary said, "but Night got killed leading the attack on Arges' house."

"You attacked Arges' house?" Calvin asked. "Geez, I missed everything. How did you find out they were together?"

"Some of the things Nightsong said about him didn't ring true. We went to confront him, and fought with his security forces."

"And Night got killed? Wow, I thought he was indestructible."

"No one is indestructible, sir," Lieutenant O'Leary replied, "although Captain Train's tougher to kill than most…"

Lieutenant Salo's Room, Bachelor Officer's Quarters, NAS Oceana, October 6, 2021

"I think it will work," Night said, leaning over a chart laid out on the table. He straightened and met the eyes of the other members of the team. "What do you think?"

"I agree with you," Sergeant Hattori 'Yokaze' Hanzo said. "If nothing else, it is our best chance for success."

"My part's easy," Lieutenant Kenyon 'Bucket' Salo, the team's pilot, said. "I don't have to do anything difficult, just fly you guys there. If you two are crazy enough to try it, I'll drive the bus."

"Yeah, Bucket's right," the shuttle's WSO, Lieutenant James 'Jamming' Miles, added. "Our part's easy. And I've already been there once, so I know the area. If you really want to try it, we'll take you there. What's the worst they're going to do? Throw us in jail?"

"No," Night replied, "if this goes badly, I imagine Arges will try to find you and kill you so no one knows this mission ever happened. Megalomaniacs aren't known for ignoring people who are threats to their supremacy."

"Then I guess you'd better not fail," Jamming replied. "I'm pretty sure my mum would be annoyed if you got me killed."

"I can do this by myself, Captain Train," Yokaze said. "Actually, I can probably do it better that way. There is no need for you to go."

"And miss out on killing Arges?" Night asked. "I don't think so. The little piece of shit tried to kill me; it's payback time. Besides, this is a two-person mission; you need someone to watch your back. Especially if anything unexpected happens."

Night turned to the last man in the room, Lieutenant Sam 'Cashman' Casher. "Can you arrange for the tech we need?"

"No problem," Cashman said, who was on leave from Department X. "I can tell anyone who asks I'm doing some off-site testing. I am, after all, to a certain way of looking at it."

"So that just leaves acquiring the transportation," Night said. "I've got some ideas on where we can…borrow…a shuttle. Hopefully, no one will notice it's missing before we bring it back."

"With all due respect, sir, I have a better idea," Yokaze said. "We don't need to steal one; I know someone who will let us have one."

"You do?" Night asked. "Can they keep it quiet? We can't allow any word of this to get out, or Arges will figure out we're coming."

"No, the person I know is very good at keeping a secret. There will not be a problem."

"Okay, you're in charge of getting the shuttle then." Night looked around the table. "There's one last thing I need to make sure everyone is aware of. We can never let anyone know about this mission. Ever. If we fail and get caught, we're going to jail. Probably for a long time. But we'll never see the end of it because something unfortunate will happen to us. We are going after the richest person in the world. Probably the richest in the universe. If we piss him off, he won't rest until we're dead, and he can finance any number of unpleasant ends for us. If you want to back out, now is the time to do it."

"I am in," Yokaze said. "The man has no honor and needs to die."

"I'm in," Bucket said. "Just don't screw it up, okay?"

Night smiled. "Just for you, I'll try not to."

"I'm in," Jamming said. "Remember, my mum will be angry if you get me killed."

"I'm in, as well," Cashman added. "Arges helped the Iranians, just for fun. There's no telling what he'll do next. He needs to die."

"We're agreed, then," Night said. "Arges must die."

Fleet Commander's Office, Fleet Command HQ, Lake Pedam, Nigeria, October 7, 2021

Admiral Wright looked up as his door opened, and a janitor in dirty white coveralls came in. He recognized the black man as one of the floor's usual cleaners.

"Thanks, but I don't need anything today," the admiral said.

"Yes sir," the janitor said as he approached the admiral's desk.

Admiral Wright recognized the automatic way he replied. The man had to be prior military. Probably Nigerian army, as the man obviously didn't speak English well enough to understand him.

"I'm sorry," Admiral Wright said. "I don't need any cleaning today, and I'm in the middle of something." He indicated the pile of paperwork on his desk with a motion of his hand. It was the last chore he had to complete prior to leaving the Terran Navy.

"I'm sure you are, sir," the man said, his English flawless; "this, however, is more important." He held out several sheets of paper to the admiral.

As Admiral Wright automatically reached for the offered papers, he noticed the hand holding it wasn't black. His eyes jerked upward in surprise to find the man had changed. No longer was the janitor African, he was now Asian…probably Japanese…and a good six inches shorter than he had been previously.

"What is the meaning of this?" Admiral Wright snapped.

"Please, sir, just read the note," the man replied. "It will explain everything, and I don't have much time."

Admiral Wright took the letter and began reading. After the first sentence, he looked up in surprise. The man looked at the letter in the admiral's hands, indicating with his eyes that the admiral should keep reading.

Admiral Wright read another two sentences and looked up again. "Who are you?" he asked.

"I am Sergeant Hattori Hanzo of Lieutenant Commander Hobb's platoon," the Asian man replied. "I am now on…detached duty…for a special mission."

The admiral nodded once. "I've heard of you," he said and went back to reading. This time he finished the letter. When he looked up again, a feral grin suffused his face. It was the first time he had smiled all week. "What do you need from me?" the admiral asked.

"Only a signature," Yokaze said, pulling a second set of papers from the inside of his coveralls.

"What is this?" Admiral Wright asked as he took the papers.

"Just a set of orders for a crew to requisition a shuttle to fly up to the moon and pick up a piece of equipment for delivery. It is all above board and totally legitimate, sir."

Admiral Wright signed the papers and handed them back.

"Thank you sir," Yokaze said. He turned to leave.

"One last thing," the admiral said. "We never had this conversation."

"How could we?" the janitor asked. He turned around, a black man again. "I was never here."

Lieutenant Salo's Room, Bachelor Officer's Quarters, NAS Oceana, October 8, 2021

"Is that really the Fleet Commander's signature?" Bucket asked.

Yokaze nodded.

"How did you get it?"

"Ninjas are experienced in the art of disguise," Yokaze said. "I disguised myself and walked into his office."

"And no one noticed you?" Jamming asked.

"I was very good at disguise *before* I met the Aesir," replied Yokaze. "When I saw the things Reeve Farhome could do, I knew having those abilities would come in handy, so I asked him to teach me. I can't do everything he can, and I used up most of the nanobots he gave me visiting the admiral, but it worked. Now I just have to figure out how to get to the Aesir home world so I can get more nanobots."

"He trained you as an Eco Warrior?" Night asked.

"No, he said the training takes 150 years. Sadly, I do not think I will have the time available to complete the program. He did, however, teach me how to control nanobots and showed me how to get them to do a few basic things."

Night looked at his watch. "Okay," he said; "time to go. Remember, we have two objectives tonight. Kill Arges and find something that incriminates him. Killing him frees our planet; getting the evidence gives us back our lives. Without it, no one from the *Vella Gulf* can ever come home again."

"*Hai!*" Yokaze said. "We will find what we need, and we will kill Arges. Honor will not be satisfied with less."

Chapter Twenty-Seven

"Nightsong got away," Captain Sheppard said to the assembled group. Since Calvin wasn't up to attending a meeting in the conference room, Captain Sheppard had moved the meeting to medical, against the wishes of the senior medibot, who had stood watching, metal foot tapping, until ordered to leave.

"I thought you said the Domans had a cruiser guarding the stargate," Calvin noted. "What happened to it?"

"They did," Captain Sheppard replied; "unfortunately, they didn't have any experience in cross-universe operations. When they saw the ship appear, they left their position to intercept it. When Nightsong started dropping things from orbit onto the planet, they assumed he was bombing their home world and sped up to intercept him sooner. Once he had them established on a track toward the planet, he jumped back into the Jinn Universe and accelerated toward the stargate. When he jumped back to our universe, he was already past the cruiser and made it to the stargate before they could turn around and go after him."

"And the *Gulf* never got a shot at him either?"

"Sadly, no," Captain Sheppard replied. "He knows all our weapons ranges and stayed outside of them while he was in the same universe we were. The problem we have is he knows everything about us while we really don't know anything about him."

"True," Calvin agreed.

"We were hoping you'd be able to shed a little light on his plans," Captain Sheppard said. "Did he tell you anything about where he's going or what he and Arges intend to do?"

"Very little," Calvin replied. "He gave me some generalities, but he didn't want to share any of the specifics." He was silent for a moment while he tried to remember everything Nightsong had said.

"Before I tell you what I know or can guess about Nightsong's intentions," Calvin continued, "there is a faulty assumption in your last question. Nightsong and Arges are not in this together. Arges caught Nightsong a long time ago…thousands of years, actually…and has been controlling his actions ever since. During that time, Nightsong has been developing a plan of his own, not only to get free from Arges, but also to get revenge for events that happened in his childhood. What we are seeing now is the culmination of these plans."

"So, they aren't working together?" Lieutenant O'Leary asked. "That would explain some of the…randomness…and why things don't seem to fit together."

"Exactly. In many cases, I think Nightsong actually was working against Arges, just to spite him, but Nightsong had to be careful. He couldn't give himself away too early and risk having Arges turn him in." Calvin paused, then added, "Of course, by this point, their paths are so intertwined that Arges really couldn't throw Nightsong under the bus without throwing himself there too."

"That would explain why the Efreet on anti-Earth weren't ready for us," O'Leary mused. "They had a huge warehouse, but it was empty. They had a walled outpost, but didn't have the weapons to defend it from anyone except maybe the Sila."

"Yeah, Nightsong jumped the gun," Calvin replied. "I heard his radio call right after he captured me. The Efreeti/Iranian alliance wasn't ready and had to adjust its plans when our troops showed up on anti-Earth. They were pissed off but had to start the war even though they weren't ready."

"In that case," Captain Sheppard said, "he actually helped us. That let us hit them before they were ready. Well, aside from the Iranians nuking Tashkent, anyway."

"What?" Calvin asked. "The Iranians nuked Tashkent? What the hell for?"

"Apparently, when Nightsong jumped the gun, that was the closest target they could hit that wouldn't send radiation back into Iran," Captain Sheppard replied. "The Iranians tried to take over the world government, but your platoon went to anti-Earth and destroyed their facilities, restoring the Republic government."

"Awesome!" Calvin exclaimed. "You guys are heroes!"

"Well, it really wasn't that much of an operation," O'Leary said. "We put together a whole big attack plan, but they didn't have the defenses in place to stop us, and we rolled right over them. Unfortunately, on the way back we stopped to pay a visit to Arges, and that cost us any accolades we might have won on the mission."

"You already said that didn't go well."

"No, not in the slightest," O'Leary replied. "He was ready for us and trapped Captain Train. The little bastard thought he killed him too, but we broke in just before Captain Train died and saved him. Part of Captain Train's combat gear included a 10-minute respirator, which he used to keep from being poisoned by Arges. We realized something would have to be done about the little piece of shit, so Captain Train stayed behind with Yokaze and a shuttle crew to take him out."

"Umm…isn't killing civilians kind of illegal?"

"Killing Terran civilians is definitely illegal," O'Leary replied. "However, killing *alien* civilians is more of a gray area. We looked; Arges never got citizenship anywhere on Terra. Countries just let him stay within their borders because he is a huge celebrity, and he pays a *phenomenal* amount of taxes, so they turn a blind eye to his nationality. Besides, if we don't take him out, who will? He controls *all* the information gathering and disseminating services, and he can turn public opinion against *anyone* in a very short time. If Arges thought we were still after him, he would have all the law enforcement agencies dropping what they were doing to find us, just to get him off their asses. The only way we had a chance to get him was if Captain Train stayed "dead," and it looked like we all fled. Hopefully, his guard will be low enough that they will be able to get into his castle and terminate him. If we don't kill him, everyone on Terra will always be under his thumb. And, since he is immortal, I do mean *always*."

"I see," Calvin said. "I wish them the best, although two people against the best security force money can buy seems somewhat…inadequate, even if one is a ninja and the other's Night. Still, you tried the direct approach, and that didn't work, so I can see why you went with something a little more discreet." He sighed. "Nothing we can do about it now, anyway. Hopefully, they'll be successful; I'd like to go home again sometime." Calvin shrugged. "So, where does that leave us?"

"Now that we know for sure Nightsong is in the courier ship, we need to run him to ground," Captain Sheppard said. "I have a lot of questions for him, and he is the only person who can corroborate the story against Arges." He paused then added, "And even with what you've told us about Nightsong working for Arges, I still don't think we know everything that's going on."

"Why's that, Skipper?" the *Gulf's* XO asked.

"Well, there's the technology gap for one thing," Captain Sheppard replied. "It just doesn't sit right with me. How can the Efreet have such crappy technology in some places, yet have sophisticated weapons like their time bombs in others?"

"They can't," Calvin said. "And they don't."

"What do you mean?" Captain Sheppard asked.

"The one thing I got from Nightsong is the Efreet don't have time bombs. When I asked who had them, he just said, 'someone else.' He wouldn't tell me who, but he made it very clear there is another race out there. The war with the Efreet is a bunch of bullshit, sir. The Efreet are rubes, and the war with them is nothing more than a red herring, something to distract us while the real danger draws closer and closer."

"The citizens of Tashkent wouldn't consider them unimportant," the XO commented.

"No, they wouldn't," Calvin admitted. "And I guess it's also possible Nightsong was lying about them. Lord knows, he lied about everything else…however, this actually makes sense. I think there is another race out there Nightsong didn't want us to know about, so he gave us the Efreet as an unwilling adversary. We haven't seen an Efreeti presence yet that was a worthwhile opponent; hell, the Sila were about to try to overthrow them on their own on anti-Keppler-

22, and they barely had any weapons. The Efreeti weapons are crap, their ships are crap and their technology's crap. The only thing they have that's worth a shit is their electromagnetic pulse bomb, which is designed to *do away* with technology. They have engines that can jump across the shroud of the universe, and they have a good robot, but I'll bet neither were invented by them. Some other race is supplying the Efreet with equipment; *that* is who the Jotunn are allied with."

"So who is that?" Captain Sheppard asked.

"I have no idea," Calvin replied. "The only other race we've heard mentioned is the Shaitan, but whether it's the Shaitan or someone else, I have no idea."

"Basically, you're telling me we need to catch Nightsong and beat it out of him before the next threat gets here and we're unprepared for them," Captain Sheppard said.

"Pretty much," Calvin replied. "And I think I know where he's going."

Cargo Bay, *Shuttle 529*, 100,000 Feet Above Switzerland, Terra, October 9, 2021

"*Two and a half minutes to jump!*" Jamming said.

"*Understood,*" Night said, walking to the end of the ramp and sitting down.

Yokaze walked out and sat down next to him, with nothing to see but the blackness of space. He wondered why Night had wanted to know exactly 2.5 minutes prior to the drop, but he hadn't wanted to ask. He looked over at Night but couldn't see anything through the captain's polarized face mask. He watched the officer for the next two minutes, but Night didn't move. As a yellow light began flashing, indicating 30 seconds to jump, Yokaze caught a glimpse of Night's face. His eyes were closed, but his lips were moving. Trained in lip reading, Yokaze watched him say, "…have him win, the Green Beret."

Night's eyes snapped open, and he nodded his head once. Yokaze saw a moment of something…sentimental?...pass through his eyes, then it was gone. Night was once again the harbinger of death Yokaze had always known.

"*May I ask?*"

"*My father used to sing the "Ballad of the Green Berets" to me when I was young,*" Night said, still staring into the black. "*It's very focusing.*" He turned to look at Yokaze. "*Are you ready?*"

"*Hai!*" replied Yokaze.

Night snapped a hook to Yokaze, tethering them together.

"*Here we go!*" Night said. He pushed off, and the two men began the long journey down.

Medical, TSS *Vella Gulf*, Epsilon Eridani System, October 23, 2021

"You know where he's going?" Captain Sheppard asked.

"Well, I don't think there's anything you can know that's 100% with Nightsong," Calvin said. "I think he's a psychopath and a pathological liar. I'm not even sure he knows all the times he's lied. He did, however, relate a story about how, at least in his mind, he is the legitimate ruler of the Aesir. He also has some plot for getting back at the Jotunn for killing his twin sister when they were kids."

"What's his plan?" Lieutenant O'Leary asked. "Better yet, how do we stop it? No, better yet, how do I get my hands on him so I can kick his scrawny ass?"

"Be careful what you ask for," Calvin said. "Not only is he an experienced Eco Warrior with fire, he's also very good with life-based nanobots. That's how he has been able to move around in our society so much; he can appear to be anyone he wants. There's no telling if he can do earth and air and water as well, but I wouldn't bet against it. He's had a lot of time on his own to practice, and Arges' nearly unlimited funding to get him what he needs. We may not have seen all of his abilities."

"Okay, how do we get our hands on him so I can *carefully* kick his scrawny ass?"

"I'm betting he is heading for the Aesir home world. I don't know what he intends to do when he gets there, but I guarantee he has a plan…something that has been a long time in the making. What scares me most is he doesn't seem to be worried we are following him."

"Why is that?" Lieutenant O'Leary asked.

"Because he either thinks his plot is foolproof and can't be stopped, or he has something nasty prepared he thinks will kill us. Regardless, he is extremely dangerous, and he's probably even more unstable than he is dangerous. There is no telling what he has planned…"

Above Chateau de Arges, Beckenried, Switzerland, October 9, 2021

Night watched the radar altimeter on his wrist. As it counted down through 2,500 feet, the drogue chutes on their packs deployed, stabilizing their fall, and Night untethered himself from Yokaze. At 1,000 feet, the main paragliders deployed, braking their fall to 1.5 feet per second, while giving them a glide ratio of over 25:1. This let them fly nearly horizontally, and the two men steered their parachutes in from north of the castle.

The defenders weren't expecting an attack from above the sheer face of the cliff, and their attention was on the front and sides of the castle, not the rear. The four guards never knew what hit them as Night's and Yokaze's laser rifles silently reached out to kill them. The landing area secure, Night and Yokaze pulled up on their chutes, braking their forward momentum, and dropped silently onto the roof.

Both men quickly took off their suits, and Night pulled out the two small boxes Cashman had given him. He pushed the blue button on the first box, and a green light illuminated after five seconds. "No monitors or transmitters up here," whispered Night. He pushed the red button on the second box, and both men watched as the system analyzed its surroundings. After 14 seconds, the main light turned green and their comm systems came to life.

"I think Manchester United is going to take Chelsea tomorrow."

"You're out of your bloody mind if you think that's going to happen, ya stupid wanker."

"You're both out of your minds. If the boss catches you bullshitting on the comm net, he'll have your asses."

"Better that than falling asleep from boredom. Then he'd really go bonkers."

"If you're going to bullshit, do it over the radio and not the comm system."

Yokaze nodded; his comm system was synchronized with the security network. Both men silently searched the four bodies on the roof.

"What do you think, Diederich?" asked a voice. Night looked down and saw it was coming from the earbuds of the man he was searching.

There was no answer. Night looked down at the dead man's name tag. It read, 'Ehrlinger.'

"You there, Diederich?"

He quickly moved to the next body. The Aryan-looking man's name tag read, 'Diederich.' Shit. He waved to Yokaze, who was already sprinting toward him, and pointed to the body at his feet. As Yokaze ran, his features turned into those of a Caucasian man with blond hair.

"Dammit, Diederich, you moron. Can someone see if he's sleeping?"

"Naw, he's awake," a voice with a U.S. southern accent radioed. *"I can see him. Just a sec."*

Yokaze arrived and touched the body's throat while he touched Night's throat with his other hand. Night felt a tickle as his voice box changed shape. Yokaze nodded.

"Sorry," Night said, talking into the dead guard's radio. *"I thought I saw something moving, but it was just a rabbit. As for the football match, who gives a shit, anyway? The Bundesliga is the only league that matters."*

"Shut the fuck up, you idiots," a voice full of authority interjected. *"I'm not going to get busted by the boss for your stupidity. Just do your damned jobs and* shut the hell up!"

Night shook his head and blew out a deep breath. "That was close," he said. "Thanks."

"No problem, suh," replied Yokaze with a smile.

Night looked at his watch. 0155. Five minutes until they changed the guard.

Chapter Twenty-Eight

Bridge, Aesir Battle Station *Cerberus*, Gliese 221, October 24, 2021

"Sir, we just had a momentary gate activation," the Aesir sensor technician said.

Fleet Admiral Valendil looked up from the report he was reading. "What do you mean, 'a momentary activation?' Did a ship enter or not?"

"Well, yes sir, a ship entered, but then it disappeared."

"Did it leave or did it cloak? What type of ship was it?"

"I'm not sure, sir," the technician replied. "The ship was destroyer-sized, so it could have cloaked. We didn't get a second stargate activation, so it must still be here."

"General Quarters! Activate the minefield!" the admiral ordered. "Send a message back to Golirion advising them we have intruders, and get me the ship's captains on screen."

Within moments, the grim visages of Captain Lyra Caelerian and Captain Klaern Edernil appeared on the front screen. Admiral Valendil's 'fleet' consisted of the battle station and just two battleships. Not enough to stop a determined invasion force…but the two ships were all he had available. "Did you also pick up the gate activation?" the admiral asked.

Both nodded their heads. "Aye," Captain Caelerian said. "Are you worried our new enemy has finally made its appearance?"

"I am," the admiral replied. "It is either a cloaked destroyer here to spy on us or one of the Efreeti ships that has gone to the other universe. I find it more likely this is an Efreeti ship. It probably saw where you were; move your ships and be ready for it to pop back up at any moment. By shifting out of our universe upon entering our system, they have already announced their attentions are other than honorable. If you see them, destroy them on sight."

"Yes sir," the two captains replied.

"Additionally," the admiral said, "I expect this is the first indication of a larger, impending attack. The minefield will stay active until further notice. Anything coming through the stargate is assumed hostile and will be destroyed on sight. We must hold this system until reinforcements arrive."

Chateau de Arges, Beckenried, Switzerland, October 9, 2021

Night flowed down the stairs, Yokaze a shadow behind him. They had eliminated the oncoming guards, but now they were on the clock; it wouldn't be long before someone noticed the new guards weren't responding, or that part of the off-going watch hadn't arrived in their quarters.

They reached the second floor landing and checked for guards, but the hallway was empty.

"Check here or go down to the main floor?" Yokaze whispered.

"The Psiclopes don't normally sleep much, so I doubt he's up here," Night replied. "I'm guessing he's down in his office."

They didn't see anyone as they continued down the stairs to the first floor. There was no one visible in the first floor hallway, either.

"I don't like this," Night said under his breath. "It's too easy."

Yokaze nodded his head while his eyes stayed in motion. "I don't often get uncomfortable," he said, "but I have a bad feeling…"

The two men crept down the hallway to the door into Arges' office. The door was different from the other doors they passed; Arges' door was massive and ornate. Intended to cow visitors into submission, it had the opposite effect on Night; it just pissed him off.

Night tried the door and found it unlocked. "Ready?" he asked.

Yokaze nodded.

"Here we go." Night slowly pushed open the door, and found himself looking into the wrong end of three laser rifles, held by the security force's three officers.

"Come in, Mr. Diederich," Arges called from behind the desk on the other side of the room. "You too, Mr. Haywood." One of the men motioned with his rifle at Yokaze. Both soldiers entered the room. There were three more of the security force waiting inside; all had weapons drawn and aimed. Arges' wife, Brontes, was standing behind him at the desk.

"I guess you've never heard of these things called 'security cameras,'" Arges said, as two of the guards came forward to take the soldiers' weapons. "Oh, your little box didn't find them? That's because it's not supposed to." He pushed a button on his desk, and a large monitor came to life behind him. The picture was from the roof, showing a number of bodies in the foreground. "I spare no expense when it comes to my own safety."

"You are a hard man to kill, Captain Train," Arges continued. "I thought you were dead when I had to abruptly leave during your last visit; I won't make the same mistake twice. I believe you brought along Sergeant Hanzo, is that correct?"

Yokaze nodded crisply once. "Hai!"

"I thought I recognized you before you changed into Mr. Haywood. I can see you've been spending too much time with the Aesir." He motioned for the men to come closer. "Come, come," he said. "I want to try this again."

As Night and Yokaze approached the desk, he pushed another button and, once again, glass walls sprang from the floor to encase them in two glass boxes that ran from floor to ceiling.

"Is this really necessary?" Brontes asked. "I understand the need to kill them, but can't you just shoot them and be done with it? Why do you have to go through all this?"

"Why?" Arges repeated. "Because the box was designed to kill Captain Train, and somehow he escaped it last time. I can't have him beating my traps. This time, he's going to die like a good little boy, aren't you, captain?"

Arges walked over to stand in front of Night's box. "What? You aren't so tough now that I have you again? No taunts or threats for me tonight?"

"No," Night said, "I think I'll save them for when I'm standing over your rapidly cooling body."

"Too bad," Arges replied; "I was so looking forward to hearing them." He shrugged. "The last time you were here, I think I told you that it was time for you to die. Now, it really is."

He smiled and walked back to his desk. "Would you like to do the honors?" he asked Brontes.

"No," she replied. "You can do your own dirty work."

Arges pushed the red button on his desk and gas began billowing into the boxes.

Bridge, Aesir Ship *Shimmering Falls*, Gliese 221, October 24, 2021

"Pop-up target off the port bow!" the laser officer announced. "Range to enemy vessel 950,000 miles."

"Engines to flank!" Captain Lyra Caelerian ordered. "Fire all weapons as they come within range!"

"Missiles firing," the missile officer announced, pressing the button that launched the chase missile mounts on the bow.

"We're still outside of effective laser range," the laser officer noted.

"Understood," replied Captain Caelerian. "In past engagements, missiles haven't been effective, but lasers were. If we can get within laser range, we may have a chance against them. Unfortunately, they can shoot their torpedoes further than we can shoot our lasers. Every other ship they have fought has run from them, though. We're not. Maybe it will surprise them."

"Stargate activation!" the sensor officer cried out. "Jotunn battleship! Another activation! More Jotunn!"

"Ma'am, the *Cerberus* is calling," the communications officer said, his voice more controlled than the sensor officer's. "Admiral Valendil has ordered us to destroy the Efreeti vessel. He said the *Cerberus* and *Western Aurora* will deal with the Jotunn."

"Tell them we will comply," Captain Caelerian replied.

"Ma'am, I am getting the indications from the Efreeti ship that we were told precede torpedo launch," the sensor officer said.

"Understood," Captain Caelerian said. "We may get hit going in." She turned to the helmsman. "Helm, if the Efreeti ship starts moving, follow it, but do *not* overrun it. I want to turn this into a knife fight." With 25 broadside lasers, she liked her chances in a laser duel with the much smaller vessel.

"Yes ma'am," the helmsman replied.

The Captain could see her confidence was contagious. Although her crew had sounded nervous at the thought of going up against an unbeaten foe, they were all calming down nicely.

"Missiles ineffective," the missile officer noted. "When they would have hit, the ship blinked out. Once they were passed, the ship jumped back in again."

"As expected," the captain said. "We knew they could do that." She paused, considering. "Hold fire for now. We may need the missiles later against the Jotunn."

"Yes, ma'am."

"The Efreeti ship is firing," the sensor operator noted.

"Understood," the captain said. "No one's intercepted one before; let's be the first. Retarget all weapons onto the torpedo and fire!"

"AMMs launching," the missile officer said. "AMMs missed," he added shortly after.

"Lasers firing," the laser officer reported. "Lasers ineffective," she said after a pause.

"Five seconds to impact," the defensive officer called. "Anti-missile lasers firing. Chaff launching."

"Torpedo hit on the bow," the damage control officer said as the ship rocked. "Damage control crews are responding."

"We've lost the chase armament," the missile officer announced. "We'll have to swing broadside to fire at the enemy."

"Ma'am, the enemy ship is underway," the sensor officer said. "It looks like they are trying to run."

"Understood," Captain Caelerian replied. She looked at her tactical display. "Keep the power up, helm. We need to finish this one off and get back to the battle." At least six Jotunn vessels were now in-system, and four were pounding on the battle station. At least one quadrant of the battle station was already out of the fight. It was bad…but might still be salvageable if she could get back quickly to help. The Jotunn ships had all been damaged by the minefield, and she could see two had been destroyed, but the minefield was spent. It was all on them now.

"One minute to laser range," the laser officer said.

"Ma'am! Another Efreeti destroyer just came through the stargate and jumped out of our universe," the sensor officer called. "Now another! Now a fourth! The last one was larger than the rest!"

This made the situation exponentially worse. Captain Caelerian knew they had to hurry with the ship they were fighting; with so many ships able to jump back and forth to the other universe, they ran the risk of being surrounded. That many Efreeti ships made things dicey…if not unwinnable.

"The Efreeti ship is preparing to launch more torpedoes," the sensor operator said.

"Coming up on laser range," the laser officer said. "Batteries need to unmask!"

"Kill the drive," the captain ordered. "Spin the ship."

"Drive off," the helmsman replied. "Rotating the ship."

The laser officer held her finger over the enable switch as the ship spun agonizingly slowly. "Stand by…*firing!*" She flipped the switch and 25 coherent beams of light lanced out, spearing into and sometimes through the enemy ship.

"Oh my!" the sensor operator exclaimed. "We must have hit part of their torpedo system; there were at least three torpedo detonations onboard the destroyer. It's hard to tell how many, exactly, as there were several sympathetic detonations that followed. The ship has been destroyed."

"Outstanding," the captain said. "Helm, get us back to the fight. Head toward the *Western Aurora*; it looks like they could use some assistance." The other battleship had a Jotunn battlecruiser on both sides. Like everything else with the Jotunn, though, their battlecruisers were oversized. Unlike Aesir battlecruisers, which would have been about three-fourths of a mile long and just over 900,000 tons, the Jotunn battlecruisers were each a mile and a half long, with a mass of nearly six million tons. The *Western Aurora* was just under 4.5 million tons, so *each* of the Jotunn vessels outclassed it; together, they were obliterating the *Aurora*.

"Ma'am, I don't get it," the laser officer said. "The Efreeti ship didn't have any shields. How could the Efreet have something like the time bomb and not have any sort of shields?"

"I don't know," the captain replied. "We don't know enough about what we're facing. Maybe it's because of their torpedo launcher. Maybe it fills all the space so there isn't enough room for a shield generator. Maybe having a shield would interfere with the launch of their weapon. Maybe they just never thought of it. Who knows? I'm just happy they don't."

She looked at her tactical display. Over half of the battle station was now unpowered, with most of it open to space. Two more Jotunn ships had been destroyed, but the battle station was taking far more damage from the remaining aggressors than it was returning. It wouldn't last much longer.

"Time to missile range on the Jotunn battlecruisers?" she asked.

"Two minutes," the missile officer replied. It was going to be close.

"Pop-up target!" the laser and missile officers called simultaneously. "New target three million miles off the starboard beam," added the missile officer.

"How long to brake and turn to intercept?" Captain Caelerian asked.

"10 minutes before we could begin an intercept," the helmsman replied.

"Continue toward the Jotunn vessels," the captain ordered. "Spin the ship and fire missiles when in range."

"I have another pop-up target five million miles behind us," the sensor operator noted. "It is the bigger of the Efreeti vessels. I'm classifying it as a cruiser. It is turning to follow us, as is the vessel on our starboard beam."

"When we turn to fire on the Jotunn, fire the other broadside at the larger Efreeti vessel."

"In range of the Jotunn battlecruisers!" the missile officer called.

"Spinning the ship," the helmsman said.

"Both Efreeti vessels are preparing to fire," the sensor operator said.

"Port batteries firing on the Jotunn," the missile officer said. "Starboard batteries firing at the Efreeti cruiser."

"Torpedo launch!" the sensor operator cried. "Multiple launches from both Efreeti vessels. At least 15 torpedoes inbound!"

Captain Caelerian looked at her tactical display. Their missiles would hit the Jotunn before the torpedoes carved her ship up like a block of cheese. They had that going for them, at least.

"Good hits on the Jotunn battlecruiser," the missile officer said. "At least one hit on the magazine; I'm seeing sympathetic detonations. It's out of the fight!"

"No hits on the Efreeti cruiser," the sensor operator said. "It blinked out when the missiles would have hit it and then blinked back in."

Captain Caelerian shook her head. The cruisers could do it too. Damn. "Understood," she said aloud. "Concentrate our fire on the Jotunn vessels. We'll deal with the Efreeti afterward."

"Five seconds to torpedo impact," the sensor operator said.

Captain Caelerian looked down at her tactical display again. An experienced officer, she knew there wasn't going to be an afterward.

Chateau de Arges, Beckenried, Switzerland, October 9, 2021

Night crumpled to the floor, using the motion to reach inside a pocket. Finding the two-inch-wide puck, he thumbed off the safety and activated the device. Reaching up, he slapped it on the glass wall, as Yokaze did the same in his cell.

Two of the guards took a step forward to see what the devices were; the officers and the third guard dove to the side. The dives saved their lives as the shaped charges exploded outward, shattering the glass and filleting the two guards with shards.

The two Terran soldiers were in motion before the glass hit the ground, but the security force personnel were already rising as well. Yokaze vaulted into a forward somersault, and then pushed off to spring upward. His heels slapped together as they came over his head, and blades sprang forth from the toes of his boots. He took one step and spun, the blade in his right boot slicing across the throat of the remaining guard in an explosion of blood.

Night also rolled forward and came up on one knee. Reaching into his sleeves, he pulled out heavy throwing knives in both hands. In one smooth motion, he brought them back and threw the knives at the two lieutenants, striking one of them in the chest. The other, the man known as Jackson, once again dove out of the way, and the knife sailed over his back.

Knowing he had a split second, Night spared a glance at the security force leader, and lunged out of the way as the man fired a laser pistol at him. Night continued rolling as the pistol tracked him, but then a throwing star slammed into the leader's wrist.

"Mother fucker!" the man yelled, switching the gun to his left hand. A throwing star appeared in that wrist as well. "Dammit!" screamed the man, turning to Yokaze. "How many of those fucking things—" He never got a chance to finish the question as a third star sliced into his throat.

Night started to rise, but sensed motion and dove to the side. Jackson's knife ripped through his right shoulder, narrowly missing his throat. Jackson followed the spinning Night and pounced on him, holding the knife point-down to stab Night. Rolling onto his back, Night grabbed Jackson's wrist in both hands, stopping the blow. As Jackson fell forward onto Night, the special forces soldier forced his legs under Jackson's body and kicked out, throwing the guard over Night's head. The knife hand was pulled from his grasp, but not before he twisted it, wrenching the man's arm out of the socket.

Night rolled to his stomach, the pain in his shoulder threatening to blind him. Something gave in his shoulder as he got his legs underneath him, and he knew his arm was useless. Reaching down, he drew his boot knife with his left hand and waved away Yokaze, who had been moving to intercept Jackson. "Mine," he grunted. "Get Arges."

Jackson was already up and moving to meet Night as he turned, and both men squared off against each other with knives in their left hands. The men slashed at each other, and both were quickly bleeding in a multitude of places. Night knew he wouldn't last as long as Jackson. The wound on his shoulder was bleeding too heavily; he would have to do something to end the fight sooner rather than later.

Getting Yokaze to kill the man never entered his mind.

Night stumbled, hoping to draw the guard closer, but the man was too much of a veteran to fall for the trick, and he pulled back out of reach. Night had counted on that, and as he stumbled forward he threw himself into a headfirst dive that turned into a forward somersault. He came down heavily on his back and shoulders, and a wave of agony threatened to overwhelm him again. Blocking out as much of the pain as he could, he rolled onto his left shoulder and kicked out, sweeping Jackson's feet out from under him.

Jackson crashed down, his head striking the wooden floor with a heavy thud. Stunned, he began rising groggily, but Night was on him before he could shake off the concussion, plunging his knife into Jackson's chest.

Night fell forward onto the dead man, breathing heavily. He took several seconds to catch his breath, then pushed off with his good arm and got to his feet. Turning, he saw Yokaze with his hands up; Arges had some type of small rifle trained on him.

"Bravo, Captain Train," the Psiclops said. "That was well done. He was the best killer I could find. Now, I'd appreciate it if you would come over and join Sergeant Hanzo. Please do not try anything stupid."

"Why's that?" Night asked. "I'm known for doing stupid things."

"You may not recognize this weapon, but it is a disintegrator." Brontes gasped, mouth open, from behind Arges. "As you can guess from my wife's reaction, being shot by a disintegrator is something you *really* don't want to do."

Bridge, Aesir Ship *Shimmering Falls*, Gliese 221, October 24, 2021

"Uncontrolled fire aft of the galley," the damage control officer said. "Repair parties do not believe they can extinguish it before it reaches the magazine. We also have smaller fires around what's left of Missile Mount 17, aft berthing and the machine shop. All starboard laser and missile batteries are out, and port laser batteries are out too."

His voice sounded abnormally metallic, thought Captain Caelerian. Probably because they were operating on emergency power drawn from the one remaining engine.

"Five more torpedoes inbound from the Efreeti cruiser!" the sensor officer called.

Captain Caelerian had heard enough. "Comm, send my apologies to Fleet Admiral Valendil, and let him know we are abandoning ship." She switched to the ship-wide communications system. "*All hands, this is the Captain. Abandon ship! I say again, abandon ship! It has been my honor to serve with you. Captain Caelerian out.*"

She had hoped to never see the red lights on her ship, but they began flashing as the damage control officer gave the signal to abandon ship. She looked around the bridge. None of the crew had moved; they all continued to do their duties, fighting the ship to the end. She couldn't be any prouder of them.

"What are you waiting for?" she asked. "*Abandon ship!*"

Her heart sank as she looked at the tactical display one last time. She had waited too long. As the bridge crew began racing to their lifeboats, the next volley of torpedoes struck the *Shimmering Falls*, including one centered on the bridge.

Chateau de Arges, Beckenried, Switzerland, October 9, 2021

"A disintegrator?" Night asked. "Sounds like fun. What is it?"

"It is a product of Aesir technology," Arges said.

"Illegal technology," Brontes interrupted.

"Yes, it was outlawed," Arges agreed with a smile as he watched Yokaze down the barrel of the weapon. "When fired, it shoots a round loaded with Aesir nanobots. These are special nanobots; their only purpose is to disassemble whatever they come in contact with, down to the molecular level. It was made illegal because having your body parts disassembled is quite a painful process, I understand, especially if part of you is left to feel it."

Night walked over to Yokaze. "Okay, I'll bite. Why haven't you shot him yet?"

"A couple of reasons," Arges said. "First, even if I hit him, I know Sergeant Hanzo is extremely fast. He might not be completely disabled, and he might have a chance to kill me before I can fire a second shot. Also, these weapons were made to use at long distances outside. When I shoot him, some of the nanobots may spray around the room; I would rather not get hit by any wayward disassemblers."

"That makes sense," Night said. "So what are your intentions?"

"I intend to get out of here alive," Arges replied, "and I am willing to make a deal. As it turns out, I need a new head of security. My old one was not up to the job."

"I don't think so," Night said. "You make my stomach turn, and I don't think I could deal with that on a daily basis."

"I am in a position to make you a very wealthy man," Arges argued, "well beyond your wildest dreams. I have money hidden in places no one will ever find. You want millions? Billions? They are yours. I will also drop the charges against you so you don't have to live your life on the run."

"How do I know you're going to follow through on that and not have me killed once you're free?"

"I'll give you my word on it," Arges replied.

"I think I'll pass," Night said. "What else have you got?"

"How about this?" Arges asked. "If you let me go, you will still get the money. I'll transfer the rest of my money into something that's easily convertible, and I will move to another system, far from here, so our paths never cross again."

"While it might be fun to be rich, I still don't have any guarantee you'll actually do what you say. How do I know you won't call the police as soon as we leave and make up a story about what happened?"

"You'll just have to trust me."

"Still not gonna happen," Night said. "Got any other options?"

Arges sighed theatrically. "My only other option would be to kill you. I was really hoping we could avoid that."

"I'm not a fan of that one, either," Night said. "How about you give yourself up and let us take you in? You could get a fair trial. Heck, with your money, you'd probably buy all of the judges and never spend a day in jail."

"I don't think so," Arges replied. "I built this shitty world, and I am *not* going to let it put me on trial."

"Well, then I guess we're just going to have to find out how good a shot you are with that weapon."

"I guess so." Arges started to pull the trigger. "Ahhh!" he cried, as Brontes shot him in the back with her laser pistol, causing his aim to go high. The round struck the ceiling and detonated, throwing disassemblers into the air above Arges' desk. Yokaze and Night dove backward, away from the cloud.

Brontes screamed, and the Terrans watched as the arm holding the pistol began to come apart, dissolving in front of their eyes.

"Arges…was a good man…once," Brontes said, tears streaming down her face. Taking the pistol in her other hand, she held it up to her head and pulled the trigger. She fell backward onto the desk, which was slowly collapsing in upon itself. Brontes began dissolving with it.

Night walked over to Arges, carefully avoiding a hole that had opened in the floor. He looked down and saw the hole went through the basement floor below, as well, and down into a sub-basement. He took the disintegrator and rolled Arges over.

No taunting was needed; Arges was already dead.

"Captain Train?" Yokaze asked from behind.

Night turned to find Yokaze looking through the hole in the floor. He looked down and saw the sub-basement had a number of pallets with something shrink-wrapped on them. The nanobots had eaten through the shrink-wrap on one prior to deactivating. Green pieces of paper could be seen through the hole.

"I believe we have found one of Arges' money stashes."

Fleet Commander's Office, Fleet Command HQ, Lake Pedam, Nigeria, October 10, 2021

"Sir?"

Admiral Wright looked up from a classified after-action report. "Yes?" he asked his aide.

"There are two men here to see you, a Mr. Diederich and a Mr. Haywood. They say they are part of Arges' security detail and need to talk to you. Would you like to speak with them?"

This ought to be interesting, the admiral thought. "Yes; please show them in."

The two men walked in, and the aide closed the door. The taller one's right arm was strapped to his midsection. Both men had a number of cuts and bandages on them.

"This may be a dumb question," the admiral said, "but before we start, are either of you Sergeant Hanzo?"

"Hai!" the shorter of the two exclaimed, coming to attention. "I am, sir!"

The admiral looked at the other man. "And you are?"

"Captain Train, sir."

"So…you aren't dead anymore?"

"No sir. Reports of my demise were greatly exaggerated. Reports of Arges' death, when they come, however, are going to be spot on. And it's a damn good thing too."

"What do you mean?"

"When we looked around his house, we found several sub-basements. One had an enormous amount of money…and another had a half-assembled transporter. It looked like he was setting up a way station in his castle to the Jinn Universe, sir."

"I take it the transporter has been rendered…non-functional?"

"Yes sir, it has. Arges also had a weapon called a 'disintegrator,' which pretty much does exactly as the name implies. Apparently, it was created by the Aesir, but was outlawed as it completely disassembles the target down to its component atoms. A couple of rounds were…inadvertently fired at the transporter, and large pieces of it were completely disassembled, including the control mechanism and anything else that looked important."

"Good," the admiral replied. "What about Arges?"

"For the record, neither of us killed Arges; in the end, Brontes shot him rather than let him disintegrate us. She then killed herself when she got splashed with the disintegration round. Both of the Psiclopes' bodies were disintegrated, so the crime scene is going to be very hard to put together."

"So, what *are* the police going to find when they get there?"

"They are going to find a lot of security force bodies and holes in the floors, but no Psiclopes. It will be impossible to determine what happened, as his computer and all the security camera footage was also disintegrated somehow. What they *will* find is a partially disassembled transporter, which is illegal and will make Arges a criminal, and millions of dollars in cash, which I'm sure will look like ill-gotten gains. I don't know the rules, but I would bet a case could be made for calling him an outlaw and impounding all his possessions…including his courier ship." Night smiled. "That might be a nice addition to the fleet, especially for senior executive travel between here and Domus."

"Indeed it might," Admiral Wright, who had always hated traveling, replied. "So what do we do with you?"

"Well, we sort of have a problem," Night said. He turned to Yokaze. "Tell him."

"Hai! Unfortunately, I do not have enough nanobots to turn us back to ourselves. Until we can get to the Aesir home world, we are stuck like this."

"Arges had several stacks of Aesir currency," Night said. "We kept those so we could purchase more nanobots for the team. The only problem is getting there. We kind of need a ride to Golirion."

"That is actually something I can arrange," Admiral Wright said. "With the Iranian and Efreeti alliance taken care of, I have convinced the government to send the dreadnought *Thermopylae* and the battleships *Hood* and *Yamato* on a shakedown cruise. The *Vella Gulf* was trying to chase down Nightsong; sending the other three ships to Golirion may provide them additional assistance along the way. My guess is Nightsong is headed to Golirion although I don't know what he intends to do there. The Aesir may need the assistance. We are also sending a delegation there to discuss diplomatic relations with the Aesir; I'm sure the *Thermopylae* must have room on it somewhere for a couple of extra emissaries named Diederich and Haywood."

"Thank you, sir," Night said. "It will be good to rejoin the unit…and even better to do it as myself again."

"One last thing," the admiral said as the two soldiers turned to leave. Both turned back around.

"The press got hold of your exploits on anti-Earth," continued the admiral, "and they are making you all out to be heroes for 'saving the Earth.' Despite the fact that most of your unit is under threat of criminal prosecution for the first assault on Arges' house, I have been ordered to give you all medals for the operation."

"Really sir?" Night asked. "It wasn't much of a battle; the Efreet were way outmanned and outgunned by us."

"I don't know how the press could come to such a conclusion, myself. Maybe there is something romantic about parachuting in on an LCAC and using it to attack a fortified castle…regardless of how poorly it was actually fortified. In any event, you're all heroes, or at least you will be when the Arges thing gets put to rest. With all the positive media coverage you're about to get, I have a feeling the Swiss police will quietly drop the charges, too, especially after they see his house. You should be able to return, whenever you want, without having to worry about anything…awkward."

"How did the press get that information?" Night asked. "Wouldn't that still be classified?"

"I'm sure I have no idea how information like that could have gotten out to the press," Admiral Wright said. "Maybe my aide mumbled something in his sleep. I think he's dating a reporter." He smiled. "Who knows?"

Chapter Twenty-Nine

CO's Conference Room, TSS *Vella Gulf*, Epsilon Indi System, November 7, 2021

"I thought it would be good to do a little planning before we jump into the HD 69830 system," Captain Sheppard said, "especially since Lieutenant Commander Hobbs has now returned to a duty status again. Ops?"

"Yes sir," the operations officer, Commander Dan Dacy, said. "We are about two hours from the jump into the Aesir's home system. Nightsong made the jump about 10 hours ago, so he will have half a day's head start on whatever he intends to do there. All of our weapons systems are operational."

"Are we expecting to jump into a combat situation?" Calvin asked. "Have we heard anything from the Aesir?"

"No, we haven't," Captain Sheppard replied, "and that has me a little worried. I know the Aesir aren't the galaxy's biggest communicators, but I kind of expected to see at least a ship or two of theirs in transit. So far, however, nothing."

"So, for all we know," Calvin said, "the Jotunn and their new allies, whoever they are, may already have taken the Aesir's home world of Golirion."

"That is correct," Commander Dacy said.

"That would make following Nightsong…dangerous…if the Jotunn and their allies are in the system," Calvin said, "especially if he has worked out some sort of alliance with them."

"Yes it would," Captain Sheppard agreed. "If any of the Jotunn ships are in the system, they will probably outclass us, making combat with them problematic, especially if they can jump between universes."

"I wonder…" Calvin started, before trailing off.

"You wonder what?" Captain Sheppard asked.

"Well, sir, I'm wondering if the Jotunn's allies have shared the secret of their jump modules with them. When we last saw the Jotunn, they didn't do any jumping between universes; they just let their allies do all the work for them. If the Jotunn had the capability to jump, they wouldn't have gone through everything they have. They would have just gone to Golirion and blown it up, or captured it or whatever they intend to do."

"That makes sense," Captain Sheppard said, "but I wouldn't want to bet our safety on it. If they do have them, and we get too close to one of their monster spaceships, we will be destroyed. No ifs, ands or buts. We'll be dead."

"Yes sir, I understand that," Calvin replied, "but let's look at it from the Jotunn's ally's perspective. The giants are enormous and have enormous spaceships with correspondingly large weapons. The ally's ships, however, seem to be more our size, if not smaller." He looked at Captain Sheppard and raised an eyebrow. "Would *you* want to give the Jotunn the ability to come into *your* universe if they were your allies, or would you rather keep them in their own universe where they couldn't get at you?"

"I'd rather keep them at an arm's length."

"Yeah, I would too. I can't think of anything the Jotunn have that they could use as leverage to make their ally give them the secret, either. If the ally didn't like what the Jotunn were doing, they could always just run back to their own universe where the Jotunn couldn't get them." He shrugged. "They could always attack them, too, like they did the Aesir. It would take longer to destroy a Jotunn ship than an Aesir ship, but if you were determined enough, you could certainly do it."

"But what if the Jotunn were the ones that developed the jump modules and gave them to their allies?" Commander Dacy asked.

"If the Jotunn had developed them, wouldn't they have gone straight at the Aesir like we already discussed?"

"Yeah, I guess they would have," the operations officer admitted.

"So, the ally has the jump module and meets up with the Jotunn somehow," Captain Sheppard said. "They decide to work together for some reason and strike up an alliance. Then, the Jotunn convince the ally to help them with the Aesir, their long-time enemies. The ally probably thinks, 'sure, that will be easy,' especially after the first combat or two with the Aesir go their way. They think it will be easy for them to help the Jotunn, and they'll get whatever reward the Jotunn have promised them."

"Then we show up and destroy their ship," Calvin said.

"Yes, and that may have called for a re-evaluation of their agreement. All of a sudden, the ally is taking losses. Their leaders may not have liked that. If nothing else, they probably don't like *us*. And, if we show up again in the *Gulf*, they might go out of their way to destroy us. They certainly didn't seem to have a problem destroying the Aesir ships or attacking us with no warning."

"Whatever code they fight by," Lieutenant O'Leary said, "it ain't chivalry."

"No, it's not," Calvin said. "So, if the ally is in the next system and they see us, we might not have any choice *but* combat."

"That certainly sounds like we're heading toward a worst case scenario," Captain Sheppard said.

"I think the worst case scenario would be a mixed force of Jotunn and their ally's ships," Calvin said. "If the Jotunn don't have jump modules, like we suspect, we could use their ally's maneuvers against them and jump back and forth between universes while we attack. It would take a while to destroy a Jotunn vessel, but we could do it." He shook his head. "If there are some of the ally's ships there, though, they'll be able to jump back and forth with us. I'm not sure how such a fight would end up, but it would make fighting the Jotunn at the same time a lot more complicated."

"We would have to fight the ally's ships first," Captain Sheppard said, visualizing the fight in his head. "Maybe even fight them in their own universe where the Jotunn couldn't get at us."

"I think we'd probably want to," Calvin agreed; "the problem would be making them stay in a single universe to fight, without jumping back and forth. We'd be handicapped if we had to stay in one universe and they didn't. We'd have to chase them down where we could use our lasers; they'd never let any of our missiles hit them."

"I had an idea on that," mumbled a voice from the end of the table.

"What?" Captain Sheppard asked. "Who said that?"

"I did, sir," Lieutenant Bradford said. "I've been giving a lot of thought to fighting the ally's ships, and I have an idea or two on how we might do it better."

"By all means, Lieutenant, tell us what you've got."

"The only reason our missiles are ineffective against the ally's ships is that they jump to the other universe to avoid them, right?"

Lieutenant Bradford asked. The CO nodded, so the lieutenant continued, "So, we just need to keep our missiles from flying past them. We need the missiles to wait in place for them and blow up when they get back."

"Okay, how do we do that?" Commander Dacy asked. "The missiles use all of their fuel accelerating to attack speed. How are you going to stop them when they don't have any fuel remaining?"

"We can't," Lieutenant Bradford acknowledged.

"I don't see how that's helping, then," the operations officer said in exasperation.

"We can't stop the missiles," Lieutenant Bradford said, "but we don't need to." He turned back to the CO. "All we need to do is either stop the warhead or jump the missile, like they do. For the first option, if we can make some sort of ejection system for the warhead that slows it down significantly, that might work, especially if the missile was chasing the ship from behind and the closing velocity was less. For the second, I was wondering if we could make a scaled down version of the jump module and attach it to some of our missiles. I don't know if the ally has a different type of jump module on their missiles that allow them to jump back and forth, but if we could design something like that, we could really be effective against them. That way, when their ships jump back and forth, our missiles can jump back and forth too, and they can track them no matter where they go."

"That would certainly be helpful," the CO said with a nod.

"It would be really cool if I could get that to work," Lieutenant Bradford said. "Since they don't appear to have shields, our missiles would do even more damage than normal to them."

"That's great," the *Vella Gulf's* executive officer, Commander Russ Clayton, said, "and I hope you figure it out. The problem is going to be staying alive. Have you come up with anything to defend against the torpedoes they're shooting at us?"

"It's a very similar problem," Lieutenant Bradford said. "We want to keep our missiles from flying through the ally's torpedoes when they jump to the other universe. We either need an ejection system, like I discussed earlier, or maybe some new programming that loops our anti-missile missiles in from behind the torpedoes where the velocity differential won't be as great. Both of these options have the potential for success."

"One question," Captain Sheppard said.

"Yes sir?" Lieutenant Bradford asked.

"What are you doing sitting here talking about it when you should be on a laptop or at a terminal somewhere, making it work?"

"Oh! You want me to leave and work on these ideas?"

Captain Sheppard turned to his XO. "XO, why is he still here?"

"I'm leaving, sir!" Lieutenant Bradford said. He jumped up and sprinted out of the room.

"I had another idea," Calvin said.

"You did?" the CO asked.

"Yes sir," Calvin said with a smile. "Being laid up gives you a lot of time to think. My thought was that, at least until Lieutenant Bradford works out something better, one stopgap method for fighting the ally would be to change the way *we* do business."

"What do you mean?" the operations officer asked.

"Normally, we fire our missiles in a salvo, which helps us defeat our traditional adversaries' defenses. In this case, though, it makes it easier for our new enemy to avoid them. If we fire our missiles sequentially, they won't be able to jump back and forth as quickly. They will have to stay out of the universe longer…which we can use to our advantage."

"What do you mean?" the operations officer asked.

"One idea would be to set up a coordinated strike between the *Gulf* and the squadron," Calvin said. "How about this? The *Gulf* ripple fires some missiles while the fighters are fairly close to the enemy ship. When the enemy jumps out of our universe, the fighters fire their missiles. Hopefully, the enemy ship jumps back in as the fighters' missiles arrive, and it doesn't have a chance to avoid them." He sat back with a smile. "Boom."

"I like that," the CO said. "Ops, have your folks work with the squadron planners and develop some tactics for a coordinated strike. Until we have something better, it's at least worth a try."

"Yes sir," Commander Dacy said. "We'll put that together when we're done here."

Captain Sheppard nodded. "Good. Hopefully, we won't need it, but if they're in the next system, I want to have something new to try against them." He paused, then asked the operations officer, "What are your thoughts on system entry?"

"If I may, sir," Calvin interrupted, "I also had some thoughts on that…"

Bridge, TSS *Vella Gulf*, Epsilon Indi System, November 8, 2021

"Ahead dead slow," Captain Sheppard ordered.

"Ahead dead slow, aye," the helmsman repeated in a muted voice.

The atmosphere on the bridge was tenser than any time Captain Sheppard could remember; the crew was even more nervous than when the ship had gone behind the enemy lines against the Drakuls. It was the unknown, he thought; the Drakuls were evil and the odds were high, but at least they knew what they were getting into then. Here, there were so many things that could go wrong…it was even worse because they had stopped to mount the ship's stealth modules and were now over a full day behind Nightsong. Although necessary for their deception plan, Captain Sheppard begrudged every minute spent mounting the equipment; it gave Nightsong additional time to set his plans in motion.

"Give me a systems check," Captain Sheppard said.

"Engines ahead dead slow," the helmsman said. His voice was so tight the CO could barely hear him. "Stargate entry in two minutes."

"General Quarters set," the duty engineer said. "Stealth modules operational and active."

Captain Sheppard knew the stealth modules would fail when they made the jump through the stargate; they always did. Just about anything electronic was disrupted for a brief period traveling through the portal; the stealth modules would have to be re-engaged on the other side. The ship would be visible to anyone watching the stargate for a brief period; there was nothing they could do. Their only hope was to enter the system as slowly as possible, which minimized the electromagnetic pulse a stargate emitted when a ship transited. The faster the ship was going, the bigger the pulse. By going dead slow, he hoped their transition into the next system wouldn't be noticed.

It was a risky plan. If they were noticed, they would be going too slowly to maneuver effectively. They would be sitting ducks. And he absolutely *hated* the term 'dead' slow.

"All defensive missile systems and lasers not covered by the stealth modules are manned and ready," the DSO reported. Since the stealth modules blocked the weapons' ports, the CO knew they would have to forego half their offensive and defensive weapons systems. Not only would they be sitting ducks; they would be nearly unarmed sitting ducks.

"All offensive missile systems and grasers not covered by the stealth modules are manned and ready," the OSO added.

"Fighters manned and ready," Lieutenant Commander Sarah 'Lights' Brighton said.

"All communications systems in standby," the communications officer said. The CO didn't want anything transmitting upon entry that would give them away…but he wanted the ability to try to talk his way out of trouble quickly if it was needed.

"All sensor systems in standby," Steropes added from the sensor station.

"Making the jump," the helmsman mumbled a few seconds later…

Bridge, TSS *Vella Gulf*, HD 69830 System, November 8, 2021

"System entry," Steropes said. "Passive systems only coming online."

Even Steropes' voice sounded muted, thought Captain Sheppard. "Roger," the CO said. "Stealth up when able. Jump to the Jinn Universe when able."

"Stealthing…now," the duty engineer replied. "Making the jump…now."

Bridge, TSS *Vella Gulf*, Anti-HD 69830 System, November 8, 2021

"System entry into the Jinn Universe," Steropes said. "Still using only passive systems."

"Stealth coming on," the duty engineer said.

"Well, what do you think?" Captain Sheppard asked, unable to contain himself. "Did we make it through without them noticing?"

"Unknown," Steropes said. "There was nothing by the stargate that would have picked us up, but I cannot say for sure."

"Did you pick up anything that might help us figure out what's going on there?"

"I'm still analyzing the data, sir, but it doesn't appear any Jotunn ships, or those of their ally, were in orbit around Golirion or are here in the Jinn Universe. There were a number of Aesir ships near the stargate to Jotunn space, including at least one super dreadnought; their focus appeared to be in that direction. They were stationary, though; the ships were definitely *not* in combat."

Captain Sheppard could hear a collective release of breath around the bridge, and the tension eased noticeably. "So, whatever it is Nightsong has planned, it hasn't started yet."

"No sir," Steropes replied; "it doesn't appear it has,"

"Want me to jump back to the other universe, sir?" the helmsman asked.

"Contact!" the DSO called. "I've got engine harmonics, and lots of them, from in-system."

"Can you identify them?" Captain Sheppard asked.

"No sir, I can't," the DSO replied. "They look like engines, but they aren't in the database, nor are they like anything I've ever seen before."

"Solomon, are you seeing them?" the CO asked the ship's AI.

"Yes, I see what the DSO is looking at, and I agree they are probably engine harmonics, but they are dissimilar to all known systems."

"Any ideas, Steropes?" the CO asked.

"Long range photos coming in now on the front screen," Steropes answered. "This picture is from the vicinity of the asteroid belt between the second and third planets."

The front screen lit up to show a fuzzy image of the asteroid belt. Although the belt was "dense" by astronomical standards, with over 1,000 asteroids larger than 100 miles wide, and over 200,000 larger than half a mile wide, the average distance between asteroids in the main belt was still over several thousand miles. While the small scale image showed the belt as somewhat of a smear, the larger scale photos only showed a single asteroid. As the image focused in, Captain Sheppard could tell the asteroid in question was different than the rest.

"Steropes, is that asteroid…brighter…than normal?"

"Yes sir, it is," the Psiclops replied. "I believe we are seeing a number of motors from behind."

"So, there are unknown ships operating in the asteroid belt?"

"We are too far away to tell for sure," Steropes said, "but I believe the ships are attached to an asteroid."

"Attached to an asteroid?" the CO asked. "Why would they do that?"

"Initial analysis indicates the ships, if they are indeed ships, are pushing the asteroid in the direction of the third planet."

"Are they trying to hit the planet with it?"

"It is too early to tell," Steropes replied. "We will need to get closer and gather more data."

"Helmsman, all ahead full," the CO ordered. "Let's find out what's going on here."

CO's Conference Room, TSS *Vella Gulf*, Anti-HD 69830 System, November 8, 2021

"Although we are still too far out to be sure," Steropes said, "and a little variation in power could make a big difference, it appears the Jotunn's ally is accelerating the asteroid toward an impact with the third planet in this system. By the time the asteroid gets there, it will be going at a significant velocity, and the damage will be substantial."

"What do you mean by, 'substantial?'" the CO asked.

"Are you familiar with the Chicxulub asteroid?"

"Isn't that what killed off the dinosaurs on Terra?"

"Yes it is," Steropes replied. "An asteroid hit the Yucatan peninsula of Mexico 66 million years ago, leaving a crater nearly 110 miles in diameter. The impact led to the extinction of the non-avian dinosaurs as well as a majority of the world's Mesozoic species. Not only did it devastate a huge region in the area of impact, it also cast up a poisonous dust cloud that blocked the sunlight for some time, probably years. The lack of sunlight killed the plants, which in turn starved the dinosaurs."

"How big an asteroid are we talking about?" the *Gulf's* XO asked.

"It is estimated the asteroid that hit Terra was about six miles in diameter," Steropes replied. "The impact of such a blow would have released the energy equivalent of 100 trillion tons of TNT. The asteroid you can see on the screen is over 10 miles in diameter, almost twice the size of the one that hit Terra; when this one hits, it will be devastating."

"I know what they're doing," Calvin said.

"Oh?" Captain Sheppard asked. "What is that?"

"The Jotunn said they had initiated Ragnarok, right? If you remember, Nightsong said that, in addition to a major battle and some other natural disasters, Ragnarok ended in the submersion of their world in water. At some point in its travel, the ally must intend to jump the asteroid into our universe so they can hit Asgard with it, causing tsunamis that will fulfill the Jotunn's prophecy of submerging the planet."

"And this is their Ragnarok?" Captain Sheppard asked.

"Yes sir," Calvin replied. "I looked it up, and the prophecy is fairly specific on some of the events. The sun becomes black while the earth sinks into the sea, the stars are supposed to vanish and flames touch the heavens. If an asteroid hit the planet like we're talking about, it would bring about all of these events."

"Okay, I understand the Jotunn want to get Asgard back from the Aesir," Captain Sheppard said, "and they probably intend to wipe out the Aesir as part of their plans, but why would they bother with running the asteroid into Asgard? Just to make it look like some ancient prophecy is coming true? Why bother? Wouldn't it make more sense if they jumped it into our system and slammed it into Golirion, killing all of the Aesir?"

"If I may answer that," Steropes said, "hitting Asgard with the asteroid is very much in line with their racial psyches. The Jotunn believe in doing what they say and in fulfilling promises. If they were somehow able to destroy the Aesir, but Asgard was never destroyed by water, their prophecy would remain unfulfilled and their racial destiny would seem somehow incomplete; they would never have their 'happily ever after.' If they are able to pull this off, then all of the Jotunn will believe the prophecy was right all along, and their destiny is complete."

"*And*, if the end of the prophecy is near," Calvin said, "that means the Jotunn must be expecting to initiate the final battle the prophecy talks about too. That battle was supposed to result in the death of a number of major figures on both sides, so they must be planning to have it here, and have it soon."

"That also makes sense," Steropes agreed.

"I guess the main question I have," Captain Sheppard said, "is, 'Do we really care?' If the Jotunn's ally jumps this asteroid into our universe and hits Asgard with it, what damage will it cause on Goliri-on? Do we care about what they're doing enough to stop them?"

"In most cases, sir, no we would not," Steropes replied; "however, I believe the Jotunn's ally has made a mistake."

"What do you mean?"

"Well, sir, it has been noted on several occasions that time in this universe runs a little differently than in ours. While we always end up in the same place when we jump back and forth, it has been noted that the inhabitants have changed slightly. I do not believe our enemy has taken this into consideration. Depending on when they jump the asteroid into our universe, there is a good chance that Golirion will not have cleared the area of space they intend for the asteroid to travel through in its journey to Asgard."

"What do you mean?"

"I think what Steropes is trying to say, sir," Calvin interrupted, "is that the Jotunn's enemy fucked up; they're going to hit Golirion with the asteroid rather than Asgard."

"I believe they will," Steropes agreed, "and that collision will most likely end all life on Golirion."

Chapter Thirty

Thor's Chambers, Golirion, HD 69830 System, November 8, 2021

Captain Nightsong shook his head. "I'm sorry, my Thor," he said, "but I do not believe the Terrans will be able to provide any assistance in our fight against the Jotunn."

"That is unfortunate," Calanon Aldaenon, who ruled the Aesir as 'Thor,' replied. "Our time to prepare is running out. The Jotunn have already broken through our blockade in Gliese 221."

"What was accomplished while I was gone?" Captain Nightsong asked.

"We have recalled the fleet and brought our other battle station to this system; however, I do not know whether it will be enough to halt their advance."

"I have fought the Jotunn's new ally, and I am similarly unsure," Captain Nightsong said, looking and sounding grim. He looked up and met the Thor's eyes. "How sure are you that everything is in readiness aboard the battle station?"

"The Tyr has given me his assurance that all is in readiness."

"But you haven't been to the station to check on everything yourself?"

"No I haven't," the Thor replied. "Do you think it necessary?"

"I think a trip to the battle station would be extremely valuable for a couple of reasons. First, you would get to see the status of the station for yourself so you can confirm that all is in readiness. It will also let the troops see you, giving them inspiration for the battle to come. Who knows? That might be the difference between victory and defeat."

"You think so?"

"I know so, my Thor. If I were you, I would go as soon as possible, too. I don't think we have a minute to lose. If there is anything that needs to be fixed, we must do it *now*."

CO's Conference Room, TSS *Vella Gulf,* Anti-HD 69830 System, Unknown Date

"I can confirm they are going to hit Golirion instead of Asgard," Steropes announced. "If they had jumped the asteroid into our universe before now, they might have missed the moon, but now I believe the moon will be impossible to miss. If they are allowed to proceed, it is likely Golirion will be destroyed."

"We have to stop them," Calvin said.

"I realize that," Captain Sheppard said. "Steropes, what are we up against?"

"Almost everything on the asteroid appears to be automated," Steropes said. "The enemy has mounted four large engines to the asteroid, which are being used to push it. There are also at least 30 other metallic items attached, which are spread out uniformly across its surface."

"Do we know what those are?" Captain Sheppard asked.

"I believe so," Steropes replied. "Those appear to be jump modules, confirming Lieutenant Commander Hobb's guess that the enemy plans to jump the asteroid into our universe."

"So, we just need to destroy the jump modules, and then we won't have to worry about the asteroid, correct?" Captain Sheppard asked. "The asteroid will stay in this system and crash into the third planet or its moon here."

"We could do that," Steropes said; "however, there are two problems with that proposal. The first is that there appears to be intelligent life on the moon. The second is that there is a destroyer-sized ship flying in concert with the asteroid. I imagine if we attack the asteroid, the ship will defend it."

"Those are two big problems."

"Yes sir, they are."

"Who are the people that live on anti-Golirion?" Lieutenant O'Leary asked. "Are they our new enemy?"

"Unfortunately, they are not," Steropes said. "The society is pre-industrial, but they are definitely intelligent."

"So letting the asteroid hit anti-Golirion is out," the CO said. "Tell me about the ship."

"The ship is similar in size to the time bomb-armed destroyer we previously fought, and its engines appear to function similarly, but it has some other projections the first ship didn't have, and its hull is shaped slightly differently. It is either a modified version of the one we fought before, or an entirely different class of ship altogether."

"Any idea on its capabilities?" Calvin asked.

"Unknown," Steropes replied. "I imagine it will have a similar armament to the other version we saw, but I don't know enough about the new race to say that for sure. There do appear to be more hatches on the side of this ship, but I won't know whether they are torpedo launch tubes, lasers, or something else until they use them."

"All things considered, I'd rather *not* let them use them," the CO said.

"Not only that," Calvin said, "but once we come out of stealth, they may jump into our universe to flee, and we will have to follow them to destroy them. I don't want to get tied up with fighting the ship and lose track of the asteroid. It may already be pre-programmed to jump into our universe at a certain time or place. We need to take the enemy ship by surprise, and we need to do it soon."

"Unfortunately, most of our weapons ports are covered by the stealth modules," Captain Sheppard said. "We may not be able to take it out with the first salvo, or even damage it enough to prevent it from jumping."

"How about this?" Calvin said. "What if we take a stealthed shuttle over to the enemy ship and plant some explosives on it? We could get back on the shuttle, remotely detonate the explosives and then we don't have to worry about the enemy ship any more. Then, we just shoot a couple of the engines on the asteroid and let the others push it away from anti-Golirion. I'm sure Steropes and Solomon can figure out which engines to destroy."

"Actually sir, I kind of like that," Lieutenant O'Leary said. "We used to train for missions like that when I was a SEAL. Swim up to an enemy ship, plant explosives on it and detonate them once we were clear. I think we could do that to the enemy ship, especially if we aren't planning on doing anything else…like trying to capture it or something crazy like that."

"No, I've had my fill of capturing enemy ships," Calvin replied. "I'd be happy to just blow this one up and go find out what

Nightsong is up to. He's already had more time to set his plans in motion than I wanted to give him."

Bridge, Aesir Battle Station *Heimdall*, HD 69830 System, November 9, 2021

"Everything that can be done has been done, my Thor," Fleet Grand Admiral Aglarion said. Also known as 'Tyr,' Fleet Grand Admiral Aglarion was responsible for the Aesir military. "All is in readiness here aboard the battle station, the stargate is as heavily mined as we can make it and all of the ships that could be reached in time have come back to defend the system." He shrugged. "We have done everything possible," he repeated. "Do you have any questions?"

"Thank you for the tour of the battle station," the Thor replied. "I only have one question. Everything you have done…will it be enough?"

"Honestly?" the Tyr asked. "I do not know. Their ally's ships have proven tremendously difficult to defeat. We know Captain Caelerian destroyed one in the Battle of Gliese 221, so they can be beaten…but it is difficult. The odds are not good if we have to fight ships of both the Jotunn and their ally at the same time. If we can contain them to the area around the stargate, we may have a chance. If they get free into the system, it is unlikely we will be victorious."

"Then you should contain them here at the stargate," the Thor said.

"That is my intention," the Tyr replied; "however, enemies rarely do what we want them to."

"Stargate emergence!" one of the sensor technicians called. *"Jotunn battlecruiser!"*

"I am sorry, my Thor, but there is no time to get you back to Golirion," the Tyr said. He stood a little straighter. "It begins." He turned to the communications officer. "Alert the fleet," he ordered. "Tell them to implement Plan Gjallarhorn."

Bridge, TSS *Vella Gulf,* Anti-HD 69830 System, Unknown Date

"*Shuttle 01* is launching, sir," Lieutenant Rafaeli, the squadron duty officer, said.

"Understood," Captain Sheppard replied.

"They took the entire platoon?" Steropes asked. "Couldn't they have accomplished the mission with just a few of the soldiers and maybe a cyborg or two to do the heavy lifting?"

"They could have," Captain Sheppard replied, "but both Lieutenant Commander Hobbs and I thought it prudent to take all of their combat power, just in case. It's better to have too many guns than not enough."

North Quadrant Control, Aesir Battle Station *Heimdall,* HD 69830 System, November 9, 2021

"That's the third battlecruiser so far," the 'North' quadrant's sensor technician said. As the North side of the station was facing the stargate, they were taking the brunt of the initial fighting.

"The first battlecruiser is finished," the laser officer said.

"Minefield integrity is at 57%," the mine warfare officer said. "The mines are doing their jobs, but the shields on the Jotunn ships seem to be stronger than normal. It is taking several hits to knock them down."

"If they would just come a little more slowly," the missile officer added, hand tapping nervously on his console, "I would like it a lot more."

"Just keep shooting," the Tyr replied. "As they start to spread out, the other quadrants will take some of the load from you."

"Gods!" the sensor technician exclaimed. "Look at that monster! It's the biggest ship I have ever seen! It's got to be at least five miles long."

"Don't spare the mines," the Tyr ordered. "That will be their command ship…and it's going to take a lot to kill it."

"Sir!" the sensor technician called. "One of the ally ships just gated in and disappeared. There goes a second! Both were destroyer-sized, I think. There is a third; this one is cruiser-sized. A fourth one now, also cruiser-sized!"

"Stay on the Jotunn vessels you can see," the Tyr said. "Let's concentrate on killing them first. We'll kill their ally's ships when they start popping back up."

Bridge, TSS *Vella Gulf*, Anti-HD 69830 System, Unknown Date

"How much longer until *Shuttle 01* reaches the target?" Captain Sheppard asked.

"If they are on schedule they should be arriving at the enemy ship right now," Lieutenant Rafaeli said. "The challenging part is going to be for the pilot to match vectors with the ship. Once that happens, they can begin mining the ship. That part should go relatively quickly.”

“Contact!” the DSO exclaimed. “I’ve got ship emanations; they are definitely *not* from the ship we are following.”

“I’ve got them too,” Steropes added. “Signal strength and engine harmonics appear to be from one of the destroyers we saw before.”

“Where are they coming from?” Captain Sheppard asked.

“They are coming from the same location as the Jotunn stargate in our universe,” Steropes replied. “The ship is accelerating and appears to be turning away from us. A second ship just jumped in. It is another of their destroyers.”

“So, the battle must have started in our universe,” the CO stated. “What is the ship that we’re tracking doing?”

“Its course hasn’t deviated,” the OSO said, who was tracking it closely.

“Do you want me to call back the shuttle?” Lieutenant Rafaeli asked.

“Not yet,” the CO said. “We may need them back quickly, but as of right now, let them continue their mission. I suspect we’re going to have to kill the enemy ship eventually, and their mission represents our best chance to kill it without taking any fire in return. Any day I don’t have to dodge torpedoes is a good day.”

“Amen to that,” the DSO muttered.

“Captain Sheppard, I am reasonably confident one of the new ships just transmitted something to the ship we are following,” Steropes said; “however, I can’t break it.”

“Solomon, what about you?” the CO asked. “Can you translate it?”

"No sir," the ship's AI replied. "I am unable to translate it, but I can tell you it is definitely not the same as the Efreeti communications we saw before."

"I've got a third enemy ship," the DSO said. "This one appears to be a cruiser."

"So there are a total of four enemy ships in this system?" the CO asked.

"Yes sir," Steropes replied. "No, five of them now. Another cruiser just jumped in."

"I hope Lieutenant Commander Hobbs destroys the first one quickly then," the CO said. "This universe is getting awfully damn crowded."

Cargo Bay, *Shuttle 01*, Anti-HD 69830 System, Unknown Date

"*O*ne minute to deployment," Lieutenant Neil 'Trouble' Watson commed. "*We've matched velocities with the enemy vessel and are making our final approach.*"

"*Ramp coming down in 30 seconds,*" added the pilot, Lieutenant Jeff 'Canuck' Canada.

"*Copy that,*" Calvin replied. He switched to the platoon's network. "*One minute out. Ramp coming down in 30 seconds. Everyone check your suit seals. Mining crew, standby by to deploy.*"

Lieutenant O'Leary, Gunnery Sergeant Dantone and Sergeant Braig stood up and shuffled their way to the end of the cargo compartment where they picked up their improvised limpet mines. "Let's get this done quickly," O'Leary said. "We don't know if they have any sensors on the outside of the hull. I'd like to be gone before any-body comes out to see what we're doing."

The ramp lowered, and the soldiers saw the ship for the first time. Unlike the smooth surface of the ships that came from the Terran replicators, the surface of the alien spacecraft was littered with what looked like nuts and bolts.

"What a piece of shit," Sergeant Braig said as he got a look. "That looks like something my kid built."

"Focus, you morons," Lieutenant O'Leary said. "If I have to—"

Everything flashed, and Calvin could feel himself falling up.

Bridge, TSS *Vella Gulf*, Anti-HD 69830 System, Unknown Date

"*S**ir!*" the OSO called. "The ship we were following just jumped!"

"What?"

"It's gone sir! I think there's a problem, too. It looks like only part of the shuttle jumped with it. There are pieces of refined metal in the vicinity of where the ship was."

"I've got a distress beacon from the pilot," Steropes added; "however, there aren't any life signs. It looks like the shuttle's cock-pit was cut in half."

Cargo Bay, *Shuttle 01*, HD 69830 System, November 9, 2021

Calvin had never felt this disoriented before, including the times he had done Navy training that was *intended* to disorient him. Along with the flash, he got the familiar nauseated feeling that occurred when... "*We just jumped back to our universe,*" he commed. He looked at the cargo ramp and watched helplessly as O'Leary and the two cyborgs went spiraling off into space as the shuttle's gravity failed. Before he could say anything else, a chorus of voices started babbling on the net.

"*Holy fuck! The roof of the shuttle's missing!*"

"*The cockpit got cut in half!*"

"*Hey, where'd the gravity go?*"

"*We're drifting away from the ship!*"

"*We're all going to die!*"

Realizing he was losing control, Calvin flipped his transmitter to OVERRIDE and yelled, "*Shut the hell up and listen! We just jumped into our own universe. The shuttle is fucked. Abandon ship and fly down to the alien ship before it jumps again. Let's go! Follow me!*"

He pushed up from his seat and through where the roof used to be. Clear of the shuttle, he used his maneuvering jets to fly toward the enemy ship. Calvin came in for a landing next to Lieutenant O'Leary, who pointed behind him.

Calvin turned to see a string of soldiers following him down...and the out-of-control shuttle. Something must have broken, as it motors were on full thrust. The shuttle spun and dove into the alien vessel, slamming into it near the bow. Even from the other end of the ship, Calvin could see a huge dent and feel the contact through his feet. It probably made a huge ringing noise inside the ship, too.

"*Well, they know we're here,*" Calvin said as he watched the shuttle rebound from the enemy destroyer and dash off into space. "*Everybody come to the back of the ship, and we'll enter together.*"

Bridge, Jotunn Ship *Naglfar*, HD 69830 System, November 9, 2021

Fornjot Deathbringer, who ruled the Jotunn society as 'Odin,' surveyed the bridge of his command ship *Naglfar*. There was no fear or tension, only the joy of battle with an enemy. He would have had it no other way; in fact, he would personally have killed anyone who showed fear. His gaze met the head of his military forces, or 'Freyr.'

"Status?" the Odin asked.

"The Aesir command ship *Surt* has been destroyed," the Freyr noted. "Now there is nothing between us and the battle station controlling their minefield. We have already lost the battlecruiser *Jormungand* to their mines."

"Good," the Odin replied. "The battle station is the priority. Once the mines are gone, they will only have their fleet…and it is hardly a match for ours." There was a difference between the 'joy of battle' with an enemy and having his forces destroyed by robot mines; the minefield was a cowardly way to conduct battle. It was far better for combat to be battle axe to battle axe, or at least ship to ship.

"My Odin, there is an incoming transmission for you from…an Aesir?" the communicator asked. "Someone calling himself 'Nightsong?'"

"Put it on screen."

The front screen lit up with the image of an Aesir, and the Odin stifled a growl. After over 200 years of inbred hatred for the elven race, it was hard to stand the sight of *any* of them, even if the Aesir in question was currently helping him.

"Were you successful?" the Odin asked.

"I was," the Aesir, who appeared to be piloting a small vessel, confirmed. "The Terrans should be here soon, perhaps as early as today."

"Will they have a big force?"

"No, they only sent a cruiser."

"Bah. That is barely worth my effort. Are you sure they will engage us in combat? It is important we begin killing Terrans as soon as possible."

"I believe it to be a certainty."

"Good. You have done well, Aesir. Where will I find your Thor?"

"He is on the battle station, as you requested. Once you capture the battle station, you will be able to take him prisoner."

"Excellent," the Odin said. "You will be well rewarded." He terminated the connection so he no longer had to look at one of the hated race.

"Your orders, Odin?" the Freyr asked.

"Destroy the battle station," the Odin replied. "Take no prisoners."

"But you gave the Aesir your word you wouldn't kill the Thor."

"No," the Odin said, a grin spreading across his face. "I said that I would not kill him on Golirion for all of his people to see. But the Thor isn't on Golirion now, is he?"

The smile spread to the Freyr's face. "No, my Odin, he is not on Golirion." He turned to his chief of staff, who was supervising the *Naglfar's* offensive operations. "Retarget all batteries," he ordered. "Destroy the battle station. Take no prisoners."

"I *will* kill the Thor," the Odin gloated, "if it is the last thing I do."

"Odin, we have stargate activations!"

North Quadrant Control, Aesir Battle Station *Heimdall*, HD 69830 System, November 9, 2021

"Thor!" the communications officer called. "We just intercepted a transmission from Captain Nightsong to the Jotunn command ship. He told them you were here on the battle station!"

"That bastard!" the Tyr said. "What was he thinking?"

"I do not know," the Thor replied. "I am not aware of any complaint he might have against me." He turned to the communications officer. "Who did he give this information to?"

"Captain Nightsong was speaking to the Odin, who is aboard the command ship *Naglfar*."

"I suspected the Odin would be close by," the Thor said. "I knew he wouldn't pass up a chance to gloat about his victory." He paused and then said, "Well, let him gag on his victory. Retarget all weapons on the *Naglfar*. I *will* kill the Odin, if it is the last thing I do."

"Sir! More stargate activations!"

Chapter Thirty-One

Bridge, TSS *Vella Gulf*, Anti-HD 69830 System, Unknown Date

"**D**o we follow them?" the helmsman asked.

"Not yet," Captain Sheppard replied. "There's nothing we can do for them at the moment anyway, and we still have a mission to accomplish here." He began issuing orders. "Steropes, get me a targeting solution on the asteroid. I want to know which engines to destroy so the asteroid misses anti-Golirion. OSO, destroy the jump modules on the asteroid and the engines Steropes indicates. If nothing else, we'll keep the damn thing in this universe; they'll have to look for their Ragnarok somewhere else. Lieutenant Rafaeli, get the other shuttle manned and ready. We'll send it after our folks once it looks like the enemy ship is going to stay in one universe or the other for a while."

"Dropping stealth," the duty engineer said.

"Firing on the jump modules," the OSO added.

"Do you want the shuttle to have a stealth module?" Lieutenant Rafaeli asked. "I just spoke with our squadron's maintenance department and, at the moment, it does not."

"Yes, I do," the CO said after thinking about it for a few seconds. "We may need to sneak up on the enemy ship again, and besides, I imagine there's a battle underway in the other universe; it might come in handy for the unarmed shuttle *not* to be seen."

"Targeting sent to the OSO," Steropes announced. "If we eliminate the two engines I have highlighted, the remaining motors *should* push the asteroid off to the side of anti-Golirion."

"Should?" Captain Sheppard asked.

"Yes, they should," Steropes said; "however, I do not know the capabilities of the ones remaining, like whether they can vector their thrust. I also do not know if the engines are pre-programmed or if they have a navigation device installed so they can compensate for the loss of the two engines I suggested destroying. There are many things I don't know about their technology; I believe what I have suggested will be effective in removing the threat of the asteroid hitting anti-Golirion, but I can't be sure."

"I have eliminated 14 of the jump modules," the OSO said. "We will need to move the ship for me to target any of the remaining ones."

"That should be sufficient," the CO said. "Normally, you have to have them spread out around the object being jumped. Getting half of them should remove any redundant capability they had. Destroy the two engines, then we'll see about finding our wayward soldiers."

"Done," the OSO replied a few seconds later. "Both of the indicated engines have been destroyed."

"Understood," the CO said. "Duty engineer, stealth us back up. Helm, when that's complete, jump us back into our universe."

"Stealth on," the duty engineer answered.

"Here we go," the helmsman said. "Jumping back to our universe."

Exterior, Alien Ship, HD 69830 System, November 9, 2021

"*Well sir, it looks like you're going to get your wish, after all,*" Lieutenant O'Leary said.

"*But I didn't want to capture this one,*" Calvin replied. "*We don't know anything about them. That's a bad way to start.*"

"*Well, I'd feel a lot more comfortable inside the ship than outside,*" Lieutenant O'Leary said, "*especially with a battle under way.*"

"*Agreed,*" Calvin said. "*Get the cyborgs started on cutting our way in.*"

"*One hole only, or do you want more?*"

"*Let's go with two. If we only enter in one place, it lets them surround us more easily, especially since we have no idea where we're going or what we're looking for. Entering in two places doubles their targeting problems, while still allowing us to keep enough firepower in each group to fight our way out of whatever we get ourselves into. You take the Space Force, and I'll take the Ground Force. If we can find engineering and the bridge, we can keep the ship in one place long enough for a rescue. What do you think?*"

"*Sounds like an easy day in the life of a Terran Space Marine,*" Lieutenant O'Leary replied. "*I'm excited to be a part of it.*"

"*Great, get started on that, and—*"

"*Lieutenant Commander Hobbs, Vella Gulf. Please pass your status when able. Be advised, we have followed you back into our universe. We're going to try to get the other shuttle to you for recovery, but need to put a jump module on it in case the ship you're on switches universes again. We will let you know when the shuttle is enroute. The other shuttle doesn't have a stealth module mounted at the moment, either, so it will take some time.*"

"*Roger that,*" Calvin replied. "*The platoon is down on the enemy ship with all personnel. The shuttle was destroyed, with both crew members lost. We'd*" *love a ride home when you can get it here. In the meantime, we're going to cut our way in and see if we can't make ourselves at home."*

"*Roger,* Vella Gulf *copies. Out."*

"*All right, Lieutenant O'Leary,*" Calvin commed. "*Mount the explosives and let's see about introducing ourselves to the neighbors."*

Interior, Alien Ship, HD 69830 System, November 9, 2021

"*S*tand back, everyone; it's about to drop,*" Sergeant Declan 'Ducky' Jones said as he completed the final cut on the Ground Force entrance. With two cyborgs cutting, opening an entryway into the ship had gone quickly. Sergeant Pierce 'Big Sky' Tomas had already completed his cut; he stepped back and aimed his Mrowry autocannon.

The section dropped a couple of seconds later, and Ducky jumped back from the barrage of light beams that erupted from the creatures waiting for them; he had to use his maneuvering thrusters to return to the ship.

The Terrans had been expecting a greeting party, and four soldiers threw grenades into the opening. Big Sky looked cautiously over the lip of the opening after the explosions and fired at one of the creatures still moving below. "*Clear!*" he called. "*Going in!*"

He dropped down through the hole and felt gravity return once he was inside the skin of the ship. Another of the aliens moved, and he fired a five round burst; what was left stopped moving. "*Weird…*" he commed.

"*What's weird?*" Calvin asked.

"These…things…or people or whatever the hell they are," Big Sky replied. *"They ain't like nothing we got back in Texas, that's fer sure, and we like to grow 'em big there."*

"What do you mean?"

"Well, they look like what you'd get if you crossed a longhorn steer with a four-armed man," Big Sky replied. *"And then gave it an extra pair of eyes on a couple of antennas, just to gross everybody out. They're weird lookin' is all."*

"Are we clear?" Calvin asked.

"Oh, yeah, we're clear, sir," Big Sky said. *"There must be some sort of force field holding in the atmosphere, 'cause there's air and gravity down here. C'mon down and join the party."*

The members of the squad dropped into the ship and found themselves in a hallway that extended in two directions.

"We're in," Calvin said, looking at the bodies and parts of bodies spread across the passageway. Although they had on suits and helmets, and most of the bodies were shredded, some things were obvious. The creatures were built somewhat like centaurs, but their bodies were heavy enough to be full-grown bulls, not horses. They had two arms on each side of their bodies, in addition to their four feet, and two eyes mounted on antennae that extended from the tops of their heads between their horns, in addition to the two eyes on their 'faces.' The aliens were weird, all right.

"We're in, too," Lieutenant O'Leary commed. *"There were a few bizarre-looking creatures waiting for us, but nothing a few antimatter grenades couldn't handle."*

Chapter Thirty-Two

"**M**erde," Admiral Etienne Lambert, the strike group commander, said. He still hadn't gotten used to having different tastes in his mouth every time he went through a stargate, and now it looked like he had stepped on a nest of vipers. "Let's get this mess sorted, and sorted quickly. I want to make sure we know friend from foe here."

As strike group commander, the admiral occupied an odd position in the naval force. He was resident on the flagship (so named because of the presence of the admiral's pennant or 'flag' the ship displayed when he was embarked) and he outranked the ship's captain; however, the admiral was not the commanding officer of either the ship or the relatively small air wing it carried. Thus it was incumbent on the strike group commander to delicately balance allowing the ship's captain to command his ship, despite being both present and senior on the same vessel.

The admiral, however, did not like to be told, "No."

"Sir, you don't intend to take the fleet *into* that, do you?" the *Thermopylae's* commanding officer, Captain Hayato Nakamura, asked from the front screen. The ship's CO was on the ship's bridge, two levels down and a quarter mile forward of the flag bridge. Over the course of their cruise so far, he had become very well aware of what the admiral liked…and didn't. "We are still on our shakedown cruise and are hardly what I would call operational. Our crews are still learning to use the weapons systems. Additionally, it is just our three vessels; we don't have any smaller ships to screen us."

"Captain Nakamura, this system was chosen as our destination for a number of reasons beyond your simple 'shakedown cruise.' Not only are we here to deliver supplies and troops, we are also here to lend support to an ally. As I look at the tactical plot, I see an ally very much in need of support. I do not intend to run away from a friend in need. Not when we have a super dreadnought and two battleships that may very well turn the tide of this battle. All ahead flank! Prepare your crew, *Captain*; we *are* going to battle." He terminated the connection and the screen went dead.

"Admiral, I am receiving a message from the Jotunn command ship," the communications officer said. "Their leader would like to speak with you."

"Put him on screen."

An enormous humanoid filled the screen, wearing yellow and blue-spotted pelts. Similar to the image the admiral had seen from the *Vella Gulf's* meeting with the Jotunn, their leader wore a chain-metal shirt over his torso and a metal helmet with immense horns.

"Ah, there you are," the Jotunn said. "A Terran, huh? I was hoping to see what you looked like before I killed you. I am Fornjot Deathbringer, the Odin of the Jotunn. It was nice of you to come here, instead of making us come find you; we will be with you shortly."

"If you would like to talk, you should cease combat operations immediately," the admiral said. "We will be happy to work out a settlement between your civilizations."

"Talk?" the Odin roared. "The time for talking is long past. Now is the time for killing. I intend to kill all of the Aesir in this system, and you as well."

"What have we done to you?" the admiral asked.

"I am told you destroyed one of our ally's ships. They do not take kindly to such an affront, nor do I. Your nation must be punished."

"What do you mean by 'punished?'"

"I'm sorry," the Odin said. "Did I say punished? I meant destroyed!" He broke into laughter, which was echoed by all of the crew that could be seen.

"You intend to destroy our ships?" the admiral asked when the Odin's laughter had slowed.

"Your ships?" The Odin asked, still chuckling. "Not hardly. I intend to destroy Terra!" He began laughing again and terminated the transmission.

"I see we've come to the right place," the admiral said. "It will be my pleasure to help the Aesir against such uncultured barbarians."

"Sir!" the strike group communications officer said. "The Aesir are calling. I have an incoming transmission from their Thor, who is on the battle station by the stargate."

"On screen," the admiral ordered. The front view screen lit up with the image of a dark-haired Aesir in a space suit with his helmet off. The skin that could be seen was pale blue, and only a small circlet around his forehead marked him as royalty. The circlet was hard to see through the smoky haze in the air, and the battle station's devastation was evident behind him. Flames leapt from a console to one side but were put out by an off-screen extinguishing system.

"I am the Thor," the Aesir said. "I apologize for the lack of formalities, but we are under some stress at the moment. My communications officer tells me you are from Terra. Might I ask your intentions?"

"It looks like you could use a hand," the admiral said, "and I intend to give you one. We are inbound at flank speed to assist you."

"Thank the gods," the Thor replied; "we could certainly use your aid. The battle station is nearly out of missiles and is only at—," he looked at something off screen, "47% of its normal operating status. If you have something that can kill the ships that keep jumping into and out of our universe, it would also be very welcome."

"Our scientists have been working on that, and I think we have a few surprises for them," the admiral replied. "If you could send us your tactical picture so we can sort out who's who, we would appreciate it."

"I will have our technicians send it to you immediately."

"Hold on, Thor, we're coming. *Thermopylae* out."

Bridge, TSS *Thermopylae*, HD 69830 System, November 9, 2021

"Madness," Captain Nakamura muttered. "This is nothing short of madness."

"What is madness, sir?" the *Thermopylae's* XO, Captain Peotr Baranovsky, asked.

"It is lunacy to take our fleet into that…that mess out there. We are unprepared. Our crew is not fully trained, we have untested weapons and our tactics to use them are still, as yet, unproven. We are going against ships that can jump in and out of our universe, and none of our ships can follow them when they go. They haven't figured out how to install jump modules on a super dreadnought, and the battleships were supposed to get theirs when we returned." He shook his head and repeated, "It is madness."

"Well, we do have the ship's AI to help the crew," the XO said. "Also, at least we are aware of the capabilities of the Jotunn's ally and have thought about how to defeat them. They aren't going to catch us unaware like they did the Aesir ships and the *Vella Gulf*."

"Speaking of the *Vella Gulf*," the CO replied, "aren't they supposed to be around here somewhere? I wonder where they went?"

Bridge, TSS *Vella Gulf*, HD 69830 System, November 9, 2021

"Stargate emergence!" Steropes called.

"Jotunn or ally ship?" Captain Sheppard asked.

"Neither. The ship entered from the other stargate and is broadcasting Terran codes…It's the…it's the *Thermopylae*, sir! Fleet command must have sent it to help the Aesir. More ships incoming. The battleship *Hood* is also here, as is the *Yamato*."

When Steropes didn't say any more for several long seconds, the CO finally asked, "What about screening ships? Battlecruisers? Cruisers? How many destroyers?"

"None, sir," Steropes replied. "Those three ships are the only ones that came through the stargate."

"Really?" Captain Sheppard asked. He shook his head. "I hope they know what they're doing." He turned to the communications officer. "Comms, put out a line so we can contact them and get me the *Thermopylae*."

Within seconds, the image of a Terran admiral filled the screen. "Ah, there you are, *Vella Gulf*," the admiral said. "I am Admiral Lambert. You are to be integrated with my strike group. Come and attach yourself to the group as we go to the immediate aid of our illustrious allies."

"Yes sir," Captain Sheppard replied. "We are working to recover our platoon of space marines from one of the enemy ships. Once we get them back, we will join you enroute."

"*No!*" Admiral Lambert screamed, his face purpling. "I said for you to join us now! You will cease the recovery efforts and position yourself within the strike group where my operations officer tells you. *Am I clear on this?*"

"Yes sir," Captain Sheppard replied. "Very clear. *Vella Gulf*, out."

"Well that's fucked up," the helmsman said.

"No shit," the duty engineer agreed. He looked back to the CO. "He can't be serious, can he? Just abandon our guys and go join the strike group? Just like that?"

"Did you hear any room for delay in the admiral's orders?" Captain Sheppard asked. Without waiting for an answer he added, "Neither did I. Let's get that shuttle launched ASAP! Helm, proceed to a rendezvous with the *Thermopylae* strike group. Best speed."

Task Force Calvin, Alien Ship, HD 69830 System, November 9, 2021

"*L*ieutenant Commander Hobbs, Vella Gulf. *Be advised, there has been a change of plans. The* Vella Gulf *has been ordered to join the* Thermopylae *strike group,* *which just arrived in-system. Recovery will have to wait until after our battle with the Jotunn."*

"What? You've got to be fucking kidding me. You're just going to leave us here on an alien ship?"

"The CO sends his apologies. He tried to argue with the admiral, but the admiral wouldn't listen to him. Frankly, you're probably better off there. I just saw the plot and the Jotunn have a ship that's freaking huge, *in addition to a bunch of smaller ones. Plus all the ones that keep jumping back and forth between universes that are hard to even* count. *Good luck, guys.* Vella Gulf, *out."*

"*Those mother fu—,*" started Lieutenant O'Leary, but he was cut off by another incoming transmission.

"*Just heard you started the fun without us,*" Night commed. "*You guys are* on *one of the ally's ships? Was it time to add another unit to Lieutenant Commander Hobbs' personal collection of captured ships?*"

"*Yeah, we're on it,*" Calvin replied. "*That wasn't our intention; it just sort of happened.*"

"*You 'sort of' invaded an enemy ship? This I have to hear.*"

"*Yeah, well, we're sort of busy right now and the* Thermopylae *just screwed us. They cancelled our recovery shuttle and made the* Gulf *go join the strike group.*"

"*You're right, that's screwed up. I'm on the* Thermopylae; *let me see what I can do,*" Night said.

"*Thanks,*" Calvin replied. "*Let me know how it turns out.*"

"*I will. Stay safe. Night out.*"

Flag Bridge, TSS *Thermopylae*, HD 69830 System, November 9, 2021

"**A**dmiral, the Aesir have begun transmitting us their tactical picture," the sensor operator said. "Whoa! The Jotunn have the biggest ship I have ever seen. It is over five miles long!"

"Steady," the admiral said. "At three miles long and 10 million tons, we bring a lot to the fight, too. With the *Hood* and the *Yamato* at our side, and the Aesir battle station assisting, I feel confident we can take them."

The admiral switched to the strike group net. "*All ships, this is the admiral. Our first target will be the Jotunn dreadnought. If we can get them out of the fight, it will be easy to defeat the rest of the fleet in detail. Although we intend to engage the dreadnought, weapons are free enroute. Maintain formation on us, but if you get a shot at any of the enemy on the way in, take it! Admiral Lambert out.*"

Bridge, TSS *Thermopylae*, HD 69830 System, November 9, 2021

"**A**wesome," the CO said with a truckload of sarcasm in his voice. "Not only are we going to charge into that hornet's nest, we are going to start out with their largest vessel." He switched to the ship-wide network. "*All hands, this is the Captain. We are headed for a Jotunn dreadnought to help relieve the pressure on the Aesir battle station. I know some of our weapons systems are new, and we haven't had much of a chance for practice, but remember, we are Terran sailors, and we have never lost a battle. Stay alert, as the*

Jotunn's ally may show up anywhere, at any time. They weren't expecting us; let's show them what Terra's got!"

"OSO, I want all systems ready to fire, *now!* Don't let those bastards pop up on us without us putting some steel back on them. Duty engineer, set General Quarters."

"We're kind of a long ways out," Captain Baranovsky noted. "Do you want to set General Quarters so soon? The men may get tired if they have to stand ready the entire time."

"Unless you can tell me where all of the enemy is hiding, and I do mean *all* of the enemy, I want us to be as ready as we can be. That means offensive and defensive systems manned and ready, and the ship buttoned up. I may disagree with the admiral that this is the best course of action, but we will fight the ship the best we are able."

Chapter Thirty-Three

Task Force O'Leary, Alien Ship, HD 69830 System, November 9, 2021

"*H*ey, *Lieutenant, they must have gone to General Quarters or something,*" Sergeant Marcus 'Spud' Murphy said. "*We're at a dead end and all of the doors seem locked; at least, they aren't opening. None of them have handles, either, so I'm not sure how to get them open. What do you want us to do?*"

"*I want you to show a teeny tiny bit of fucking initiative,*" Lieutenant O'Leary said. "*Get one of the cyborgs up there and cut a way through. Also, let's try to cut our way through some of the other doors here. I don't want to leave a bunch of them behind us so they can hit us from the rear when we least expect it.*"

"*I'm on the door at the end of the passageway,*" Sergeant Jacob 'Chaos' Braig commed.

"*I'll start working my way down the corridor and see if anyone's home,*" Gunnery Sergeant Dantone said. "*Fire Team One with me for fire support.*"

There was a flash and a moment of disorientation.

"*Dammit,*" Lieutenant O'Leary said, "*I wish they'd make up their minds on what universe they want to be in.*"

Task Force Calvin, Alien Ship, HD 69830 System,

November 9, 2021

"*H*ey, sir, the passageway ends up here in a wall," Sergeant Richard 'Shipwreck' Shipley said. "*I passed a few things that looked like doors on the way, but none of them have handles or any other way of gaining entrance.*"

"*Yeah, I saw one,*" Calvin said. "*Looks like they must have some sort of key card or something that grants access to the spaces they're allowed to go. Apparently, they haven't given us access to any of them, so I guess we'll have to cut our way through. Let's all move to the end of the passageway and then we'll have the cyborgs cut through the doors as we come to them. At least that way, they won't pop up behind us.*"

A call came in on the comm network. "*Lieutenant Commander Hobbs,* Shuttle 02. *We are enroute your position for recovery. Help's on the way, no matter which universe they take you to.*"

"*Awesome. We're looking forward to your arrival. We are on the interior of the ship, so let us know when you're five minutes out.*"

"*Wilco. 02 out.*"

Everything flashed as the ship jumped universes.

"Dammit," Calvin muttered. He switched to the platoon-wide network. "*You guys found anything yet, Lieutenant O'Leary? All we've got is a dead-end passageway with locked doors. We're about to start cutting into them.*"

"*No sir. We've got the same thing over on this side. I would have expected stairs or a ladder or something, but so far, nothing. We're about to start cutting, too.*"

"*Look for a way to go forward and down,*" Calvin replied. "*The spaces we're looking for will probably be the ones that are hardest to get to.*"

"*Roger, sir; we're looking.*"

North Quadrant Control, Aesir Battle Station *Heimdall*, HD 69830 System, November 9, 2021

"Tyr, the East Quadrant just took a hit in their control space," the damage control officer said. "Repair teams are responding, but it sounds like the quadrant is going to be down until we get it into a space dock. Remaining defenses, what few there are, have gone to local control."

"Understood," the Tyr replied.

"What is—," the Thor stopped to cough. The smoke was becoming thick enough that it was starting to work its way into their suits' recyclers…even though that was supposed to be impossible. "Our status?"

"The East and the South Quadrants are both out. If any of the missile or laser batteries are still functional, they are being controlled by their local operators. The other quadrants are heavily damaged and shields are down throughout the entire station. The only quadrant with minimal damage is the Lower Quadrant." The Tyr paused to cough. "Unfortunately, the motor control relay used to spin the ship took a hit, so we are dead in space. If we can fix that, we can spin the station and take the Jotunn under fire again. Until then, the rest of our systems are down to about 25%, and the Jotunn are trying to stay in our blind spots. I wish I could get you out of here, my Thor, but the Jotunn have destroyed every evacuation pod that has launched so far."

"The bastards."

"Yes, my Thor. My sentiments, exactly."

"Tyr! I have motor control restored!"

"Good. Spin the ship to orient the Lower Quadrant on the Jotunn command vessel. Tell the Lower Quadrant control officer to fire everything she has at the *Naglfar*."

"Aye aye!"

The Tyr smiled. "We'll see how they like this."

Bridge, Jotunn Ship *Naglfar*, HD 69830 System, November 9, 2021

"Freyr, the battle station is in motion," the sensor technician said. "It appears to be spinning."

"Why would they do that?" the Odin asked.

"They are probably trying to bring a less damaged side of the station to face us," the Freyr replied. "Frankly, I am surprised it has taken them this long. We have pounded that side to scrap; if I were in control over there, I would have spun the station long before this. They must not have much remaining."

The Freyr looked at his tactical plot. "Our allies are doing an excellent job on the Aesir ships," he said. "They are doing too well, actually; they have already destroyed the majority of the Aesir fleet. We will have to hurry with the battle station, or there won't be any left for us."

Bridge, TSS *Thermopylae*, HD 69830 System, November 9, 2021

"Contact!" the OSO said. "One of the Jotunn ally's ships just popped up on the other side of the *Hood*, sir. It is approximately eight million miles beyond the *Hood!*"

"Can we fire?" Captain Nakamura asked.

"No sir," the OSO replied. "It is in range; however, we would have to shoot across the *Hood.*"

"Understood," the CO said. "Prepare a targeting solution that takes the missiles around the *Hood,* in case we're needed."

"Sir, the ally ship is preparing to fire torpedoes!" the sensor operator shouted.

"Calm down," Captain Nakamura said. "Make your reports like you have been taught."

"Sir, the enemy ship is preparing to fire torpedoes," the sensor operator said in a more normal, although excited, tone of voice. "The ship is larger than the one the *Vella Gulf* fought; this one is cruiser-sized."

"Much better," the CO replied. "DSO, if the torpedoes come toward us, are you ready?"

"Yes sir," the DSO replied. "Decoy systems operational, manned and ready."

"Very well."

"Sir!" the communications officer exclaimed. "The *Hood* just asked for us to shoot over them at the enemy ship. They were not at General Quarters, and their systems aren't fully manned."

"OSO, take the enemy under fire," Captain Nakamura ordered.

"Firing, sir."

The crew could feel the ship jolt slightly as the broadside of 35 anti-ship missiles launched. "Birds away," the OSO said.

"Sir, the enemy ship has launched," the sensor officer said. "10 torpedoes inbound toward the strike group." His tone was back up half an octave, the CO noted.

"Can we do anything to assist the *Hood?*" Captain Nakamura asked.

"No sir," the DSO replied. "Unless the torpedoes are targeted on us, they will be outside the range of our defenses. The *Hood* is on its own."

Flag Bridge, TSS *Thermopylae*, HD 69830 System, November 9, 2021

"Admiral, all 10 torpedoes hit the *Hood.* At least one of her engines has been destroyed; she is beginning to drop behind."

"Should I tell the rest of the strike group to slow to match the *Hood?*" the flag watch officer asked.

"No," the admiral replied. "I told the Thor we would come at our best speed, and I intend to. If the *Hood* can't keep up, they'll just have to get there when they can. Leave them."

Bridge, TSS *Vella Gulf*, HD 69830 System, November 9, 2021

"Skipper," the communications officer said, "Captain Train just commed me. A couple of our squadron pilots and platoon members are onboard the *Thermopylae.* He's asking us for a shuttle run to come get them before combat starts. He said, and I quote, 'I'd feel a lot safer on a ship run by someone who wasn't an idiot.'"

"I'd love to get them, but our shuttle already has a priority run. Please let him know we can't get them at this time."

"Excuse me, sir," the sensor officer interrupted, "but one of the destroyer-sized ships just popped up on the opposite side of the *Hood* from the first one. It's preparing to launch, too."

"Geez," Captain Sheppard said. "This is just like watching a World War II German submarine wolf pack at work. Cut out the weak and destroy them in detail. Helm, how long until we join up with the strike group?"

"30 minutes," the helmsman said. "And then another 30 minutes until we are in range of the Jotunn dreadnought."

"This is ludicrous," the CO muttered. "Get me the admiral, please."

Admiral Lambert appeared on the screen. He didn't look happy. "Yes?" he asked. "We are busy fighting a battle at the moment. Is there something you absolutely need?"

"Yes, admiral. You may not know it, but the *Vella Gulf* can jump between universes like the enemy can. I am requesting permission to jump to the Jinn Universe and hunt the enemy ships there."

"Permission denied," the admiral replied. "They have to jump into our universe to fire at us; we will fight them here. Continue toward the strike group and take the *Hood's* screening position to our starboard. When you are there, de-cloak. That should give them pause."

"Aye, sir, we will take the *Hood's* position. Can we get a shuttle run to bring our crew members over to us before combat begins? You have two of our pilots; we may need them for the fight."

"We don't have time to send a shuttle there and back. I'm going to have to say—,"

"We already lost a shuttle and the command ship has two extra," Captain Sheppard interrupted. "I'd appreciate it if we could borrow one of yours until we get a replacement."

"Sure, whatever, just get in position ASAP!" Admiral Lambert ordered. "And get your fighters into formation *now!*"

"We're on our way!" Captain Sheppard replied. The communication terminated.

The CO turned to the comms officer. "Let Captain Train know they are cleared to bring a shuttle over." He shook his head. "Staying in this universe is lunacy, but at least that part went well."

Chapter Thirty-Four

Bridge, Jotunn Ship *Naglfar*, HD 69830 System, November 9, 2021

The Freyr watched the plot as another salvo of missiles hit the defenseless battle station. Although a few missiles launched sporadically from its few remaining silos, coordinated actions had ceased several minutes before. "The Aesir fleet has been destroyed," the Freyr said, "and if that is all the battle station has left, we should shortly be able to turn our attention to these Terrans who have so graciously shown up to be destroyed."

"The remaining two ships will be in range within 10 minutes," the missile technician said. He looked at his scope again. "Wait, there are three ships…no, four ships in the Terran fleet now!"

"Four ships?" the Freyr asked. "Where did the two new ones come from? Are they anomalies in your system?"

"I have them on my system, too, my Freyr," the sensor operator said. "I do not believe them to be anomalies."

"Well, are they some sort of countermeasures system? Are the Terrans capable of deceiving our systems?"

"I do not know, sir," the sensor operator said. "One of them, cruiser-sized, just appeared and has remained stable. The other target has fluctuated, growing larger then smaller. That one may be a deception. Certainly, it does not move like a ship; its acceleration vector just changed like no cruiser I have ever seen before."

"What ships do we have remaining?" the Odin asked.

"In addition to the flagship, we have two *Wind*-class battleships, the *Hurricane* and the *Sirocco*, and four *Raptor*-class battlecruisers, as well as a few cruisers and destroyers," said the Freyr. "Most of the screening ships did not make it through the minefield. We have more than enough combat power to deal with the Terrans, despite their ability to pull ships from thin air."

"I agree," the Odin said. "Prepare our line of battle. Once we deal with the Terrans, we can finish off the battle station and watch the show on Asgard."

Cockpit, *Shuttle 617*, Onboard TSS *Thermopylae*, November 9, 2021

"**W**e're out of here," Bucket commed. "*I just spoke to the crew of the Gulf's shuttle. They are going to meet us enroute and take you guys to rejoin your unit. The ship they're on is currently in the other universe, and the shuttle has a jump module to take you there.*"

"*Rendezvous will be in about 10 minutes,*" added Jamming.

"*Can you make it nine?*" Night asked.

"*We'll try.*"

Bridge, TSS *Vella Gulf*, HD 69830 System, November 9, 2021

"**D**etach all stealth modules!" the CO ordered.

"Detaching stealth modules," the duty engineer repeated. "Modules detached; we are now visible."

"Understood," the CO replied.

"We're coming up on the firing point," the OSO said.

"Roger," Captain Sheppard replied. "I want you to launch our missiles five seconds early."

"Yes sir," the OSO said. "Launch our missiles five seconds early." He paused, then asked, "Umm, sir, you know the admiral is going to have a stroke if I do that, right?"

"I am well aware of what is likely to happen when we launch our missiles early; however, I am also aware of their new capabilities, which the admiral is not. I would tell him, but I don't think he'd welcome another call from me at the moment."

"Yes sir," the OSO said. "I'll launch five seconds early."

"Those are the modified missiles?" Lieutenant Bradford asked.

"Yes they are," the CO replied. "They're going to work, right?"

"I hope so."

"Do you know how much trouble I'm going to be in if they don't?" the CO asked.

"Yes sir," Lieutenant Bradford said; "I can well imagine." He shuddered noticeably. "They will work." He paused, but couldn't help himself. "I hope."

"Too bad we didn't have any of the time bomb thingies to put on them," the DSO said. "That would have been a nice touch."

"Oh, I think we'll be all right without them. 10 pounds of antimatter will work just fine," the OSO replied. "I wouldn't want to be on the receiving end of it, anyway."

Bridge, TSS *Thermopylae*, HD 69830 System, November 9, 2021

"The Jotunn dreadnought is launching," the DSO noted.

"Weapons free," the CO said. "Defend the ship. I expect they will try to take us out first; let's be ready for them."

"52 missiles inbound from the Jotunn command ship," the DSO said. "All but one are targeted on us. Anti-missile missiles (AMMs) launching." Beads of sweat began appearing on the DSO as the missiles approached.

"Approaching missile range," the OSO noted.

"Understood," Captain Nakamura said. "Coordinate with the *Yamato* to launch in concert with them. We want our missiles to arrive at the same time as theirs. We need to overwhelm their defenses and start getting some hits on their dreadnought."

"Yes sir," the OSO said. "Targeting the dreadnought, designated as contact 'Sierra One.' I am holding the fighters until the *Gulf* launches; their missiles have a shorter range than ours."

"Second salvo of AMMs firing," the DSO said.

"Captain, another 10 torpedoes just hit the *Hood*, sir," the sensor officer said. "She has been destroyed."

"Launching!" the OSO called. "Confirmed launches from the *Yamato*. 66 missiles launched."

"Defensive laser clusters firing," the DSO said, "The *Yamato* is also providing defensive fire support, but we're not going to get them all."

"Notify the crew," Captain Nakamura reminded.

The DSO nodded and switched to the ship-wide comm network. *"Missiles inbound,"* he said. *"All hands brace for shock!"* He lapsed back into his commentary. "Defensive lasers continuing to fire…six, no five missiles remaining…two seconds…"

The ship rocked with the impacts.

"Hit alpha, hit alpha," the duty engineer commed. *"Missile hits fore, midships and aft. Damage crews responding. Radiation alarms at Frames 17 and 213. I repeat, radiation alarms at Frames 17 and 213."*

"What the hell did they hit us with?" Captain Nakamura asked.

"Looks like they used nukes," the DCO said. "Really, really big ones. They overwhelmed the shields in some places, irradiating the ship. Shields at 78%."

"What about our missiles, OSO?" the CO asked.

"They're arriving now," the OSO reported. He paused and then added. "Most were intercepted or absorbed by the shields." He shrugged. "That's okay; it was just the opening round, and we haven't played our hole card yet." He paused again, then said, "Coming up on second launch…Fire!" He pushed a button on his console and commed, *"All fighters launch!"*

Cockpit, *Asp 01*, HD 69830 System, November 9, 2021

"Five minutes to the firing point," Lieutenant Commander Sarah 'Lights' Brighton said.

"Formation still holding pretty well for all of these newbies," her pilot, Lieutenant Carl 'Guns' Simpson, replied. "Some of the Wildcats are all over the place, but most of the Blasters and Pukin' Dogs are where they're supposed to be. Our folks are all in position."

Lights switched her display to show the formation. Like the *Vella Gulf*, each of the new ships was based on an Eldive model and had its own squadron of space fighters attached. Lights didn't know if it was the most efficient use of space onboard the capital ships, but it gave them a certain flexibility lacking in the other races' ships. The Eldive hadn't cared about efficiency. Avian in nature, they put fighters on all of their ships for one simple reason; they liked to fly.

The Terrans had improved on the concept by adding electronic countermeasures to the fighters. Each of the new fighters carried a reflector and a jammer on one of its weapons stations, making the formation appear to be a larger warship…but only when they were in the proper formation. With three squadrons of the new fighters (the *Hood* had launched her fighters before she was destroyed), they appeared to be a cruiser, or would if the SF-4 Wildcat pilots would stay in formation.

"Wildcat 03, Wildcat 08 and Wildcat 10, tighten it up and get into formation!" she commed. If the *Gulf's* fighters had the same gear, the four squadrons could have spoofed the enemy's systems into thinking they were a battlecruiser; more fighters translated into bigger ships. She didn't bemoan the new fighters' absence onboard the *Gulf*; her squadron had a better surprise.

"Targeting in the air!" she commed as she passed the targeting solution to the other fighters. Because the other crews were all relatively 'green,' all the fighters would use her data. That would also let them launch all their missiles at the same time, a trick the Mrowry had taught the *Vella Gulf's* WSOs. All the other crews had to do was push the 'Accept' button, and they'd be set. *"Don't forget to push the Accept button, located on the lower right panel."* She didn't care if they thought

her a mother hen for reminding them; it beat not getting the missiles off on time.

"*ECM off!*" she commed 10 seconds prior to launch. Time for 'the big reveal.' She looked to her right and watched as the reflector was ejected downward from the Blue Blaster fighter there. At least one got it right, she thought.

Three seconds prior. "*Stand by!*"

"*All fighters launch!*" she heard the OSO on the *Thermopylae* comm. "*Fire!*" she ordered, pushing the 'Launch' button. 60 missiles launched from the *Gulf's* 12 fighters; another 140 from the 36 fighters from the *Therm's* air wing. After three long seconds, the remaining four missiles launched from *Wildcat 08*.

"*All missiles launched,*" she commed, shaking her head. Had she ever been that green?

Guns turned the fighter toward their holding point, and Lights smiled as she watched the missiles race to intercept the Jotunn vessel on her display. This time, you bastards, the joke's on you.

Chapter Thirty-Five

Bridge, Jotunn Ship *Naglfar*, HD 69830 System, November 9, 2021

"The repair teams are reporting minor damage in several compartments, but nothing that can't be fixed."

"This shouldn't be too hard, then," the Freyr said. "Those were the missiles from their super dreadnought and remaining battleship. All they have to add to that are their two cruisers, which shouldn't complicate our defenses too much."

"Freyr," the sensor officer said, "their second cruiser is not a cruiser. It was a deception; the contact is really a mass of fighters. They are launching…almost 200 missiles are inbound from that line of bearing. Initial analysis indicates they are all targeted on the *Naglfar*."

The Freyr glanced down at the plot. "The Odin must be protected. Inform the *Sirocco* that it is to move between the missiles and the *Naglfar* to provide anti-missile defense."

The Freyr turned to the Odin. "With that many missiles, some are going to get through to the *Sirocco*, but that has to be all the missiles the fighters have. Even if we lose the *Sirocco*, we have more than enough ships left to destroy the Terrans."

Bridge, TSS *Thermopylae*, HD 69830 System, November 9, 2021

"Those morons on the *Vella Gulf* launched five seconds before everyone else," the OSO said, as the ship rocked from the second wave of Jotunn missiles. "There's only nine of them to start with, and now they're all going to be wasted. Morons."

"Shields down," the DSO said. "Any additional missiles that get through the defenses will reach the ship."

"Then let's try to be perfect from now on," Captain Nakamura said.

"Sir!" the sensor operator cried. "The Jotunn are launching again. Their battleships and battlecruisers launched this time too! Almost 250 missiles inbound!"

"All right, DSO," Captain Nakamura said, "here's where you earn your pay."

"Oh, fuck," the DSO muttered under his breath. His screen was so crowded he couldn't see the individual missiles. Response time was growing shorter too. "Yes sir…AMMs firing." He pushed the release button, and the first 35 defensive missiles went down range.

"One of the battleships is moving to intercept the missiles from the fighters," the OSO said. "Designating the contact as 'Sierra Two.'"

"Understood," Captain Nakamura said. "Continue targeting their dreadnought; put in waypoints so the missiles fly around the battleship if you have to. We have to take the dreadnought out ASAP!"

"Yes sir," the OSO said. "Continue firing at the dreadnought. Next salvo firing *now!*"

"Second salvo of AMMs launching," the DSO said, three seconds later. He hated having to wait, but had to give the offensive missiles some separation so the AMMs didn't get distracted and try to target them instead. They were small enough that it was unlikely, but the weirdest things happened in combat. "First salvo effective," he added; "31 missiles destroyed." *Out of 247, he said silently. Fuck. We're doomed.* Sweat dripped onto the console. "Third round launching."

"Shields down on Sierra Two," the OSO said. "Multiple hits on her. She's venting atmosphere in a number of places and is dropping out of the line of battle."

"Sir!" the sensor operator called. "Some of the fighter missiles missed the battleship and are continuing toward the dreadnought! No, they didn't miss, sir; they're jumping in and out of our universe like the enemy ones!"

"I'm seeing the same thing with the ship-launched missiles from the *Vella Gulf*," the OSO added. "They're jumping out of our universe when the enemy AMMs target them!"

"Lasers firing," the DSO said, still looking at over 150 missiles on his screen. "*All hands brace for shock!*" The lasers weren't going to get them all; there was no way they could. They wouldn't even destroy enough of them to matter. *Dammit, this was going to hurt.*

Bridge, TSS *Vella Gulf*, HD 69830 System, November 9, 2021

"The *Thermopylae* has been destroyed," the DSO said.

"Destroyed?" Captain Sheppard asked.

"How do you destroy something that's three miles long?"

"With about 100 missiles," the DSO replied, "especially if each of them has a 50 megaton warhead."

"Understood," the CO said. "Contact the *Yamato* and—"

"Woohoo!" the OSO yelled, looking up from his display. "Sir, we got them! Most of the new missiles worked! The fighters got at least 43 hits on the dreadnought, and at least 6 of our missiles hit too."

"Good," the CO said. "Damage to the dreadnought?"

"Major damage, sir," the OSO replied. "At least two of our missiles hit the stern; the dreadnought is down to one engine, and the rest of them won't be coming back! We took down the dreadnought's shields with our missiles, and the rest of the fleet's missiles struck home. It looks like the *Therm's* missiles must have had at least 20 pounds of antimatter in them; the bites they took out of the Jotunn ship are *immense!*"

Bridge, Jotunn Ship *Naglfar*, HD 69830 System, November 9, 2021

"Freyr, the shields are down and only one engine is operational," the damage control officer said. "Most of the compartments in the stern are wrecked. If we try to accelerate too quickly, we may very well overstress the frame and snap the ship in half. I don't know what was in those missiles, but the ship is no longer operational. Power is out across most of the ship, and we no longer have missile launch capability."

"Odin, I am receiving a call from the Aesir battle station," the communications officer said. "The Thor wants to know if we surrender."

"Tell him to go to hell," the Odin said. He turned to the Freyr. "Do we have the ability to steer the ship?"

"Yes, Odin. It is limited, but we could still escape."

"Escape? Escape is for the weak. The prophecies said we would die in this battle, and die we shall, if it will help us take back our homeland. I had hoped to avoid this outcome, but it is impossible to avoid your destiny. Steer toward the battle station and give the ship as much power as it can handle. If I have to die to fulfill the prophecies, then by the gods, so does their Thor."

Chapter Thirty-Six

Bridge, TSS *Vella Gulf*, HD 69830 System, November 9, 2021

"Sir, we have a call from the *Yamato*."

"On screen."

The image of an Indian man appeared on the screen. "Captain Sheppard, I am Captain Patel; I do not believe we have met. I am senior and am taking over command of the fleet, or what is left. If you have the ability to jump universes, use it. Do whatever you can to cover our retreat. There is nothing further to be gained here. Patel out." The screen went blank as the transmission ended.

"Sir, the *Yamato* is flipping over to decelerate," the helmsman said. "Do you want me to match them?"

"No," Captain Sheppard said. "There is still the Jotunn battleship and all of the battlecruisers. I think we'll stay a bit longer to ensure the *Yamato* gets away. Shift fire to the other Jotunn battleship and *fire*."

"Firing at the undamaged Jotunn battleship, designated as Sierra Three," the OSO said.

"The Jotunn dreadnought is turning toward the battle station," Steropes said. "I believe they intend to ram."

"Is there anything we can do to stop it?" the CO asked.

"No sir," Steropes replied. "Even if we shot out their last motor, their momentum would still take them into the battle station."

"Then let's concentrate on what we can do. Keep firing at the other battleship. Helm, be prepared to jump to the other universe when they shoot at us. While we're in the other universe, make a course change so we don't come out where they expect."

"Aye aye, sir."

"OSO," the CO continued, "Work over the battleship until we knock down its shields, then hit it a few more times. After it's bloody, pick a battlecruiser and start on it. We don't have enough missiles to kill all of them, but if we make it painful enough for them to stay, maybe they'll leave."

"Aye aye, sir," the OSO replied. "What about the other enemy?"

"Hopefully, when the Jotunn leave, they'll take the others with them. Besides, we'd just be wasting missiles shooting at them that would be better spent on the Jotunn ships we know we can hit. How many more missiles do we have that can jump?"

"Only 18 sir."

"Four per ship, then; do what you can."

"Captain Sheppard, the *Yamato* is under attack by the Jotunn's ally," Steropes said.

"Say a prayer for them then," the CO said; "it's all we can do right now. They ran for it; hopefully, they'll make it out. We're too far away to help them. They're on their own."

Task Force O'Leary, Alien Ship, HD 69830 System, November 9, 2021

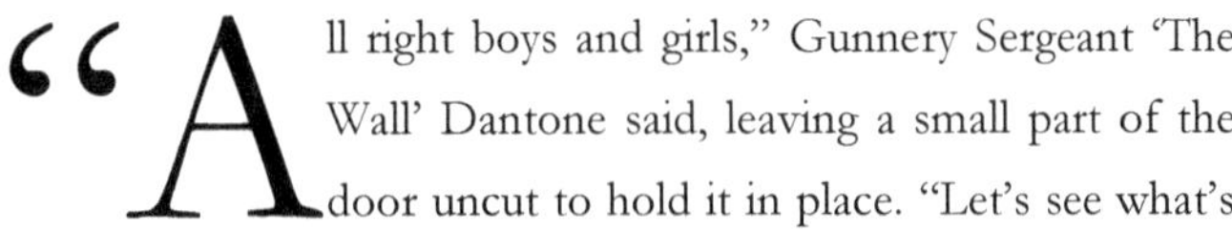

"All right boys and girls," Gunnery Sergeant 'The Wall' Dantone said, leaving a small part of the door uncut to hold it in place. "Let's see what's behind Door Number One." The cyborg retracted his cutting laser and reached back over his shoulder to pull out his Hooolong pulse rifle. As it spun up to speed, he leaned back and kicked the door in…right into the face of the creature waiting for them.

The creature's weapon was jarred out of its claws as it fired, sending a blast of light into the overhead.

Already leveled and ready, The Wall's pulse rifle fired 30 rounds into the alien, striking it in the chest of the 'human' half of the creature and nearly severing it. The creature crashed to the floor where it lay kicking. It emitted a high pitched shrieking noise that left goose bumps on some of the humans in the group until The Wall strode over and fired a three round burst into its head.

The legs kicked a few more times then went still.

"Fuck me," Sergeant Marcus 'Spud' Murphy said, looking up at the ceiling. "That weapon had some punch. It melted a hole six inches deep into the overhead, and it's metal." He watched another drop of liquid metal fall from the ceiling. It sizzled when it hit the deck. "Just think what that would do to you."

"Any idea what that was, Wall?" Lieutenant O'Leary asked. "You had the best view."

"No idea, sir," The Wall said. "Some sort of directed-energy weapon more powerful than our lasers, at least up close. Maybe a particle-beam weapon of some sort; I don't know. All I know is I *don't* want to get hit with one."

"No shit," Spud said. "And just think what it would do to us poor biologicals."

"*Lieutenant Commander Hobbs, we just found our first living alien,*" Lieutenant O'Leary commed. "*They can take a lot of hits before they go down.*

Be advised, they also have some sort of particle-beam weapon that can melt metal. Recommend extreme caution."

"Aside from not opening any of the doors, I don't think we can be any more cautious," Calvin said. *"Keep looking for the bridge or engineering."*

Task Force Calvin, Alien Ship, HD 69830 System, November 9, 2021

"All right, you heard Lieutenant O'Leary," Calvin said. *"Watch out for their weapons."*

"Always good advice," Gunnery Sergeant Stasik said.

"What did he say they had?" Corporal Sam 'Mental' Ward asked.

"Particle-beam weapons," Gunny Stasik replied. *"It's a weapon that shoots a high-energy beam of atomic or subatomic particles. The particles have massive amounts of kinetic energy and cause catastrophic superheating when they hit you. Aside from disrupting your atomic or molecular structure, it will also hurt like hell and probably kill you, depending on where it hits. Just try not to get shot, all right?"*

"You got it, Gunny," Mental replied.

Cockpit, *Shuttle 617*, HD 69830 System, November 9, 2021

"We've got them," Shuttle 02's WSO, Lieutenant Thomas 'Mays' Yilmaz, said. *"Proceeding on mission."*

"Copy that," Jamming said as the other shuttle jumped to the Jinn Universe. The transfer of the two soldiers to the other shuttle had

gone smoothly and quickly. He looked across the cockpit. "So, where do you want to go?"

"Well, let's see," Bucket said. "We could take our unarmed and mostly unarmored shuttle into the middle of a major battle to link back up with the *Gulf*, or we could find somewhere else to sit on the sidelines, *out of the way*, and watch. Maybe even pray that we've got a ship to recover on when it's over. I think I'd rather watch at the moment than try to recover onboard the *Vella Gulf* in the middle of a battle. How about you?"

"Works for me." Motion on his tactical plot caught his peripheral vision. "Oh, shit! The enemy vessel just jumped back! Come right! *Max power!*"

Cockpit, *Shuttle 02*, Anti-HD 69830 System, November 9, 2021

"**D**umbass aliens," Mays said. "Boy, they can't make this easy, can they? They just jumped back to our universe."

"What the hell are they doing?" his pilot, Lieutenant Miguel 'Ghost' Carvalho, asked.

"Probably trying to make it difficult for additional forces to land on their ship, I imagine," Mays replied. "Here we go, jumping back." He threw the switch and everything flashed as they jumped.

"Oh, shit!" Mays said. "The other shuttle is still here! The enemy ship is firing!"

"They don't have jump or stealth, do they?"

"No, dammit, they don't. Either of them. They're sitting ducks…Aw, fuck. *Shuttle 617* has been destroyed."

Chapter Thirty-Seven

Bridge, TSS *Vella Gulf*, HD 69830 System, November 9, 2021

"That's the last of our missiles," the OSO said. "That's all I've got, unless you want us to close to graser range." His tone indicated he didn't think that was a very good idea.

What a waste, thought Captain Sheppard as he looked at his tactical plot. The three biggest ships in the Terran fleet had been destroyed. The Jotunn had also lost three of their capital ships, including their second battleship when a lucky strike from the *Vella Gulf* hit the armory and the ship detonated. It was impossible to tell how many ships the Aesir had lost from the piles of wreckage floating through local space; it had to be at least 10, as well as their battle station. The tangled remains of the station and the Jotunn dreadnought weren't good for anything except scrap for the replicators.

And now he was out of missiles. He agreed with the OSO; he had no intention of mixing it up with four ships larger than his own, even if they were all damaged. The Jotunn's allies hadn't been seen since they destroyed the *Yamato*, but he expected them to pop up at any moment to complicate his life. All he had to fight them with were his grasers, which meant running them down across two universes. That should be fun.

And the fighters? He was at a loss for what to do with all of the fighters.

The battle had gone on for over 24 hours now, and he was dead tired. His decisions were starting to be suspect…and now he was so tired that he had begun talking to himself.

What else could go wrong?

"Sir, one of the Jotunn battlecruisers is calling," said the communications officer. "It's the *Soaring Eagle.*"

Never ask what else can go wrong, thought Captain Sheppard. Never. "On screen."

The image of the Jotunn commander filled the screen.

"I am Fenrir, son of Loki, and captain of the Jotunn ship *Soaring Eagle*," said the giant.

"I know," Captain Sheppard said, "We met once before."

"We did? You puny ones all look alike to me." Fenrir shrugged. "We seem to be at an impasse. All of our leaders have been killed, and we are out of missiles. Judging from the fact you haven't fired at us recently, you are out of missiles, as well. I doubt you want to bring your insignificant vessel close enough for us to destroy it, and since you can jump to the other universe, we are unable to make you fight us if you are too afraid to do so. I also haven't heard from our allies in a while, but they do not seem to be in a hurry to fight you, any more than you want to fight us."

"That appears to be a pretty accurate assessment of the situation," Captain Sheppard replied. "What do you suggest we do about it?"

"When I arrived here, I believed this would be the conclusion of Ragnarok; however, Asgard has not been drowned in water as it should have been by now. I suspect you had something to do with that." He paused, looking for confirmation, but Captain Sheppard just looked at him blankly, neither confirming nor denying.

"Everything else occurred as forecast, but without the drowning of the world, this is not Ragnarok. I must return to my world to form a new council to determine what this means for the prophecy. We will also rearm, and then we will return to finish the conquest."

He paused and glared at Captain Sheppard. "Make no mistake," Fenrir continued, "Ragnarok is *not* over, and we *will* return to take back what is rightfully ours. You have only postponed what has been forecast, not prevented it."

"Yeah, well, I'm kind of tired, so I'll take 'postponed' for now," Captain Sheppard replied. "Have a nice tribal council, or whatever it is you're planning on doing. If you think about it, roast a marshmallow over the fire for me. We'll be waiting for you when you get back."

"You would be better served to learn manners while I am gone," Fenrir replied, "or I will pull your disrespectful tongue from your mouth when I return and roast *that* over an open fire."

"Yeah, okay, buh bye," Captain Sheppard said. He started to terminate the link, but then another thought came to him. "Hey, when you come back, are you going to bring more of your allies? I'm looking forward to a rematch with them."

"The Shaitans?" asked Fenrir. "I do not think you want to make them any angrier at you than you already have. They neither forgive, nor forget. You have already destroyed one of their ships; for that, your entire civilization will pay. They will be coming for you, Terran, and they will be coming for you in greater numbers than you will be able to turn away. You will wish you had died here today before they are through with you. Their high lord has decreed that your civilization will be destroyed for your insolence in attacking his forces."

"As I remember it," Captain Sheppard said, "they attacked us, but I doubt that's important any more. I will say one thing for them, at least they are better fighters than you."

Fenrir's face went scarlet, and he started to stutter a reply, but Captain Sheppard terminated the connection before he could say anything coherent.

"Was it really wise to antagonize him like that?" Steropes asked.

"Probably not," the CO said, "but honestly, I'm too tired to care. Besides, at least we now have a name to put on their allies."

"Speaking of their allies, the other enemy ships just appeared," the DSO said. "They are at the stargate and it looks like they're leaving."

"That is interesting," Steropes said. "In order for them to already be at the stargate, they must have decided to leave some time ago, certainly well before the Jotunn decided *they* were leaving."

"What do you suppose that means?" the CO asked.

"Unknown," Steropes replied. "One thing that can be inferred is that the Jotunn are not in charge of their allies; if anything, it is a loose alliance. It could also be possible the Jotunn are subordinate to the Shaitans."

"What if the Jotunn told them to leave a while ago, and only told us now?" the OSO asked.

"That is possible also, I guess," Steropes said. "It seems the nature of their alliance will have to remain a mystery for now."

"It would seem so," Captain Sheppard said. "Okay, on to the next mystery. Let's go find our troopers."

Task Force Calvin, Alien Ship, HD 69830 System, November 9, 2021

"*If the dumbass aliens would quit jumping back and forth,*" Mays commed, "*it would make coming to get you a lot easier.*"

"*Understood,*" Calvin replied. "*We're trying to find the bridge or engineering…something to get them to stop.*"

"*As soon as you do, we'll be right there for extraction. We wouldn't mind if you hurried, either, sir; being in stealth this long is eating our fuel pretty quickly. If we don't get you soon, we won't be able to make it back to the* Vella Gulf."

"*Yeah, I know. We're doing what we can.*"

Everything flashed as the ship jumped back to the Jinn Universe.

"This is really starting to piss me off," Calvin said.

"Hey, sir," Gunnery Sergeant Jerry 'Wolf' Stasik said. "We've checked all of the doors on this passageway except the one on the end. They all look like living spaces, or what I think living spaces might look like for cowtaurs."

"Cowtaurs?" Calvin asked.

"Yeah, the guys said the aliens looked like a cross between a cow and a centaur, or whatever that half-man/half-horse thing was. Cowtaur."

"Got it," Calvin said. "All right, let's see what's behind the last door. It's gotta lead somewhere."

"You heard the man, Ducky," Wolf said. "Knock it down."

"Sure thing, Gunny," Sergeant Declan 'Ducky' Jones replied. The cyborg finished his cut and took five steps back from the door while he strapped his rifle to his back. "Here goes." He lowered his shoulder and charged the door, pushing off as he slammed into it. The remaining portion holding the door attached was ripped apart, and

Ducky and the door flew through the air, crashing into a group of three Shaitans waiting for them.

Behind the door was a circular ramp that descended into the ship, curving to the right as it circled back on itself. The Shaitans waited at the curve, and the door cut the legs out from under one of the cowtaurs, while Ducky crashed into another, knocking it down. A third Shaitan, partially around the bend in the ramp, began firing and was met by answering lasers from several of the Terrans and Big Sky's Mrowry autocannon. It dropped after firing five rounds.

Ducky rolled and came eye-to-eye with the eyestalks of the Shaitan he had knocked down. Without thinking, he reached up and grabbed them in one of his armored hands and squeezed. A horrible scream filled the space as the eyes exploded in his hand, and the cowtaur began kicking out in every direction. Ducky released the remains of the eyestalks and drew his laser pistol, firing it repeatedly into the creature's head.

The Shaitan stilled, and the Terrans killed the third alien as it started to rise.

"Ouch," Sergeant Richard 'Shipwreck' Shipley said into the silence that followed. He looked down at the hole through his chest, then fell forward onto his knees and then his face. Sergeant Simon Douglas, the squad's medic, rushed over, but Calvin could tell from the size and placement of the hole that the medic wasn't going to be able to help.

"We're about to open the door at the end of the corridor," Lieutenant O'Leary commed.

"We just opened ours," Calvin replied. *"Ours goes to a ramp that leads down into the ship. Beware, several of the Shaitans were waiting for us."*

Task Force O'Leary, Alien Ship, Anti-HD 69830 System, Unknown Date

"*There may be a ramp behind the door,*" Lieutenant O'Leary commed on the squad's network. "*Be ready; the skipper said there was a welcoming party behind their door.*" Several troopers adjusted their weapons. "*Okay, Chaos, open 'er up.*"

"*You got it, LT,*" Sergeant Jacob 'Chaos' Braig said. The cyborg cycled both of his shotguns to full auto, then said, "*Here we go.*" He leaned back and kicked the door open. Already weakened with a plasma torch, the door crashed backward onto a circular ramp with a resounding '*boom!*'" The ramp turned counterclockwise as it descended, and the door slid a quarter turn down the ramp.

The area was empty.

Keeping the shotguns ready for close quarters work, the cyborg walked onto the ramp and looked into the center of the well. "*Looks like an opening halfway around,*" he commed.

"*Roger, that,*" Lieutenant O'Leary said. "*You've got point. Let's find out where this goes.*"

Chaos worked his way around the ramp with the rest of the squad close behind. He reached the opening and pulled a small mirror from a pocket.

"*Big, tough cyborg's afraid to look around the corner himself?*" Corporal Jonny 'Dark' Minion asked.

"*Big, tough cyborg was a biological once,*" replied Chaos, "*and he remembers what it was like to get shot to shit. If you'd rather look, go ahead.*"

"*Nah, that's all right. Go ahead and use your mirror.*"

"*If you insist,*" Chaos replied. He attached it to the end of his middle finger and eased it into the passageway. Before he could turn it to see down the hall, a blast of plasma took off the mirror and the last inch of his finger. "*Bitch!*"

"*Spud, throw some grenades in there and soften them up,*" Lieutenant O'Leary ordered.

"*Sure thing,*" Sergeant Marcus 'Spud' Murphy said. He adjusted his trident and fired a string of double strength grenades into the opening.

"*That ought to do it,*" Chaos said. He jumped forward into the opening.

"*Ziiiiiip-PEW! Ziiiiiip-PEW! Ziiiiiip-PEW!*" Plasma bursts struck him in the head and chest, and he fell backward onto the ramp, the hole in his head still smoking.

"Bastards!" Corporal Calvin 'Bossman' Davis shouted. He dove into the opening, firing before he hit the floor. He continued firing down the passageway as several plasma bolts went over his head. "*Ro—*" he commed, as two plasma bolts went through his head. A third struck his rifle, shattering it.

Sergeant Anne 'Fox' Stasik dove across the gap, several plasma rounds narrowly missing her as she crashed to the ground on the other side. "*There are three of their robots side-by-side in the passageway,*" she commed as she came to rest. "*They look bigger than the ones we fought in the Jinn Universe.*"

"*Understood,*" Lieutenant O'Leary said. He switched to the command network. "*We've got several robots blocking our path. They're armed with plasma weapons and have already killed two of my squad.*"

"*Is there any way to get around them?*" Calvin asked.

"*We may be able to get by them, but they may also be guarding where we need to go. Also, if we bypass them, they could pin us down somewhere. Their weapons are extremely powerful; I don't want them behind me.*"

"Roger that. We haven't run into any of them yet. Why don't you hold your position and maybe we can find a way to take them from behind."

"Okay, I will hold here. O'Leary out." He switched to the squad's network. *"Everyone just sit tight. The CO is going to try to hit them from behind."*

"Lieutenant!" Corporal 'Bill' Obillossilllolis screamed. *"I have movement from behind us. Cowtaurs behind us!"* O'Leary could hear the Kuji firing his rifle faster than what it was rated for.

"I'm on it," Gunnery Sergeant Dantone commed. *"Fire Team Two with me! Jones, you're on the left. Rozhkov, you're right. I've got the middle."*

Lieutenant O'Leary could hear antimatter blasts and lasers firing from above him, then the distinctive sound of a Hooolong pulse rifle on full automatic.

"We may need to do something about the robots," Gunny Dantone commed 30 seconds later. *"We've got an ass load of cowtaurs coming from behind us. Looks like they've gone outside the ship and are coming in through the entrance we made."* There was a pause, then he added, *"Fuck. These have some sort of combat suit on, and they are taking even more firepower to bring down. Look out!"* Another blast of pulse rifle. *"Lieutenant, we'll need to bypass the robots; we're not going to be able to hold them here for long."*

"I've got an idea," Spud said.

"Have I ever told you I hate it when you have ideas?" Lieutenant O'Leary asked. *"Is this something likely to get you killed?"*

"I hope not," Spud commed, dialing up the setting on his trident. *"I'm going to try to bounce some antimatter grenades off the wall behind the robots so that it hits them in their softer spots. Wish me luck."*

He dove into the passageway with his trident at the ready, coming to rest against Corporal Davis. He was able to fire three times before one of the plasma rounds struck him in the face.

Task Force Calvin, Alien Ship, Anti-HD 69830 System, Unknown Date

"*T*he good news is we're past the robots,*" Lieutenant O'Leary commed. "*The bad news is there are cowtaurs coming in from behind us in large numbers. Watch your back, sir!*"

"*Yeah, we've got them here too,*" Calvin said. "*Keep pushing on, and we're bound to get somewhere important. We're going to start at the bottom of the ramp and work our way up. Try to find out whatever it is that the robots were guarding.*"

"*Wilco, sir; we're on it.*"

Calvin switched to the squad's network. "*Let's go down to the bottom and start there. The other squad is going to start on the top.*"

"*Sir, Gunner's down with a plasma bolt through the chest.*" Calvin watched as Sergeant Milan Vranjesevic's life signs went to zero. Ironic, Calvin thought. The Serb had survived NATO bombings early in his Army career, only to be killed by a cowtaur in a system he had probably never heard of.

"*Leave him,*" Calvin commed. "*If we don't hurry up and find a way to stop this ship from jumping back and forth, we're not getting off it.*"

"*Sir, I'm at the bottom of the ramp, five turns down,*" commed Staff Sergeant Alka Zoromski. "*Looks like we got robots in the passageway here too. Sal's dead.*" It had to happen sometime, Calvin thought. Corporal 'Sal' Sallissollosiss was the unit's first Kuji fatality.

"*Is there any way to get some antimatter behind them?*" Calvin asked. "*That was how the other squad got past their robots.*"

"*It's going to be difficult, sir,*" replied Staff Sergeant Gurney. "*The ramp ends in the passageway where the robots are, and it's going to be darned difficult to fire anything down the corridor without giving them the chance to shoot back at us. Let me see what I can do."*

"*Hang on, Staff Sergeant,*" Calvin commed. "*Wait until I get there.*" He hurried around the last two turns of the ramp. "*Oh, crap,*" he said, arriving at the Big Gurn's position. "*That sucks.*" There was no way to get an angle on the robots without the robots being able to shoot first.

"*I've got an idea,*" said Sergeant Declan 'Ducky' Jones. "*What if I drop down the center of the ramp well. They'll be focused on the ramp, and I may be able to get off a few shots before they reorient on me. Gurn can come down the ramp right after, and while they're shooting at me, he can fire off a few rounds too.*"

"*You're going to be pretty exposed there,*" noted Calvin.

"*Not really,*" said Ducky. "*I think I can fire, then dive under the ramp. As long as they aren't too fast, it could work.*"

"*Whatever you're doing sir, you're going to need to do it faster,*" said Wolf, who was rear guard. "*They must have emptied the ship to get this many cowtaurs behind us, but there's a whole pile of them back here.*"

Calvin looked into Ducky's eyes. "*Yes sir. I can do it.*"

"*It's a good plan,*" said the Big Gurn. "*We can do this.*"

"*Okay,*" Calvin said. "*Do it.*"

"*Let me know when you're ready,*" said Ducky. The cyborg put a leg over the railing, his mortar at the ready.

The Big Gurn moved to where he was just out of sight. "*Ready.*"

"*Here we go,*" said Ducky. He jumped.

Chapter Thirty-Eight

Task Force O'Leary, Alien Ship, Anti-HD 69830 System, Unknown Date

*"T*here only be one door on the left side of the passage-way,"* Sergeant Margaret 'Witch' Andrews said, *"but there be five doors on the right side."*

"Any idea what's behind them?" Lieutenant O'Leary asked.

"No mon, I mean, no sir," Witch said, *"but whatever's behind the single door must be pretty big. I vote for that one."*

"All right, Dantone, get up here and cut through the single door," Lieutenant O'Leary ordered. *"Wraith, you've got rear guard."*

"I'm on it, Lieutenant," Staff Sergeant Park Ji-woo replied.

Task Force Calvin, Alien Ship, Anti-HD 69830 System, Unknown Date

Ducky hit the ground and stood up. Knowing he didn't have time for his brace to extend, he leaned into the shot and fired a high explosive round. The force of the launch drove him back several feet; the force of the blast pushed him back even further as the mortar reloaded. He leaned into the shot and fired again. Silver thermite.

The pyrotechnics of the round detonating was the most beautiful thing he had ever seen. The silver sprayed everywhere in the passageway, reacting with everything it touched, turning it into radioactive slag.

It was also the last thing he ever saw, as the remaining robot reoriented on the cyborg and fired, the plasma bolt going completely through his head, killing him instantly.

The Big Gurn ran down the ramp as Ducky fired his first round. As he aimed his trident, the world exploded in yellows and silvers as Ducky's second round detonated, and he was hurtled backward off his feet to slam into the unyielding surface of the ramp. Stunned, he watched in horror as the robot on the right turned to fire at Ducky. Having miraculously avoided the spray of silver thermite, the robot shot Ducky in the face with the first shot and then twice more as the cyborg collapsed.

Having finished with the cyborg, the robot turned back toward the Big Gurn. Gurney threw himself to the side as it fired, and its first shot missed. Up against the ramp, the Big Gurn had nowhere else to go, so he aimed his trident and fired. The round struck behind the robot and detonated, destroying the robot…just milliseconds after it killed the Big Gurn.

Task Force O'Leary, Alien Ship, Anti-HD 69830 System, Unknown Date

"*H*ere goes the door, Lieutenant*,*" Gunny Dantone said. "*Fire Team Two, ready on support.*" He looked around and all were sighted down the barrels of their weapons. "*Now!*" He kicked the door, and it fell inward.

The heavy door slammed down with a clatter.

"*Is this what I think it is?*" Gunny Dantone asked.

"*Yeah, it is,*" Lieutenant O'Leary said.

"*Then where are all the people, or creatures, or whatever?*" Gunny Dantone asked.

"*Yeah, dude,*" Sergeant Jamal Gordon added, "*like, where are all the aliens?*"

Task Force Calvin, Alien Ship, Anti-HD 69830 System, Unknown Date

"*T*wo doors, both sides of the passageway,*" Wolf reported. "*All four of them are damaged by the silver thermite round Ducky used. Looks like some of that shit has gone through the floor…I hope there isn't anything too valuable down there.*"

"*Pick one and start cutting,*" Calvin said.

"*I'll start on one of the damaged ones, if you don't mind, sir,*" replied Big Sky. "*I've probably got enough juice left for one more door after that.*"

"*Go ahead,*" Calvin said. "*That will probably be faster—*"

The ship rocked as something below them exploded.

Chapter Thirty-Nine

Task Force O'Leary, Alien Ship, Anti-HD 69830 System, Unknown Date

"*What the hell was that?*" Gunny Dantone asked as the ship shuddered noticeably.

"*No idea,*" Lieutenant O'Leary replied. "*The CO must be having fun somewhere.*" He looked around the open chamber. "*I'm more worried about why the damn bridge is empty. I mean, this has* got *to be the bridge, right?*"

"*You've spent more time on them than I have,*" Gunny Dantone replied, "*but it sure looks like all of the ones you see in the movies. Big console in the middle for the CO, lots of stations and monitors and shit on the sides. Except all of these are blank.*"

"*Not 'dis one,*" Witch said, "*and I got me a bad feelin' about what it be doin' mon.*"

Lieutenant O'Leary hurried over to where Witch was standing, and she pointed at one of the monitors in the central console. The monitor had a single symbol on it. After three seconds, it switched to another symbol. After another three seconds, it switched again.

"*Yeah, I've got that same bad feeling,*" Lieutenant O'Leary said. He switched to the command net. "*Hey, boss, I think we found the bridge,*" he commed.

"*Great!*" Calvin replied.

"Not great," Lieutenant O'Leary replied. *"The bridge is deserted, and it looks like there is some sort of countdown running. You don't suppose they'd blow up their ship, would they?"*

"To keep the technology out of our hands? Yeah, they might well do that."

"Yeah, well, in that case, we better get the hell out of here because this thing is going to blow."

The ship shuddered again.

"We might need to leave, anyway," Calvin replied. *"Ducky used a silver thermite round and slagged a bunch of shit down here. Some of it went through the floor, and it's reacting badly with whatever's underneath us. Trash the bridge and get topside; we'll meet you there!"*

"See you there," O'Leary said. He switched to the squad's net. *"Set some explosives and let's get the hell out of here! The ship is going to blow!"*

Task Force Calvin, Alien Ship, Anti-HD 69830 System, Unknown Date

*"F*orget the door,"* Calvin commed. *"We're leaving!"*

"I don't know where you're planning to go, but I wouldn't recommend 'back,'" Staff Sergeant Zoromski commed. *"There's a bunch of them back here. Better continue in that direction and find another ramp up."*

"All right, Wolf," Calvin said.

"I heard him," Gunnery Sergeant Stasik replied before Calvin could complete the sentence. *"Going forward."*

"Good man."

"Hey, sir, I'm through the door," Big Sky said. *"Looks like an engine room."*

"Awesome," Calvin said. *"Set some charges quickly if you've got them. If not, shoot it up and let's get the hell out of here."* The cyborg was obviously out of explosives as the ripping sound of a Mrowry autocannon on full auto reverberated through the hallway.

"I'm at the end of the hallway," Wolf reported. *"Looks like the door opens out. I think a cyborg could knock this one down without having to burn through it."*

"On it," Big Sky said.

The autocannon firing stopped, and the cyborg clomped past Calvin in the passageway a couple of seconds later. "A cyborg's work is never done," Big Sky said in passing. He accelerated as he approached the end of the hallway, lowered his shoulder and smashed through the door. A ramp going up awaited behind it.

"Quickly! Up the ramp!" Calvin ordered. He switched to the squadron net. *"Ghost, Mays; either of you up?"*

"Yes sir," said *Shuttle 02's* WSO, Lieutenant Thomas 'Mays' Yilmaz. *"We're standing by."*

"We're about 200 yards away from the ship," added his pilot, Lieutenant Miguel 'Ghost' Carvalho. *"There were some extraterrestrials on the side of the ship when we got here, but they've all gone back inside. We can swoop in whenever you're ready for extraction."*

"Roger that," Calvin replied. *"We're on our way out for immediate evac. It looks like they've set the ship to self-destruct."*

"Well then, hurry on out, sir," said Mays. *"We'll be waiting."*

"We're hurrying. Calvin out."

Cargo Bay, *Shuttle 02*, Anti-HD 69830 System, November 9, 2021

"*H*ey, Mays," Night commed. "*You can see the alien ship?*"

"*Yeah, we're alongside.*"

"*And there aren't any aliens?*"

"*No; they all went back inside.*"

"*Then why the hell are we sitting out here? Do me a favor and* get us the fuck over to it! *People are dying over there, and Yokaze and I can help!*"

"*You want us to land now? Before the Skipper is ready?*"

"*I want you to land* right fucking now, *or I will come up there and land this fucking tub myself.*"

"*Well, why didn't you say so? We'll have you there in 30 seconds.*"

"*About damn time!*"

Task Force O'Leary, Alien Ship, Anti-HD 69830 System, Unknown Date

"*I* think I've got the skipper's group coming from beneath us on the ramp," Staff Sergeant Park 'Wraith' Ji-woo commed. "*Sounds like a damn cyborg's stomping up the ramp, anyway.*"

Wonderful, Lieutenant O'Leary thought. At least they didn't have to go looking for them. "*Ground Force, be advised we're above you at the top of the ramp,*" he commed. "*Space Force, don't shoot them as we link up.*"

Within seconds, O'Leary heard the heavy footfalls of the cyborg, too, and then the Ground Force reached the top of the ramp. "*Good to see you, sir,*" O'Leary said as Calvin approached. "*We hold one of the openings to the roof and will start falling back to the shuttle. It's going to be a bit dicey for the last couple of folks out; we're holding off a bunch of them on this level. Since we're already in place, why don't you leave me Big Sky and take your squad to the shuttle?"*

"Sounds good," Calvin said. *"Ground Force, to the shuttle. Big Sky, you're with the Space Force for covering fire."*

"Dark's down," Staff Sergeant Jones said as several explosions were heard. *"We need a medic and a little help down the passageway. They've got some kind of explosives launcher."*

"Lucky, go check out Dark," O'Leary pointed down the passageway. *"Big Sky, get them out of there,* now!"

Fire Team Two, Alien Ship, Anti-HD 69830 System, Unknown Date

"*Good to see you,"* Staff Sergeant Jones said as Big Sky and the medic arrived. The former CIA operative pointed at the ramp, just visible through the smoke. *"Sky, I need you to keep them off us while we pull back, and then join us on the run. Got it?"*

"Sure thing, Staff Sergeant," the cyborg said. He took cover in a doorway and fired at movement on the ramp. Several blasts of plasma erupted from the ramp, narrowly missing him. "Damn," he said as he reflexively jerked backward out of the line of fire.

"No shit," Staff Sergeant Jones said. "Watch out for the arrows. They blow up. That's what got Corporal Minion."

"He's dead," the squad's medic, Corporal Shaun 'Lucky' Evertson, said.

"Fuck," said Staff Sergeant Jones. "Jonny was a pain in the ass, but he was still one of ours." He shook his head. *"Fire Team Two, fall back to the shuttle. Lucky, you too. Big Sky will cover us and then fall back.*" He stepped up behind the cyborg and slapped him on the shoulder. "Got it, Sky?"

"Yeah, hurry it up," the cyborg replied. "I'm starting to run low on ammo."

"Okay, I'm gone. Give me three seconds, then follow me." Big Sky fired several rounds into the ramp well to cover Staff Sergeant Jones' departure, then threw his two remaining grenades. As the first one detonated, he turned and ran down the passageway after Staff Sergeant Jones.

He had only taken three steps when a plasma bolt hit him in the back of the right leg.

The servo mechanisms failed, and his leg went out from under him. Big Sky crashed to the floor, his momentum slamming him into the bulkhead on the right side of the passageway. He looked down at his knee and saw a two-inch hole through the section where his control wires ran. Crap. That wasn't going to be fixable.

"*I'm hit and down,*" he commed. "*My right leg is inop; I'm going to need assistance to get out.*"

"*On my way,*" Gunny Dantone replied, the only remaining member of the team able to lift the cyborg.

"*Lucky, go take a look, too,*" Lieutenant O'Leary ordered.

Big Sky sat up and began pushing himself backwards down the hall, firing a couple of rounds every few seconds to keep the Shai-tans' heads down. He had covered nearly half the distance when Dantone arrived, followed immediately by the medic.

"What's up?" asked Dantone, firing at movement from the stairwell. A blast of plasma burned past his head in reply. "Oh? You want to play?" he asked. He dropped his pulse rifle, allowing it to hang from the magazine on his back, and unhooked his trident. Selecting the 50 nanogram setting on the antimatter projector, he fired a single round into the ramp well. The size of a small bomb, the antimatter round destroyed the upper section of the ramp, with the shockwave from the explosion pushing them several feet down the passageway. "That ought to keep their heads down," he added.

"Can you do anything?" Big Sky asked the medic as he continued pushing himself down the passageway.

"I don't know what you expect me to do," Lucky said. "I'm a corpsman, not a damned auto mechanic. I didn't even *take* shop in high school."

"Well, let's get him up and out of here before they come back," Dantone said. He clipped his trident to his back and reached down with both hands to lift Big Sky up onto his good leg. "I've got him," Dantone said; "you can head up to the shuttle."

"No," the medic said. "You don't have anyone to cover you. I'll stay, just get going."

Big Sky put his right arm over Dantone's shoulders and the cyborgs began awkwardly walking down the passageway to where Wolf waited for them, firing in the opposite direction. "Hurry!" he called; "lots of them coming from this way."

"No shit," Lucky muttered. He ran forward to join Wolf, firing furiously at the approaching cowtaurs.

"You need to eat a salad," said Dantone, grunting for effect as he boosted Big Sky up to the overhead exit. "Heavy fuck."

"You need—" Big Sky said. Several plasma rounds cut off the rest of what he was going to say, along with most of his head, and the cyborg fell over backward, overbalancing Dantone. Both cyborgs crashed to the floor.

"Shit," said Wolf, diving out of the way from a hail of plasma. He looked back to see Lucky collapse, with several holes through his chest. Wolf knew he was screwed. He couldn't get up without getting shot; there were too many of them coming. He continued firing, the counter on his battery rapidly approaching zero. He hoped the stupid cowtaurs would at least give him a chance to swap out the battery…although the next one would be his last.

An enormous cowtaur, bigger than any he had seen before, emerged from the smoke. It had to be an important one; it had a sash running across its upper half filled with shiny emblems. It also carried a bigger gun than anything even the cyborgs carried.

Wolf sighted on the creature's head and pulled the trigger. A weak bolt fired; the end of the battery. The laser bolt only succeeded in singing the Shaitan's fur, and the cowtaur roared. Its weapon came down to point at Wolf as he struggled feverishly to change out the battery; Wolf knew he didn't have enough time.

Wolf was close enough to see the creature's claw start to tighten on the firing mechanism and gathered himself to dive out of the way.

The creature exploded as Night's first antimatter round struck it in its bovine chest, painting the passageway with its purple blood. Night landed in front of Wolf and continued firing his trident into the mass of aliens until nothing in the corridor moved.

Wolf slammed in the new battery and searched for additional targets, but all that remained were pieces of aliens; there wasn't a whole one visible. *"Glad you could join us,"* he commed. *"Thanks."*

"I couldn't let you guys have all the fun," Night replied. *"Now let's get the hell out of here before this damn ship explodes."*

"Yes sir!"

Cargo Bay, *Shuttle 02*, Anti-HD 69830 System, November 9, 2021

"We're all aboard," Calvin said as the suit identifying itself as Night's came up the cargo ramp. He caught a look at the occupant's face, and it didn't look anything like Night. "*Let's get the hell out of here,*" he added, deciding to worry about it later. He toggled the switch to bring the ramp up.

"*Roger, that,*" the shuttle's WSO replied. "*Detaching now!*"

Calvin saw the ship begin moving before the ramp finished closing. He also got a glimpse of the cowtaurs approaching from beyond the curvature of the ship's skin.

"*Hurry,*" Calvin urged. "*If you've got stealth, now would be a good time for it, too.*"

"*I just stealthed us,*" Mays said. "*I don't know what it is they're shooting, but we've got a three inch hole through the wing. It's a good thing that fuel tank was empty.*"

"*Let me know when we're clear so we can blow it,*" Calvin said. "*I don't want to give them time to disarm the presents we left them.*"

"*I don't think that will be a prob—*" Lieutenant O'Leary began.

"*Holy shit!*" the shuttle's pilot, Lieutenant Miguel Carvalho exclaimed. "*The ship! It just blew up! Did you guys do that, or did it self-destruct?*"

"*As I was saying, I don't think there will be a problem with them disarming our weapons,*" Lieutenant O'Leary said. "*Even if the other ship didn't self-destruct, I made the charges tamper proof. Either way, I don't think we'll be seeing that ship again.*"

"*In that case,*" Calvin commed. "*Take us home, Mays. Let's go back to the Gulf…assuming it's still around.*"

"*Hey, Skipper,*" said Lieutenant O'Leary. "*I've got a question.*"

"*Yeah?*"

"*Who the hell's wearing Night's suit?*"

Chapter Forty

Bridge, TSS *Vella Gulf*, HD 69830 System, November 10, 2021

"That's the last of them," the DSO said as the last Jotunn vessel hit the stargate. The departure of the Jotunn had been delayed while they recovered their survivors from the battle the day before.

"Recall the fighters," Captain Sheppard said. Although they had been rotating the pilots, all of them had greatly exceeded the rules for 'mandatory' crew rest. It was funny how regulations went out the window when you had enemies trying to kill you.

"Sir, we are getting a call from Golirion," the comms officer said. "The new Thor wishes to speak with you."

"On screen, please," Captain Sheppard said.

The screen illuminated with the visage of the former Captain Nightsong. "Thank you for your assistance fighting the Jotunn," he said. "As you may have noticed, they are departing. It is now time for you to depart as well."

"What do you mean?"

"We are a private people," Nightsong replied, "and your presence is not desired. Please leave."

Captain Sheppard looked incredulous. "What? You want us to leave? All of your fleet has been destroyed, and your battle station is wrecked. How are you going to defend your planet if the Jotunn or Shaitans come back?"

"Truthfully, Terran, that is none of your business," Nightsong said with a sneer.

"What are you going to do?" Captain Sheppard asked. "Just give Golirion to the Jotunn when they come back?"

"No," Calvin said, finally understanding. "He's not giving Golirion to the Jotunn; he intends to join with the Shaitans. He would no more join up with the Jotunn than we would join up with the Ssselipsssiss. They are the Aesir's traditional enemies. He would, however, use the Jotunn to get to where he could meet up with the Shaitans, who are the rulers of the Jinn Universe. He must have somehow made their acquaintance in the other universe while he was pretending to be Wayland, and he has been working to find them in this one. The Shaitan home world must be in the Jinn Universe, somewhere up the Jotunn chain of worlds."

A shadow passed across Nightsong's face, but then he recovered his serene gaze. "I don't know what you are talking about," he said. "Our world just lost most of its rulers, and I have stepped up to lead it through this time of troubles. We do not desire any foreign entanglements while we sort this out, so I must once again ask you to leave our system."

"*We can't leave him in charge,*" Calvin commed to Captain Sheppard and Lieutenant O'Leary. "*Not if he intends to turn over Golirion to the Shaitans.*"

"*I've got this,*" Lieutenant O'Leary said. He stepped forward from the back of the bridge where he had been standing. "What if we don't leave?" he asked. "Are you going to come make us, you overgrown fairy? All of your itty bitty ships are all busted up. I guess you'll have to use your pretty little courier ship, won't you? Oh, I forgot. All that does is run *away* from fights."

Captain Sheppard turned his head to look at Lieutenant O'Leary and frowned at him. *"That is* not *how we conduct diplomatic relations,"* he said over the comm channel.

"I know, sir," O'Leary replied. *"Trust me."*

"Just a little."

"You will leave Aesir space immediately!" Nightsong screamed.

Lieutenant O'Leary smiled at the screen. "Uh oh, looks like I made Santa's little helper angry. Are you all mad at me now?"

"I will ensure you die a slow death for your insolence!"

"You, and whose army, bark breath?"

"I don't need an army; I will kill you myself!"

"Are you challenging me to a duel?"

"Yes! I challenge you to a duel!" Nightsong shouted.

"Wonderful," Lieutenant O'Leary said with a smile. "I accept."

Captain Sheppard terminated the communications link. "What the hell was that all about?"

"Well, sir," Lieutenant O'Leary said, "Lieutenant Commander Hobbs said we couldn't leave him in charge, which meant that either (1), we couldn't leave, or (2), he couldn't stay in charge. Me, I want to go back home, so somebody has to kill the little rat bastard. I chased him across two universes, all the while swearing I would kill him; this was finally my chance."

"You do know he is proficient as both a fire and a life Eco Warrior," Calvin said. "He may know the other areas too. How do you intend to beat him if you can't get close to him?"

Lieutenant O'Leary grinned. "That's why it was important to piss him off. I wanted *him* to challenge *me* to the duel. That way, I get to choose the weapons. If I had challenged him, he would have gotten the choice, and I'm sure he would have picked something that would have put me at an even bigger disadvantage. Hell, he might even have chosen to have no weapons at all. Couldn't have that, sir. I wanted the choice of weapons…and I'll make it count."

Reeve Hall, Golirion, HD 69830, November 11, 2021

"Kind of feels like déjà vu, eh sir?" Night asked as the Terrans walked into Reeve Hall.

"Yeah," Calvin replied. "I kind of hoped to never see this place again. Especially under these circumstances."

"So this is Reeve Hall?" Lieutenant O'Leary asked, looking around. "What a dump." The underground Reeve Hall was a giant horseshoe-shaped room with a packed dirt floor. Two rows of elevated seating rose up on both sides and met at the opposite end of the chamber, over 80 feet away. The seating was terraced, with an eight-foot wall surrounding the floor of the horseshoe.

"Take a good look, Terran," Nightsong said in greeting as he walked up behind them. "It is the last thing you'll ever see."

"Don't you worry, little elf," Lieutenant O'Leary said. "I'll try not to make this hurt *too* much."

"Should you find yourself lucky enough to hit me," Nightsong said, "it will not matter. I have lived thousands of your years. I have forgotten ways of killing that you don't even know exist. And as far as hurting me…" He pulled out a knife and drew it across his arm. A few drops of blood welled up, but then the sides of the cut closed, and the wound healed as if it had never occurred. "There isn't anything you can do to hurt me, which I can't undo." He put the knife away. "Now, if you would just give me my weapon, I'll kill you quickly so all of you can leave. Where is it?"

"Here they are," Night said. He carried a large box in each hand. Setting them down on the dirt floor, he opened them up with a flourish. Two items rested in each case.

"What is this?" Nightsong asked, suspicion tinging his voice for the first time.

"It is a Sturmgewehr 44 assault rifle," Lieutenant O'Leary said. "The Germans used it in World War II." He picked up one of the rifles and snapped in a magazine, pocketing the other two. He chambered a round and then slung it over his shoulder.

Nightsong pointed to the barrel, which bent in a 45 degree angle and had a periscope attached. "They really had guns that looked like that?"

"Yes, they did," Lieutenant O'Leary said. "That's called a krummlauf. It's a bent barrel attachment used for shooting around corners." He picked up the other item. "And this is a machete. Even overgrown pixies like you can probably figure out a machete is just a big knife."

"Take your position," Nightsong said with a glare. "And prepare to die."

Lieutenant O'Leary walked to the other end of the arena while the rest of the Terrans were led away.

"Got any last words, Terran?" Nightsong asked

"Yeah, ya got any cookies, you oversized fairy?"

"Begin!" called the judge.

"Whenever you're ready, barbarian," Nightsong said.

"Oh, so we're name-calling now, are we?" Lieutenant O'Leary asked. He held up his rifle so the angled barrel pointed in the direction of the Aesir, sighted through the periscope and fired. The bullet struck Nightsong in the shoulder, and he dropped his rifle as he was knocked back.

"Gods!" cried Nightsong. "I was willing to kill you quickly, but now you're dead!" The wound started closing as his nanobots went to work repairing the damage.

"You know, you're not very good at the whole name-calling thing, tree fucker." He fired several more shots, one of them striking Nightsong in the arm and another in the leg.

Nightsong screamed in pain and limped to where his rifle lay on the ground. He picked it up and yanked the trigger back. The rifle was set on full automatic and seven rounds fired, spraying around the arena. Aesir politicians dove for the floor as ricochets buzzed around the chamber.

As the eighth bullet fired, the barrel shattered, with pieces exploding outward like a grenade. Shrapnel flew into the Aesir's face, blinding him. He fell backward, dropping the rifle again.

Lieutenant O'Leary took advantage, charging across the surface of the arena.

Knowing he had to do something, Nightsong raised his hand and a stream of flame blasted forth. O'Leary dove to the side, protecting the rifle by taking the fall on his side. Nightsong manage to open an eye in time to see O'Leary come to a kneeling position and fire.

Nightsong dove out of the way as five bullets ripped through where he had just been.

Still unable to see in one eye, Nightsong threw another gout of flame in O'Leary's direction as his nanobots worked to clear his vision. A shard of metal worked its way free of his left eye and fell away.

O'Leary threw himself to the side and rolled into a prone position. He fired once, hitting Nightsong in the center of his chest. Nightsong went down, and O'Leary emptied the rest of the magazine into the writhing Aesir.

Nightsong stopped moving, and O'Leary discarded the rifle. Jumping up, he drew his machete and charged. As he got to his opponent, Nightsong kicked out, knocking O'Leary's legs out from under him. O'Leary hit hard, and the machete went flying. He lay stunned, his breath driven from him. Before he could move, the Aesir dove on top of him, and the two combatants began rolling around on the floor, each looking for advantage.

Nightsong rolled on top of O'Leary, choking him with both hands. O'Leary kicked off with one foot and drove a palm up into the Aesir's chin, breaking the hold. Nightsong brought one hand back down to choke O'Leary again, while the other hand drew his machete. O'Leary could feel his strength waning as he reached up and grabbed Nightsong's wrist. Balling his other hand into a fist, he punched the Aesir in the throat.

Nightsong's eyes bulged, and he fell backward off O'Leary, dropping the machete. The Terran rolled and pushed himself up. Grabbing the machete from where it had fallen, O'Leary turned and stabbed, striking Calvin in the chest.

O'Leary let go of the machete, his mouth dropping open. "I'm sorry—" was all he was able to say as his commanding officer dropped to his knees, gasping his final breaths.

Calvin took the machete handle in both hands and slowly pulled it out. "That hurt," he said. "Good thing you're so damn gullible." Calvin slashed out at O'Leary with the machete, his features returning to those of Nightsong.

Dumbstruck, O'Leary was slow to move, and the Aesir slashed him across the leg, drawing blood. O'Leary fell backward to avoid the backswing of the machete, landing on top of the remains of the Aesir's rifle. As Nightsong dove after him, O'Leary held it up and drove the shattered barrel into Nightsong's stomach. O'Leary pulled it out to stab the Aesir again, and Nightsong fell on top of him, the rifle knocked to the side.

The two opponents rolled back and forth on the ground again, Nightsong changing once more; this time, his features changed to those of O'Leary, and Calvin quickly lost track of which one was the real O'Leary.

"Foul!" the judge yelled. "The match is forfeit for failing to retain your identity."

Neither man nor Aesir stopped the fight; both continued punching, kicking and clawing each other as they rolled back and forth. Calvin had no idea who was winning, or who he should be pulling for.

"Stop the match!" the judge yelled. "Somebody stop the match!"

Not seeing anyone else taking action, Calvin vaulted the wall separating him from the arena floor and drew his laser pistol as he ran to the struggling combatants. As he arrived, one of the O'Learys finally got an advantage, getting the other one in a chokehold from behind, his arm wrapped around the throat of the other.

"Shoot him," he gasped. "I'm the real O'Leary, and he's the imposter."

"Not...true," the O'Leary being choked replied. Calvin looked at both men and saw they were identical. The men looked the same, the wounds were the same, hell, even the blood splatters on their clothes looked the same.

Calvin aimed his laser pistol at the O'Leary being choked. "Not me, sir…other one…is Nightsong." It sounded like O'Leary's voice, Calvin realized, although somewhat strangled. He turned the pistol on the other O'Leary.

"Don't shoot *me*, sir," the second O'Leary said, also in O'Leary's voice. "He's the rat bastard we chased across two universes."

"He's lying…" the O'Leary being choked said. "I'm…real…O'Leary."

"You're the real O'Leary?" Calvin asked the one doing the choking.

"Indeed," he replied. "Shoot him, so we can get the hell out of here."

Calvin aimed at the O'Leary being choked, but then switched to the other and fired. The O'Leary being choked rolled free, and Calvin fired several more times into both the head and where Nightsong had said his heart was. The edges of the wounds grew closer together, but then the body stilled, and the features returned to those of Nightsong.

"Good…choice," O'Leary said, massaging his throat.

"Thanks," Calvin said, looking at the body. "I always hated how he said 'indeed' all the time." He saw O'Leary struggling to get up and motioned for him to lay back. "Medic!" he called, looking up.

Calvin knelt down and applied pressure to staunch the blood flowing from Lieutenant O'Leary's leg. There was a lot of blood. "Where did you come up with the rifles?"

"We used to shoot them…all the time… with the newbies. Losers had to…buy beers. Didn't figure…would have ever seen one before." Lieutenant O'Leary chuckled then coughed weakly. "They're fun, but they have a problem."

"What's that?"

"The barrels…too much stress…usually break…after 160…shots."

"How many had his fired when you gave it to him?"

"170."

Reeve Hall, Golirion, HD 69830, November 13, 2021

Reeve Hall looked much different than it had two days previously; the dirt floor had been covered with some sort of parquet. The wood had a hypnotic pattern that seemed to entrance anyone who looked at it long enough. In the middle of the arena floor, the Aesir had placed a dais, on which sat a large table and four chairs. There was a chair for each of the Terrans who had been invited by name to attend the court proceedings: Captain James Sheppard, Lieutenant Commander Shawn Hobbs, Captain Paul Train, and First Lieutenant Ryan O'Leary.

"You know, I've been here three times now, and this is the first time I've actually felt welcome," Night said as he took a seat at the table.

"At least you never had anyone actively trying to kill you," Calvin replied under his breath.

"No shit," Lieutenant O'Leary said, massaging his throat as he took the seat furthest to the right.

"At ease, all of you," the CO said, seated on the left. "It's still creepy being here with everyone looking down at us."

"No shit," Lieutenant O'Leary repeated. "I mean, no shit, sir."

"I knew what you meant."

The reeves stilled as an Aesir came out onto the Thor's balcony. "Reeves of the Aesir," he proclaimed in a voice that echoed throughout the hall, "now hail the new Thor!" The reeves stood, with the Terrans following suit.

A second Aesir walked forward to stand next to the herald.

"Is that Silvermoon?" Night whispered.

"Yeah, I think so," Calvin replied. The Terrans had recovered the elven prince on a prior mission after he was captured by the Jotunn/Shaitan alliance. The Aesir's hearing had to have been superb, for he turned and winked at the Terrans before turning to face the herald.

The herald placed a small circlet on the Thor's head, and the reeves chorused in loud voices, "All hail, Thor!"

"Thank you," the Thor said. "Please be seated." He waited for everyone to get settled and then continued, "I thank you for your trust in me, although I feel it may be misplaced as I am not sure I am up to the challenges that face us. Of course, no one may be up to the challenge; our situation is dire. We are without a fleet, our last battle station has been destroyed and our enemies abound. It is certain the Jotunn will return, and we must prepare for both them and their unholy allies from beyond our universe."

"And prepare we shall…but first, it is proper to recognize the aid we have received from our allies. These are the best of friends, friends who came to our aid in our time of peril when we were betrayed by one of our own to our enemies. Friends who fought alongside us, even though they were outnumbered, sacrificing their ships and their lives so our civilization would live on. Friends that crossed the very boundaries of our universe to fight the Shaitans hand-to-claw on their own spaceship. For these actions, I name them

"Friends of the Aesir," and give them honorary Aesir citizenship. These men, these Terrans, are henceforth welcome on Golirion or any other planet in our dominion whenever they wish to come."

Knowing how private the Aesir were, Calvin expected booing or some display of negativity, but he didn't hear any. Impressive.

"I have also commissioned medals to be given to your crew and the next-of-kin of the Terrans who lost their lives here," the Thor continued. "Unfortunately, they are low priority compared with some of the other issues we are faced with at the moment, so it may be some time before I can send them to Terra. I will, however, send a proclamation back with you to document this fact." He paused, then added, "I also salute you for weeding out the traitor in our midst. It is with some trepidation, however, I must unfortunately note he does not seem to be dead."

"Not dead, Thor?" Calvin asked. "What does that mean? I killed him. I shot him in the heart. Repeatedly."

"As I said, unfortunately, that does not seem to be the case. When the Arbiter of Final Rites went to dispose of his mortal remains, his body had disappeared. We don't know if an accomplice stole his body or if he wasn't quite dead yet, but his body has vanished. We suspect that, like the vampyres of old, he wasn't dead and has risen to kill again. With his abilities, he could be anyone."

"Mother fucker…" Lieutenant O'Leary muttered. "Next time…"

"Next time, *I* will kill him," Night said. "And then he will *stay* dead."

"With Nightsong on the loose, and the Jotunn/Shaitan alliance at our doorstep, it is our greatest desire for the *Vella Gulf* to remain here and help us in the defense of Golirion. If that is not possible, we would request you take our plea for assistance back to Terra at your best speed. Our replicators are working around the clock; however, my best advisors do not believe we will be prepared for our enemies' return."

"I understand your need, Thor, and we are evaluating what is best for both of our civilizations," Captain Sheppard said. "We will advise you of our intentions shortly. At a minimum, we will be leaving several of our fighter squadrons here with you. You may use them however you wish for the defense of your system."

"Will you be leaving the pilots, as well?"

"I don't have the authority to order the pilots to remain behind; however, I will ask for volunteers. Those that want to stay will be allowed to do so. I imagine there will be many who will, rather than being packed like cordwood in the *Vella Gulf* for the return home…should we choose that route."

"Anything you can do to ease our burden will be greatly appreciated," the Thor said. "We Aesir have long memories; if we make it through this period, we will always remember the assistance you have given us."

"Speaking of assistance," the Thor said after a brief pause, "Our civilization will be sending Lieutenant Commander Hobbs some…um…assistance…in his continued efforts."

The door opened beneath the Thor's alcove, and a familiar Aesir walked toward the Terran's table. The Aesir giggled twice as he walked toward them, stifling them with a hand over his mouth both times. It was the Eco Warrior and former Reeve Farhome.

"I told you once before that our lives and destinies were intertwined," Farhome said. "It was foolish of me to allow you to leave here by yourself. Hee, hee, I thought you would be able to stay out of trouble on your home planet; I did not realize you intended to try getting yourself killed in so *many* creative ways. With the problems the universe has at the moment, you are far more valuable to both our civilizations in your own body, not stuffed into some moldy old sword."

"I'd like to think so, anyway," Calvin said. "Uh, thanks…I think."

"You're welcome." He muffled a giggle. "Sorry; still trying to stop that. I'm getting much better. Really. The bottom line is I intend to come with you from now on. Don't try to stop me; I have ways around anything you might try to do to prevent it. It will be better for all of us if you just accept it."

Calvin didn't know what Farhome had in mind; he also didn't want to find out, so he simply stood and bowed. "It will be my pleasure to have the company of someone with your…many talents," he said.

"See? That wasn't so bad, was it?" Farhome asked. "We are going to be the best of friends." He turned and walked toward the door. "I will just go get my things." As he walked, he started giggling again, which turned into laughing. By the time he reached the doorway, he was laughing so hard he could barely walk.

"Umm, good luck with him," the Thor said. "I thought he was getting better, but…good luck."

Bridge, TSS *Vella Gulf*, HD 69830 System, November 13, 2021

"So, what do we do now, hero?" Captain Sheppard asked.

"First, we get you to stop calling me that, sir,"

Calvin said.

"Why?" the CO asked. "Everyone else in the universe does it; why not us Terrans?"

"For one thing, it's silly," Calvin replied. "For another thing, I can't even begin to think what the government or Fleet Command will do if they hear it. I'm not a hero; I'm just me, trying to stop the bad guys and keep from getting killed along the way."

"Okay, so now what do we do, champion?"

"I don't think that's any better, sir."

"No?" the CO asked. "How about vanquisher? Conquistador? Defeater? Subjugator? The galactic dictionary has about 500 synonyms, depending on the type of foe you're trying to defeat. Sadly, there isn't one for stopping a Shaitan menace."

Calvin heard a snort from the front table and leveled a glare in their direction; the helmsman and duty engineer both found something on their panels that needed their attention. When he looked back at the CO, Captain Sheppard was smiling.

"All joking aside, I'm curious what you think we ought to do next. I already know what my duty to the Terran Republic requires, but I'd like to know what you think."

"I think we need to go home, sir. We need to get back and check in with Fleet Command. They need to know the Shaitans are behind this, and that they are coming to get us. I don't know where they're located, but it must be somewhere down the Jotunn's chain of star systems. Once we check in on Terra, someone, probably us, needs to go find their home world before they find ours. If Nightsong was working with them, he may already have told them where to look for us."

"I wouldn't put anything by him," the CO said; "that's for sure."

"Also," added Calvin, "we probably ought to swing by the Mrowry home world and let them know what we've found out. Maybe they can send some ships to aid in the defense of Golirion. They may also have couriers going to the Archons or the other socie-ties; we can spread the word to them, too." He tapped the tactical plot at the CO's chair. "We could also bring back a few of the extra fighters we have lying around. I think we still owe Emperor Yazhak for the ones we destroyed the last time we were here. He never asked for them back, but…"

"Yeah, we owe him," agreed the CO.

"But then we need to go home."

Chapter Forty-One

Emperor Yazhak the Third's Estate, Grrrnow, 61 Virginis, November 23, 2021

Emperor Yazhak stood silently, looking out the large bay window at the rock formation several miles away. The massive sandstone monolith was nearly identical to Ayers Rock on Terra, and it glowed bright red as the sun set behind it. The glow from behind him tinged his ebony fur crimson.

"Thank you for coming down to the planet," he finally said, turning around to address the Terrans waiting for him. "Please sit; we have a lot to discuss. Some of it will not be very pleasant."

"We were happy to come," Captain Sheppard said, "as we need to fill you in on the Shaitan/Jotunn alliance and begin planning how to defend ourselves from them."

"That is important," the emperor replied, "but it isn't why I asked you to come meet with me here."

"No?" Captain Sheppard asked. "What is more important than that?"

"Only time will tell if it is more important, but this topic is certainly more time critical," the emperor answered. "The Ssselipsssiss have asked to meet with you."

"The Ssselipsssiss?" Captain Sheppard asked. He turned to Calvin. "Isn't that the race of lizards you fought on your first mission?"

"It is," Calvin said, nodding his head. "What do *they* want?"

"I do not know," the emperor replied. "I know they have been pushing harder on us the last year or two than they ever have before. For a race like theirs, that probably means another race is driving them toward us. Their war must be going extremely poorly if they are asking to meet; they haven't asked to meet with anyone since the fall of the Alliance of Civilizations."

"If they want to meet with us, I'm sure our government will send someone to talk to them," Captain Sheppard said. "Maybe someone can come from Domus; that planet is closer than Terra, and it would save a little time."

"No," the emperor said. "They don't want to meet with Terran representatives; they want to meet with Calvin."

"*Meet with me?*" Calvin asked, his eyes opening wide in surprise. "They asked to meet me? How do they even know I exist?"

"Well, they didn't ask to meet you by name, but they are well aware of our belief in hero spirits, and the fact they rise when needed. They asked to meet with the hero running our war effort."

"*But I'm not running your war effort!*" Calvin exclaimed. "I'm not even running ours. In fact, I'm only the fourth highest ranking person on my *ship*, much less my military. There are hundreds of officers senior to me."

"I am well aware of that," Emperor Yazhak said with a smile. "The fact remains that you are always where the action is, and you are the person who is accomplishing the deeds needed to ensure the continuity of both of our races."

"Well, yes, I've had the misfortune of being in the center of a few fights, but there are many others who helped me in those fights, including your grandson." He waved in the direction of Lieutenant

Rrower. "I absolutely couldn't have been successful without all of their help. I haven't done any of it alone."

"Nor could you," the emperor agreed. "Hero spirits always attract others to their side. I am tremendously proud that my grandson was worthy enough to be one of them. Hopefully, if his defining moment arrives, he will approach it with the heart of a warrior."

Lieutenant Rrower roared a very lion-like bellow, then said, "You can count on me, Grandfather!"

The emperor gazed at his grandson for a few seconds. "It is easy to say that, here and now; however, it is never as easy when the moment arrives. That is why it *is* a defining moment."

Lieutenant Rrower bowed his head. "I understand," he said in a much more subdued voice.

"What is a 'defining moment?'" Calvin asked.

"It is where you are called to give your life for your brothers and sisters," the emperor explained, "knowing full well the cost you are going to pay. It is different than dying in battle where a random laser or grenade blast kills you. A defining moment gives meaning to your life. It is when you choose whether or not to lay down your life for something you believe in. From that moment onward, you will always be defined by it, whether you are known as a hero or coward. Nearly all those who accompany a hero spirit reach their defining moment in the hero's service. I expect my grandson's will come as well; hopefully, he will face up to it in such a manner as will make our people proud of him."

"Okay, I understand all of that," Calvin said, "but it doesn't change the fact that I am not leading our war effort."

"You may not be the person charged with making all of the decisions," the emperor replied, "but you definitely make the ones that count, and you influence others at the right time and place to make the correct decisions."

"What if I were to quit?" Calvin asked. "Just retire from the Navy and go home? What would happen then?"

"You won't," the emperor replied.

"How do you know?"

"Because your country, your very race, needs you. You will no more 'quit and go home' than I will step down from being emperor. Yes, there are many difficult tasks to be accomplished, and impossible questions to be answered, but both of us have been called to our duties, and we will not shirk them." The emperor began laughing, long and hard.

The laughter was infectious, and, after a few seconds, most of the others in the room joined him. Calvin watched, red-faced. Finally, he couldn't take it any longer. "What is so funny, your highness?"

"Sorry," the emperor said, winding down. "I haven't laughed that hard in a long time. The concept of a hero spirit not participating in the events he was called forth to accomplish just struck me as humorous."

"So, hero spirits are good for comic relief?" Calvin asked.

"Sometimes," the emperor said, still smiling. "Especially when the people around them need it."

Calvin shrugged, realizing he wasn't going to change the emperor's mind. "So, what is it the lizards want?"

"They also believe in hero spirits, after a fashion," the emperor replied, "although all of theirs seem to have gone missing at the moment. In fact, the war is going so badly for them they sent a ship into HD 40307 with a white flag. They have promised to give us anything we ask if our hero would assist them in their war."

"Can we trust them?"

"Not as far as you can throw them," Emperor Yazhak replied. "They have very short memories for promises, and they are nearly amoral."

"You need not look any further than what happened on the planet Typhon," Lieutenant Rrower said.

"What happened there?" Calvin asked.

"What happened? We taste good to the Ssselipssssiss. They used a sneak attack under the cover of a truce to land their troops there and take it from us. By the time we could get additional forces to the system, they already had defenses in place around the stargate. There was no longer any need to fight for it, either; they had already killed all of our colonists."

"How do we know they are negotiating in good faith this time?" Captain Sheppard asked.

"There's no way you can," Lieutenant Rrower said. "You know the old joke about how to tell when a Ssselipssssiss is lying to you?"

"No," Captain Sheppard said. "How do you tell when they're lying to you?"

"Their forked tongues are moving."

"Okay, we can't trust them," Calvin said. "What would you recommend we do, Emperor?"

"I would suggest you go and see if you can help them."

"Why would we want to do that?" Calvin asked. "After my first contact with them, I'd be pretty happy to just let them fight it out to the end with their adversaries."

"It might seem so at first, but if you would listen to someone who has spent a lifetime studying strategy, I would tell you that it makes good strategic sense for you to help the Ssselipssssiss, especially if it turns out they are also fighting the Shaitans, as I suspect they are. If you can help them put more pressure on the Shaitans, it will relieve some of the weight from the Aesir. From what my grandson's told me, the Aesir are at the point of being wiped out. Although they are reclusive, the Aesir have always been good allies, and I would not want to write them off if they can still be saved. Besides, the Ssselipsssiss have been fighting their enemy for several years. They may have developed weapons and tactics to deal with them that are more effective than what we currently have."

"Well, that at least makes sense," Captain Sheppard said.

"If you ask for payment from them for your assistance, make sure they give it to you up front," Lieutenant Rrower said. "They have a tendency to forget about promises they've made after the danger has passed."

"Payment?" Calvin asked. "Like what?"

"You are still a developing civilization," the emperor said. "I would make them give you a couple of their replicators. That way, you can build up your forces faster after this conflict is over, and you won't have to worry about them immediately attacking you."

"I can imagine the Ssselipsssiss having fewer ships would be something very beneficial for the Mrowry, too, wouldn't it?" Captain Sheppard asked. "Perhaps even more so since you are closer to them?"

"It certainly would," the emperor replied, smiling broadly. "I wouldn't have suggested it otherwise. Besides, they are excellent laser technicians; getting their replicator data banks would be very helpful in arming your ships."

"And I'm sure you wouldn't mind if we then shared this technology with you?"

"A little technology transfer in the interest of diplomatic relations would certainly be appreciated."

Captain Sheppard sighed; he could see he'd been had. "Okay, we will go meet with them, but I would appreciate it if you could send a courier ship to Terra to let them know what happened to our fleet and where we are planning to go."

"Nothing could be easier. My pilots are getting to know the route quite well."

Bridge, TSS *Vella Gulf*, 61 Virginis, November 23, 2021

"I had a question I wanted to ask you," Calvin said.

"Anything," Lieutenant Rrower replied. "What do you need to know?"

"It's about something your grandfather said when we were talking about hero spirits."

"Yes?"

"He said that nearly all those who accompany hero spirits will reach their defining moment in the hero spirit's service. Is that what you really believe?"

"Yes," Lieutenant Rrower replied. "It is something that has been borne out on many occasions. Look around you…how many of the men and women in your service have fallen along the way while you continue to press forward?"

"That's not fair," Calvin said. "I've been wounded, too. I even chose to fly my fighter into an oncoming missile to save the *Vella Gulf*. That should have killed me."

"That is true, and yet here you are, still alive. Obviously, you are the hero spirit." He said it as if no evidence in the world could dissuade him.

"Okay," Calvin said, "I'll go along with that, at least for the moment. My question, though, was about you. Knowing that I am a hero spirit, and that most of the hero spirit's followers end up dying, you still chose to come with us. Why?"

"What you are doing may save our races from annihilation or enslavement. That alone makes it a worthy cause for a warrior. Additionally, I know that by being with you, I will be part of events that will shape the future of my race. Depending on my defining moment, I may even be remembered by future generations for the sacrifice I make. And finally, there is a definite possibility I might survive. It is a tremendously small one, but it exists nevertheless. Everything we have done and continue to do will make wonderful stories to tell by the fire when I am a white-hair. Maybe my stories will even inspire one of my grandchildren on to greatness. That is why I do this."

"You're crazy."

Lieutenant Rrower cocked his head, considering. He smiled. "That is a possibility, too, I guess."

Chapter Forty-Two

Bridge, TSS *Vella Gulf*, Kepler 62 System, December 1, 2021

“**S**ystem entry into the Kepler-62 system,” Steropes said. “This is a five-planet system about 1,200 light-years from Earth in the constellation Lyra. Kepler-62 is a star classified as a K2 dwarf. It is about two thirds the size of the sun although it is only one fifth as bright. At seven billion years old, the star is several million years older than the sun.”

“Steropes!” Captain Sheppard exclaimed.

“Oh, sorry; it’s been a while since we went anywhere new,” Steropes answered. “The system is held by the Ssselipsssiss, and we are going through their minefield. They appear to have it turned off.”

Captain Sheppard thought he heard something about “a six-pack of duh” from the front table, but he couldn’t be sure.

“I have indications of at least three Ssselipsssiss starships in the vicinity, as well,” Steropes continued. “It looks like a battleship and two cruisers.”

“That’s it?” the CO asked. “Three ships and a minefield to hold a contested system? Doesn’t that seem pretty thin to you?”

“Yes sir, it does,” Steropes replied. “At a minimum, I would have expected at least a dreadnought and several battleships, along with their attendant smaller ships.”

“Where do you suppose they are?”

“Unknown, sir. I do not believe they are stealthed, so they must be in another system.”

"I only show the three lizzie ships, too," the DSO said.

"Me, too," the OSO added. "I don't have any indications of anything else in the system, aside from some ground-based defenses on the planet."

"They don't have enough here to hold the system if the Mrowry wanted to take it from them," DSO said; "about the only thing they could do with those ships is destroy us."

"True," Steropes said. "And, having seen how thin they are here, it is unlikely they will let us go if our negotiations with them go poorly as they will be afraid we'll tell the Mrowry."

"I guess negotiations had better be successful then," the CO said.

"At a minimum," Steropes agreed.

"I have a call coming in from the battleship," the communications officer said. "Their CO is calling, sir."

"On screen."

"It is audio only, sir."

"On speaker, then, please."

"Terran ship, this is Captain Skrelleth. I have been bidden to welcome you. Welcome. You will proceed to the fifth planet. Our ambassador awaits you there. Captain Skrelleth, out."

"Not the warmest welcome," noted the CO.

"The Ssselipsssiss are not known for their hospitality," Steropes said; "however, that was short, even for them."

"Why do you suppose that is?"

"Also unknown, sir. It is possible the captain disagrees with our mission here. It is also possible he just doesn't like us. More information is needed."

"What can you tell me about the fifth planet?"

"The fifth planet used to be held by the Mrowry, who called it Typhon. It is in the habitable zone and orbits the star every 267 days. It is about 40 percent larger than Earth, with a surface gravity of 1.1 of Terra's, although over 60% of the surface is covered in water. The fourth planet in the system is also habitable but is 100% covered in water. This system is interesting in that all of the planets are oriented straight up and down in their orbits; none of them would have seasons like Terra."

"I just received the coordinates of the meeting site," the communications officer said.

"All right," the CO said. "Pass them on to the helmsman and let's get going. I'd like to get this over with as quickly as possible."

"Sir, one of the cruisers is moving to tail us," the DSO said.

"And maybe even sooner," the CO added.

Keppler 62 'e' (Previously "Typhon"), Kepler 62 System, December 2, 2021

Three of the maroon Ssselipsssiss waited for them on the platform. The central lizard appeared to be unarmed, a politician perhaps, while the creatures on either side had both arms and armor; definitely warriors. Although Calvin had fought them before, he hadn't had time to stop and look at them closely. The fact that they were actively trying to kill him at the time probably had something to do with that. He took a long look at the central Ssselipsssiss as the Terrans approached.

Bi-pedal lizards, the Ssselipsssiss looked more humanoid than the allied Kuji; their arms were normal length for humans, if not slightly longer, with sharp claws adorning both hands and feet. At seven feet, the lizards looked down on him, but Calvin could still see the tips of their two small horns. Their tails flipped back and forth in agitation, allowing Calvin to see the sharp tips on them; metal spikes reinforced the ends of the warriors' tails.

Calvin knew from experience the rifles held by the warriors were high-powered lasers.

"Welcome," the unarmed Ssselipsssiss said as Captain Sheppard, Calvin and Night neared. "My leaders wished me to thank you for coming. If you would follow me."

Without waiting for an answer, the Ssselipsssiss turned and began walking toward a large sand-colored tent close by the platform. When the Terrans didn't immediately follow, the two soldiers motioned with their rifles that the Terrans should go with their leader.

"They always this friendly?" Night asked raising an eyebrow.

"No idea," Calvin said. "At least this time they're not shooting at me. That's a plus."

The Terrans followed the Ssselipsssiss, who had stopped and was waiting for them at the opening of the tent. When the Terrans approached, he held open one of the flaps and motioned for them to precede him.

The interior of the tent was cool and dim compared with the outside, and it took a few moments for the Terrans' eyes to adjust to the gloom. For all of its expanse, the inside of the tent was sparsely furnished; its one piece of furniture was a large, central table, behind which two Ssselipsssiss waited.

Where the first Ssselipsssiss had worn a simple tunic and kilt, the two waiting creatures were far more ornately dressed. Both wore red velvet robes with black trim, along with what looked like black stretch pants. Although slightly different, each of the robes had a small golden patch on the left side, and both of the lizards had gold jewelry around their necks and wrists.

"I am Ambassador Gresss," the taller of the two said. At seven and a half feet, he stood three inches above his companion. "This is my assistant, Sub-Ambassador Kressiss. My government wishes to thank you for coming today."

"It is our pleasure," Captain Sheppard said. "I am Captain James Sheppard, the commanding officer of the Terran Ship *Vella Gulf*. The two men with me are Lieutenant Commander Hobbs and Captain Train. How can we be of assistance?"

"We understand you have experience fighting the enemy from beyond. Is this correct?"

"We have experience fighting a number of races," Captain Sheppard said. "Can you be more specific on which enemy you are talking about?"

"We are fighting an enemy that uses time as a weapon," the ambassador replied. "Have you fought such a race?"

"Yes," Captain Sheppard said. "We have fought them on several occasions. They are skilled at using those weapons to their advantage as well as jumping back and forth between our universe and theirs."

"Ahhh, so they *are* going to another universe," the sub-ambassador replied. "We did not know where—"

"Yes, that is our enemy," the ambassador interrupted, giving the sub-ambassador a sharp glance as he cut his subordinate off. "We have been fighting them for some time. Despite the bravery of our ship captains, their ability to 'jump back and forth' as you call it makes them difficult to fight, and we have been forced to concede many of our systems to them."

"We have been fighting them in another chain of systems," Captain Sheppard explained, "so their reach appears to be substantial. They have also allied with other races, which has given them additional capabilities."

"Yes, we have noticed that as well," the ambassador replied. "There is one race that can barely figure out which end of the laser the light comes out of, but there are other races who are more capable."

"But they all appear to be under the leadership of the enemy who has the time weapons?"

"Yes, they do," the ambassador agreed.

"That race is the Shaitans," Calvin said. "I have fought them at close quarters, and I can tell you they also have a directed energy weapon that can melt metal. They are a difficult opponent."

"Where did you fight them like that?" the sub-ambassador asked. "We haven't been able to get close—"

"Sub-Ambassador Kressiss was a ship captain before becoming part of my staff," the ambassador interrupted. He gave his counterpart another look. "Sometimes he forgets his new position does not deal with battle tactics." The ambassador turned back to the Terrans. "Still, this time, the question is valid since we have been unable to get close to the enemy…the Shaitans, as you call them. We have successfully defeated their allies a number of times, but the Shaitans have proven more difficult."

"Actually, I fought them inside one of their own ships," Calvin replied. "We didn't intend to fight them there, but we got stranded on their ship and had to fight our way out."

"So you know the taste of our enemy."

"Um, taste?" Calvin asked. "We didn't eat them."

"No," the ambassador said, "I mean the nature of the enemy. What they are like. We do not even know what they look like. They have never even communicated with us. They just show up and kill us until we flee."

"We haven't communicated with them, either," Captain Sheppard said. "The first time we met them, one of their ships appeared and attacked us. We were lucky to escape with our lives."

"And yet, escape you did. Not only once, but in other engagements as well."

"Yes, we did," Captain Sheppard replied.

"We have a saying among our people," the ambassador said. "'A first victory may go to the lucky, but never a third.' At some point, it ceases being a matter of luck and becomes one of having better skill, equipment or tactics. Unfortunately, we do not have any of those in our fight against the Shaitans, which is why we have come to you."

"That does bring the conversation back to the point," the CO agreed. "So, putting aside all of the diplomatic niceties, what exactly is it that you want from us?"

"What do we want?" the ambassador asked. "That is easy. We want you to go to the Dark Star and kill the Shaitans. All of them. And, while you're on the way to the Dark Star, we want you to kill every single one of them between here and there."

"You saw that we have a cruiser in orbit, right?" Captain Sheppard asked. "Not a fleet of super dreadnoughts, but a single, solitary cruiser? How do you expect us to go to this planet and kill them all?"

"If we knew how to do it," the sub-ambassador said, "we would have already done it ourselves. We expect you to do it with the same skills, equipment and tactics that have kept you alive so far."

"What can you tell us about this planet?" Calvin asked. "Where is it?"

The sub-ambassador reached under the table and pulled out a large chart, which he unrolled and snapped into clips mounted to the table. "Here is what we know," he said. He pointed to the chart, which had a line of 10 star systems. "We are here at this system on the end. The Dark Star is here at the other end of the chain. This is where we first found them."

"I'm not a sailor," Night said, "but it appears that most of the information that should be on this chart is missing. The only information is the name of each system. It doesn't tell us about the systems' planets, other stargates or anything else that might be helpful. Am I missing something?"

"No," Calvin said. "You're right; this chart should have more information."

"Our leaders asked us to withhold information on our systems until you agreed to help us," the ambassador said.

"I understand that," Calvin said, "but if what you say is true, you no longer own some of the systems on this chart."

"That is true," the ambassador said. "We hold this system and the next two. After that, they are currently being held by the enemy. I would like to say we are preparing an assault to return them to our control, but that would not be accurate."

"So we have seven enemy systems to transit in order to get to this 'Dark Star,'" Captain Sheppard said.

"Three of them do not have any inhabited planets," the sub-ambassador offered; "it is unlikely you will find any of the enemy there."

"That still leaves four enemy-held, populated systems," Captain Sheppard said.

"Yesss, that is true," the ambassador replied. "You will have to find a way, whether by stealth or by fighting your way through."

"So, what will we find at the end of this chain?" Calvin asked.

"You will find the Dark Star, and around it the Dark Planet."

"And what exactly is a Dark Star and a Dark Planet?

"It is exactly as it sounds," the ambassador replied. "The star is dark, not full of life like the one in this system. It is a brown dwarf, a body that is in between the mass of the heaviest gas giant planets and the lightest stars. Although it formed independently, like a star, it didn't have enough mass to ignite like a normal star. The Dark Star is at the upper end of the brown dwarf spectrum. It is able to fuse lithium but not able to fuse hydrogen. Still, it gives off enough heat and light to create a habitable environment on the sole planet orbiting it, the Dark Planet."

"And this 'Dark Planet' is the home world of the Shaitans?" Calvin asked.

"We do not know," the ambassador replied. "Certainly, their home world is not on that planet in this universe, or we would have known about it much sooner. We mapped the system a long time ago, hundreds of years ago, in fact, but it wasn't on our list for colonization. Although life might be possible on the planet, there isn't enough 'normal' light for anyone to want to go and settle there. Even at noon, the planet would never be brighter than what you would have at late-twilight here."

"Although the planet wasn't marked for colonization," the sub-ambassador added, "the system has a second stargate, so we had a small observation post there, in order to watch for alien invasion.

The outpost was unprepared for having the enemy appear alongside it, and the station was destroyed. A ship underway at the time made it out of the system and brought back word of the attack. Since then, the enemy has appeared more and more frequently, and in greater numbers. It is like trying to hold back the water from a dam that has burst."

"So…if the Dark Planet is the home of the Shaitans, it is in the other universe, not ours," Calvin said.

"That is correct," the ambassador agreed. "We can't confirm their home world is the Dark Planet; it may be somewhere else, but that is where the enemy appeared. We know the Shaitans didn't arrive through one of the stargates; they just appeared there."

"So that is where we must go," Captain Sheppard said.

"It seems so," Calvin said. "Another desperate mission against incredible odds. At least we have an advantage in that we're already familiar with their technology."

"Unless they've changed it," Night said.

"Yes," Calvin agreed, "unless they've changed it."

"I only have one more question," Captain Sheppard said. "How do you intend to reimburse us for our efforts?"

The ambassador hissed in dismay. "You would charge us in our hour of need?"

"Your civilization still owes us for damage you did to our ships in the Tau Ceti system. There is also the matter of the war with the Mrowry that the emperor asked me to remind you of. How is it that you expect us to risk our lives and equipment for you, on a task you cannot do yourself, without expecting to reimburse us for our efforts? I'm afraid that just doesn't seem very equitable, especially since it is quite likely we will be killed in the attempt."

"We will cease all offensive operations against the Mrowry, as soon as I can get the word to my commanders," replied the ambassador. "Unfortunately, we have no money to repay either you or the Mrowry; the war has bled us dry."

"We would accept a battleship-sized replicator or better as repayment," Captain Sheppard said, "especially if it came complete with all of the latest technology."

"I would like to do that, but I can't promise it without speaking to my superiors," the ambassador said.

"What can you promise without speaking to your superiors?" Captain Sheppard asked.

"Not much, unfortunately," replied the ambassador. "At the moment, we have very little we *could* give you. We are almost to the point of eating our young or conducting an all-out final attack on the Mrowry. If you will attempt this mission for us, I will promise not to attack the Mrowry. If we *are* forced to attack them, it is likely our civilization will be destroyed, and theirs will be unprepared for the Shaitans when they shortly arrive." He paused, then added, "It is the best I can do. Even then, we will still probably be forced to eat our young."

"I understand," Captain Sheppard said, "and I hope it will not come to that for you. I will take your offer back to Emperor Yazhak and see what he has to say while you discuss our requests with your superiors."

"We have one final request then, if you are to leave," the ambassador said.

"What is that?" Captain Sheppard asked.

"While you are gone, we would like to have the services of your hero."

"What? You want us to just leave him here with you? Why? As some sort of hostage?"

"You can view him as a hossstage if you would like," the ambassador hissed, "but you have seen our defenses, and I'm sure you realize we could not stop a determined assault by the Mrowry if it should occur. I would prefer you not urge them to make that assault, and I would like to keep your hero as insurance you won't. From a more practical perspective, our admiral would like to have him inspect our defenses. Perhaps he will identify something we missed. Our situation is so grim we are willing to try anything, even listening to a Terran's advice."

Officers' Mess, TSS *Vella Gulf*, Kepler 62 System, December 2, 2021

"What did they offer in return for helping them?" Lieutenant Rrower asked.

"We got a whole lot of 'Would like to' and 'We can't promise that," Calvin said. "They were very evasive about what they would do for us if we helped them. They told us the war was going poorly for them, but they may not have told us *how* badly. I wonder if it's even worse than they indicated."

"It is possible," Lieutenant Rrower said. "I don't think they would have come asking for assistance if there had been any way for them to do it themselves. They may no longer be in control of the replicators or technology you asked them for. What information did they have for you on the Shaitans?"

"The only thing they gave us for now, until we agreed to help them, was this chart." Calvin unrolled the chart on a table. "There isn't a lot of information; it's just a chart showing a chain of 10 star systems. It goes from where we are now," he pointed at one end, "to where they say they first discovered the Shaitan." He pointed to the other end. "They also said they only hold the end system, plus the next two in line."

Lieutenant Rrower looked at the chart. "I see why they are negotiating with you," he said. "To use one of your sayings, 'they're fucked.'"

"Why?" Calvin asked. "What do you mean?"

"You said they only hold the three systems closest to the end?"

"Yeah," Calvin said with a nod.

"I've heard of the fourth system. I haven't been there, but I know its name. It's the Ssselipsssiss home world. The negotiators here? They're fucked. They've lost their capital. They may not even be in contact with any of their leaders any more…if they even exist." Lieutenant Rrower shook his head. "The reason they can't promise you anything for helping? They've just about lost it all…and if we don't help them, the Shaitans will be into our systems next."

Epilogue

Keppler 62 'e' (Previously "Typhon"), Kepler 62 System, December 3, 2021

The shuttle touched down gently, and the ramp started down. With a sigh, Calvin picked up his sea bag and smaller duffle bag.

"You don't have to go," Captain Sheppard said. "Say the word, and we'll go back to the ship. I doubt they can jump to the other universe so we could probably make it out of here with only minimal damage."

"No sir, it's okay," Calvin replied. "I'll be fine. Just…um…don't take too long getting back, okay?"

"Hee, hee, we're going to have lots of fun with the, what did you call them? Lizzies?" asked Farhome. "We're going to have lots of fun with the lizzies. I can just tell!"

"You don't have to come," Calvin said; "they only asked for me."

"If you think you're going without me, you're crazier than I am," Farhome said. "I thought you'd be safe on your own home planet, and look at all the trouble you got into. Here? The universe is the limit! You'd probably fall into a super nova or something. At least I'll be here to see it! I've never been close to a super nova, so that will at least be a new experience for me, hee, hee. No. If you're going, I'm going with you." He picked up a bag smaller than Calvin's duffle bag. "I'm ready."

"That's all you've got?" Calvin asked. "We may be there for a while."

"It's all I ever need." Farhome smiled.

"I've got my bags, too," Night said. "I really think you ought to reconsider and let me come. You know they're just using you. When it goes bad, which it will, you'd be able to kill a lot more of them with me there than if I'm with the *Gulf*."

"I know," Calvin said, "and while I'd love to have you, I need you to reconstitute the platoon. We took a lot of casualties, and we're going to need reinforcements. I need you to get them up to speed and ready for combat because I know there's going to be more. A lot more. We have to be ready, and I know you're the man to prepare the unit."

"If you say so, sir," Night said. "I still think you're making a mistake not taking me along."

"I may be," Calvin said. "It wouldn't be the first time."

"Just don't get dead, okay?"

"I promise," Calvin replied. He turned to Farhome. "All right, let's go."

Calvin and Farhome walked out of the shuttle and over to where the ambassador stood. Calvin turned and watched as the ramp went up and the shuttle lifted off. Within seconds, it disappeared into the turquoise sky. There was no way home until the Terrans came back. If they ever made it back. And if he was still alive to greet them. Calvin turned to the ambassador.

"So? What's next?"

# # # # #

1st Platoon, "A" Company, 1st of the 1st Terran Space Force (Prior to Anti-Domus Operations)

Commanding Officer	LCDR Shawn 'Calvin' Hobbs
Executive Officer	Captain Paul 'Night' Train

<u>Space Force</u>

Space Force Leader	Master Chief Ryan O'Leary
Squad 'A' Leader	Gunnery Sergeant Patrick 'The Wall' Dantone, Cyborg
Fire Team '1' Leader	Staff Sergeant Park 'Wraith' Ji-woo
Laserman	Sergeant Marcus 'Spud' Murphy
Laserman	Sergeant Margaret 'Witch' Andrews
Laserman	Sergeant Dan 'Giseman' Geisenhof
Laserman	Corporal Calvin 'Bossman' Davis
Fire Team '2' Leader	Staff Sergeant John 'Mr.' Jones
Laserman	Sergeant Jamal 'Bad Twin' Gordon
Laserman	Sergeant Austin 'Good Twin' Gordon
Laserman	Corporal Irina 'Spook' Rozhkov
Laserman	Sergeant Anne 'Fox' Stasik
Fire Team '3' Leader	Staff Sergeant Eric "Willie" Williamson
Laserman	Sergeant Ismail "Mailman" Al-Sabani
Laserman	Sergeant Jacob 'Chaos' Braig, Cyborg
Laserman	Corporal Dan 'Danny Boy' Anderson
Medic	Corporal Shaun 'Lucky' Evertson

<u>Ground Force</u>

Ground Force Leader	Master Gunnery Sergeant Bill Hendrick
Squad 'B' Leader	Gunnery Sergeant Jerry 'Wolf' Stasik
Fire Team '1' Leader	Staff Sergeant Alka 'Z-Man' Zoromski
Laserman	Sergeant Richard 'Shipwreck' Shipley
Laserman	Corporal Robert 'Fury' Scott, Cyborg
Laserman	Corporal Donald 'Triple D' Drake
Laserman	Corporal Rus 'Overkill' Rogers
Fire Team '2' Leader	Staff Sergeant David 'Market' Hirt
Laserman	Sergeant Rajesh 'Mouse' Patel
Laserman	Corporal 'Bob' Bobellisssissolliss
Laserman	Corporal 'Doug' Dugelllisssollisssesss
Laserman	Corporal Brenton 'Butcher' Davis
Fire Team '3' Leader	Staff Sergeant Ryan "Big Gurn" Gurney
Laserman	Sergeant Milan 'Gunner' Vranjesevic
Laserman	Sergeant Pierce 'Big Sky' Tomas, Cyborg
Ninja	Sergeant Hattori 'Yokaze' Hanzo
Medic	Sergeant John 'Gags' Russert

1st Platoon, "A" Company, 1st of the 1st Terran Space Force (Anti-Domus Operations and Beyond)

Commanding Officer	First Lieutenant Ryan O'Leary
Executive Officer	Second Lieutenant Cristobal Contreras

<u>Space Force</u>

Space Force Leader	Gunnery Sergeant Patrick 'The Wall' Dantone, Cyborg
Squad 'A' Leader	Staff Sergeant Park 'Wraith' Ji-woo
Fire Team '1' Leader	Sergeant Marcus 'Spud' Murphy
Laserman	Sergeant Margaret 'Witch' Andrews
Laserman	Sergeant Dan 'Giseman' Geisenhof
Laserman	Corporal Calvin 'Bossman' Davis
Laserman	Corporal Jonny 'Dark' Minion
Fire Team '2' Leader	Staff Sergeant John 'Mr.' Jones
Laserman	Sergeant Jamal 'Bad Twin' Gordon
Laserman	Sergeant Austin 'Good Twin' Gordon
Laserman	Corporal Irina 'Spook' Rozhkov
Laserman	Sergeant Anne 'Fox' Stasik
Fire Team '3' Leader	Staff Sergeant Eric "Willie" Williamson
Laserman	Sergeant Jacob 'Chaos' Braig, Cyborg
Laserman	Corporal 'Bill' Obillossilllolis
Laserman	Corporal 'Skank' Misssollossissos
Medic	Corporal Shaun 'Lucky' Evertson

<u>Ground Force</u>

Ground Force Leader	Gunnery Sergeant Jerry 'Wolf' Stasik
Squad 'B' Leader	Staff Sergeant Alka 'Z-Man' Zoromski
Fire Team '1' Leader	Sergeant Richard 'Shipwreck' Shipley
Laserman	Corporal Sam 'Mental' Ward
Laserman	Corporal Joshua 'Prince' King
Laserman	Corporal 'Sal' Sallissollosiss
Laserman	Corporal 'Phil' Fillississolliss
Fire Team '2' Leader	Staff Sergeant David 'Market' Hirt
Laserman	Sergeant Rajesh 'Mouse' Patel
Laserman	Corporal 'Bob' Bobellisssissolliss
Laserman	Corporal 'Doug' Dugelllisssollisssesss
Laserman	Sergeant Declan 'Ducky' Jones, Cyborg
Fire Team '3' Leader	Staff Sergeant Ryan 'Big Gurn' Gurney
Laserman	Sergeant Milan 'Gunner' Vranjesevic
Laserman	Sergeant Pierce 'Big Sky' Tomas, Cyborg
Ninja	Sergeant Hattori 'Yokaze' Hanzo
Medic	Sergeant Simon 'Dougie' Douglas

Space Fighter Squadron-1

CO	Lieutenant Commander Shawn 'Calvin' Hobbs
XO	Lieutenant Commander Sarah 'Lights' Brighton
Pilot	Lieutenant Carl 'Guns' Simpson
Pilot	Lieutenant Kenyon 'Bucket' Salo
Pilot	Lieutenant Samuel 'Sammy' Jakande
Pilot	Lieutenant Hans 'Schnitzel' Hohenstaufen
Pilot	Lieutenant 'Tex' Teksssellisssiniss
Pilot	Lieutenant Jim 'Sweets' Sweeny
Pilot	Lieutenant Jerry 'Brick' Johnson
Pilot	Lieutenant Jiang 'Tooth' Fang
Pilot	Lieutenant Simon 'Straw' Berry
Pilot	Lieutenant Pablo 'Bob' Acosta
Pilot	Lieutenant Jeff 'Canuck' Canada
Pilot	Lieutenant Tatyana 'Khan' Khanilov
Pilot	Lieutenant James 'Speedy' Swift
Pilot	Lieutenant Denise 'Frenchie' Michel
Pilot	Lieutenant Miguel 'Ghost' Carvalho
Pilot	Lieutenant Steve 'Heartbreak' Ehrhardt
Pilot	Lieutenant Phil 'Oscar' Meyer
NFO	Lieutenant Tobias 'Toby' Eppler
NFO	Lieutenant Neil 'Trouble' Watson
NFO	Lieutenant James Alfred 'Jamming' Miles
NFO	Lieutenant Dan 'K-Mart' Knaus
NFO	Lieutenant 'Olly' Ollisssellissess
NFO	Lieutenant Faith 'Bore' Ibori

NFO	Lieutenant Erika 'Jones' Smith
NFO	Lieutenant Jim "Ozzy" Osbourne
NFO	Lieutenant Sasaki 'Supidi' Akio
NFO	Lieutenant Gwon 'Happy' Min-jun
NFO	Lieutenant Brian 'Sherri' Bouchez
NFO	Lieutenant John 'Trudy' Douglass
NFO	Lieutenant Thomas 'Mays' Yilmaz
NFO	Lieutenant Poon 'Harpoon' Yee
NFO	Lieutenant Ali Ahmed 'Sandy' Al-Amri
NFO	Lieutenant Reyne 'Rafe' Rafaeli
NFO	Lieutenant Aharsi 'Swammi' Goswami

The following is an excerpt from Book 3 of the Codex Regius:

The Dark Star War

Chris Kennedy

Available from Chris Kennedy Publishing

Winter, 2016

eBook, Paperback, and Audio Book

Excerpt from "The Dark Star War:"

Sssellississ System, December 14, 2021

"The enemy approaches," Sal said, pushing himself back from the lip.

Calvin let the lizard slide past him and took his place in the narrow opening of the cave mouth. He slid forward until he could look down on the procession below. The creatures looked like the centaur-like beings you'd get if you crossed a longhorn steer with a four-armed man and then added on an extra pair of eyes on antennas. They were creatures out of his nightmares.

Shaitans.

They herded along three of Sal's Ssselipsssiss countrymen with some sort of electric prod, laughing to themselves as they used it on the helpless lizards.

He pushed himself backward before one of the Shaitans could look up and see him.

"Yeah, that's our enemy too," he whispered. "Those are Shaitans, and it looks like they have captured three of your people. We've got to find a way to free them."

"They are as good as dead," Sal said, "just like the rest of this planet. It is more important to find a way off this planet and take word back to my people."

"What are they going to do with the information?" Calvin asked. "Just knowing the name of the race fighting you isn't going to help defeat them."

Sal hissed, his annoyance evident.

"It doesn't matter whether you like it or not," Calvin said; "it's the truth. We have the same problem. We know *who* we're fighting, but we don't know where their home planet is, or anything else about them. All we know is they have at least a limited mastery over time because they use it as a weapon. If they can do other things with it…more powerful things…then we are well and truly screwed."

"My race is already, as you say, 'screwed,'" Sal replied. "They have taken most of our planets, including my world and our capital planet. If we don't find a way to stop them, and soon, we will be annihilated."

Having fought them before, Calvin wasn't sure the loss of the Ssselipsssiss race was something the galaxy would mourn, but he shrugged internally. Better the enemy you know than the one you don't.

"If nothing else," Calvin said, "at least we now know we're fighting a common enemy. If we can put pressure on them in another place, maybe that will help your race at least hold on to what you still have. To do that, though, we have to get the word back to my people."

"Truth," Sal agreed. "How do you suggest we do that?"

"I don't know," admitted Calvin. "Do you think your people will come looking for you?"

"No," Sal replied, with another hiss. "They are barely able to hold on the defensive. They will not send an offensive expedition to look for us. What about your people?"

"We may be even worse off than you," Calvin replied. "We just lost our only super dreadnought fighting the Shaitans and one of their allies. We also lost two of our battleships. Unless we've built a lot more while I was gone, that only leaves us with a cruiser and a couple of battleships."

"That's all?" Sal asked. "You are even worse allies than I thought. I knew allying with you was a mistake. We should have just fallen back on your planets and taken them as ours."

"You would turn your back on our agreement? That quickly?"

"If it meant my race had a little longer to live and find a solution to the Shaitan menace? Yes, I would. Faster than I could kill you."

"Well, happily for Terra, then, you're marooned here with me, and that knowledge won't make it back to your people if we don't get off this planet."

Sal hissed again.

"You know, you hiss a lot," Calvin noted.

"We do that to show anger or frustration."

"We do something we call sighing," Calvin said. "I'm told I do that a lot too. If nothing else, at least we have that in common." He held out a hand to the Ssselipsssiss. "Truce. At least until we make it back."

Sal looked at his hand for a few seconds, causing Calvin to wonder if he would take it or bite it. As the alien had a mouthful of extremely sharp teeth, Calvin hoped for the former.

"Truce," Sal said finally. "At least until we get back."

"Fair enough. Now let's go see if we can find a way off this rock."

* * * * *

ABOUT THE AUTHOR

A bestselling Science Fiction/Fantasy author and speaker, Chris Kennedy is a former school principal and naval aviator with over 3,000 hours flying attack and reconnaissance aircraft. Chris is also a member of the SFWA and the SCBWI.

Chris' full-length novels on Amazon include the "Occupied Seattle" military fiction duology, the "Theogony" and "Codex Regius" science fiction trilogies and the "War for Dominance" fantasy trilogy. Chris is also the author of the #1 Amazon self-help book, "Self-Publishing for Profit: How to Get Your Book Out of Your Head and Into the Stores."

Titles by Chris Kennedy:

"Red Tide: The Chinese Invasion of Seattle" – Available Now

"Occupied Seattle" – Available Now

"Janissaries: Book One of the Theogony" – Available Now

"When the Gods Aren't Gods: Book Two of the Theogony" – Available Now

"Terra Stands Alone" – Available Now

"The Search for Gram" – Available Now

"Beyond the Shroud of the Universe" – Available Now

"Self-Publishing for Profit" – Available Now

* * * * *

Connect with Chris Kennedy Online:

Facebook: https://www.facebook.com/chriskennedypublishing.biz

Blog: http://chriskennedypublishing.com/

Want to be immortalized in a future book?
Join the Red Shirt List on the blog!

Available Now from Mark Wayne McGinnis!

"Scrapyard Ship" by Mark Wayne McGinnis

Lieutenant Commander Jason Reynolds has had a string of bad luck lately—evident by the uncomfortable house arrest bracelet strapped to his right ankle. Worse yet, he's relegated to his grandfather's old house and rambling scrapyard. But it's through a bizarre turn of events that Jason is led to a subterranean chamber hundreds of feet below ground. There he discovers an advanced alien spacecraft that complicates his life further. The adventure begins… and with it new troubles for Jason. Everyone, including his raucous Navy SEAL buddies, are clamoring to fight a new alien interstellar threat. Catapulted into the Captain's chair, Jason's impetuous decision-making certainly makes for danger and excitement. At stake is the very existence of the human race. This is a full-length novel—first in the science fiction adventure series of Scrapyard Ship.

- Mark Wayne McGinnis, Author of the Scrapyard Ship,
Lone Star Renegade, Tapped In and Star Watch Series

Catch up with Mark Wayne McGinnis at:

Amazon: http://www.amazon.com/-/e/B00FI0N7W0/

Website: http://markwaynemcginnis.com

Facebook Fan Page:
https://www.facebook.com/MarkWayneMcGinnisAuthor?ref=hl

Twitter: @MarkWMcGinnis

Available Now from PP Corcoran!

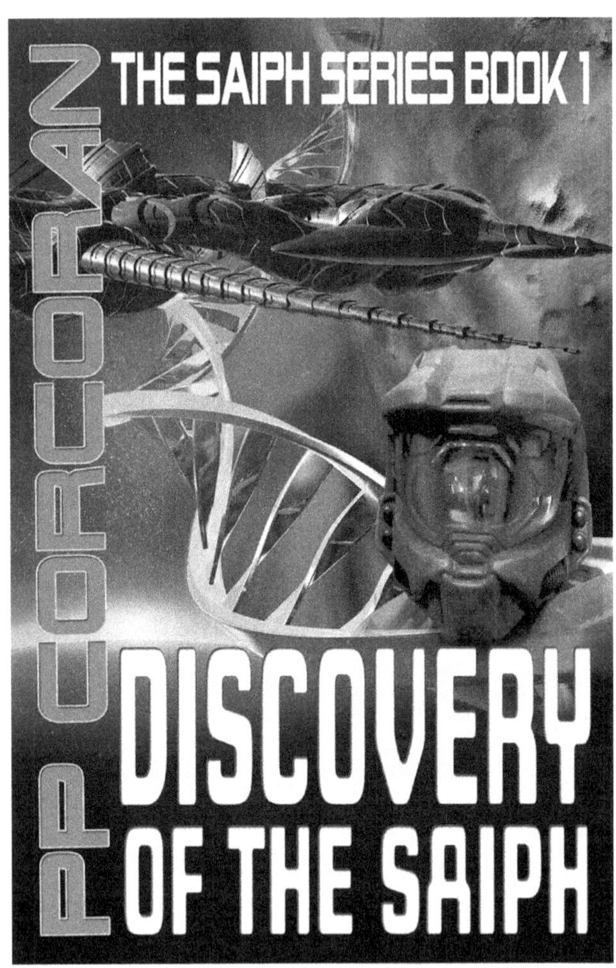

PP CORCORAN'S: DISCOVERY OF THE SAIPH

In the not too distant future humanity can travel faster than light. This remarkable development leads to the construction of the TDF *Marco Polo*. Captained by David Catney he leads humanity's exploration outside its Solar System and ultimately to the Discovery of an ancient, dead, civilization, The Saiph, an alien species who bear an inexplicable likeness to humans.

The Saiph's technology is submerged deep within an extinct planet but it leads to a shocking revelations of their existence and instructs others how to survive what the Saiph could not...war with The Others.

Praise for PP CORCORAN'S Best Selling Saiph Series:

"...amazing, epic space battles, space colonization, the discovery of new alien cultures, desperate missions behind enemy lines, and a many and varied cast of believable beings, it was a heart jarring, mind blowing joy ride through the cosmos that I could not put down."

"Intelligent, well written story... This book has everything from exploration to huge space battles in a terrific story. This is the book space opera fans will love."

The Saiph Series comes highly recommended from fans of the Honor Harrington and Lost Fleet series, the works of Jack McDevitt, The Mote in God's Eye by Niven and Pournelle, Asimov and Arthur C Clark.